The Shadow Watchers

Ellie Crofts

Serenade Publishing

Copyright © 2025 by Ellie Crofts

All rights reserved.

No part of this publication may be reproduced, distributed or transmitted in any form or by any electronic or mechanical means, including information storage and retrieval systems, without written permission from the author, except for the use of brief quotations in a book review.

Publisher's Note: This is a work of fiction. Names, characters, places and incidents are a product of the author's imagination. Locales and public names are sometimes used for atmospheric purposes. Any resemblance to actual people, living or dead, or to businesses, companies, events, institutions or locales is completely coincidental.

Serenade Publishing

www.serenadepublishing.com

For Scarlett, Darcy, Clara, Tilly and Austin

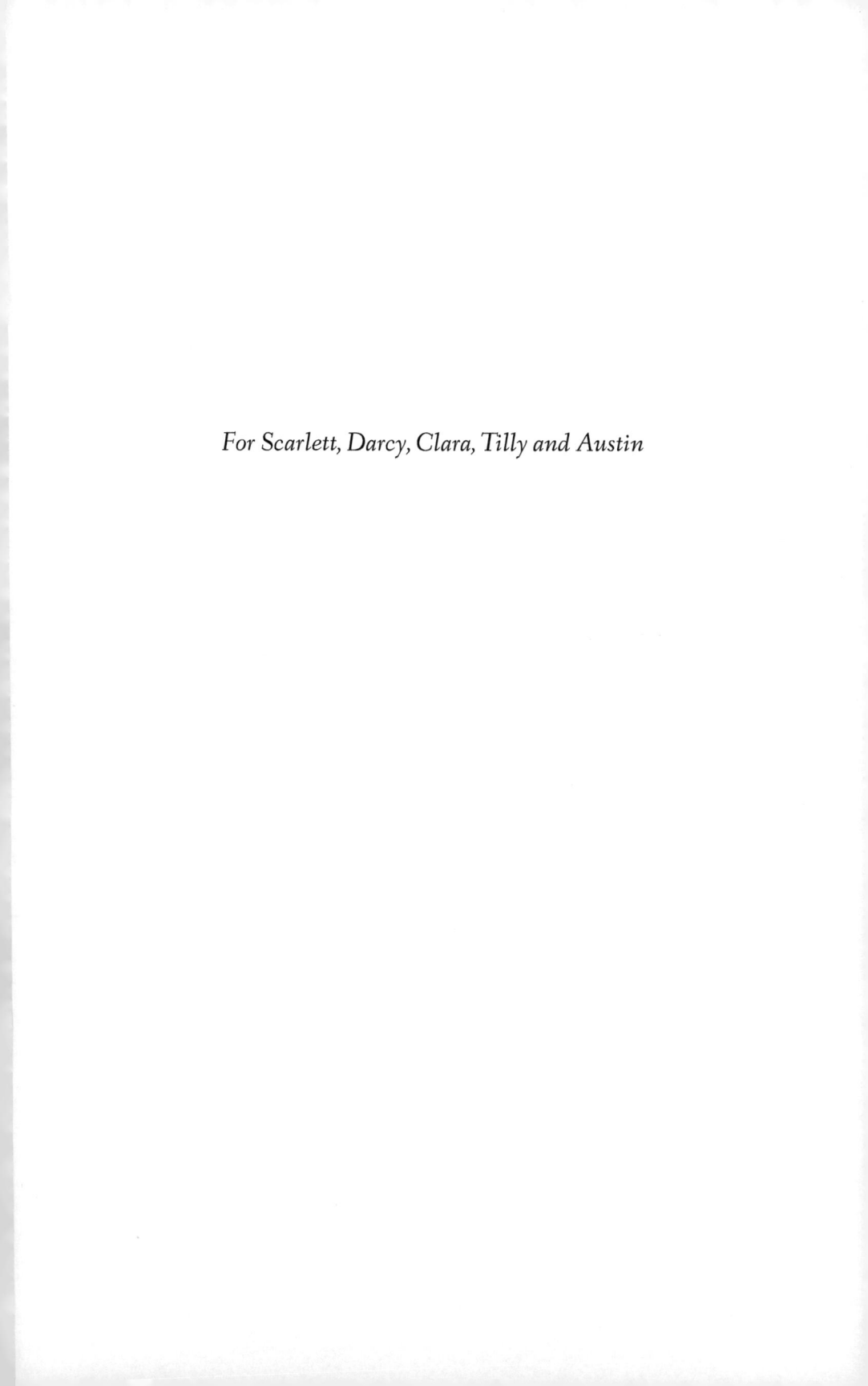

Chapter One

"God, I look a fright!" My face looked ghastly pale in the bathroom mirror, with shadows under lacklustre green eyes. Rebellious locks of tawny auburn hair refused to obey the hairbrush. Grimly I applied blusher.

"Now I look like Worzel Gummidge's Aunt Sally." I muttered, rubbing off most of it. I didn't know why I looked as if I'd drunk too much wine the night before. I hadn't, but there was no denying an uncomfortable sensation in my stomach.

In the kitchen, Evie, my flatmate, spread a thick layer of marmite onto a slice of toast and bile rose unpleasantly into my throat. I gulped in panic. "That looks disgusting," I snapped, and Evie stared at me, toast halfway to her mouth.

"Who's got out of bed on the wrong side this morning?"

I sagged into a chair. "Sorry, I don't know what's the matter with me. Yes, I do! I've got a bad case of collywobbles about the Skype meeting set up this morning with the New York Trekkers."

"It's only a Skype call to New York, for goodness' sake, and from what you've been telling me about a thousand times already, the bike trekking outfit you are getting pally with in the US is like yours and Will's business so you've got lots of common ground." Evie resumed her chomping, and I stared at the table instead of looking at her eating.

"Yes, I know," I sighed. "It's just that it's all on my shoulders; I researched this New York outfit and started contact. Considering expansion in North America is an appealing opportunity before our clientele get bored with the same treks in Europe. Will wasn't keen until he saw the picture of Rafaella Benotti, the brains and beauty behind her outfit." I rummaged through my tote bag for phone, notebook, wallet, office key. "Will was transfixed by her profile on their Social Media account. All glossy hair, perfect teeth, and skintight Lycra!" I sighed moodily.

Evie shoved her glasses on top of her head and picked up the ancient-looking document in front of her. "I ought not to be looking at this with food around. It's been languishing in the basement storage area of the Museum of London for decades, part of a set of diaries."

Evie Cranston, my best mate from university days, freelance archivist and historian, and my flatmate. Always ready to share her knowledge and enthusiasm. "What's this woman got that has made you so jealous?" she demanded.

"I'm not jealous!" But it might explain my moodiness this morning. I brought up Rafaella's profile and Evie agreed she had a certain celebrity attraction. "Will's seen plenty of Lycra clad females on his bike treks. I'm sure he'll cope with another one! You have nothing to fear from him."

Our customers are not as alluring as Ms Benotti in Lycra. On my crowded tube journey to our business office, Tough Treks, in Whitechapel, I had time to reminisce on Evie's remark.

Will Payne-Ashton, my fiancé, and I ran a bike trekking company. I met Will at University when I joined the cycling club, which headed out of town most weekends. We didn't think we were serious about one another until he graduated a year ahead of me and came back to see me every weekend. A year later, after I graduated; he told me of his plans to set up his own bike trekking business. His mother had offered initial financial backing, and he wanted me in on it as well. We were amazed and thrilled when our company, Will Payne-Ashton and Clemency Wyatt Bike Treks Abroad, proved popular right from the start and gradually we could expand, employ more staff and change our name to Tough Treks. We'd been successful for several years, hence my bright idea to expand into North America.

In our cramped office, we waited impatiently, or nervously in my case, for the appointed Skype call time. New York was a few hours behind London. Eventually, our small team gathered round my PC screen. Will drummed his fingers on the desk. Hugo Young, our second trek leader, sat to one side with a notepad on his knee. I moved someone's coffee to another surface. The smell of it made my stomach perform anxious flips. *Butterfly nerves.*

"Hi, good morning from New York!"

Sultry Italian American tones preceded the image, then the screen lit up, and there was an indrawn breath from someone as Rafaella Benotti appeared live on screen, burnished dark hair cascading over her shoulders, her teeth displayed in a dazzling white smile.

"It's so great to see you all and thank you for choosing us as potential partners in your quest to expand trekking routes. We have just about the most awesome places to show you, but first let me introduce you to my great team: Jimmy, Ruby, Sam, and Dunc."

Partners? We were exploring options, not going into business with her.

Her team waved, and it was my turn to introduce our team, then Will stuck his head close to the screen and I rolled my eyes as he gushed how the descriptions and pictures of her trek routes had filled him with excitement at the prospect of exploring the routes.

From being the only one of us expressing doubt on setting up treks on the North American continent, he was now embarrassingly overly enthusiastic.

Rafaella showed large-scale maps on the walls behind her with national parks highlighted. Although I'd done research, it looked incredible that all this natural beauty lay within reach of New York.

"Wow, that would be amazing!" Will crowed, and I dragged my attention back to the screen.

Chatter erupted around me. What had Will or Rafaella said?

Will turned to me. "Rafaella has just suggested that I go out there and explore some routes before we make a final decision."

"You and Clemency or Hugo will be very welcome.," Rafaella broke in. "Some of the terrain is tough and I don't know about your customers; whether they're prepared to fly out before trekking, but if you want to win in any business, you mustn't be afraid to play hardball."

Before I could speak, Will jumped in enthusiastically. "Exactly! We're on the same wavelength, Rafaella. I'll get Clemency to arrange flights. Do you mind if we come over right away? I can't wait to get started!"

"Not at all. We feel privileged you chose us and we'll make sure you have a great time. I'll get Ruby to book hotel rooms for you and Clemency or Hugo as soon as we get email details of your flight."

We ended the link-up buzzing. Will, who'd been the only one pessimistic about a North American itinerary, was suddenly tasking Kim Lee, our admin assistant, to find flights as soon as possible. Was his change of heart because of the prospect of trekking unknown adventurous trails as well as instant infatuation with Rafaella?

Hugo announced that Will, and I should be the ones to travel.

"Clem's got the business and logistical head for details and you can test out the terrain, Will."

A thrill of excitement ran through me. A visit to New York was a prospect we couldn't pass up.

Kim brought up all flight details. Will would have jumped on a plane that night, but we opted for a flight tomorrow and she verified the details in an email to Rafaella.

Later, as we all left the office, a cold damp mist from the river spread tentacles along the street

"I'd better go back to Evie's to pack tonight," I said to Will. "It'll be too awkward travelling back and forth from my place to yours with an early start tomorrow. We'll meet up at Heathrow."

Will nodded, "Makes sense. I'll be too wound up to oversleep and I'll ring you first thing. This trip is gonna be a good one, Clem. I can feel it in my bones!"

"Well, you were certainly drooling over the prospect, going by your reaction to Ms Benotti!" I teased him with a straight face.

"What? I wasn't!" In the glare of the street lighting, I swear he coloured up.

We hugged and parted for our respective tube stations. As the business had grown and more treks added to the seasons' itineraries, I'd rattled around feeling at a loose end in Will's flat when he was away. Evie didn't object when I moved back to our shared flat in a converted mews stable and in truth, I'd never moved much of my stuff to Will's. The arrangement just continued down the years, with Will regularly staying at the mews flat.

All the way home, the queasiness increased, and I barely had time to shrug off my coat before dashing to the bathroom and heaving my guts up. It continued all evening, and I was hot, light-headed, and if I moved too quickly, another bout of nausea overcame me.

Evie arrived home from work and stayed clear of my bugs.

When Will phoned late to check that all systems were go for

tomorrow, I lied to him from my bed, hoping by morning whatever had upset my stomach would have passed through my system. I managed to fall into an exhausted sleep, but when my alarm went off extremely early and I staggered out of bed, nausea and faintness overwhelmed me. Evie eventually put her head round my bedroom door, looking concerned.

"You've got to phone Will," she said firmly. "You can't get on a plane like this in case you're contagious."

"But I've got to go on this trip; Will's counting on me to get the best deal." It was an effort to talk.

"You know Will is as canny as you are and he'll soon have Rafaella eating out of his hand with his boyish charm. Phone him, get him to cancel this flight. You can always get a later flight when you're better."

I knew Evie was speaking practically, but I also knew Will; when he decided on a course of action, a dose of food poisoning wouldn't deflect him. Besides, I felt sick at the thought of trying to hold a conversation without rushing to the bathroom. If this bug was contagious, it would be selfish to sit on a plane with unsuspecting passengers. Evie pushed my phone towards me, but I shook my head feebly as the room spun round.

"OK, let's see what he suggests." She closed the door behind her and I heard her voice, quiet and reasonable at first, then becoming loudly querulous and I knew Will would get on the plane without me. When Evie returned, shaking her head, I was relieved that I didn't need to make any more efforts.

"Will's very sorry, and says not to worry. He'll be fine. Try to get some water down you before you dehydrate. If you don't improve by this afternoon, you must get medical help."

I was grateful to rest in bed, having no energy to argue or feel disappointment, and fell deeply asleep. When I woke and saw the glass of water Evie had left by my bed, I gulped it down thirstily.

Bad mistake, because a horrible sensation rose immediately and I only just made it to the bathroom in time.

Evie appeared; her specs perched on the end of her nose. "OK, you're still not right, so I'm phoning the medical centre," she said, sounding like an elderly aunt. "I'm working from home today so I could keep an eye on you."

"Doctors don't do home visits anymore," I gasped.

"I'll take you there myself, as long as don't throw up in my car." I almost laughed because Evie had recently become a proud car owner after years of resisting. Her work as an archivist researching documents and contents of old buildings could take her anywhere in the country, and she had admitted that travelling by public transport was a handicap.

∽

Hours later, I was in hospital, an IV drip hooked up to my arm treating my dehydration and I was waiting for the results of a routine urine sample. If I had a urine infection, a course of antibiotics would set me right and I could fly to New York. Even in my febrile state, the thought of Will acting like a besotted schoolboy in front of Rafaella filled me with disquiet. Had he asked Hugo to go in my place?

My groggy head throbbed. Antiseptic and air fresheners did nothing to dispel the distinct, vaguely unpleasant smell of hospitals. Clattering trolleys, loud voices, and hurried footsteps outside my cubicle all disorientated me.

The cubicle curtain swished back.

"Hello, Clemency, I'm Dr Fleming," said a young woman carrying an iPad. "I have the results of your urine sample. It's positive, which means you are pregnant," she announced.

"That's impossible!" I declared, shocked out of my muzzy

state. *Was it? I was on a contraceptive pill, but there were times when I'd forgotten....*

Doctor Fleming smiled. She'd probably heard those words countless times. "You are experiencing extreme morning sickness, which we call hyperemesis gravidarum. It can be quite debilitating at the start of pregnancy."

She felt my abdomen - it was tender, and I winced.

"I'd estimate you're about ten to twelve weeks, but I'll arrange for you to go and have an ultrasound scan right away. I can prescribe some anti-sickness tablets, they won't harm the foetus," she reassured me when she saw my dubious expression.

The doctor used her mobile phone to arrange the scan, disconnected the IV, and soon after, a porter arrived with a wheelchair to take me to the Maternity Unit.

"God, do I have to use this?" I muttered, embarrassed.

"Just get in it. The Maternity Unit is probably further than you can manage in your state," Evie ordered. As we trundled along corridors I kept repeating: "I can't be pregnant, it's a mistake."

Evie had no sharp quip to counter my mutterings, and I was called forward after a very short wait.

I climbed onto the couch and the sonographer smeared gel onto my stomach and moved the probe around. Murky, grainy shadows appeared on the screen.

"Oh, my God!" Tears sprang to my eyes, as, lying snugly in its little cave, I saw a tiny head and stumps indicating limbs.

"Now do you believe it?" asked Evie, and squeezed my hand. Sensible, no-nonsense Evie looked emotional too.

Everything was a blur after that. The size of the foetus was estimated at twelve weeks, and a healthy size. No abnormalities appeared at this stage and the estimated date of birth given as early September.

I was allowed home with instructions to rest. "I can't tell Will yet," I said to Evie in the car. I clutched the images of the scan tightly and I couldn't take my eyes off them.

"Fair enough–wait until he comes home," offered Evie. "He'd sure have a hell of a shock learning he's to be a father when he's in the middle of business negotiations."

∼

Will phoned at some point after I returned home. He didn't ask how I was, for which I felt relieved and annoyed simultaneously, and he hadn't invited Hugo over to replace me. "Rafaella met me at the airport and when she learned you were ill, Clem, she offered me the spare room in her apartment. I'm looking out of her window now, down towards Central Park." Will sounded tired, but boyishly exuberant. "The skyline is mind blowing and Rafaella's apartment is swish. We're going out to eat now and then tomorrow get down to business at her office. It's a pity you're not here, but I'll talk to you tomorrow. Bye, Darling."

The only part of his conversation that resonated was that he was staying in Rafaella's apartment. Were my newly rampant hormones making me super sensitive? I said nothing to Evie but spent the rest of the night trying to stop unwanted images flooding my mind. I had a terrible night. It was too stressful trying to get to the bathroom, so I had a bowl by my bed. Despite assurances about the anti-sickness medication, I was reluctant taking them.

Next morning, I dragged myself out of bed and showered. When Will and Rafaella Skyped from New York, I was determined to hear what they had to say. I crept out of the flat without disturbing Evie.

In the cramped confines of our office, the aroma of coffee emanating from various mugs made my stomach turn over, but I made some peppermint tea and sipped cautiously. As the morning slowly passed, I stared unseeingly at my computer screen, trying not to be obvious about my frequent trips to the loo to retch as quietly as possible. Kim glanced at me sympathetically, but said nothing. Just after lunchtime, my stomach sore and empty, I longed to return home to bed. My laptop Skype call sounded and on answering, the screen was filled with Will's beaming face. Everybody crowded behind my chair, as agog for news as I was.

"Hi guys," Will waved at us all. "Let me introduce you properly to Rafaella Benotti. I know we've spoken to her before, but being physically here with all her team is just totally mad and amazing!"

His happy grin emphasised his boyishly attractive face, his dark blond hair that wouldn't lie flat, and his blue eyes crinkled with good humour and exuberance. Rafaella smiled benignly, and her brown eyes glowed, fringed with thick dark lashes. "Would you like to ask me any questions?" she said in her impossibly sexy accent. "All my best brains are here; Jimmy Jordan, who is Trek Captain Two, Ruby Romanescu, my financial wizard, Sam Levy and Dunc Downing, planners and Trekkers."

She panned round and her young, attractive team waved and called out greetings. I tried to shrink into the background; my pale complexion was no match for Rafaella's looks, but nonetheless professionalism took over, and, inviting the others to get comfortable, the question-and-answer session got going. An hour later, we ended the call and looked at each other optimistically.

"Will looks like the cat that's got the cream and I think the deal was in the bag even before our discussions online," announced Hugo.

"Agreed! I don't think we're a big enough outfit to cause Rafaella any challenge. She also has a very small team and North America is a large enough continent to avoid crashing into each other or stealing away her clients!" I replied. Despite my misgivings, probably caused by a certain amount of female territorial jealousy on my part, I was confident. Will had pulled off this deal without my input and the resulting expansion in opportunities promised challenging new trips on our itinerary. Then, just as I was about to call it a day, feeling thoroughly wiped out, Will Skyped again. This time he and Rafaella were holding up champagne glasses to the screen.

"Guys, meet our new partners–instead of Tough Treks setting up in the US as a separate concern with Rafaella's blessing, we've decided to amalgamate resources. Grab something to toast us in our new venture as Trekkers International!"

There was a nanosecond of stunned silence. How did that happen? Who would oversee the combined teams? Would one of us would have to be permanently based in the States? Why hadn't this option come up in the discussions earlier? Why hadn't Will consulted Hugo and me beforehand? All these questions buzzed round my exhausted brain.

"That outcome wasn't in the script, mate," Hugo frowned at Will on screen. "Don't you think Clemmie and I should have been in this private decision-making process?"

Will squared his shoulders defiantly.

"Look, guys, nothing will change in structure apart from the fact that we are expanding our territories. Rafaella thought it made better sense to work together as one unit rather than constantly confirming routes and logistics with her team in case we overlapped on expeditions. It just makes sense, and you know it too. Look, it's getting late over there with your lot, so I'll email Clem and Hugo all the proposals and outlines of the structure that Rafaella and I have worked. Go through it and raise any points if you must, but I'm certain you'll all approve. It's a bloody fantastic opportunity, guys. Sleep on it and we'll talk tomorrow."

Will cut the connection and I instinctively knew that he was irritated by our reaction to his news. After emerging from yet another trip to the loo, all my energy had seeped away.

Andy, Ben and Kim were gathered round Hugo's desk, discussing the latest bombshell.

"Let's call it a day. We can't do anymore. Tomorrow we can all get to grips with the proposals and implications. Don't be afraid, any of you, to voice any fears and doubts you may have. When the email comes through, I'll forward it to each of you so nobody is in the dark."

"You look done in, Clem," said Kim. "That bug has really taken it out of you. I'll call a cab and Hugo and I will lock up. We need you bright eyed and bushy tailed for tomorrow!"

A cab, yes! Travel by tube was the last thing I needed. My phone bleeped: a voice mail from Evie. "Hope you felt better today, Clem. You must have left early. I didn't hear a thing! Anyway, I'm just catching up on stuff at work, so I'll see you later. And TAKE IT EASY!" *Thanks Evie, I'm too exhausted to do much else!*

∼

At home, I heated and hungrily spooned down a bowl of soup, praying I'd retain it, then ran a bath, adding soothing lavender essence. The warmth enveloped me and my eyelids drooped, only to snap open when the image of Will staring at Rafaella with a stupid, besotted expression imprinted itself on me. Not once during the meeting had, he singled me out, even with just a fond smile. Nor had he asked how I was faring after my bug, which wasn't a bug but extreme morning sickness. Will wasn't aware of that. Would my news, when I had the chance to have a private conversation with him, wipe that euphoric smile from his face?

Pragmatically, it was a momentous time for Tough Treks and Will's dedication and enthusiasm were paying off, so of course our business future was top priority. Will would be raring to go on his first trek on the North American continent.

I couldn't wait to get into bed and give my body and brain a rest. Evie hadn't returned home by the time I turned in.

Sometime in the early hours, I woke, remembering the detailed email that Will had promised. Cautiously, I got out of bed to power up my laptop, aware of a nagging ache in my back and lower abdomen. Will had laid out all the facts and figures so that they were easy to read and assimilate. I suspected Rafaella had been the author, because of the American phrasing. Hugo had obviously read the proposals during last evening because there was an email from him recommending the proposals and in his opinion the deal, although suddenly sprung on us, was sound. There was no doubting the facts: Trekkers International was bound to attract new biking enthusiasts. After forwarding Will's details to the rest of the team, I scoured the rest of my mail for any personal message from Will. None, so I sent him a message of encouragement and added lots of kisses.

Sleep eluded me, so I got up to make a weak cup of tea, relieved I hadn't spewed up in the night. The images of the scan still lay on the kitchen table. It was incredible that this tiny creature curled up inside me was my baby, our baby. Will and I were to be parents, a life-changing event for both of us. Tears rolled down my cheeks. I wanted to phone Will right there and then, but I wanted to share the news when we were together. A shattering thought lodged in my mind. What if Will didn't welcome the news? He was so wrapped up in the future of Trekkers, would he react negatively or positively? All I knew at that very moment was that I would do everything to keep this incredible life growing inside me safe and secure. In Will's absence, it was easy to surmise he wouldn't be jumping for joy at the news, but I had no right to judge his reaction. A baby wouldn't stop him from trekking, nor should it. It was his job.

How difficult would it be for me to manage my job, an infant, and an absent father several times a year? Countless other parents faced the same dilemma, and each decision made was unique for those parents. I could take a tiny baby into the office and feed and change him and even cradle him at my desk. But what would happen when he/she grew out of sitting placidly in a pushchair and wanted to crawl and then walk and generally cause chaos in a small space with lots of electrical equipment and cables to pull on? Childcare would be expensive. I put my elbows on the table and rested my head in my hands. *Oh, Will, I want you here so badly right now.* My head spun, and I felt sick as all these wild notions whirled uncontrollably through my mind.

The image of Will and Rafaella sharing affectionate looks and clinking glasses reared up in my vision and the churning, sinking feeling in my stomach was nothing to do with nausea. *Could they be starting a relationship? Will looked besotted in her company.* As I rushed to the bathroom, I sent the kitchen chair crashing on its side. When I emerged, feeling wretched, Evie was filling the kettle, yawning.

"OK, now?" She righted the upturned chair and helped me into it again as I stood shivering.

She placed a mug of tea in front of me on the table. Evie had made coffee for herself and I couldn't help wrinkling my nose at the smell.

"Sorry, I'm going to have to take note of triggers and cravings from now on!"

"Plenty of triggers, but I'm not craving anything yet. Just sleep!"

After I'd given her a brief update about Trekkers International, she shrugged. "It all sounds perfectly doable to me," she said.

"I can't get my head round being pregnant and focussing on what's going to happen at work and the New York office and... and ... things." I put my mug down and ran a reviving shower, dressed, applied moisturiser and blusher to my wan face, and brushed my hair. If there was to be a lot of Skyping today, I could never rival

Rafaella in looks, but I would make sure to match her in professionalism.

"You shouldn't even be thinking of going into work," clucked Evie when I emerged from my room at last. I stuck my tongue out at her.

"Needs must, but I'm not looking forward to Tube travel. I can't keep taking taxis, they're not cheap!"

"Wait for me, and I'll travel part of the way with you. And take some paper bags with you just in case...." said Evie, disappearing into the bathroom. Her whacky sense of humour was just what I needed to stop me wallowing in self-pity and walking to the underground station with her arm linked through mine gave me much needed support.

There wasn't a lot of day-to-day work going on when I finally reached our office and thumped heavily down onto my chair, relieved I hadn't disgraced myself by throwing up on the London Underground and grateful for Evie's diverting chatter before she changed trains.

Listening to conversations, I quickly gathered that they all accepted the merger of the two companies, excited at prospects, so I suggested they write their questions on the whiteboard on the wall.

Ben, our graphics expert, queried website developments. Andy, fresh from college, just expressed a keen interest in trekking in the States. Kim worried about possible job losses. That had been one of my concerns and it wasn't difficult to work out that I'd be the redundant one, although I wasn't telling my colleagues I was pregnant until I'd told Will.

Hugo asked if there was a likelihood of one of us re-locating to the New York office. There was a lot of uncertainty before the merger was settled. Kim ordered in pizzas while we waited for our Skype call. Starving myself would not cure morning sickness, so I forced myself to eat a tiny slice.

"If Will thinks he can hog the States and that gorgeous Rafaella all to himself, he can think again!" burst out Ben, shovelling down a slice of pizza loaded with pepperoni. "Hugo, Andy and me all want to explore over there."

"We'll have an empty office and angry clients if you all decamp to the States," I said mildly, but understood their mood. Rafaella had mesmerised the men just as much as she had Will.

"Have we finished with the pizza? Let's get our brains into gear and get those New Yorkers out of bed!" said Hugo smartly.

It was an unfortunate remark to make. Hugo wasn't to know how my thoughts had dwelt on unbidden images.

Hugo commanded the screen when the Skype meeting began. The rest of us clustered round him. Will looked belligerent: was he expecting us to mutiny? He ranged round our faces while Rafaella spoke pleasantries. Will's eyes locked on my face, and he frowned. His face cleared when Hugo gave our unanimous approval.

"Guys, I could hug you all! It's great news, isn't it, Raf?" he grinned and spontaneously put his arm round Rafaella's shoulder. That slight gesture rattled me.

After questions and reassurances, it was agreed that Hugo fly over to explore trails that Jimmy Jordan had mapped out. Will's impatience was palpably obvious.

"If you can get Hugo booked on a flight, *pronto* Clem, we can get the show on the road. You can limber up in Central Park, Hugo, like Rafaella had me doing this morning!"

Chapter Two

Kim brought me a cup of tea and returned to the animated discussion going on around Hugo's laptop. Efficiently she'd booked a flight for Hugo while I looked on, unable to shake off the weariness and nagging ache which accompanied my nausea. Seeing Will gazing at his new business partner and his body language did nothing to lift my spirits.

I grabbed my coat and bag and slipped out.

The cold, drizzly afternoon matched my mood, so I flagged down a cab and sank gratefully into the back seat.

Evie was still out at work and I barely had the energy to remove my outer clothes before rolling shivering into bed, wrapping the duvet tightly round me.

The ping of a message arriving on my phone woke me. It was 8.30pm and my body was heavy and sluggish. The message was from Evie saying she was out to dinner with colleagues and was I OK?

I replied:

> Yes, enjoy yourself, I'm fine!

Slowly climbing out of bed, I stretched carefully and wrapped my fleecy dressing gown round me. Will had commented that I looked like a cuddly teddy bear in it and a longing for his physical presence swept over me. I ate scrambled eggs on toast, accompanied by a mug of chamomile tea. Watching a couple of episodes of Friends on TV emphasised my loneliness. There would be emails from the office and more proposals and plans from everybody, but at that moment I couldn't think of positive and encouraging words for my team.

My mood lifted after a scented bath. I had arrived at a decision. Tomorrow I'd put a private call through to Will before Hugo arrived, because if Rafaella whisked them off to distant trails, it could be days before we had a chance to catch up. Will had to know our news before anyone else in the office; I intuited Kim suspected, so imagine his shock if he was the last to hear!

Mum and Dad's reactions to my news would be entirely different. Dad would be over the moon. Mum wouldn't be. The relationship between my mother and me was strained. I didn't conform to her rigid set of principles and although I knew I could always rely on Dad's support and love, Mum regarded me as a disappointment. She'd made it clear on more than one occasion that our joint business was precarious and we'd given very little thought about financial security in old age. Mum liked tidiness and neat solutions–in her home, in her life and, where possible, this extended to her children. My older brother, Thomas, shared her neat outlook. He had qualified as a dentist, married Anna, a teacher, who patronised me for my lack of ambition. They had two sons, Alfie and Charlie, my nephews, who, at the tender ages of eight and ten, were already destined for lucrative careers. When I had provocatively suggested that they might become footballers or pop stars, Anna had practically banned me from visiting! Mum got on better with her daughter-in-law than with me. Thomas and

Anna gave her no sleepless nights. They had pensions, a tidy house, and their futures mapped securely.

I knew instinctively that when I gave them the news of my pregnancy, Mum's reaction would be the shame of an unmarried daughter in the family, even in today's relaxed society. Dad had learned to keep his head down and let Mum take the helm. He had semi-retired as a company accountant, keeping a handful of clients who kept him ticking over so that he could enjoy days on the golf course or whittling in his shed, which Mum called his workshop.

My reverie left me slightly shameful about my criticism of Mum's outlook on life. I knew I had consciously rebelled against an orderly existence and deliberately chose an unstructured lifestyle, which suited Will probably more than me. Intuitively, I guessed his infatuation with Rafaella was because I had never made any demands on him, emotionally or otherwise. The ring on the third finger of my left hand, a classic flower design studded with tiny diamonds and a central sapphire, had been bought on an impulse, delightful and unplanned, but no commitments had been made then or since. Tough Treks was our baby and consumed our time and energies. Now there was a real baby that would demand even more time and energy and, above all, love.

Evie returned home, surprised to see me still up.

"You must be feeling better," she said, throwing her bag and coat on a chair and kicking off her boots.

"I have eaten, and it's stayed down.," I announced, holding up two crossed fingers. "That's a major plus point in my day! I'm phoning Will in the morning before he goes off trekking. Hugo's flying out to join him and I can't keep my morning sickness hidden all the time. I'm sure Kim suspects something, but she's been the soul of discretion."

"You should take time off work until your hormones adjust," Evie said, massaging her feet.

"I'm just taking one day at a time and now I'm off to bed. I had a good nap earlier, but I feel so tired all the time."

∼

I awoke in the early hours in urgent need of the loo and was horrified to find I was losing blood. My first reaction was that I wasn't pregnant at all, but the results given to me at the hospital and the images were solid confirmation. I froze for long seconds and before panic took over; I tried to think calmly. Shivery with shock, I entered my predicament into a search engine and rapidly read a sample of the many entries that came up. I latched onto a phrase explaining that sometimes "spotting" occurred in the early stages of pregnancy; nevertheless, it was wise to monitor further signs if it didn't clear in a couple of days or the blood loss increased. I wondered how much 'spotting' amounted to imminent disaster. The nagging back pain I'd felt yesterday was still present. I had no option. I needed professional help. Shivering, I knocked on Evie's door and she listened to my panicky outburst.

"Evie, I'm bleeding and sick at the same time. I feel so dreadful..."

"Ambulance," she said without preamble and made the call on her mobile before I could say anything about not wanting a fuss. She helped me dress in jogging bottoms and thick fleece and in a surprisingly short time the ambulance arrived. The paramedics, two women, were quietly reassuring and carried me down the stairs. Evie said she'd follow in her car, but they told her to get in the ambulance as well.

By now, I was quite tearful. "What's Will going to say if I'm losing this poor baby when he doesn't even know I'm pregnant?"

"Wait till you see a doctor or midwife, you must keep calm."

Once again, I was in hospital, lying on an examination couch in Gynaecology. A midwife took my blood pressure, which was raised, not surprisingly. She gently examined my nether regions and listened to the baby's heartbeat using a stethoscope, smiling as she listened for a full minute. She wiped the earpieces and offered them to me. Hearing the rapid whooshes was incredible and scary; there was still a life force growing inside me!

"I'm sure the bleeding is what we call spotting; it does not appear heavy or continuous." the midwife spoke in a practised comforting voice. "You can go home now, but take some time off work. However, if the bleeding does become heavy and continuous or clot, and you experience contraction like pains, call an ambulance immediately. This is very scary for you at the beginning, but I'm sure it's likely you'll have a successful pregnancy. We'll make appointments for you at the maternity clinic for regular checks, which should reassure you." She patted my arm as I rearranged my clothing and Evie made a relieved face at me and I burst into tears.

"We'll get a taxi home," she said, taking my arm, "but first we'll have a cup of tea. We're both suffering from shock!"

She led me to the cafe on the ground floor. I gratefully sipped the ginger tea and even had a couple of bites of croissant which Evie put firmly in front of me. My phone pinged a message from Kim.

> Are you OK? Was a bit worried when you didn't turn up at the office. Hugo's flight has departed so he'll be arriving in New York later.

I phoned her immediately. I didn't want her to jump to conclusions without Will knowing first. "Hi Kim, I had a rotten morning (which was true!) so I've decided to take some time off to really recover. I'm sorry not to have spoken to you earlier. If you have any queries, don't hesitate to phone or email me. Can you let me know if Hugo gets in touch to say he's arrived? Thanks, Kim, speak to you soon."

"I've really got to phone Will now. I can't hang on any longer. Kim is being discreet, but it's not fair to her or the others." I said. "I'll call a taxi from here, Evie, if you want to go straight to work. You've been a star so far, but I don't want you to get into trouble not turning up for work either."

"I phoned them earlier, so no need to worry about me. Let's get you home. No arguments. I'm coming with you."

Dear Evie, I know I would have been in pieces without her unflustered and calm support. Soon I was installed on the sofa, wrapped in a duvet with lots of cushions and a carton of soup defrosting in the kitchen.

Evie left for work after making me promise not to do anything silly, like cleaning windows or moving furniture. "Evie, I can hardly muster enough strength to phone Will at the moment!" I answered.

I turned my phone over and over in my hands, trying to rehearse what I must say to Will. There was no point beating about the bush. However, I tried to phrase it, my announcement would still be a shock. I scrolled to his name and pressed call. As it dialled, my heart was thumping so noisily I thought Will would hear it when he answered. When a female voice answered immediately, recognisable as Rafaella's sultry tones, I was struck dumb. "'Ello, 'ello, who is this please?"

"It's Clem... Clemency," I faltered. "I need to speak to Will."

"Ah, Clemency. Will is using my laptop. Let me get him for you. He thought there might be news of Hugo's arrival. We will pick him up later. How are you in London? Has the weather improved? We put bikes in my pickup yesterday and have been cycling."

"Oh, how nice," I said politely. "The weather is a little better, but damp and grey as usual." *How could he think of Hugo's arrival and not spare a thought about me?*

I sounded like a gibbering idiot and was relieved when Will picked up.

"Hi Clemmie, is everything ok? Rafaella said you sounded odd. You didn't look right yesterday, and I reckoned your bug had really knocked you sideways. We ventured out of NY yesterday. I did not know there were so many wonderful trails in the vicinity. As soon as Hugo arrives, we can hit more trails." Will's tone was breezy and unconcerned. Of course, he had no presentiment that I was about to turn his world upside down.

"Will, listen, I'm pregnant." I blurted out, desperate to tell him and hear some comforting words. "That tummy bug turned out to be extreme morning sickness." I took a shuddering breath. "but I've had a little scare and now I must take time off because I might lose the baby. I'm so sorry." Tears coursed down my cheeks.

The silence on the phone unnerved me. "Will, I'm truly sorry - this is a shock for you. It's a shock to me too and then just as I'm coming to terms with having a baby, I might lose it if I don't rest for a bit." And then I hiccupped to a halt as tears became sobs.

"Jesus, I don't know what to say, Clem. What a... shock! Clem, don't cry, we'll sort something out." I visualised him in Rafaella's 'sumptuous' apartment, trying to focus on my phone call instead of planning exciting trails with Rafaella.

When I continued to sob down the phone, unable to speak, he said, "I'll get the next available flight home; just stay put and I'll let you know when I'm arriving." He cut the call, and I sat and sobbed. I cried because I'd bottled up my emotions and was so distressed that I couldn't control them. There had been no words of comfort or joy from Will, which wasn't surprising under the circumstances. I was relieved he was coming home, but what did he mean when he'd said we'd sort something out? But I cried more for this tiny being inside me that was in now in danger.

Will phoned an hour later. He was booked on a flight and would be arriving at Heathrow late that night. He would ring me when he landed and if I was too tired to stay up, he would wait till tomorrow, otherwise he would come straight round. He sounded hesitant and subdued.

"Come straight round, Will, please. I...I need you." Tears threatened again. I needed to see him in the flesh and hold him and have him hold me. I needed to see how my news had affected him; he had many hours on the plane to stew on it. I needed to convince him that having a baby was not a disaster and that the life he loved would not be ruined. If anything happened to this baby, this foetus, my life would be altered.

Chapter Three

It was well past midnight when Evie reluctantly retired to her room. She had become protective in Will's absence, but I didn't want any additional confrontations when Will arrived. I'd tried not to look as if I was at death's door, showering, putting on fresh clothes, and brushing my hair. Thank God the blood loss hadn't increased, but I still fretted, and it was emotionally exhausting waiting for Will.

There was a slight noise, and Will stood in the doorway, looking haggard. He had let himself in quietly in case I was in bed, but he laughed in relief when he saw me.

I stood up, slowly, for I was conscious of every movement I made, and he put down his rucksack. Instead of enveloping me in the caring hug I so desperately needed, he held me at arm's length and ran a critical eye from my face to my stomach and back.

"I thought - imagined all the way over that you'd be in hospital or having an op or laid up in bed. And here you are looking just the same, only thinner! Tell me you *are* feeling ok, Clem. Eight hours is a long time for the imagination to be in overdrive."

"I'm sorry to have sprung this on you, Will."

He threw himself down on the sofa and I followed more carefully.

I'd also had many hours thinking about what I would say to him when I saw him. Pessimistically, I'd imagined him suggesting an abortion, and I'd prepared myself to give back his ring and tell him I would have this baby alone. Will looked shattered; I had irreversibly altered both our lives. Neither of us was prepared for a baby in our lives, but I was strong enough to help the both of us to adjust.

Unfortunately, the trauma of the day, the waiting, and now the nervous climax on seeing Will culminated in me visibly crumpling before his eyes.

"You need to get some rest," said Will and stood up to help me to my feet. "Go to bed now and we'll talk tomorrow. I'm seeing spots in front of my eyes too!" I must have hesitated because he said gently, "I'll be in shortly, just need to freshen up first."

He gave me the briefest of embraces, as if I was too fragile to touch, and pushed me gently towards the door. I retreated to the bedroom, understanding that the ground on which we were treading was akin to walking on broken glass.

After a short while, he gently slid into bed beside me. I didn't wait to see if he'd keep his distance, but turned and threw my arm round him. I wanted to tell him how much I'd missed him, but sobbed into his shoulder instead. He drew me to him and rubbed my back, but was silent. Eventually, I relaxed into sleep.

In the morning, I was awoken by Will bearing a steaming mug of tea. His towel dried hair stood on end. He looked fresh and very handsome, but his eyes still held that wary expression he'd had last night. It was as if I'd suddenly transformed into an alien creature he no longer fully recognised.

"Evie's gone to work and sends her love and instructions to take care," he said. "Shall I make you some breakfast?"

"No thanks! Mornings are horrific!" His eyes widened. I threw off the duvet and rushed past him into the bathroom.

Sometime later, I emerged, showered and better. There had been some spotting while I'd been sleeping and I prayed to whatever gods were listening to keep my child safe.

Will had refrained from producing his usual fry up, probably because the fridge was depressingly empty.

"Can you eat a bit of toast?" he asked, slotting bread into the toaster.

I grimaced. "No, thanks!"

"No wonder you're looking skeletal, then. You need to eat for two!"

Despite trying to make light-hearted conversation, we were two strangers eyeing each other warily.

"When I was sick and didn't make it to New York with you, I really thought it was just a bug. I kept thinking I'd be ok the next day. If it hadn't been for Evie, I wouldn't have even bothered to see a doctor. Then I was told I was dehydrated, and had to take a pregnancy test as routine, and Will, when it came back positive, I just kept denying it to the doctor and she just looked at me. She'd probably heard that a thousand times before from silly sods like me."

Will reached over and gripped my hand. "You aren't a silly sod, you silly sod!" he said, making me smile.

I moved aside the junk mail on the table and found the images of the scan. Wordlessly, I pushed them over to him. Frowning, he picked them up, obviously having trouble working out the shapes. Then he swallowed hard and his face just crumpled. I was round the table and cradling him in a heartbeat.

"I'm sorry," he croaked. "I thought it was all a mistake and a false alarm. All the way over on the plane, I kept telling myself you'd had a false alarm. But now......" He broke off, raising the image. "It's real. It's a real baby."

I kissed his tears as happiness flooded through me. All

thoughts of Will demanding an abortion because a baby didn't fit into Trekkers International plans were swept away in an instant. The next few months would be a challenge, but we'd do it together.

"Trekkers is expanding and the last thing I want is for you to suffer because of a silly mistake of mine. I couldn't tell anyone and you were so far away and you and Rafaella looked and sounded as if Trekkers would be such a big success in the States and it was just too much to deal with."

Will had withdrawn his hand at the mention of Rafaella's name and gripped his mug. "It wasn't your mistake, Clem. I'm not saying it's a mistake at all, not now, not after seeing these." He indicated the images again.

"I can work from home, even with a baby. It's not as if I'm a Trek Leader. Kim is quite capable of running the office and I worked out that if, now we've merged, and there might be some staff adjustments, I'm the one who's dispensable. I'd worked it all out, Will. I wasn't going to ask you to commit, not now you have the States to conquer. And then, and then…" I pressed my lips together; I would not break down. "The thought of losing the baby made me realise I wanted it more than anything." I went over to the sink to get a glass of water.

"Of course you've got my support," said Will. "It's a shock for both of us and sure, it is bad timing, but the baby is not to blame. You're not dispensable, Clem. You're the glue that holds us all together. And I've also come to a decision about making sure that you rest properly and not take risks."

I looked at him quizzically as the water splashed out of the glass into the sink.

"Before she went to work, Evie filled me in on how bad you've been feeling. No, it wasn't a lecture," he grinned when he saw my face. "You scared her, and that's saying something about Evie who can scare the hell out of me! If you stay here, you'll want to come to work and refuse to take proper care. So, while you were in the land of nod, I did a bit of phoning. You'll probably try to refuse, but, Clemmie, I want to make sure you are ok and the baby has the best possible chance. So, I'm taking you to my family home in Wiltshire so you can be looked after and have a break for however long you need or want."

"Family home? What family home? You've never said anything about Wiltshire before! Your mother lives in France!" I said incredulously, water spilling everywhere. For as long as I had known Will, he had always lived in London.

Will pulled an embarrassed expression and fiddled with a knife. "I've never really lived there apart from school holidays with my father. My mother separated from my father when I was a nipper and I went to live with her in London. The house has always been in my father's family and after he died, I never went back there. You don't need to worry. Joe and Serena manage the house and grounds, they live in so it won't be full of dustsheets and cobwebs!"

"What about your mother?"

"She prefers to live in France. She paints and loves it there in her cottage. Please, Clemmie, just say yes. Serena, the housekeeper, is preparing a room for you. The country air will do you good, you won't be tempted to work, and we'll keep in touch with you about everything, and you can get plenty of rest and good food. It'll only be until enough time passes and the medics say the baby is in no danger."

I chewed my lip while doing calculations. I had a midwife appointment in a couple of weeks and had been advised to contact the hospital immediately if the blood loss became significantly heavier or I experienced contraction like pains. Two weeks' rest would not be too tiresome and I could always return whenever I liked. It would give me some time to sort out my emotions. Will still hadn't expressed pleasure at the thought of being a father, but then he had to come to terms with the future as much as I did. Besides, I was downright curious about his family home.

"All right," I said slowly, "as long as you don't forget about me if I'm to be stuck in the middle of nowhere."

"You'll love it, Clem. If you feel up to it you can explore the countryside around. Joe and Serena really will look after you. Just so long as you don't try to overdo it. And stay off a bike."

"Who pays this Joe and Serena? Surely your salary can't cover an annual income for them both. And if this place has so much going for it, why aren't you there more often?"

Will shrugged. "I was mainly brought up in London, so regard here as home now. Joe and Serena's salary does not come out of Trekkers income. Now, go pack and I'll retrieve the Range Rover to drive us down."

"We have to tell everyone at the office before I go."

"You phone Kim and I'll let Hugo know. I had an email from him. He's arrived in New York and in the hotel. Between them, both the news will spread like wildfire!"

"What about Rafaella in New York? You must have told her before you jumped on the plane home." My pregnancy should mean nothing to her as I was not one of her team. I should have asked Will directly if she knew we were engaged, but again, was my emotional state exaggerating any mutual attraction between them? My mind slid from the reality of knowing.

"She promised not to say anything until I officially announced it," he said rather brusquely. "I'll be back as soon as I can, so get packing, woman!"

Will was animated by his solution and he left without a backward glance, a kiss, or a hug.

I reluctantly packed a small case with plenty of warm tops and trousers in case it was a draughty old house. I'd forgotten to ask its exact location in Wiltshire so I could look it up in Google Maps. It occurred to me he was relieved to be packing me off somewhere 'safe' so that he could concentrate on the New York connection. When I'd packed, thrown things out and repacked, I added my laptop and e-reader, then phoned Kim at the office. Naturally, she was not at all surprised at my news. She'd already guessed, of course, but it was lovely just to hear her sounding thrilled. She was the first person who'd expressed congratulatory words, and I dripped a few tears.

Then I phoned Evie, who, surprisingly, wholeheartedly endorsed Will's suggestion. "I know you," she said. "You'd be getting bored and start decorating or turning up for work when you are supposed to be resting. And besides, I've got to go away myself for a few days research, so there'll be no one to keep an eye on you!"

"I just have a feeling I'm being packed off to some remote place and left to languish like Miss Haversham in Great Expectations. Did Will tell you where exactly his family home is?"

"No, but Wiltshire is not that far from London and Miss Haversham was dressed as a bride, and not a pregnant one either! I'm only at the end of a phone if you get lonely."

So still feeling moody, I paced around for a bit, tidying here and there in a distracted fashion. I was about to make a flask of coffee, then remembered that the smell of it rendered me queasy. I phoned Kim again to tell her where to find latest figures and itineraries on my computer, but she'd already found them and spoken to Ruby in New York who needed some figures. *All sorted, I'm redundant already.*

Will arrived and picked up my case. "There is a washing machine at Harthill House," he said, quirking his eyebrows, "so you didn't need to pack for an expedition! Are you ready? Traffic won't be too bad at this time of day for getting out of town, and we should be there before it gets dark."

Stepping into Will's Range Rover was a step into the unknown in more ways than I could possibly have imagined.

Chapter Four

Will was quiet as he concentrated on driving through London heading west, accompanied by his favourite rock classics. I had a million questions to ask about his home in Wiltshire, but I waited for the traffic to ease before bombarding him. Will was a good driver; he didn't crash gears, hurl the car round corners, or brake abruptly and eventually my head nodded.

When Will shook my leg, I blinked awake blearily.

"Clem, we're almost there," he said. "We're just bypassing Salisbury and in another twenty minutes, we'll be there. Feast your eyes on the Wiltshire countryside, even if it is only February."

We were driving along a narrow road which twisted and turned through a valley filled with ploughed fields and pastures. Cattle clustered around feeders full of hay and trees of all shapes and sizes grouped in copses or stood like solitary sentinels in the middle of fields, their skeletal branches stark against the grey sky. Over a wall bordering the road on the right, I glimpsed what looked like stone turrets and exclaimed.

"No, that's not Harthill House, "laughed Will. Now I was

fully awake he was quite animated. "That's the home of an earl and it is open to the public occasionally. Wiltshire is full of much grander homes than Harthill House. Wilton House, Longleat and Stourhead are probably the most famous and then there's Bowood in the Savernake Forest. And there are several in Dorset and Hampshire."

I looked askance at him, amazed at his sudden divulging of place names he'd never mentioned before. "My father dragged me round all those large houses when I was growing up," he said, as if he was embarrassed to admit it. "He wanted to compare them with our small estate. A lot of our land was sold after the First World War by some not-so-illustrious ancestor. Harthill House is certainly not on the same scale as Longleat, whose house and grounds are extensive, plus they have room for a Safari Park as well!"

"I can't believe it! I can't believe you're talking about stately homes and estates," I said, my mind reeling.

"It's of no consequence." Will shrugged over the steering wheel. "The main thing is making sure you rest until the medics tell you all is well. There is a surgery in Bridgeford, which is only a few miles from Harthill House, and I'll feel happier knowing a doctor is not far away."

Before I could express anything, he nodded forward. "Look," he said quietly.

We had turned a corner and fields fell away towards a silver thread of river as the road suddenly rose steeply into an escarpment densely packed with trees that rose like a huge curtain wall before us. The effect was quite dramatic as the road climbed and twisted through the middle of this dark forest of spiky branches and twisted limbs. Will indicated and swung right on a steep corner where the trees gave way to a pair of old wooden gate posts, an open white painted wooden gate, and a lodge on the left. It was built of brick and flint with gables and I had to screw my head round to confirm that I'd seen two Elizabethan style spiralling chimneys rising from the roof. The driveway, for that is what Will had turned into, ran along the top of the ridge, and was bordered by the dense trees on the right and farm fields on the left. A magnificent old tree some metres up the drive dwarfed the other trees lining the drive.

"The old ash is still standing," remarked Will. "Joe gets tree surgeons to assess its health every year as it is older than the house."

"Just how old is your house?" I began and stopped as I glimpsed movement on the other side of the ash tree. Two people emerged from behind the trunk's considerable girth and stared at the car. I craned round to see if they were walking in the same direction as we were. Both were dressed similarly, and I supposed they were walkers or farm workers, but in the dimming light it was hard to be sure.

"Do you know those people?" I asked.

Will glanced in his rear-view mirror. "What people?"

We rounded another tree filled bend and there was Harthill House before us and my mouth fell open. Will had given few clues about the size but it was literally large. A central building rose three stories with a pair of two storied wings on either side. The entire house was built in warm red brick with lines of white facing stones between each storey. Some of the tall sash windows were shuttered and chimneys stood outlined against the sky. Will crunched noisily on the gravel before a front entrance sheltered by an impressive central pillared portico and I was speechless.

"Welcome to Harthill House," he announced. He helped me out of the car because I was still stunned and the wide entrance door opened and a man and woman who looked in their fifties stepped out, closely followed by two very boisterous golden retrievers. They immediately ran up to Will, weaving round him, barking madly. He bent down to stroke them, and they nuzzled into him rapturously. Then they saw me and came to sniff, although their tails still waved furiously. "Get away, you big mutts!" said the man. He was tall and broad shouldered with dark hair. His face was weathered and crinkles formed round his eyes as his wide mouth stretched into a welcoming grin. The woman was slightly behind him, almost as tall as the man, her dark hair tied back. Smiling warily.

"Clemmie, meet Joe Hudson and his wife Serena who look after Harthill House and are waiting to take good care of you."

Joe wrung my hand heartily, and I was glad of his friendly countenance. Serena gave me a tentative handshake and her wary grey eyes assessed me before she said, "I hope you'll use this house as your home for as long as you want, Clemency. William has explained the circumstances and we hope everything will be fine." She moved towards Will and gave him an affectionate hug. "You've been away too long," she scolded. Joe also wrung Will's hand and gave him some hearty welcoming thumps on his back.

"Let's get in out of the cold," said Joe and ushered me in through the main doors into a huge, high-ceilinged room which soared up into shadows. Niches on the walls held statues of neoclassical figures. Plaster reliefs of decorative swags of leaves, flowers and fruit ran along the walls in a frieze and on the ceiling. A huge fireplace dominated one wall where a log fire cheerfully crackled. Opposite the main door, another set of imposing polished doors were closed. The wooden flooring glowed and a Persian rug faded with age lay in the centre under a round table. A vase filled with winter jasmine and willow twigs adorned the table and if I'd been overwhelmed by the exterior, nothing had prepared me for the interior so far. The smell of polish and wood smoke was comforting and the table lamps on either side of the fireplace cast a warm light.

"There's a pot of tea and a sponge cake in the kitchen," said Serena and led us to a door in the corner of this grand hall, the two dogs preceding us, tails high, leading the way. "Joe and I will show you around later, or tomorrow, if you prefer to rest."

Will just stood and grinned. He was enjoying my dumbstruck amazement.

"I'll take Clem's stuff up to her room first. She's in the blue bedroom, isn't she, Serena?" Serena nodded affectionately to Will. Whenever did they get to see him?

We passed out of the grand hall and into a large airy vestibule with an elaborately curved and highly polished staircase. Will charged up it with my bags.

The kitchen in the basement was accessed by a steep narrow staircase, which seemed at odds with the dimensions of the house. The kitchen contained the biggest Aga I had ever seen. The dogs flopped down on a rug spread before it after noisily lapping from a decorated chamber pot full of water. A huge tabby cat also lay on the rug, unperturbed by all the commotion. A wooden dresser with shelves of old looking crockery occupied the wall opposite the Aga and the wall behind the door had a recessed cupboard whose open doors revealed shelves of jars, tins, packets, and containers, as well as pots and pans. Shelves were fixed to the wall between two windows, holding books and dishes above a worktop and cupboards. A long oak table dominated the middle of the room. A laptop stood open at one end, with a pile of books and magazines next to it and a jug of early daffodils in the middle. Serena bustled about, setting plates and cups and saucers. She uncovered a Victoria sponge cake on the table. It was the first homely impression so far, and I sank gratefully into a chair. One dog pushed his nose into my hand and I stroked the silky head.

"That's Bess, "said Joe. "She's Jasper's mother and a bit calmer than Jasper, sometimes."

I was too intimidated to ask any questions: the enormity and age of the place robbed me of speech. I was not normally shy with people, but at that moment, I wanted Will by my side. Joe cheerfully chatted while washing his hands at the Belfast sink about the rarity of William's visits, but now he'd brought me down hopefully visits would be more plentiful.

"We have plenty to fill our time," he explained, sitting down opposite me. "We have the grounds and woods to manage and parts of the riverbank have fishing rights. Home Farm is next door, although Matt Crane, the farm manager, looks after the farming and livestock, and I give him help when needed. Serena is the housekeeper and looks after the kitchen gardens and flowerbeds and the house, but you probably know all this."

Serena nodded as she cut generous slices of cake.

I was reluctant to display my total ignorance and shock on discovering that Will was a landowner and owner of a private stately home. Who paid these people? Will had said their income did not come from Tough Treks finances, so who looked after the financial affairs of this country house and estate? I accepted a cup of tea in a lovely bone china cup decorated with roses and butterflies, as were the plates, and cut my cake into small portions as I was feeling queasy with nervousness again. It was best to be honest with Serena and Joe, so at last my tongue unstuck itself from my dry mouth and I asked where the bathroom was, just in case I needed to rush away. Serena looked mortified.

"Of course, my dear, I'm so sorry, I'm forgetting my manners! There is one here in the basement, just a little way up the passage on the left. Your bedroom has a bathroom attached, not exactly en suite, but near enough for emergencies, and there's another on the ground floor."

Will strode in and sat down next to me. He didn't speak until he'd taken a mouthful of sponge cake, then sighed and wiped his lips on the paper napkin. "You haven't lost your touch, Serena, light as a feather and delicious." He turned to me. "Serena makes jams from all the fruit grown here, and the farm sells milk to local dairies who turn some of it into butter and cream and sold locally under our name."

"I hope you can cast an eye on things while you're here, William," said Joe, helping himself to another slice. I had managed half a slice, and it was as delicious as Will said, but I feared embarrassing everyone if I had to rush out, even though I hadn't eaten anything so far today.

"Not this time, I'm afraid, Joe," said Will with his mouth full. "I was just about to say to Clem- something's come up at the office, so I'll need to leave shortly."

I turned in consternation to him. I wanted to say please Will don't leave me on my own so soon, but instead I said, "What's come up?"

"I'll tell you after tea when I take you up to your room. And besides, you are not to take on any problems while you're here." He smiled affably, helping himself to more cake as if I would accept his decision meekly.

"We've just made an epic decision at Tough Treks to set up in the States," he explained to Joe and Serena, who were leaning in eager to hear more. "So there's lots of stuff to sort out."

"Are there problems?" I asked sharply. It hit me suddenly that I was about to be sidelined, put out to pasture in the country, out of harm's way. I glared at Will to say that I was still his business partner when Serena asked if anybody would like more tea, obviously trying to smooth over a budding domestic drama.

"I think I would like to go to my room now," I said, trying not to sound rude. Will and I had to talk without Serena and Joe hanging on our every word. I didn't want these strangers to know that a chasm had opened between us: on one side, me and a precarious foetus, and on the other Will and Rafaella and the lure of the States. Although Will acted blissfully unaware of any chasm. I stood up and stared at Will meaningfully. He got up in his relaxed way and, with a "see you later" to his house custodians, opened the door for me and ushered me through.

"I can see you are rattled," he said as I clambered up the steep staircase from the basement. "Even your curls are quivering!" I almost spluttered into a giggle, but remained indignant.

"We're going to have to go up the grand staircase as well." Will took my arm to help me up, but I shrugged him off.

"I'm not an invalid," I retorted and stamped up the beautiful, curving staircase, gripping the smooth, polished balustrade.

At the top was a wide space, lit from above by a cupola reflecting very little daylight now as darkness fell. There were a couple of doors opposite each other on this landing, but Will led me down a passage and opened the first door on the left-hand side and felt for a light switch. Momentarily, my breath stopped as I entered a large bedroom graced with a bed crowned with soft blue drapes at its head. A blue silk quilted coverlet matched the drapes, as did the curtains at the two huge sash windows opposite the door. Will crossed to the windows to close the shutters.

"All the shutters and windows are original. You might hear the wind sighing through the sashes if you're lucky! It will sound like moaning ghosts!"

He drew the curtains over the shutters and turned on the bedside lights. It was truly a delightful room. The walls were covered in very pale blue watered silk fabric, maybe original. The room should have felt cold as there was so much blue, but the effect was calming. An ornate white marble fireplace with a modern electric fire in the hearth was opposite the bed. There were radiators under each window, but the fire gave out comforting warmth. I turned to Will, who was watching me with a quiet amusement, almost drinking in my astonishment. My irritability was forgotten.

"I've set your laptop on the dressing table and you'll be pleased to know there is broadband connection in this remote outpost of the empire. You can communicate and shout at us and no doubt think of things we've forgotten to your heart's content." I made to swipe at him and he ducked away.

"Honestly, Clem, there is no secrecy. I've got to go back to New York to sign all the legal documents. Rafaella has been working hard to make sure our enterprise is legally formalised. Hugo's already there and met the team. We'll both sign the contract; everything will be legalised and we'll be up and running in the spring! If you had been well, you would have signed instead of Hugo, but I won't let you fly, not now."

"I'm sorry, Will. I shouldn't have jumped to conclusions. All this on top of everything else has wiped me out." I slumped into the deep armchair near the fire.

"It means I have to go now, though, Clem. I've got to drive back tonight so that I can catch an early plane tomorrow. I am truly sorry, but timing is critical."

"But I don't know my way round the house. I never in my wildest imagination believed your family owned such a grand mansion. And I've only just been introduced to Joe and Serena," I wailed.

"Joe and Serena will look after you twenty-four seven. Their living quarters are on the floor above, so you won't be alone. Your bathroom is the next one in this passage. Sorry it isn't en-suite, but we can't knock through walls in a Grade One listed building!"

"How can you afford all this, Will? Who pays Serena and Joe?"

"Ah, the house and estate are in a Trust. I won't bore you with details now, but it's to do with inheritance. Serena and Joe are paid by the Trust, so nothing comes out of the business profits, Clem."

He came up to me and took my hands. "I must go now, darling. Don't be cross with me. I'll stay in touch and I'll tell Serena that you might like supper in bed tonight." He leaned down and kissed the top of my head. "Stay safe", he said and disappeared out of the door before I could protest. He'd kissed the top of my head like I was his sister or an elderly aunt! I rushed to the door, almost fearing he'd locked me in, but the passage was empty and the thought of chasing after him, and bumping into Serena or Joe and trying to pretend everything was fine overwhelmed me. I dashed to the bathroom next door and emptied the very little contents of my stomach. It was a modern bathroom unit, the floor was thickly carpeted, fluffy towels hung on the heated rail, and pretty watercolours hung on the walls. There was a shower over the bath shielded by a glass screen and a thick white bathrobe hung on the back of the door. I threw my clothes on the floor and climbed into the shower. I expected a feeble trickle but was proved wrong and the shower cream was expensive and smelled exquisite.

I dried with the fluffy towel and put on the bathrobe, feeling more relaxed and struck by the absurdity of the situation. I was staying in a gothic mystery mansion! I dug out my pyjamas from my case, which Will had left on the bed, and by the time I had donned them and the bathrobe again, I eyed the bed longingly. I should have guessed Will had no intention of staying, because he hadn't brought any luggage with him. There was a light knock on the door. Will! I rushed to open the door with a huge smile. Instead of Will, Serena stood there wearing a sympathetic expression.

"Will has explained his situation, that he has to go back to the States," she said. "I am so sorry he couldn't stay; we don't see him enough. And you must be feeling lonely without him and overwhelmed by all this. I'll bring up some supper for you in a little while."

Feeling overwhelmed was an understatement. Although I would have gone straight to bed without bothering to eat, it would have been churlish to refuse and I had to eat, even if it didn't remain long inside me.

"Thank you, that would be lovely, but I can't eat anything

heavy, I'm afraid. I hope this nausea doesn't last too long as I normally eat like a horse! And it has been a strange day so far," I said tiredly.

"I'm glad you've found the bathroom as well," Serena smiled, which transformed her rather grim countenance. "I'll be about half an hour; I have a chicken casserole in the Aga so you can eat as much or as little as you wish."

Tomorrow, I would make a fresh start and find out as much as I could about Will's life here and about Harthill House itself.

I looked at my phone and there was a text from Evie:

> Hi, Sweetie, how are you? Sorry I had to rush off this morning, but I knew you and Will had a lot to catch up on! How's it going? Hope you have kissed and made up; you can both be a little stubborn LOL. And send me pics of your hovel in the country please and hope you are not out gathering sticks for the fire!!! xxx

I fired off a reply:

> The house is Definitely Not a hovel and my mouth is still hanging open! I will send pics tomorrow as it is dark now and I'm about to have supper. (Yes, I am being looked after). My bedroom is very sumptuous and you would be green with envy at the size of the house! xxx

I didn't say anything about Will rushing off again; I was too tired to have to go through more explanations. I was about to move to my laptop when there was a tap on the door again. Joe and Serena were both outside. Joe carried a tray with a couple of covered dishes on it, and a bottle of water and Serena carried a tray with a kettle, and an array of different flavour tea bags and a packet of biscuits.

"Supper served", said Joe and set it on a low table by the armchair. "And a kettle, in case you feel like a hot drink in the night. It's a long trek to the kitchen, so these are emergency rations."

"Thank you, you are being very kind. I must apologise for being a bit, well, off, when I arrived," I said sheepishly, not accustomed to being waited on.

"No apologies, love, as William explained, you have had a fright and it's not over yet, so we will make sure you don't overdo things." Joe beamed at me and I responded with a smile. Serena had disappeared but then returned with my clothes picked up from the bathroom floor and folded. She placed them on the bed and waved away the apology which had formed on my lips.

"We hope you have a peaceful night, but here is my mobile number in case you get panicky. We are upstairs, but it will seem like a million miles away to you. We'll give you the royal tour tomorrow if you are up to it." Joe handed me a piece of paper with his number written and I felt childishly reassured.

After they'd gone, I cautiously lifted the lid covering the dish. A wonderful aroma assailed me, making me realise I'd been starving myself the last couple of days so that I wouldn't be sick, but of course it made no difference. I sat in the chair with my tray and spooned down chicken casserole hungrily. I sat back after a little while, not risking eating the lot, but completely satisfied and a feeling of well-being spread through me. I was warm and fed and cosy. Bleeding had not increased. Will would contact me in due course. There was nothing I could do but surrender to my welfare here and make the best of it. I gazed dreamily at the portrait paintings hanging on either side of the fireplace. There were four small oval ones each portraying a young woman and from her hairstyle and upper garments I guessed they were early nineteenth century. Was she one of Will's ancestors who had lived in this house? I couldn't quite get my head around the fact that this place had a story to tell and Will was part of it.

Chapter Five

When I woke the next morning, I lay for a few seconds adjusting to where I was, confused that daylight was glimmering from a different direction than my window at home. I sat up shivering and pulled the bathrobe around me. The familiar crampy twinges got me out of bed to creep hastily to the bathroom before realising that there wasn't anybody near to disturb. It was a strange scenario, like staying in a hotel where all the other guests had mysteriously vanished. Serena had tidied the bathroom from last night and I was relieved that the 'spotting' had decreased.

Back in my bedroom, I sat quietly for a while until the nauseous sensations subsided. Curiosity drew me to the windows, and I opened the shutters fully, letting the clear morning light in. The windows looked out on the back of the house. The trees opposite were part of a thick wood separated from the end of formal gardens by a wide meadow. I could hear the cawing of rooks. There was an ornamental fishpond surrounded by a low wall and formal flowerbeds on either side, in front of stone steps which must lead to a doorway beneath my room. To my right, the gardens stretched in lawns to a high hedge with a wooden door in it. Beyond that the meadow broadened, revealing the dark line of a river glimpsed through winter trees. On the rising ground across the river, chequered fields and small copses of trees rose gradually to a rounded hill crowned with trees. Movement drew my gaze to the left as a herd of black and white cows progressed across the meadow, tearing at the sparse winter grass as they slowly ambled. Two men were standing under a tall leafless beech tree by the fence bordering the wood opposite, gazing upwards towards my windows. They looked very like the people I'd seen in the drive yesterday and I guessed they were the herdsmen, or dairymen. Something about their style of dress made me stare hard. Both wore straw hats and baggy smocks which hung down towards their knees and belted with what looked like rope. They appeared to be wearing breeches and old-fashioned strips of cloth-like gaiters and boots. One of them had a pipe in his mouth and both held long knobbly walking sticks, probably to drive the cattle. Their faces were in shadow under their wide-brimmed hats, but they were looking intently towards my window. I fetched my phone and, half hidden behind the shutter, took a photo of them. It was presumptuous of me, I know, but when I met them, I would ask if they minded and really see if they were dressed in what looked like outfits from a Thomas Hardy novel. After the last of the cows had passed, the men remained staring in my direction and didn't follow the cattle. I took another couple of shots of the views from my window, such a contrast after city streets. Then I scrolled back through them so I could send them to Evie. The first one I'd taken showed the start of the procession of black and white cows meandering into view, a stretch of meadow, the fencing separating the wood, the beech tree, but no men.

I frowned at my screen suspiciously. I was sure I had centred the men on my screen before clicking, but the picture just showed a rural winter scene. Neither of them was in the field when I peered through the glass again.

I dressed quickly and gathered all last night's supper dishes. Negotiating the highly polished staircase with a tray was daunting, but at last I reached the basement. Serena must have heard the rattling dishes because she came out of the kitchen and relieved me of the tray.

"I was just going to bring a breakfast tray up to you," she said. "You look more rested today, my dear."

The kitchen was warm, and the two dogs vied to say hello.

"Sit yourself down. I'm just doing scrambled eggs for you," Serena commanded.

"You don't need to......" I started to say, but at Serena's questioning look the words 'put yourself out for me,' froze on my lips and I sat down obediently. She and Joe had been instructed to look after me, and that's what they were doing. A plate of scrambled egg on toast appeared before me and adding seasoning, I took a mouthful of the deliciously smooth texture and grinned my thanks.

Joe came into the room, rubbing his hands. "It's a bit parky out there. Good morning to you, Clemency, hope you had a good night?"

"Yes, I thought that with being in a strange bed in strange surroundings and no London traffic noises, I wouldn't sleep a wink, but I think the quietness helped. The only thing that unnerved me was when I switched the lights off and it was totally black!"

"Ah, no streetlights here! You could leave the passage light on so that it shines under your door for orientation if the dark bothers you," said Joe.

"I just undid the shutters. That helped," I replied.

"You'll soon get used to it all." Joe attacked a plate of bacon, eggs, and sausage and as the smell reached over to me, my stomach rebelled.

The cat stood and stretched languidly before coming over to sniff my feet. I leaned down to scratch his or her head and it arched its back before returning to the rug.

"That's Tabby. She appeared a few years ago and decided to stay. She pleases herself, so don't be disappointed if she ignores you!"

"Do you have a family?" I asked.

"Yes, two strapping lads, both in farming," said Joe. "Christopher is up in Cumbria, Andrew in Wales, with a growing family. They were brought up on a farm, like me and my father and grandfather, so it's in their blood. Anyway, Clemency, I'll give you the promised tour of the house after breakfast, but there's no need to rush anything. I'll meet you in the hall, say in half an hour?"

That would give me time to deal with any repercussions from a delicious breakfast and the nausea inducing smell of bacon.

In my room I stood at the window, taking in the tranquil view under a clear cold blue sky, then peered round as far as I could see in case the two strangely dressed farm workers were still lurking.

On the wall on either side of the pretty fireplace carved with swans and bulrushes were the four miniatures set in oval gilt frames I'd noticed last night. Three depicted the same young lady, with a heart-shaped face and a sweet smile which lit up her blue eyes as if she had been enjoying her time sitting with the artist. A loosely tied bonnet rested lightly on her corn-coloured hair. But the composition of the fourth one made me hastily compare with the other three, as this one depicted her with hair covered by a mob cap, from which tendrils of hair framed her now sad face. Her eyes were heavy lidded, shadowed, and sombre, and her mouth a straight line. She gazed into the distance as if her thoughts were elsewhere. I searched for a name and at the bottom right of each picture were the initials HW. *Was this girl one of Will's ancestors or just pictures bought at an auction? There might be a family tree somewhere in the house.* I stepped carefully down the stairs to meet Joe.

We started with the ground-floor rooms. Opening off the great hall was the salon or drawing room, light reflecting off the yellow walls and silk drapes. Beautifully upholstered sofas were arranged away from the walls, with antique occasional tables next to them. Mirrors reflected the light from the long windows, of which the central one opened like a door onto the steps outside. A white and gilded sideboard without a back held a lamp and the fireplace was carved marble. Beyond that large room lay the library, and I gasped when Joe turned on the lights as the windows were still shuttered. Shelves reached almost to the ceiling with long drawers at waist height and were situated on either side of the fireplace. Books of all sizes, some bound in leather or cloth coverings, filled the shelves. Leading off that room and the hall was a wood panelled room which was sparsely furnished with a couple of winged armchairs and a small table. "This is called the Gentlemen's Parlour," said Joe. "Apparently, in days of old, this is where the gentlemen retired after dinner, but it's not used for anything now. And through that door is a loo."

He led me through a door in the Great Hall, which Joe described as a cube because of its equal dimensions, and I was flabbergasted by another staircase, much narrower and carpeted. "This is the service staircase," grinned Joe, enjoying my amazement. "It's what the servants used, as it runs from the basement to the top of the house."

There was an exquisite dining room on the left of the front entrance. It was small compared to the size of the house and the centre filled with a long oval table with chairs tucked under it. There was another marble fireplace, sideboards, and oil paintings. I was running out of expressions of surprise and amazement!

"We'll do downstairs next if you feel up to it." Despite tiredness, my curiosity won the battle.

Joe led me down the corridor, linking the central block with the South Wing. The niches in the walls were empty now but had apparently been occupied by sculptured figures. Down a stone staircase under the South Wing was a cavernous room with worn stone flags. "This is the original kitchen," he said, twirling round. One wall was filled by the enormous stone fireplace and ovens, now rusting and flaking. In its heyday, it would have been warm in the winter when pies and pastries, dishes of fowl, venison and mutton were prepared for the family, hellishly hot in summer. Did Will's ancestors entertain lavishly? There were dark rooms leading off the kitchen, and I'd watched enough period dramas to know that kitchen maids and skivvies would have been kept relentlessly busy washing up and preparing food in them. We retraced our steps to the stairs leading down to the basement. "Once the original kitchen and the basement corridor were connected, but must have vanished under the garden years ago!"

"The servants must all have been very fit running along these passages and up and down the stairs," I said, as out of the corner of my eye I glimpsed a figure in a white apron scurrying along. I turned but saw nothing.

"And exhausted! Up before dawn and no bed until the master and mistress retired! The kitchen we use now used to be where all the staff ate. Where the Aga is now, there was a fireplace. And this room opposite, the boiler room, was the sewing or linen room. It's good for drying stuff now." Joe indicated strings of washing line crisscrossing the back of the warm room.

As he led me up the corridor, I stopped suddenly, as shadowy figures glided past me and disappeared through open doors in the long passage and alarmingly through the wall where the staircase was. Joe, thinking I was resting chatted on about the different uses of the little rooms which he called pantries: the butter pantry, where blocks of cold butter were patted into dainty shapes using wooden paddles, the bread pantry containing wired shelves, and the china room which still contained some exquisite sets of china that were part of Lady Therese's trousseau. *Who is Lady Therese?* As Joe stopped in front of a closed door, I distinctly saw a footman wearing breeches and a black waistcoat over a white ruffled shirt. His hair was tied back in a ponytail. Joe unlocked the door as I stood gaping at the silent spectacle and Joe was completely unaware! "This is where the silver is kept," he said, holding the door open so that I could see in. It was a windowless room, and the walls lined with shelves and cabinets. Candelabra and silver salvers, flagons and jugs and bowls occupied the shelves. "Most of it is locked in the cabinets, but I act as the butler by cleaning it occasionally."

Still dumbfounded by my 'vision' of footmen, I backed out of the room and hurriedly stepped out of the way as a maid in a voluminous white apron over a grey dress, her hair tucked under a mob cap passed me carrying a tray of dishes. I kept glancing at Joe, but he was oblivious and I wanted to break out into nervous giggles. He led me to the very end of the passage, with me glancing behind.

"This is the old scullery. It's still freezing cold in here. I pity the poor people who had to scrub the family's dirty linen!" I blinked several times as I watched a young girl, lanky hair trailing from her cap, leaning over one of the two deep stone sinks, red chapped hands rubbing a piece of material. Through her ethereal body, I saw the modern washing machine and tumble dryer against the wall behind her. "The sinks are good for washing the dogs now," Joe said. I still couldn't speak, but I didn't feel afraid. A door led out into an open area between the main house and the North Wing, which was partially open to the skies. Hooks in the walls were clues that this was where the family laundry was hung up to dry on good days.

The whole of the downstairs must have thrummed with the multitudinous daily tasks to ensure smooth running of the household. Was I so absorbed in Joe's descriptions that my vivid imagination had conjured up people from the past? The formal rooms upstairs were richly decorated and echoed the tastes and designs of that era, but none held the busy atmosphere of the lower level. If I was seeing ghosts from the past, I wasn't alarmed by them. I had never had any such experience ever in my life.

Joe opened a heavy oak door opposite the silver pantry: the wine cellar. I was reluctant to go down the stone steps into that dark cavern, despite the installation of electric lighting. The brick lined walls absorbed the light and the thought of going down there with a flickering candle or lantern held aloft two centuries ago searching the wooden racks for the master's wine or brandy or port brought goose bumps over me.

By the time Joe guided me briefly round the unoccupied rooms on the ground floor of the North Wing, I was sagging and was conscious of continually glancing back. I wasn't alarmed; more amazed by this newfound 'gift' of seeing presences I'd suddenly acquired. I didn't want to alert Joe to these presences. He was obviously unaware of them. He happily prattled on, explaining that this wing hadn't been in use a for a century and had to be assessed regularly for damp, dry rot, and woodworm. The plaster had been removed, exposing original bricks. The other cellars used for hanging game and storing wood and coal were down steep steps beneath the South Wing. I was showing signs of fatigue and imagination overload by then and Joe said he'd show me the upper floor and stable block another time, although there were no horses now; Will's father had been the last person to ride and hunt.

Joe escorted me to my room. We just peered into bedrooms on the way.

"Thank you, Joe. The house is incredible and I'm truly fascinated by it. I'll be ready to continue when you're not busy another time, and I'll have a wander myself."

"There aren't that many bedrooms on this floor, considering the size of the house," he said as I flopped on the bed. "That's because the hall is two storeys high. Serena will bring you up some soup for lunch." He raised his hand as I protested. "We all have soup, so it's no bother. Then I'll be off to give Matt a hand."

"Thank you so much again, Joe. The house is a real treasure, but I hope I haven't kept you from your tasks."

"No bother at all. I'll see you later." Joe galloped off down the stairs before I could ask him about the two farmworkers I'd seen.

∼

"Harthill House is huge, Evie, and I've yet to see the top floor and the stables and the grounds!" I sat cross-legged on the bed, gazing at the trees out of my window. "I can't understand why Will has never mentioned this place before or brought me here on a visit. If it was a tumble-down cottage with the roof caving in, I would understand why he conveniently forgot about it but the rooms are seriously grand, the views spectacular and there are woods and a farm and fishing rights on the river and goodness knows what else providing income."

"Perhaps he's ashamed in an inverted way," suggested Evie. "He might think everybody will think he's a Hooray Henry and not take him seriously." I conceded the point.

"Evie, I've forgotten how many rooms already, and they all have names. The drawing room opens onto the formal gardens and with the yellow walls and drapes, it is very light and graceful. There's a library stuffed from floor to ceiling with shelves of books and there's even a little room off the great hall called the Gentlemen's Parlour so you can imagine the bewigged gentlemen leaving the ladies and taking their port and cigars or pipes to discuss the price of wool and silk, and stocks and shares in the trade from India and the Far East –and probably gambling! Apparently, Will allows some groups to meet in the year, mainly history or literary or architectural societies. I don't know why he hasn't applied for a licence for marriages to be held here. It would be magical..." I paused as my heart lurched. Would I ever marry my baby's father?

Evie took up the cue. "It sounds amazing, Clem, but I think you've been watching too many period dramas and your imagination has taken off. But that's not a bad thing! Is Will still with you?"

After a moment's hesitation, I decided truth was best. "He's flown over to New York again and Hugo's there as well to sign the deal with Rafaella." A sudden thought hit me. "Evie, why don't you come and visit me? There's plenty of room. I'll phone Will to OK it and make sure Serena and Joe don't think I'm taking advantage of them. I'm not sure whether to regard them as servants or House Managers like they have in the National Trust. They seem more at home here than Will."

"Clem, that would be amazing! Can I come soon? I've only got some reports to finish, and the library you described sounds exciting."

Her voice bubbled with enthusiasm and I longed to see a familiar face with whom I could share my thoughts instead of treading carefully around Joe and Serena, although so far, they had been unfailingly helpful. And did I really see ghosts in the basement passage? They weren't remotely frightening, just getting on with their daily tasks. They appeared unaware of me and Joe. There was a knock on the door and I opened it to admit Serena bearing a tray with soup, bread, and fruit.

"Joe was a superb guide, but I wilted before he could finish," I said as she put the tray down on the table by the fireplace. "Thank you for going to all this trouble, Serena. You must be kept busy keeping all the rooms clean and tidy."

"I don't do it all myself and as the rooms are rarely used, they just need maintaining. Mollie Crane, who lives in the cottage by the gates, comes in twice a week. You'll meet her tomorrow."

"I'm going to phone Will shortly as my flatmate Evie would love to see the house, but I don't want you to be overloaded with extra cooking and cleaning. Evie took care of me when I was sick, when Will was away."

"You don't need to ask my permission, Clemency," said Serena. "Having company makes a nice change from rattling round on your own while William's away."

I warmed to Serena. She must get rather lonely here, especially as her sons were so far away.

"Thank you. We can always rustle up our own meals if it's too much for you."

"It's no more effort to add one or two more to the table, and I enjoy cooking," said Serena affably, and I decided it was more tactful to fit in with her plans.

I ate as much of the soup and fruit as I dared and then brewed up a cup of chamomile tea. Had I only been in this house for twenty-four hours? There was so much yet to discover and without Will here, it was difficult to comprehend that he was the owner of this property. He must have arrived in New York by now, so I quickly rang his number and drifted to the window. There, surely in the deep shadow of the wood opposite, was movement. Frowning, I peered into the wooded shade. Will answered his phone, and I turned away, happiness surging through me at the sound of his voice.

"Clem, how are you? I've literally just landed! Look, I really am sorry for ditching you last night, but there was no choice. Are Serena and Joe taking good care of you? They really are the best of people. They've been at Harthill House since before my father died, and you couldn't be in safer hands."

"I might forgive you for ditching me, as you put it, and yes, I am being spoiled. Why on earth haven't you told me about this place before, Will? It's not as if its size is insignificant!"

"I'll give you the full story when I'm back, I promise, but right now I've got to find my transport to Rafaella's office. Hugo's there already, plus Raf's lawyer."

"Before you rush away again Will, is it ok if Evie comes to stay? Serena has no objections."

"Of course she can! Evie's company will cheer you up. Got to push on. Clem, hopefully Rafaella will show us some trails tomorrow, so speak to you soon."

He was gone. I made my way down to the kitchen before brooding on the brevity of Will's conversion. His tone was upbeat, despite the long flight and his focus was very definitely on the States. *And Rafaella?*

Serena was tapping at her laptop on the kitchen table. "Leave the tray on the side and I'll add them to the dishwasher later."

"I can do that," I said, adding my few dishes. "Will doesn't have any objection to Evie coming to stay, so can I give you a hand getting a room ready?"

"No, no, there'll be no need, Clemency. Mollie will be in tomorrow, so she can freshen up the Green bedroom on the other side of your bathroom, then you'll be near each other. Do you mind sharing the bathroom?"

"Gosh, no! Thanks, Serena. How do I get to the gardens?" I asked, noticing the sun outside. The windows were lawn level, reminding me I was in the basement. "I need some fresh air."

"The back door is next to the boiler room. Just go through the yard to the steps and turn right to get to the gardens or left for the front of the house. Better take your phone with you, just in case..."

Glancing in the boiler room opposite the kitchen on my way out, I noticed various forms of outdoor wear hanging up with an assortment of wellington boots lined up below them. My jacket was warm, but one of those waterproof coats would be useful if it rained, as would the wellies. They must belong to Will's relations in the past. His life was a complete mystery to me. He owed me explanations when he returned.

The back door opened into an enclosed courtyard and the steps out of it passed under the south wing. There were sturdy wooden doors on either side of the brick arch and I guessed these were the cellars or storage cellars Joe had told me about. Emerging at the top of the steps, I turned right, as instructed. Going through an ornamental gate, I found myself in a small garden enclosed by low hedges and ornamental trees. Stone urns graced each corner, and I imagined them filled with crimson geraniums in the summer. Beyond the hedge lay fields and away to the left I glimpsed a roof and chimneys through a copse of trees which must be Home Farm. A wooden gate in the hedge to my right took me into the formal gardens and I followed the low box hedge until I saw the wrought-iron gate which opened onto the meadow. Snowdrops glowing in the woods on the other side of the meadow enticed me through the gate to the wood opposite, avoiding the many cowpats. A chained and padlocked gate offered entry into the wood, but was easy to climb over. Looking back to the house, the rays from the westering sun reflected in the many windows and the red brick glowing warmly as I clicked away on my phone camera happily. It was a very attractive house, geometrically balanced with equal spaces between each window and a double door in the middle of the ground floor, leading into what I now knew was the Drawing Room. Steps from a terrace led down to the small pond flanked by more of the stone urns. It would be a lovely spot to relax with drinks on summer evenings. My heart twinged at that distant possibility.

The wood was in deep gloom, in contrast to the luminous snowdrops. Bare-branched trees stretched into a dark silent distance, although brown buds were already forming. Surrounding the snowdrops were straggly box hedges, long neglected. I sniffed deeply as the tiny flowers perfumed the air with delicate earthy sweetness and I swiftly gathered a large posy for my bedroom. When I straightened, darkness settled under the trees as the sun slid behind a ridge on the far side of the valley. All was still in the cold air. Even the rooks had fallen silent, high in their rookeries. I quickly picked my way through the tangled undergrowth to climb back over the gate and, as I swung my leg over the top, I felt a prickle on the back of my neck. I glanced behind me in the dark pools between the trees and the shadowy shapes of two people appeared.

"Hello," I called out, unnerved by the silence but thinking they were the herdsmen. There was no reply and my imagination played tricks: the shapes moved closer without disturbing the bushes and clumps of dead grasses and their silence was unnatural. The prickly feeling intensified into panic as they drew closer. I stumbled back across the meadow and ran through the garden gate. In the hedge's shelter, I plonked down on a stone bench to get my breath back. It was stupid of me to panic and I'd missed the opportunity to speak to the herdsmen and introduce myself. They might have presumed I was a trespasser. I scrolled through all the photos I'd taken to select some to send to Evie. They should whet her appetite and amaze her as much as Harthill House amazed me! When I got to the first one I'd taken from my bedroom, I still couldn't fathom why the men hadn't appeared on it.

Evie quickly answered the phone. "I'll be there as soon as I can," she said, delighted, when I told her she was welcome at any time. "Then we can explore every nook and cranny as long as we don't upset Mrs Danvers."

"Evie, Serena is nothing like Mrs Danvers," I laughed at her comparison with the creepy housekeeper in Daphne du Maurier's *Rebecca*.

The cold of the bench soon persuaded me to move, and I met Bess and Jasper coming from the other direction as they plunged down the steps and barked at the back door. Joe appeared from the direction of the front of the house. "You look a bit flustered."

"It got dark rather quickly in the woods, and the silence was unnerving. I must be more of a city girl than I thought!" I held out the snowdrop posy as a reason for entering the wood in the near dark.

"They're putting on a good show this year. Those in the wood must have been planted when it was still part of the garden to the house. That bit is called the Ladies' Bower and apparently there used to be little paths lined with clipped hedges and ornamental trees. Lavender still grows in there in the summer, but it's all gone wild after years of neglect. William's father had plans to restore the parkland to its former glory all the way down to the river. There's a plan in the library showing the extent of the estate in its heyday."

He opened the back door, and the dogs rushed in to drink noisily and sloppily out of their drinking pot. Joe moved the kettle onto the hot plate.

"Sit down and I'll make tea. You look, well, a bit stricken, if you don't mind me saying. Please don't overdo things. There's no need for you to rush around. Serena's at her WI meeting in Bridgeford, but she should be back any minute and then she'll be planning her cakes that she sells at the WI market on Friday mornings."

I relaxed as Joe prattled on as he drank his builder's tea leaning against the warm Aga with the dogs stretched out on the rug before it, and I sipped at my weak peppermint tea. Tabby rubbed against my legs, then returned to the warm Aga.

"Joe, do you have many farm workers here at the moment?"

Joe shook his head. "In the summer months, I get someone to lop the high hedges and we check and prune some trees as necessary. William leaves it to me to decide whether we need tree surgeons in to clear any dangerous boughs or trees. I do all the mowing and other hedges and Serena does the weeding and planting in the gardens and in the veg and fruit garden behind the North Wing. Matt only uses casual labour at lambing and harvesting. The farm is part of the estate and Matt pays rent to William, or rather, to the Estate Trust, so he can't afford workers permanently. He works very hard and I give him a hand at milking times sometimes and with the lambing and calving and harvest time."

The picture of rural life here that Joe was painting was so far removed from the life I lived with Will in London that I shook my head in disbelief.

"I've seen the same two people two or three times," I said.

"Probably walkers; the path through the woods is a public right of way, but some take advantage and wander round the grounds."

I frowned at his remark. Those two silent figures moving towards me in the woods didn't look like casual walkers.

"It's another world that Will inhabits. While he's off doing treks and completing business deals in New York, you are all beavering away down here. He has never spoken to me about this place, you know." I felt disloyal discussing Will like this to Joe, but he shrugged and seemed to understand.

"William trusts us to manage it all and we do. Once or twice a year, the Estate Trustees meet with the Solicitor and Accountant in London and we go over finances and plan out priorities. William has told us he has no plans to sell up; legally, it would be difficult for him to do that, anyway. The estate is entailed."

"Sorry, what does entail mean?"

"It means the estate has been willed as a life estate passed down to the male heirs. If you'll forgive me for speaking plainly, if there is a little heir on the way, William might make a bigger effort to turn Harthill House into a family home again."

Bess suddenly gave a little bark as Serena entered the kitchen and dumped her bag on the table. After the dogs had duly received fondling of ears, they subsided onto the rug again.

"Whose family home are we talking about?" she asked as she pulled off her woolly hat and unwound her scarf.

Joe looked a little shamefaced. "I think I was speaking out of turn, talking about the new arrival."

"Yes, I think you were and you should apologise to Clemency. It's none of our business."

"Really, there is absolutely no need to apologise," I protested. "If anything, it should be me apologising for asking too many questions. I came here totally unprepared for this house and all the work going on behind the scenes. If Will was here, I'd be grilling him instead!"

I thought Serena's attitude was unnecessarily brittle, but I couldn't risk saying or doing anything to jeopardise their kindness in looking after me. I took my mug over to the dishwasher and asked Serena if she needed any help.

"No, thank you for offering. When supper is ready, I can bring it up to you or you can eat with us in the kitchen if you'd like."

It was an olive branch, and I grasped it. "Yes, please, it would be lovely to join you." Serena gave me an estimate of the time supper would be ready and I escaped. At the foot of the stairs, I turned and headed for the library instead of going up to my room. Joe had mentioned an old plan of the estate in its heyday, and I assumed that would be the best place to find it. The hall was lit by an outsize table lamp on the oak side table and it cast muted light around the large space and the polished floor gleamed. There was no fire in the huge hearth today and the windows were shuttered. I opened the door to the library and groped for the light switches. An overhead chandelier burst into light and recessed lighting in the bookshelves responded to the light switches. The two sashed windows hadn't been shuttered yet and the reflection against the winter evening outside reminded me of the mysterious unknown Twins, as I now called them, outside. Quickly I drew the long thick curtains at both windows and I felt a little less exposed.

Apart from the window wall, all the walls were lined from floor to ceiling with bookshelves and drawers. The wall above the marble mantelpiece was filled by an oil painting of Harthill House painted at an angle to soften the geometrical lines of the house and the driveway swept up to the porticoed front entrance. The foreground was dotted with shrubs and bushes and tall elms, beeches, and a cedar tree filled the corner of the canvas rather like a Constable painting. A glass domed ornamental timepiece stood in the centre of the mantel shelf, flanked by two miniature blue Chinese willow pattern vases. The clock's mechanism glinted in the light of the chandelier. Long drawers at waist height lined either side of the fireplace.

I thought of Will's light and airy flat in London, filled with light wood and chrome fittings and leather sofas with not a chandelier or oil painting in sight.

Where to look for a map? There's certainly no room on a wall in here. I perused the shelves on my left nearest to the door. Tomes were packed in, mostly leather or cloth bound with gilded titles. Some were clearly ancient: I gingerly picked out a cloth covered volume. It was a biblical atlas, dated 1798 in Roman numerals, and it was filled with folded hand drawn charts of Old Testament locations and the fine text described locations and finds. Sketches of Middle Eastern peoples, garbed in black or white robes, haughty camels and women at wells with covered heads and pottery ewers and dark-haired children by their sides interspersed the writing. The author's name was unknown to me; was he related to Will's family? I put it back carefully and picked out a slim volume like a diary. It was filled with exquisite sketches and delicate watercolours of flowers, fruits, and animals. The descriptions were written neatly by hand in faded ink. I looked at the frontispiece and read the name Helene Wallington. Higher up, I spotted a thin volume with a stamped title proclaiming *'Lettres de Champollion'*. I recognised that name as the Frenchman who had decoded Egyptian hieroglyphs. The upper shelves were filled with books about Egyptology and archaeology of the Middle East. Which one of Will's forebears was a follower of archaeological discoveries or even an archaeologist? I felt a flicker of exasperation aimed at Will for choosing to ignore his past. What had happened to cut himself adrift from his family history?

I was fascinated by the range of subjects from art and music to science and astronomy; it was a true library. The shelves next to the fireplace housed modern fiction, crime, thrillers, historical romances, and biographies. I pulled my attention away from the books and looked at the drawers. One contained old books that needed attention with broken spines or loose pages and the drawer beneath held maps. I espied what seemed like a hand drawn chart, on thick paper, curling in on itself and I carefully lifted it. At last! An ornate, hand printed decorative scroll at the top proclaimed: *Harthill House. Commissioned by Sir Horace Barnard Bt. in the year of our Lord 1731 to shew Layout of New Estate since the Building of Harthill House Anno Domini 1730.*

I laid the map on the beautifully polished table in the middle of the room and used books to weight the corners down. I rubbed my hands together, as my fingers were stiff with cold.

The map was exquisitely produced. The house was drawn in fine detail, but minus the wings, which had been added a few years later. I loved the sketches of trees, some small and fat, others tall and graceful with sweeping boughs. The river swept past the estate and tiny fish were depicted while on the banks I recognised perfect representations of herons and otters. My eyes roamed over the map, but suddenly the clock on the mantelpiece chimed softly, making me jump and returning me to the present. Nearly time for supper and I was very conscious of not wanting to be in Serena's bad books. I left the map on the table, switched off the lights and hurried upstairs. I had barely finished freshening myself and was dragging a brush through my ever-unruly hair when there was a knock on the door and Joe called out that supper was ready.

Serena had prepared a fish pie, which meant that I could scoop a little out of the dish. As I hadn't caught any of the cooking aromas, I'd escaped the evening nausea so far, but I wasn't ready for taking too many risks. It was warm and comfortable in the kitchen with both dogs looking alert in case a morsel should find its way to the floor. It felt like a normal domestic setting except for my awareness of the number of rooms above and around us. And the presence of busy ghostly figures in the passage outside.

"I've been in the library, Joe, after you showed me round and I was gobsmacked at the number of old books and literature in there. Were some of Will's ancestors archaeologists or historians or artists, or did they just fill up the library to impress the guests?" I asked.

"Well, all of those, I believe," said Joe. "Geoffrey Payne-Ashton, William's father, took great care that the rare items were archived and catalogued, but I don't think the task was ever finished. We know that some of the family in the distant past pursued interesting lives. They didn't have to hold down day jobs like we do now because of inherited wealth. I'm sure I remember William's Uncle Daniel telling us that one of Sir Horace Barnard's sons, Laurence, was an archaeologist and naturalist and one of his daughters, Helene, was a gifted artist and naturalist. Sir Horace was the one who built the house, and it's been in the same family ever since."

I recalled the name of Sir Horace Barnard at the top of the map when Serena said, "Joe, when you've finished your plateful, why don't you fetch the family tree scroll from the library? William's Uncle Daniel prepared it years ago." It was as if her reluctance to part with information had suddenly vanished. Perhaps it had dawned on her I would one day be mistress of this domain. I felt exasperated with Will for deliberately ignoring their loyalty when they were doing all they could to preserve his inheritance. Serena began clearing away the plates while Joe went on his errand to the library.

While Serena dished out bowls of fragrant blackcurrant Creme Fraiche, Joe unrolled a long parchment scroll and weighed it down with various heavy objects. It took up half the length of the table and I was momentarily lost for words. "Good grief," I uttered faintly in disbelief. "it's a very long tree."

"It starts with Sir Horace Barnard, who was a wealthy merchant trading with the East with shares in the East India Company, if I have my facts right. He married a French aristocratic heiress in 1727 and with her dowry and inheritance, they commissioned Harthill House to be built when he received a knighthood and granted land by George II."

I looked along the row, counting the names of the offspring of Sir Horace and Lady Therese. "They certainly had a large family," I remarked, counting ten offspring. Looking at the dates of birth and death, some had died early in infancy. In history modules from my Levels, I'd studied source materials of death rates and child mortality in the seventeenth, eighteenth and nineteenth centuries which were acute in cities and especially those born in poverty. Plague and dysentery were rife, but surely living in the country and in wealth should have been a preventative.

The daughters of Sir Horace and Lady Therese all had French names: Marie-Therese, Helene, Elise, whilst the sons bore English names. Their first son was born in 1728 and their last child, a son named Gerard, born in 1750. The lines of descent stretched across and down the creamy parchment–like paper and without taking any names in I quickly scanned to the bottom and there was Will's name, William Gyles Payne-Ashton, born 5th April 1979.

The significance of his lineage was mind-boggling. Will had never acknowledged his pedigree once in the years I had known him, and especially since we'd been together. Perhaps he believed that if he'd revealed he owned an estate in the country, I would have stayed with him, hoping to cash in on his inheritance. Perhaps he didn't really know my character after all and preferred to keep me ignorant of his family background. A new realisation hit me. Despite being pregnant, would he ever marry me? *Why am I getting excited about his family tree when Will apparently shows no interest? Will he be resentful of me taking an interest when he obviously ignores his background?* I was conscious of being at one end of a dark tunnel and Will was at the other.

It was apparent that living the life of a country squire was not in his restless character. It would stifle his exuberance and enthusiasm for exploration. The qualities that had drawn me to him in the first place. Will wasn't cut out to spend his days surveying his estate and entertaining the neighbours like one of the landed gentry.

And a realisation bubbled up in me: I was carrying the next heir to Harthill House. If I gave him a son, would he inherit all this?

My head grew hot and there was something wrong with my vision. Serena sounded like she was speaking underwater.

"Look out, she's going to faint," Joe shouted and grabbed hold of me. I'm sure I didn't faint dead away because I was conscious of their voices coming over a great distance, but I couldn't respond and trembled all over.

Through the buzzing in my head. I faintly heard Serena say she was calling the doctor." Can we get her to her bedroom?"

"Not up two lots of stairs," said Joe. "I'll get her to the sitting room and she can lie down there while you phone Doctor Laidlaw."

Joe put his arms under me and carried me up the first steep flight of stairs from the basement kitchen to the ground floor as if I was weightless. Under the grand staircase was a door which I hadn't noticed before and Serena flicked on the lights. Joe laid me carefully on a sofa facing a fireplace.

Gradually, my sight and hearing cleared, but my head ached, and my limbs were heavy. "I'm so sorry. What must you think of me?" I stammered.

Serena handed me a glass of water, which I sipped cautiously. "Dr Laidlaw will come out; he used to be the family doctor. He's semi-retired but still visits old patients when necessary. We promised William we'd look after you and that's what we are doing." Her voice was kind as she tucked a throw gently round my shoulders. She eyed me doubtfully while Joe put a match to the kindling in the fireplace.

"Have you fainted before?" Serena asked.

"No, I'm sure I'll be ok in a little while," I said shakily, my head still aching. Serena's mobile phone rang, but Joe snatched it up to answer. He murmured a few words briefly.

"Doctor Laidlaw is on his way. He's coming from Salisbury so it won't take long, as the roads will be quiet at this time of night."

"I'm so glad we didn't go up to the flat and leave you on your own." Serena said anxiously. She fetched another woollen throw from the back of a chair and tucked it round me, and I settled back on the cushions in relief. It was a shock that I could feel so fragile and exhausted.

Joe fed small logs onto the now blazing fire and the warmth emanating from the flames made me sleepy. Serena sat in the armchair near the fire while Joe paced. "I'll go and wait by the front door with the dogs," he said and left the room, quietly shutting the door behind him.

I looked around this little room with fuzzy, detached interest. My eyes were still blurry, so I didn't want to make sudden movements. The walls were a soft pink and the curtains at the two windows were a rich cream with pink edgings. The deep piled carpet was cream, and a multicoloured rug lay before the hearth.

The sofa and armchairs were piled with colourful cushions. It was a cosy feminine room, made intimate by several framed photos which stood on the writing bureau between the windows. Water colours adorned the walls, but I still could not focus clearly.

"This is William's mother's sitting room," explained Serena. "Not that she's used it for some time. The pictures on the wall were painted by her as well. She's very talented and lives in France now where she has a studio, but I expect you know that." I nodded, acknowledging that at least I knew that fact. We heard the dogs barking and Serena got up to open the door. Bess and Jasper rushed in, tails high like banners, announcing the arrival of Joe and Doctor Laidlaw. Delightedly the dogs threw themselves on to the rug before the blazing fire and stretched out their golden limbs.

Doctor Laidlaw was elderly, tall, with a shock of white hair. His face was weatherbeaten as if he spent his days in all elements, and his intelligent eyes assessed me calmly before crinkling into laughter lines as he smiled down at me. He wore a thick Arran sweater and comfortable red corduroy trousers. He looked every inch a typical country resident, but he conveyed a sense of security to me. After introductions and shaking hands, he sat down on the sofa next to me. "Well now, I have great pleasure indeed meeting William's intended," he said, pulling a blood pressure kit from his bag. "It was my pleasure to deliver the young rascal into the world in this house a tad prematurely. From what I gather from his lifestyle, he's certainly made up for his small size and shaky start at birth by becoming a master of physical endurance!"

He took my temperature, felt my pulse, and then took my blood pressure, all very calmly. I answered his questions about my sickness and visit to the hospital and he nodded satisfactorily.

"Blood pressure is a little under the norm, but nothing alarming. If you wriggle down on the sofa, I'll have a listen to the baby's heartbeat. I apologise for my old-fashioned equipment, but it's still functional."

He produced a funnel shaped instrument and pressed it against my tummy after I'd lifted my sweater out of the way. After a few moments, he nodded again.

"Baby has a good strong heartbeat in there. Fainting in the first trimester of pregnancy is usually caused by blood vessels naturally relaxing and dilating because of the progesterone hormone and this can lower your blood pressure. Also, because you are suffering hyperemesis gravidarum, you are feeling weaker than normal. However, your blood pressure and temperature give me no cause for concern. Rest as much as you can and try to eat little and often. I know that's hard when you can't seem to keep anything down. I'll phone tomorrow afternoon and if you have any concerns, I'll come out again. Don't hesitate to call me." He addressed Serena and Joe as he said this, and they nodded gravely.

He patted my hand and stood up, tidying away his equipment. "You're in good hands with Serena and Joe and we'll all make sure you are well looked after. I'm in semi-retirement, so I will always have time for you." He paused for a second or two, as if considering what to say next. "I must say this house will be all the better with a young family in it. William is a very lucky chap, even though I haven't seen him for some time."

He refused the offer of a hot drink, and Joe and the dogs escorted him from the room. Just outside the sitting-room door, I heard him say, "By the way, Joe, check your security. I saw two fellows loitering by the old ash tree when I passed. They may have been on their way to visit Matt or Mollie in the Lodge, but they looked a bit shifty to me in the car headlights."

Chapter Six

Serena put her hands on my shoulders and blew out her cheeks. "What a relief, Dr Laidlaw said all is well! I'm sleeping in the Green Bedroom tonight, for my peace of mind as well as yours. Mollie can freshen it up tomorrow before you friend arrives."

I'd forgotten all about Evie and as I'd left my phone upstairs, I had no idea when to expect her. Will would be exploring trails with Hugo and Rafaella, so there'd be no contact from him yet. Joe returned and with both their help, I managed the stairs.

"Would you mind if I used the sitting room during the day?" I asked as I sat on the bed. It would be a private bolt hole compared to the grand reception rooms, chilly library, and Serena's territory in the kitchen.

"Yes, by all means. It's a cosy room." I was curious to know when Will's mother had last lived in the house, but held my tongue. It was better to let little snippets of information be revealed by Serena in her own time rather than bombard her with questions, as I had witnessed her hostility when Joe had tried to elicit information about any plans for living at Harthill House in the future. Joe was more open and keener to impart any information that he saw fit. As I dragged my clothes off and threw them tiredly in a heap and donned a warm sweatshirt to sleep in, Serena came back with a hot water bottle in a rather dilapidated furry teddy bear cover.

She grinned as she held it out to me. "Sorry about the cover. It belonged to Andrew, our son; it even went with him to agricultural college and much used! I'm only down the corridor if you need me, so I'll say goodnight and hope you have a restful night." She turned to leave, then faced me apologetically again. "Earlier, when Doctor Laidlaw was here, I tried to call William. He had his phone switched off, so I left a voice mail, telling him we were concerned about you. I hope he doesn't panic when he gets the message and calls you and you wonder how on earth he came by the news."

Serena was more certain than I was that Will would call. There had been a missed call from Evie and then a message saying that there was a hitch at work, but she was hoping to come down Saturday morning. It gave me a couple of days to get back to normal to explore with her. Normal! After all my experiences in the last few days, I began to think that my definition of normal had disappeared forever.

Despite tiredness and the comforting hot water bottle, I didn't slip into sleep instantly. I still had a vague headache and images of the family tree scrolled before my eyes, especially the line of children Lady Therese Barnard had borne all those years ago—the beginnings of a family dynasty in which I was to play a part. Childbirth then was risky, so what must the Mistress of Harthill House have felt each time she carried a child? Gladness to be providing her husband with sons and heirs? Fear of losing a child in pregnancy or just after birth? Faith in God and the promise of life everlasting comforted women back then. Sir Horace would have ensured the best physicians and midwives attended his wife. I knew that grand houses such as this had huge numbers of staff -

butlers, chatelaines, footmen, housemaids, serving maids, cooks, kitchen skivvies, scullery maids, gardeners, stable lads - a veritable army of servants, because Evie, a natural communicator, shared such knowledge whilst researching and archiving, and hadn't I witnessed for myself such activity in the basement passage?

Seeing Will's name at the end of the family tree standing out alone had been the cause of that overwhelming sense of history bearing down on me like a great weight. The sense of threat and fear that accompanied the silent appearances of the two strangers who didn't seem to be part of this household also filled me with disquiet. I sat up and switched on my bedside lamp. *Stupid woman, you are letting your imagination run riot over nothing at all.* I bashed my pillow and settled back again, switched off the light and lay looking through the window at the blackness of the night outside and the distorted pinpricks of starlight. Doctor Laidlaw's words came back to me clearly as he had left the sitting room. "Two fellows loitering...... looking a bit shifty to me..." The warmth of the hot water bottle relaxed me at last and I let go of tumbling thoughts as my eyelids closed.

The ringtone on my phone dragged me from strange dreams of bewigged gentlemen, ladies in rustling silk, children in long dresses running about on a lawn. My room was still dark as I grabbed the phone and saw Will's name. "Hello, hello," I croaked, struggling with the duvet, pleased, yet groggy with sleep.

"Clemmie, it's me, Will. I've had my phone switched off all day because we were out riding and when I got back, I picked up a message from Serena. What's happened?"

"I just had a funny turn and Serena called out Doctor Laidlaw. Do you know him? He said my blood pressure was low but the baby's heartbeat is fine and nothing to worry about. He was quite reassuring, and he's going to check up on me tomorrow, well, today now. I'm feeling better now I've had a sleep."

Will was silent for a few seconds; he'd probably forgotten I was pregnant, I thought cruelly. I had a feeling that he wouldn't want to jump on a plane again just as he'd returned to the States and thrown himself into exploring.

"How are things going over there? I'm looking forward to seeing some of your routes mapped out soon."

"Yes, we'll get down to doing that in the morning, but the prospects are great. We drove out a way and then rode some trails with awesome scenery. We've decided that we can run treks on two levels – one for those who want their baggage taken ahead to overnight stops and sleep in comfort and one where we carry minimal camping gear and camp in the wild for a real experience of forests and lakes."

He sounded fired up with enthusiasm, and I laughed. "Sounds like you'll be opting for the second option."

Will answered with a huge yawn resounding down the phone. "Sorry, Clem! It's been a full-on day and I'm knackered. Rafaella certainly pushes the pace! Are you sure you're ok?"

"Joe and Serena are keeping a good eye on me and spoiling me and Evie is coming down on Saturday and she'll definitely go into strict matron role so don't worry about me."

"Good! I'm ready for the sack. Raf has got another muscle screaming trek planned for tomorrow." He stifled another yawn. "If you're sure you are OK, I'll say goodnight, Clem, love, and please take care of yourself."

"Love you," I murmured down the phone, but he'd already gone. At the mention of Rafaella's name, my little bubble of intimacy with Will burst.

An insistent whining noise made me start up in bed. Daylight was streaming through the open shuttered window, revealing a pale blue sky. It was nine thirty, and I struggled out of bed and was beset by nausea. I grabbed the bathrobe and threw open the door to rush to the bathroom next door, almost colliding with a diminutive woman, pushing a vacuum cleaner along the passage. I charged past her and managed to get to the bathroom just in time. Afterwards I washed my hands and bathed my face and leant on the washbasin for support, waiting for my heaving stomach to subside. I couldn't face the woman outside yet so ran the shower. Hot water sluicing over me quelled the shivers.

When I'd dried and pulled the bathrobe around me, I opened the door. She was still there dusting the pictures on the walls of the passageway, as if she'd been waiting for me to emerge. She stopped and appraised me with extraordinarily bright blue eyes which looked far too young in contrast to her lined and weathered face. A cloud of white hair sprang madly round her head in a wiry halo.

"Be you feeling better now?" she asked in a drawn-out lilting dialect. "I'm sorry if I disturbed you, I would 'ave taken me Hoover to another part of the house if I'd knowed you be still abed."

She followed me halfway into my bedroom, so I climbed back into bed and felt a rush of relief to lie back again. "Mornings are always like this at the moment. I'm Clemency, by the way, Will's partner," I held out my hand, smiling apologetically.

"Aye, I know who you be, my lovely. Serena told me you were taking care of your little burden." The tiny woman nodded towards my abdomen as she gripped my hand in her small hand, which felt rough and calloused against my soft palm. "I be Mollie Crane; I live at Snowdrop Lodge by the gates and help in the house."

"Oh yes, Serena told me about you." I was amazed and amused that an elderly lady as small as Mollie could manage the upkeep of a house as big as Harthill, although I had to acknowledge a wiry strength emanating from her. "I'll get dressed now and see if I can keep a bit of breakfast down. I've been instructed to make sure I don't starve myself!"

Mollie fixed me with her disconcerting blue eyes. "Aye, keep vittled up. You need the strength. Joe be down at the barns with my Matthew tending to the early lambin' ewes. February's a fickle month for lambing – weather can be like this," she said nodding towards the blue sky outside, "then an icy spell, and lambs get frozen to death. I used to scoff at them when lambin' in barns became the modern way, but when I remember trudging through blizzards with me dogs looking for ewes and lambs hoping they be alive, it makes sense knowing they would be where you can keep an eye on them. Livestock farming is all about money these days." She sniffed heartily, then seemed to remember where she was. "Better get on, I'll tidy bathroom and Green Bedroom and yours and then come down for me cuppa."

She marched out, and the hoovering begun again. I dressed quickly and then shut my laptop in a drawer under some of my clothes and dropped my phone into my pocket. I suspected Mollie would snoop amongst my belongings, although I had nothing to hide, but she knew Will and it would be natural for her to try to find out as much as she could about me! She'd referred to 'my Matthew' in her introduction and I assumed she must be related to Matt, the farm manager I hadn't met yet. I passed her in the Green Bedroom, changing the bed linen where Serena had slept last night. This bedroom where Evie would sleep was smaller than mine, with one sash window overlooking the wood. The walls were lined with wallpaper of a pale green background carrying a design of huge cabbage roses in pale greens and pinks. It should have looked hideous, but in a room in this house the effect was dramatic. Heavy green curtains framed the window and next to it stood a mahogany chest of drawers on which stood a decorated antique china washbasin and jug.

Downstairs, I pushed the kettle onto the hotplate and looked for the herbal tea bags. A sourdough loaf had been left on the breadboard and I cut a slice to toast, hoping it would stay down. There was no sign of Serena or the dogs and the family tree scroll was still on the table where we'd left it last night. I sat down in front of it with my mint tea and dry toast. Whoever had created this tree had added little notes in neat handwriting in the margins, with guidelines ruled towards the relevant person in the tree.

Mollie bustled in and busied herself making tea and adding milk and sugar, and fetched a biscuit tin from the cupboard. When she sat down, she exclaimed when she saw the family tree.

"Well now, what've we got here? This be good, but I could probably recite all these names to you because my family's been here as long as Master William's. I reckon this was done by Mr Williamson." She slurped her tea and bit deeply into a chocolate digestive and when I looked questioningly at her, she looked smug.

"He be William's Uncle Daniel. He married William's Aunt Pauline. Look 'ere he is on the chart." Mollie pointed towards the bottom of the tree and there I read that Will's father, Geoffrey, had been born in 1935 and his sister Pauline in 1939. The date of her marriage in 1960 to Daniel Williamson was recorded, as was her death in 1962.

"Oh, how sad," I exclaimed. "They'd only been married two years before she died. How awful for him. Is he still alive? Did he marry again?"

"Yes, he's still alive. And no, he's never married again. He lives in Salisbury in the Cathedral Close. He used to teach music and history in the Cathedral School, so that's why I reckon he did this tree. He's very clever,"

"How sad that he was only married for two years, though. How did she die?"

Mollie took a deep breath, opened her mouth, then closed it abruptly. "Not my place to say," she muttered. "I'll just say she met with an accident." And she went over to the sink to rinse out her mug.

I stared at the entry. Pauline Williamson would have been only about twenty-two or twenty-three at the time of her death, younger than me. One of the ruled lines led from her name to a boxed note in the margin. It read: 'Baby Archie stillborn 1962.'

Tears pricked my eyes, and I instinctively put my hand on my abdomen. Had he been born because of the accident Mollie mentioned and both tragically dying? I gazed out of the window. Why should I be bothered about a family tragedy that had happened half a century ago? Mollie looked like she would enjoy a good gossip, so there must be a mystery that the family wanted hushed up. Perhaps Will would know. His father Geoffrey had been married to Roberta for nine years before Will came along, but there were no recordings of any siblings. Will's grandfather, Michael Payne-Ashton, had been married three times before Geoffrey and Pauline were born. Childbearing was a risky business, I thought, as I saw that Michael's first wife had died in childbirth and the poor baby had died not long after. An uneasy feeling crept over me. Baby deaths were not rare in this family. I rinsed my breakfast dishes and went upstairs. I needed fresh air to blow these gloomy thoughts away.

Mollie was trundling her unplugged Hoover up the passage. "Your rooms are all spick and span now, me duck. Have you seen the nursery on the top floor?"

Joe had promised to show me the top floor, so I shook my head. Mollie looked pleased. "Come along with me and I'll take you up there."

She led the way up the servants' staircase. Joe and Serena also lived up here; the long passage had been closed off at mid-point with a private door. The doors leading off this passage may have been where some live-in servants had slept. Mollie opened a door behind the top of the staircase to reveal a large square room filled with light from windows on two walls. I was drawn to a frieze of exquisitely painted animals from the Beatrix Potter tales.

"Master William's mother painted them," Mollie nodded

towards the frieze. "She were a good artist, but upped sticks and left soon enough."

The nursery was empty apart from a painted white chest of drawers and a rocking chair, and the floor was uncarpeted and dusty. The fireplace was small with a Victorian green tiled surround. Two windows overlooked the Ladies' Bower and wood stretching into the distance, and the window on the other wall looked out over the roof of the North Wing and tops of tall beeches and stables beyond. Connected to the nursery was a smaller room with an old white painted metal bedframe. A wooden crucifix hung on a nail above the bed.

"That were the nanny's room," said Mollie, "although Master William's mother didn't have one. I remember playing up here with his father and aunt when they were tiddlers. I were a tiddler meself then – same age as Mister Geoffrey and a bit older than Miss Pauline. My mother worked in the house, so I spent a lot of time up here with them running around the house and getting into trouble! Mr Geoffrey and Miss Pauline had little beds in here. Then when he were older, he demanded a room of his own. He acted quite grown up by then and I used to follow him around like a little shadow until he'd tell me to clear off! Mr Geoffrey's father, Mr Michael, didn't like a din; he was always in the Library with his head in one of they books, or writing and he went abroad a lot. Your affianced was a babby in here, too." She said, fixing her bright blue eyes on me.

"His mother went into premature labour and Mister William was born in this very nursery. It was quite a kerfuffle, and we staff kept out of the way while Mr Geoffrey hopped around in a state waiting for the midwife and Doctor Laidlaw. I used to nanny Master William or walk him up and down the drive in his big pram when he wouldn't settle. He had a big pair of lungs on him, I can tell you! He wanted to run and climb afore he could walk properly, that lad. When he got older, he was allowed out on the estate in his school holidays and that's when he and my grandson Matthew became friends. They'd be off on their bikes or fishing or swimming in the river. He were accident prone, was young William–branches falling on him, nearly swept down the millstream! His parents and me and my hubby used to tell 'em off for swimming- that river looks slow and lazy, but the currents are swift and dangerous. He were grounded for telling lies when he said two strange people pushed him in once." Mollie paused for breath, her cheeks pink with exertion and her eyes bright with memories. "Sorry, I was off in my head remembering then. It's been a long time since we had children here..."

I sat in the big rocking chair and rocked, fascinated, while she'd reminisced.

"You have some amazing memories, Mollie! I know so little of the family history, but now I'll know who to ask!"

"Aye, well, some history is best kept to itself, as you'll soon find out, and the past is always present in this house," she said cryptically. "Good golly, better finish me chores. Serena will be wondering what I'm up to if she's back."

She hurriedly left, and I heard her humming as she went down the stairs and then it was silent. I had been quietly rocking in the chair. Even without cushions, it was soothing. Had Will sat here being nursed on his mother's lap? Why had she left Harthill House to live in London and only let Will return on his school holidays? Her relationship with her husband had obviously not been straightforward and after his death, she had chosen to live in France rather than return here. The chair creaked comfortingly as it rocked backwards and forwards on the bare boards, and I could feel my eyes drooping. It was very quiet up here at the top of the house except for the distant caw of rooks in the woods opposite and a gentle cooing of a pigeon which echoed down the chimney into the empty hearth. I could see the tops of the leafless trees swaying in a wind. It was very chilly in the room.

Distressing cries of a very young baby, then a shattering scream: "No, no, no," repeated over and over, filled my head and the room. I shot out of the chair and rushed to the window, my breath misting the cold panes of glass. I cleared the glass impatiently and saw the two strangers standing in the Ladies' Bower close to the fence, very definitely looking up at this window in the old nursery on the corner of the house. This time I could see their upturned faces pale under their battered straw hats, old and grim, with their mouths set in identical sneering lines. I pulled back from the window, feeling exposed and vulnerable and confused. Where could the noise of a baby crying be coming from? I risked another peep out of the window. The two men had gone. The chill in the nursery had intensified, and the silence was oppressive-even the pigeon had stopped cooing and the rooks were silent. Then I heard a faint sound of sobbing disturbing the silence. Shivering I started down the back stairs, chastising myself. Of course, the nursery would be cold; nobody could afford the luxury of heating an unused room. What had Mollie just said: 'the past is always present in this house'. The house was haunted. Hadn't I witnessed servants in the basement passage? If, and it was a big if, Will and I lived here, I would not be using that old nursery when our baby was born even after Mollie's reminiscences.

The strangers' appearances troubled me. They were apparently stalking me.

My mobile trilled as I reached my warm room, my heart still thudding. Evie had texted:

> Good news, all niggles (human ones!!) sorted, so I'll be down tomorrow. Send me your postcode and I'll attempt to find you by satnav Love Evie xx.

After texting back, and a lot cheerier, I went downstairs to the kitchen to tell Serena. The dogs greeted me boisterously. Tabby blinked and Serena stirred a pan on the hotplate. It was such an ordinary domestic scene that I doubted experiencing the frightening episode in the nursery and seeing strangers outside.

"There you are! I was getting a little worried because I couldn't find you when I came back from walking the dogs. Doctor Laidlaw said he'd ring about lunchtime to check on you, so he would have been alarmed if I'd told him you were missing."

"I slept late this morning, and I was quite nauseous when I got up, and then I met Mollie while she had her tea break. She showed me the old nursery. Oh, and Evie is coming tomorrow. Mollie was doing her room earlier."

"I'm glad you'll have a bit of company; it is a large house to rattle round in if you haven't got anything to occupy yourself with. I'll take up some clean towels later. Can you fetch some soup bowls from the dresser – Joe'll be in shortly after helping Matt with some early lambing."

As if on cue, the dogs barked and rushed out of the kitchen. A minute later, Joe appeared, followed by a younger man. When he snatched off his beanie hat, my mouth fell open because, with his tousled dark blond hair and blue eyes, he could have been mistaken for Will's brother.

"Clemency, this is Matt Crane, Mollie's grandson. Matt, this is Clemency Wyatt, Will's fiancée," said Joe.

Matt rubbed his hands down straw covered overalls. "Let me wash my hands first. You wouldn't want to shake my hands after where they've just been!" He washed them vigorously in the sink, then wiping them on the towel on the Aga handrail turned back to me. "I'm very pleased to meet you, Clemency," As I took his hand, he enclosed it firmly with both of his and grinned; an almost identical smile to Will's but warmer, that crinkled his eyes and lit his face. I felt quite discombobulated! How many more surprises would this house spring on me?

"I brought Matt over, hoping there'd be enough soup to go

round, love, because we'll go back straight after. All's quiet for the moment, but not for long, eh, Matt?" He gave Serena a kiss on her cheek. I fetched another bowl and cutlery and Serena placed a large loaf on a board in the centre of the table alongside a block of cheese and a jar of chutney, but before doing that she quickly rolled up the family tree scroll and placed it on the dresser.

"How are you this morning, Clemency?" asked Joe, carving thick slices of bread while Serena dished out tomato soup. "Has Doctor Laidlaw called back yet?"

"I'm feeling better as the day goes on. I feel such a fraud scaring you both last night," I said, sipping the soup tentatively.

"How do you like it here, Clemency?" asked Matt, turning his blue gaze on me. "I heard Will had been called away to New York, which is a pity because I haven't seen him since last year's Trustees' Meeting and it would be good to catch up with him."

Embarrassingly, I felt my face grow hot under that gaze so like Will's. "It's an amazing house and Joe and Serena are absolutely spoiling me." My words stumbled out: I couldn't get over how much he resembled Will. Did they both realise the similarity? And surely such a shrewd woman like Mollie must be aware. "Am I allowed to see the lambs at some point?"

"Come back with us after lunch. You should be able to watch some lambing. Oh, unless it might upset you?" Matt had clearly just remembered that I was pregnant and looked embarrassed.

The phone on the dresser rang. "It'll be Doctor Laidlaw," said Serena. "If you'd like to speak to him in private, take the call in the small sitting room."

I convinced Dr Laidlaw that I was fine now, and he kindly reiterated his availability at any time.

Chapter Seven

Will

Will prowled his room, unsettled. The day had been fantastic; driving out of the city with Rafaella at the wheel of the SUV, Hugo and himself in high spirits and their bikes secured on the back. Snow lay on the ground after a long drive reaching the outer suburbs, lying in deep drifts. The trail through the forest was clear and the silence uplifting after the roar of the city. Crispy dead leaves crunched under their tyres as Rafaella led them uphill through tall conifers, the trail covered in layers of pine needles and it was still and brooding in the cold, windless air. When they broke out of the forest onto a ridge overlooking a valley of deciduous trees, all stripped of their leaves, they saw a descent into a river gorge. They'd ridden hard down a steep trail no more than a narrow track, full of hairpin bends which had tested their muscles. At the bottom was a wooden bridge, and the trail had ascended to another ridge thick with conifers wearing crowns of frozen snow. At the top of that ridge, they could see the forest spread below them and rising again in steeply undulating contours.

"There are trails for miles," Rafaella had said. Her cheeks were flushed with exertion and her eyes sparkled. Hugo was intent on plotting the distances on his phone. Will was certain her eyes flashed come on signals to him and his puppy eyes betrayed his feelings. She laughed softly and sped down the steep incline. Will and Hugo, taken by surprise, scrambled to take off after her. The trail twisted round enormous tree trunks, and it took all their concentration and skills to avoid rocks and holes filled with frozen snow. They reached a level clearing where felled conifers lay piled up, topped with a blanket of snow. Rafaella was waiting, laughing, and had lifted off her helmet, shaking out her long dark hair when they pulled up alongside her, sweating despite the cold.

"Just testing you boys, "she'd laughed.

The way was blocked by a deep ravine filled with white water crashing over rocks and boulders.

"There's a narrow trail along the edge of the ravine to a waterfall which can be crossed in summer when the water levels have fallen. It's too risky to try now in these conditions and I don't want you boys being swept down in that torrent. Neither do I want to lose good machines," she said, pointing to their bikes. Hugo congratulated her.

"It's a great place, "Hugo had said. "Our clients will love it. Can't wait to start mapping routes, Rafaella."

She'd taken all her team and Hugo and Will to a restaurant that evening and the excellent menu, beer and wine had loosened them all up. Later in his room at the hotel, he toyed with his phone, knowing he had to suppress his instinct to call her. He saw he'd had a voice message from Serena in Wiltshire and, with foreboding, he listened to it. When he'd heard Serena's voice telling him that Clemency had fainted, but Doctor Laidlaw had checked her over and had seen no cause for concern, Rafaella's spell cast over him vanished. He phoned Clemmie immediately, even though it would be the early hours of the morning in the UK. When Clemmie answered sleepily and apologised for causing a silly scare, he felt immediately relieved. He had no idea that nausea in pregnancy could be so debilitating, but she really did sound OK. Overwhelmed with tiredness after a busy day and evening, he'd described his day and rung off. It had been stupid of him to think Rafaella was attracted to him and even stupider to think he would respond.

Normally the only challenges life presented him were those while on treks, testing terrain, muscles, and nerves. Now bothersome clouds had appeared in his personal life that made him question his directions. One cloud was Clemmie and a baby. Clemmie and he had drifted over the years, their relationship tied to their joint venture. They were akin to an old married couple: close and comfortable, with occasional sparks of passion. They had drifted along in a cosy, unpressured bubble, but as soon as he'd been in Rafaella's physical presence, he was dramatically aware of the effect she had on him. He gave a short, bitter laugh. Lust! He was a bloody fool. Clem needed him.

Rafaella was dangerous: he'd need to watch his step.

His mind refused to quieten, and on impulse, he found his mother's number. After a few moments, his mother answered. "Will darling, what a pleasant surprise and so early. I was just getting my coffee ready. How are you, my darling, and where in the world are you calling from now?" Roberta Payne-Ashton was quick to detect Will's hesitation before answering.

"What is it Will? You haven't had an accident on one of your adventures, have you?"

"No, Ma, all's well with the trekking. I'm in New York right now. We've just made a fantastic deal with a similar company over here that trek all over the States and we've joined forces. We can start organising trips over here soon, concentrating on the Northeast, as well as continuing in Europe. I was finding it hard to wind down after a brilliant day,"

"Is Clemency with you?" asked his mother. "You said we and I know she's as keen as you are about your trekking."

"No, Hugo is with me. You probably remember him from Uni days."

Will hesitated and then plunged in; it wasn't worth beating about the bush and his mother would have to know one day. "Actually, Ma, Clemmie is pregnant."

"Oh, Will, how lovely!" She sounded delighted, then after a beat, "planned, or a surprise?"

"A total surprise, well, a shock, really, for both of us. Even now I'm telling you I still haven't got to grips with the news yet."

"Ah, it will soon sink in. Your life is full of dashing around on two wheels, so I don't suppose it ever occurred to you that the arrival of a baby might happen one day. What about Clemency? How is she? She doesn't gad about as much as you, so perhaps it is a big hint for you both to settle down?"

Will's heart sank when he listened to her last sentence. "It was a shock for her, too. She thought she had food poisoning and was due to fly over here with me. But she's had a threatened miscarriage before she's even come to terms with being pregnant."

Roberta exclaimed down the phone, sounding distressed. "Oh darling, how awful for her–for you both. How is she? Are you with her?"

"No," said Will, rubbing his forehead, aware of how selfishly he'd acted in the last few days. "I flew back to London and took her down to Wiltshire to rest for a couple of weeks. Then I had to fly back to New York, as our negotiations were at a critical stage." How hard and glib he sounded.

He heard his mother inhale sharply. "Wiltshire? You mean Harthill House?"

"Yes, I thought it the best place for her to rest, as Joe and

Serena can keep an eye on her. Clemmie would only want to go into work and what with that and commuting, she'd put herself at risk again. Joe and Serena are there twenty-four seven and she's assured me she's being spoilt."

His mother gave a funny strangled cry down the phone and he frowned. "Will. you mustn't leave her on her own down there. She isn't familiar with the place and she's bound to feel lonely without her friends and colleagues, and you."

Will answered defensively. "Clemmie's not alone. Ma. Joe and Serena are looking after her and Doctor Laidlaw has checked her over and says she's fine. I've talked to her, and she's told me she feels fine. Her best mate Evie is coming to stay this weekend. This is all happening at a critical time for the future of our business. I couldn't put this deal on hold, otherwise a once in a lifetime opportunity to expand would have been lost. Clemmie understands. She knows this deal is important for our company, Ma. She hasn't demanded that I stay with her and I'll be returning soon, anyway."

"I do understand, my darling, but if Clemency wants to return to London, you won't try to stop her, will you?"

"I know you hated Harthill House, Ma. God knows why, you never told me and it made me indifferent to it as well. I don't know if I could live there permanently. When you weren't there when I was growing up, it never felt like my home."

"I will explain to you, one day, darling," she said in what Will thought was suspiciously false brightness. "But promise me you'll join Clemency as soon as you can to give her the support she needs at the moment."

"Evie is coming down in a couple of days, Ma. I can't leave here right now unless something terrible happens." Will knew he sounded petulant, rather like a teenage boy resenting being told what to do. "I've got to go now, Ma. It's late here and we have a busy day schedule tomorrow, so I need some shuteye. I promise I'll call again and keep you updated."

He finished the call abruptly before his mother could say more. From the brief phone conversations he'd had with Clemmie, she'd given him the impression that she'd started to like Harthill House. Would she want to live there after the baby arrived? Why was his mother so insistent that he persuade Clemmie to leave as soon as possible?

The reading of the Will after his father's death had been a shock to him. The house and estate were all entailed on him and his heirs in perpetuity. The scene in the Drawing Room replayed in his head.

"But I don't want to live here," he'd said, dismayed at the prospect of having the responsibility of the estate.

The family solicitor, Douglas Pargeter, had held up a placatory hand. "Your father foresaw your reluctance in living here and running the estate, William, so he set up a Trust to oversee the management of the house, farm, and estate. The Trust will convene once a year at my London offices and will consist of myself, or one of my nominated partners; the estate accountant Joel Phillips, yourself, Roberta, Daniel Williamson, Joseph and Serena Hudson and Matthew Crane. Travel expenses and hotel accommodation will be borne by the Trust. Geoffrey hoped that this way you could be part of Harthill House Estates and enable you to carry on with your own career."

Will had been visibly cheered by the disclosure and accepted the conditions without qualms.

When he returned to the UK, he must tell Clemency all this. He'd conveniently put Harthill House and the estate on the back burner. His mother would be reminding him of his responsibilities often, from now on. Sighing, he got ready for bed.

Chapter Eight

In contrast to the cold outside, the barn smelled strongly of animals and hay. It was divided into pens with a central passage through the middle and, forgetting about my city, bred trepidation, I knelt down in front of a pen containing a ewe and a tiny lamb. It lurched unsteadily towards its mother and foraged underneath. The ewe stamped and moved and I cried out in distress as the lamb rolled over. "A stroppy Mum," Matt said, crouching beside me. "We always keep an eye on the newborns in case of rejection, but so far none have been." The lamb struggled up and turned to its mother again. This time, it found the source of nourishment and the ewe stood placidly. Some lambs in the large pens were old enough to be exploring their surroundings, sniffing the straw, leaping high into the air, running to their mothers to latch on to milky teats. Matt and Joe worked well together. They watched one ewe which had separated from other pregnant ewes in the large pen as it suddenly lay down. One lamb slipped out quickly in a membrane of mucus and the ewe leaned round to lick at the struggling lamb. She bleated in distress and Matt spotted forelegs of another lamb, but no head. He and Joe quickly climbed over the straw bales and, pulling on a long plastic glove, Matt gently felt round the forelegs while Joe wiped down the first lamb to stimulate movement as it lay close to the mother. The second lamb slipped out in a wet slick. Matt cleared the mucus from its mouth and rubbed the tiny lamb's chest. There was no movement, and I held my breath. Matt inserted a length of straw up its nose and waggled it, but there was still no movement. He swiftly stood up and swung the lamb from side to side. Still no movement. I let out all my pent-up breath as tears prickled. Matt shook his head and gently laid the poor dead lamb aside as the ewe stood licking the surviving lamb. Joe shovelled up the placenta and put it in a wheelbarrow.

"Sadly, we don't always get a hundred percent success rate," said Joe noticing my distress.

"I'm sorry you had to witness it," said Matt.

"No, that's nature. I can't expect to see cuddly lambs without seeing the other side as well" I wiped my runny nose. "God, I wouldn't last a day in this job. I'd be paranoid about the dangers and risks!" I looked at Matt with respect.

"I don't like losses, but there was nothing we could do to save that one. But look!"

The surviving lamb had struggled up on wobbly legs and its tail wiggling as it suckled.

"Here, cuddle of one of the older lambs. She's quite healthy." Matt caught a lamb and placed it in my arms.

"Am I allowed? Won't the mother reject it? I've read that if the ewe senses human smell on the lamb, it rejects it."

"Sheep are used to being handled. This lamb is well bonded!"

I took the lamb delicately, but it weighed robustly in my arms as I scratched its head. When I put it down, it leapt high before running off.

"Now you smell of sheep, so you'll be accepted," laughed Joe.

"I expect you could do with a cup of tea after subjecting you to nature in the raw. I'll take you over to the farmhouse. Nan will have the kettle on. She won't have missed the fact that you are over here," Matt said.

"Right then, you take Clemency on over and I'll daub the newborn's navels with iodine," Joe said. I was impressed by the efficiency and care, but then I remembered what Mollie had said about farming, being all about money these days. Nevertheless, that Matt loved his job was transparent and Joe's experience was apparent.

The sky was darkening when we emerged from the barn complex. In the glare of security lights, we walked the short distance to the farmhouse. Mollie was putting cutlery in a drawer as Matt ushered me into the modern kitchen extension and there was a kettle steaming on the ubiquitous Aga, a freshly baked fruit cake on the scrubbed pine table, its warm aroma filling the kitchen. Matt slipped off his boots, and I followed his example. Matt's dog came flying out of a scullery attached to the kitchen. I could see it housed a washing machine, dryer, fridge freezer, and a sofa draped with an old duvet that was obviously for the dog. Pegs on the wall were festooned with all manner of tools, harnesses, rope, twine. And outdoor gear.

Matt introduced me to his dog Scout as he hurriedly drank his tea and wolfed down a couple of generously buttered wedges of fruit cake.

"I'll show you round properly one day. This farmhouse predates Harthill House. It was built in the 1600s and has mullioned windows and very low ceilings! But I've got to see to my other girls who'll be lining up impatiently!"

He laughed when I raised my eyebrows questioningly. "The herd! They'll be waiting by the gate to be milked! No rest for the wicked. I've got a shepherdess arriving tomorrow to help with lambing as it'll all be peaking in the next week or so and even with Joe's help, it's more than I can handle at this time of year. There are heifers in calf too, so they'll be arriving in spring if you're still here."

Do you have someone to help you with the cows?" I asked Matt as he was put on his boots. "Only I thought I saw two farm-workers by the fence yesterday."

I saw Mollie look sharply at me as she picked up Matt's empty mug.

"No, Joe and Diane, the shepherdess, are my helpers. Joe should be round shortly to escort you home. Nice to meet you, Clemmie. Hope to see you again soon."

He rushed off, hopping along as he pushed his foot into his other boot. I was sorry to see him go; he was a link to Will, and I wanted to hang on to it. In the ensuing silence, I looked up to see Mollie watching me with those bright eyes. "Forgive me asking you, Mollie, but I thought you said you lived in Snowdrop Lodge by the gates?"

"And you be right, my lovely. Matthew lives here by himself, but at busy times I pop over and tidy up and put something in the oven for him. I used to live here with my husband, John, when we farmed, then my son, Jack, that's Matthews's father, took over and we retired to Snowdrop Lodge. Worse thing we could have done. My John, he 'ad a stroke a year after we retired and never recovered. My son, Jack, and his wife Sandra managed the farm well, and I kept my hand in to keep busy. That was when William's grandfather, Mr Michael, was alive. There's been Cranes living here for a couple o' hundred years. Mollie paused and wiped down the worktop.

"Have your son and his wife retired now as well?" I asked, as it was clear Matt ran the farm single-handed, with outside assistance when necessary. It was still a puzzle where the two strangers fitted in around here. Nobody acknowledged knowing who they were. Mollie paused while washing up the mugs and plates, her back to me.

"Jack and Sandra were killed in a motor accident. Matthew was at Agricultural College. He came back and took over the farm. He were only twenty."

I put my hand over my mouth in shock and embarrassment. I went over to Mollie and lightly touched her arm. I didn't know her well enough to know if she would appreciate a hug. "I'm so sorry, Mollie, if I've upset you."

Mollie turned to me, drying her hands on a tea towel, her eyes fierce. "No, my dear, best you know, you would have been told by anyone round here. All water under the bridge now. I'm that proud of my grandson I could burst with love and pride every time I lay me old eyes on him. I'll just check on his casserole in the oven before I take meself off home. He could do with a wife to help him and look after him – he's always too busy to cook proper food for hisself so I make sure he keeps his strength up. If ever he's brought a girl back here, they take one look at the mud and smelly animals and disappear as fast as their high heels can carry them afore they break a fingernail!"

I laughed; the farming life certainly meant a commitment to working in all weathers and in all conditions. Although I lived and worked in the city, I was used to being outdoors and I could see the appeal and satisfaction in the farming life despite the hard work and terrible pressures to make it all work financially.

"If Joe's busy, I'll walk back to the house," I said. If Mollie was eager to get home, I didn't want to overstay my welcome.

"Absolutely not. Joe'll be here soon as Matt's back in the lambing sheds. Serena would have his guts for garters if she knew he'd let you stumble around in the dark alone in your condition!"

I was secretly relieved. I wasn't too keen on stumbling around in the dark either; not because of my condition, but because I didn't want to bump into my stalking strangers and I wasn't too sure of the way in the dark.

"And who will walk you home, Mollie?" Snowdrop Lodge seemed a long way down the drive from the farm.

"Bless you, child, I can find me way blindfolded!"

As if he'd heard Mollie's summons, Joe tapped lightly on the door. "Ready?" he asked as I pulled on my boots and fleece. He refused Mollie's offer of a cup of tea. "I'll get one back at the house. Thanks Mollie, see you tomorrow." Joe switched on a powerful torch, lighting up the ground before us.

A waxing moon tipped the tops of the trees so that the bare branches were silhouetted against the dark canvas of the sky. Joe pointed out the planets, Venus the bright one, Mars with a reddish tinge. "We hardly ever see stars in London because of the light pollution." I said, gazing upwards towards the clear star filled sky. You can almost make out the Milky Way."

I had gratefully taken hold of Joe's arm when he offered it. There were no lights showing on the ground floor of the house. I felt pleasantly tired now; my nausea had kept at bay and I relished the thought of curling up on the sofa in the small sitting room in front of a blazing fire. I'd ask Serena if I could just have scrambled egg for supper and I'd take it up there on a tray. When Evie arrived, I wanted to be able to explore with her without having to hover near a bathroom. Joe turned to close the final farm gate into the grounds of Harthill House. As he swung the torch beam onto the recalcitrant gate catch, I gazed ahead and clearly saw two figures identically dressed, just lurking in the deep shade of the hedge. They were almost near enough to reach out and touch me. I cried out involuntarily because Joe swung round all at once, concerned. "What is it Clemency? Are you in pain?"

There were no figures in the torch beam. "Sorry Joe, I thought I saw something in the hedge which startled me." I felt myself grow cold all over and had to control my shivering before Joe noticed. I focussed on my feet for the short distance to the back entrance and breathed deeply to shake away my fear. *It's my hormones*, I repeated to myself unconvincingly.

Forcing a cheery voice, I called out a greeting to Serena and went to the boot room to take off boots and coat. Joe was scrubbing his hands in the kitchen sink.

"It was a good day, today, love," he told Serena. "Diane arrives tomorrow, so at least Matt will get some respite. He slept in the barn last night, apparently because one of the ewes was worrying him. In the end, it gave birth with no complications. And I think Clemency enjoyed her educational visit, didn't you, despite having to witness a still birth."

"It must be a worrying time, all those ewes waiting to give birth, but very rewarding. And the lambs are beyond cute!" I had washed my hands and held them under the hot water tap to restore warmth. Serena noticed my pinched face. "There's a fire in the sitting room, go and get warm and supper in an hour." I opened my mouth to say I really didn't feel hungry, as I'd had a small piece of Mollie's hearty fruit cake, but Serena gave me a tart look that brooked no excuses.

"No skipping meals on Doctor Laidlaw's orders," she said meaningfully. I smiled and gave a mock salute. I went upstairs to refresh myself first, retrieve my phone and laptop, and returned to the sitting room. A cheerful fire crackled in the grate and the lamps cast a warm glow on the walls. The thick curtains had been drawn against the frosty night and the room had a warm and welcoming ambience.

I lay back on the sofa and felt my body relax after it had tensed up when I'd seen the twin strangers. I had to consider the fact that they were more ghostly figures. Much as I wanted to ridicule my own instinct, I couldn't think of another rational explanation. They couldn't be stalkers; who would want to stalk me? Nobody else had seen them or knew who they were, and they were around the grounds often. Of all people, Mollie might have known who the oddly dressed strangers were, but she hadn't commented.

If Serena, Joe, or Mollie were aware of resident ghosts, they were certainly keeping the information close to their chests, perhaps not wanting to alarm me. The figures I'd seen in the basement weren't malign presences; on the contrary, they gave the impression of busy bustling, as if life two centuries ago was carrying on as normal. Every time I saw the twin strangers, feelings of dread sapped the strength out of me. They only appeared outdoors: if they appeared when I was with Evie, I'd soon find out if she saw them as well.

Evie had left a voice mail to say that she would be leaving at the crack of dawn tomorrow, so except for traffic and losing her way, she would arrive around noon. "You never have your phone on," she'd said. "Are you sleeping through the day as well?"

There was nothing from Will, as he had said he would be trekking again. Being with Matt had been strangely comforting. He'd been warm and informative and welcomed me like an old friend instead of a stranger he'd only just met. His enthusiasm for farming had matched Will's for exploration and I speculated that somewhere down the line there was a family link, although I'm sure Mollie would have trumpeted had there been one.

Kim had emailed, although she didn't need any help or advice from me; she was running the office very capably. Instead of being jealous that she was usurping my position, I was grateful she had taken over.

Chapter Nine

Evie's face was a picture when she got out of her car just before lunchtime the next day. Her expression matched mine on first sight of Harthill House. I could see she was torn between hugging me and standing gawping at the size and architecture of the building.

"Welcome to my little hovel in the country," I laughed.

She recovered herself to hug me. "I stopped at the lodge on the corner, thinking what a cosy place to hide away! When I knocked, a little wizened, witchy woman answered. She cackled like one when I asked if you were in and directed me up the drive. I blame the satnav! No wonder she laughed. There's a bit of a difference in size!" She looked me up and down. "You don't look quite as ashen as you did a few days ago, but you're still looking peaky. Are you still throwing up like a volcano?"

"Lovely to see you again, Evie. You shouldn't be rude to the Lady of the Manor, or I'll have the butler turf you out!"

Evie's eyes widened. "You have a butler? Oh my lord, or lady, I don't believe it!"

"Only joking! Although Joe Hudson is as good as a butler. You'll meet him and Serena in a few minutes."

Evie picked up her overnight bag from the boot of her car and slung her laptop case over her shoulder. "I'm here till Tuesday morning, if that's ok."

"More than ok! I'll take you upstairs and you can drop your bags and then come down for lunch, and a tour round. There's no getting out of lunch, I'm afraid. Serena is quite a dragon where meals are concerned."

"Crikey, she really is Mrs Danvers reincarnated, then. Lead on before I get my camera out. If it's as magnificent inside as it is out here, I'm going to be busy."

We entered the front door under the portico. It was slow progress, taking Evie up to her room. She stopped dead in her tracks in the Hall and gazed around.

"Look at the size of this, it's magnificent," she breathed in awe.

"It's the height of two storeys," I said grandly, repeating what Joe had told me. She admired the arched niches and statues in them and exclaimed at the sweeping staircase as I led her up. Evie was clearly impressed and, whereas I was too constrained to ask probing questions, Evie would have no such qualms.

At last, I managed to usher her into the Green Bedroom. She dumped her bags on the floor and laptop on the bed and went over to the window. "This house is in a perfect setting on top of the escarpment overlooking the valley and river to that ridge beyond," she said. "Look, see that wooded hill on the other side of the valley? That was probably an ancient hill fort. Bloody hell, look at that Obelisk in the wood opposite! Have you been to it? Wonder why it's there? We'll have to go and look if you are feeling ok." Evie stopped as I burst out laughing. My spirits had risen considerably thanks to her infectious enthusiasm.

"Oh, I wish I could stay for longer than a weekend, "she said.

"Looking round the house will take a day and then the surroundings another day. I should start researching its history right now!"

"It must be hard being a historian in a place like this," I laughed. "A mere mortal would bounce on the bed to see if it was soft or inspect the bathroom to see if it came up to standard."

"Now you mention it, where is the bathroom? I drove straight down here without stopping in case I got lost."

While Evie disappeared into the bathroom next door, I ventured a quick look out of the window. The sky was blue, the grass green with a muddy track through the middle of the field where the cattle processed. Rooks wheeled and cawed above the treetops and down at the end of the meadow, the cattle clustered round a feeding trough piled with hay. It was a quiet, serene vista, and I breathed a sigh of relief.

Evie threw her bag on to the bed and upended it, then rummaged until she found a fleecy sweater. "I know what these big old houses can be like; the owners tend to live in a couple of semi-heated rooms and the rest are like ice tombs! Seriously though, Clem, how are you? You look better than when Will whisked you off, but you still look a bit strained."

Dear Evie, never one to miss a thing. How I longed to blurt out my pent-up fears about Will and Rafaella, and about my real or imagined sightings of my stalking twins.

"I'm still trying to get my head round the fact that this house belongs to Will," I said, fiddling with the arrangement of winter blooms on the chest of drawers. "There's also a working farm and estate, but Serena and Joe are treating me like a long-lost relative that's suddenly appeared on the doorstep. What they make of Will's reluctance to be here or even talk about it must be as much of a puzzle to them as it is to me. I really don't know whether to bother getting attached to this house in case there's no future here. I'm scared, to be honest, Evie, it's like a weird dream and I'll wake up in our flat and everything will be as it used to be."

"Will is only able to focus on one thing at a time and that's the US of A at this moment in time," said Evie. "I'm sure when the deal's secure, he'll return and focus on you and the baby. It's not as if you'll be hiding a bump for much longer. Anyway, can we find something to eat? I'm starving – I only had a quick cup of coffee before leaving so I could eat a horse now!" she'd found a brush in amongst her garments and dragged it through her thick dark hair.

"I'll take you down to the kitchen. It's nicely normal down there and I expect Serena will be back from shopping. This is my boudoir," I said, opening the door with a flourish.

"Love the silk wallpaper and marble fireplace," commented Evie. Her eye was trained to spot details like these. "We ought to be wearing crinolines, going down this grand staircase."

"The servant's staircase at the other end of the house is more suitable for the likes of us!" I retorted.

Serena was stirring a large pan of soup on the Aga as we entered the kitchen and I introduced Evie.

"I'm pleased to meet you, Evie. I hope you enjoy your stay here. And I hope you like sweet potato and red pepper soup!" Her greeting held none of the wariness at our first meeting, her smile warmly genuine.

"Shall I get out bowls and plates?" I asked.

"Yes please, you know where they all are now."

As if led by the aroma of the soup, Joe came in shortly after we'd laid the kitchen table and he greeted Evie cheerily.

"We've got some new lambs this morning. Diane, the shepherdess, arrived just in time to oversee, as it's been very busy in the barn." He rapidly spooned up soup and helped himself to bread and cheese, offering the board to Evie.

"Thank you, that soup was delicious. I was rather peckish," she said and turning to me, she said, "I hope you are managing to eat more, Clem. It was really alarming how much you couldn't keep down, back at the flat."

"I'm still cautious, but everything Serena cooks is so good!"

"If you'll excuse me, ladies, I need to get back to the farm now. I'm on clearing up duties! If you need a guided tour, Evie, I'm available later." Joe stood and started putting bowls into the dishwasher.

"You were such a good guide yesterday, Joe. I'm sure I can find my way round the house with Evie," I said.

"I'd better give you advance warning, as an historian, I'll probably bombard you both with questions, and you'll be glad when I leave," said Evie and Serena looked faintly startled.

"We'll be glad to help. See you at suppertime." Joe lifted his hand, and we heard him donning boots and jacket.

Serena waved off our offer of help. "Go and do your exploring. If you feel like hot drinks, help yourselves and supper is later this evening."

"First, I'd like to stretch my legs after the drive down. Would you come with me, Clem, or do you rest in the afternoon?"

"I'm fine," I said truthfully. We collected jackets and scarves from our rooms and when we came back downstairs, Bess and Jasper weaved between us, tails waving hopefully. Serena agreed the dogs could come, and they bounded up the steps out of the courtyard and waited to see which direction we would take.

"Can we get to the obelisk easily?" Evie asked. "I'd like to get an idea of who erected it and why."

"I've passed it, but didn't take much notice, I'm afraid. I was busy spotting snowdrops and early primroses just coming up and lots of lovely yellow celandine. I have found out it's in the part of wood called the Ladies' Bower and you'll be able to see how the ornamental hedges were laid out, though they're just straggly and overgrown now."

After they had sniffed round the formal paths through the garden, the dogs caught us up at the gate to cross the meadow and raced ahead, Jasper immediately rolling in the wet grass waving his legs in the air ecstatically, and Bess ran round him barking. "I hope he hasn't rolled in something vile," I said. "The cows pass this way every day."

The cattle were nowhere to be seen, so I gathered this field must lead through to other meadows. We climbed over the old gate into the wood, Evie insisting on helping me over. We held up the fence wires so that the dogs could pass beneath and they set to sniffing around. Evie stamped her way through the dead undergrowth to the obelisk, circling it several times and looking up and down the tall monument, snapping away with her camera before pausing and kicking away dead nettles and ivy from around the base. I was quite happy to let her do all the work as she worked her way round. Finally, she hunkered down. "Hey, there is an inscription carved into the stonework. I knew it must be some sort of memorial." She extracted a small penknife from her pocket and carefully scraped away moss and dirt and then rubbed at the inscription with a handful of grass to clear away the debris.

I crouched beside her to peer at the faint lettering.

Evie read slowly as some of the carved-out letters had almost eroded into the stone by the passage of time and weather.

This Monument was Erected in the Year of Our Lord
Eighteen Hundred and Nine
Requiescant in Pace
Eighteen Hundred and Eleven
By Honoria Barnard Payne
As a Lasting Memorial to
Gyles Payne Aged forty-five years, Beloved Husband of Honoria,
Bartholomew (Tolly) Payne aged Seventeen Years, Beloved Son of
Gyles and Honoria
Edmund Barnard Aged Fourteen Years, Beloved Son of Horace
Barnard Deceased and Priscilla

The Shadow Watchers

Who died near to this place on the Eighth Day of April in the Year of Our Lord

Chapter Ten

"Requiescant in Pace." Evie read the inscription solemnly. We looked at each other, mystified. "How could they all have died in one place?" I asked.

Evie looked around at the bushes and trees surrounding the Obelisk. "Perhaps a tree fell on them? Shot each other in a family feud? The clue is on the memorial: 'Who died near to this place…' We'll ask Joe or Serena; they may have some knowledge."

"There's a family tree scroll. It goes back to the person who built Harthill House. Serena put it out of the way on the dresser in the kitchen." I didn't tell her about my fainting episode after regarding it.

"Great," said Evie, her face animated in anticipation. "We can study it tonight and discover Will's mysterious ancestors."

Somewhere in the distance, Bess or Jasper barked, and I looked round guiltily. "We'd better find the dogs; they know their territory but we don't!"

We scrambled through tangled undergrowth until we struck a well-trodden and muddy track. Calling their names, we followed the path as it wound round tree trunks, dodging trailing brambles, dead nettles, and tall wintery stalks of grasses as the track led downhill. We passed clumps of snowdrops and sword shaped iris leaves on the banks of a long dried-up brook. The barking grew louder as we drew closer to them, renewing our shouting until they ran towards us up the muddy track, panting, in a similarly muddy state. The path divided a little way ahead: one led off at a right angle and the track we were on inclined downwards steeply. It was rutted, and the mud filled puddles looked treacherous.

"We could just see round the next bend," I suggested, doubtfully. "Will and I always said this when we were out riding. Only the next bend would lead to the next one until we were miles further than we intended!" Speaking of Will filled me with a warm glow until I remembered where he was.

"Maybe tomorrow," said Evie, looking at the sky through the skeletal branches. "You shouldn't overdo exercise just yet, and it's already getting dark."

We turned back, and the dogs happily complied with our instructions to stay with us.

"I hope Will hasn't been forgetting to keep in touch with you while he's off enjoying himself. He was keen that you shouldn't be left on your own and he insisted he could arrange something for you. He said he knew someone connected to his family who'd be available twenty-four/seven. Then he clammed up, so I left him to make the arrangements. I was as gobsmacked as you were when you said you were at his family home in Wiltshire! Who knew?"

"Who knew indeed," I sighed. I didn't tell Evie that he'd left almost as soon as we'd arrived. And he hadn't been in touch since early yesterday morning, only because of Serena's urgent message. As we walked, we heard a different sound over the bird songs and cawing rooks, and Evie pushed between young saplings that were acting like a barrier on the left of the footpath. She beckoned me through. Below us a broad river gleamed pewter in the light, and the sound of rushing water was much louder here.

"Sounds like a waterfall below us. Better keep an eye on the dogs in case they take a fancy to taking a dip. We can come back maybe tomorrow to see where the track leads to. We'll ask Joe for a local map. There's so much countryside to see, and there's still your stately home to explore. I'm not here long enough," Evie said as we resumed our tramp up the path.

"It's not my stately home, and Will is coy about telling me anything about it. Oh, I've just remembered, I found the original map of the house and estate yesterday. It's in the Library where Joe unearthed the family tree scroll."

A familiar rush of weariness washed over me, but I said nothing to Evie and linked arms with her. We didn't divert past the Obelisk and eventually a farm gate appeared in a gap in the trees and beyond, the red bricks of Harthill House glowing in the winter sunset. Evie had her miniature camera out and clicked away happily. Then I stumbled to a halt, as there, blocking the gateway, were my stalkers, still dressed identically in their smocks and straw hats and breeches and glaring menacingly at us. Bess barked once, then came to stand at my side, her tail down.

Evie lowered her camera. "What is it?" My gaze was locked on their glare. Surely Evie could see them too? I pointed, but I could tell she was puzzled.

I broke my gaze to look at Evie and when I looked towards the gate, no one was there.

"I thought I saw someone at the gate and then they vanished." I felt the familiar shivering take over my body. Evie firmly linked arms with me for the rest of the way. "Was it Joe?" she said. "Perhaps Serena was worried and sent him out to look for us, although the dogs would have recognised him and run to meet him. It was probably walkers who hurried on in case they thought they were trespassing. You can tell this path is well used by all the muddy footprints."

The farm gate opened easily, unlike the old, rusted gate

leading to the Obelisk further along the fencing. There was no sign of Joe, walkers, or stalkers. The only movement was a stately procession of cows plodding up the field towards the milking sheds and a brace of pheasants heading for shelter in the woods. As we crossed the field, the dogs raced ahead and waited impatiently until Evie let them through the garden gate and they disappeared round the corner of the house to the courtyard.

What the hell is happening to me? The dogs would have rushed to meet him if it had been Joe, and Bess had her tail down as if she didn't like something. They were the same Twins. They surely can't be my imagination, and Evie didn't see them.

We reached the courtyard. "You make a cup of tea while I dash upstairs!" I said.

Thankfully, Evie didn't appear to be aware of my strange behaviour and I hastily removed my outdoor gear and trod wearily upstairs. I stared at my reflection in the bathroom mirror as I washed my hands. My face was pale and my eyes were troubled, so I did my best to lift my expression. Two mugs of tea stood on the kitchen table and a biscuit tin, from which we extracted home-made shortbread fingers. The dogs had settled on the rug in front of the Aga and the normally aloof Tabby sat happily purring on Evie's lap. I spotted the rolled-up family tree on the dresser and waved it at Evie.

"Let's go up to the sitting room with this and we can study it in comfort." I handed the scroll to Evie, who gently dropped the big cat on the floor. I scribbled a note to Serena to say where we were, then picked up the mugs and led the way upstairs to the small sitting room where the doorway was tucked away under the main staircase. Kindling was laid, so I put a match to it and knelt in front of the fire as the kindling and small logs ignited before placing larger logs on top. Evie pulled the curtains against the gloom outside, stopping to look at the framed photos on the bureau.

"Look at this one," she said, handing me the frame. It could only have been of a much younger Will at about twelve or thirteen, his hair white blond in the photo and with a huge grin on his face. He was standing on a riverbank in the shade of a willow and holding up a large fish, maybe trout, triumphantly. Other photos showed Will together with his mother, and a larger framed one showed Will as a much younger child between his parents under the portico and surrounded by black Labradors and Springer spaniels. A small frame caught my eye showing Will and Matt as teenagers on bikes because the similarity between them was plain to see. An oil painting of his mother hung on the wall over the bureau. Will had inherited her fair good looks.

Will's mother looks fairly content with life in this painting, so what possessed her to up sticks and move to London?

Evie pulled the coffee table closer to the sofa and spread the family tree on it, anchoring it down at each corner.

"I've found Honoria Barnard Payne - you know, the person who had the obelisk erected," she said in answer to my blank look.

"She was the granddaughter of Sir Horace Barnard, who built the house. Look, she married Gyles Payne in 1789. There are a lot of names underlined in red all the way through the tree."

She silently scanned the names and linked branches as I peered at Honoria's place in the tree. I saw that she and Gyles had had two children, Edwin and Bartholomew, whose name was on the Obelisk. Edwin's name was underlined in red.

"Oh, I see it now, "said Evie. "All the heirs to Harthill House are underlined, so the tree is easy to follow. Guy is the oldest son of Sir Horace. Guy's son Horace becomes the heir, then Horace's son Edmund will inherit when his father died. But then Edmund also dies in the strange accident. Honoria's father is James and his name is underlined and he comes after his older brother Laurence. Ah, yes, it's written under their names that Laurence and his wife die without issue. That means they didn't have children," Evie patiently explained to me. "Then there's the youngest son to Sir

Horace called Gerard born a long time after his other brothers and sisters."

As Evie studied the scroll and commented aloud, my eyes grew heavy. I watched the flickering flames in the hearth and her voice dimmed. I should keep awake. After all, this family history would be part of my unborn child's inheritance. As if on cue, my phone rang. Will! With a thumping heart, I rose from the sofa and went into the Hall. It was dark and shadowy in there and I had no idea where the light switches were, so I sat on the bottom stair of the grand staircase and listened to Will as he told me excitedly of the places they'd visited.

"This place is spectacular, Clem. We could go all the way to Niagara with the right transport. Rafaella's father laid on his helicopter for us." My eyebrows shot up in amazement, but I had no time to comment before Will rushed on. "Raf is a qualified pilot, but we had another pilot today so that she could point out all the terrain and trails for miles. Clem, Hugo and I are totally blown away. The prospects are just perfect. There'll be a lot of prep work for you all at home, but Rafaella is instructing her team to give us all the help and advice we need. We have a few more trips and then we'll have to head home to do lots of homework and the bookings should start rolling in."

I was on the point of asking if he had a date in mind for returning, but Will said they were about to take off again. He hoped all was well, and I was still resting and would upload some photos of the area soon. "Miss you," I called, but he was gone when I heard a female voice calling out to him. It was clearly obvious that Will had lost his heart to the States in more ways than one. He had his team looking after his interests over here, which meant he could indulge all his passions to his heart's content. Was Rafaella included in his passions? Tears stung my eyes. What if my suspicions about them were just that, suspicions? Will and I loved each other and I should trust him.... I slowly walked back to the sitting room and waved my phone triumphantly at Evie. She was still immersed in the family tree to look up and notice me struggling to contain my emotions.

"Rafaella's father has lent them his helicopter," I said flatly. "Will says the region is stunning and he's very excited about prospects."

"Lucky man," said Evie laconically. "I hope he's remembering his commitments at home, too."

"He says he's heading home after the next round of trips," I said with a conviction I didn't feel. "But I'll probably be back in London any way soon as I've got another antenatal appointment coming up."

Evie regarded me seriously. "Why don't you transfer to the local surgery so you can spend time here and get some healthy country air? You know you won't take adequate breaks at home and you'll be back at the office and commuting as soon as you return. I know, I know, lots of women work right through their pregnancies with far harder lives." Evie raised her hands to ward off my protests. "But you are suffering extreme sickness and then thought you were losing the baby. I bet Will and Serena and Joe would rather you remain here for a while. From what you have told me, Kim is keeping everything together at the office in your absence, so why don't you let her get on with it?"

Evie's words resonated, and I had to admit that I was probably jealous that Kim was coping so well. After all, keeping in touch was easy and Kim updated me every day, so I was abreast of all developments. Truthfully, thoughts of working hadn't been my main concern recently. Even Doctor Laidlaw was on hand to treat me if I had any worries. But I knew I would probably experience loneliness after a long period, unless I had some sort of job to do here. Serena and Joe could not be expected to spend lengthy periods with me: Joe had a job managing the estate and assisting Matt on the farm and Serena had the house to care for and her own social life. The image of the Twins entered my mind and I knew I had to solve that mystery before considering lengthening my stay.

"I didn't realise that nausea would drain me so quickly, but the spotting is clearing up, thank goodness," I said.

"Then you are in the best place here," said Evie in her no-nonsense voice. "And I can come down when I'm free now I know where you live! Anyway, looking at this family tree, I can't really understand why the line of inheritance comes through Honoria. Her brother died young, ruling him out, her uncles either died young or without issue in adulthood. Her cousin Horace died when his son was a baby, so Edmund was the legitimate heir, and then he died in this freak accident. All the dates are set out in this family tree. So, why didn't the estate go to the youngest son, Gerard? It says here that he had several illegitimate offspring, then he marries in 1812 and has twin sons the same year. Perhaps he was deprived of the inheritance because of this bit of a scrum in the middle of the tree: Honoria's remaining son, Edwin, marries twice by the age of twenty-two and there's a flurry of sons born around that time and then the line continues down through Edwin."

"So, what you are saying is that Will may not be the legitimate heir after all because of some skulduggery in the past? He'd be happy about that, I'm thinking, but I'm not going to mention it to him and put my foot in meddling with his family history."

If Will was aware of his long line of ancestry, he had to all intents and purposes turned his back on it as he had with the estate. Evie was making Will's family history sound intriguing as I looked over her shoulder.

"Look, there's the annotation that confirms the dates of deaths of Honoria's husband, son, and her cousin Edmund. But not how they died."

There was a faint tap on the door and Serena came in. "You

look cosy in here," she said. "Just came to tell you that supper will be ready in about half an hour in the kitchen, as usual. Clemency, there was a phone call from William's Uncle Daniel earlier. He would like to come and meet you while you are here. Apparently, he heard from William's mother, and she is anxious to know how you are. He's also the one keen on history, so I expect he'll fill in a few gaps," she said, nodding towards the family tree scroll. "I invited him to lunch tomorrow if that's agreeable. You'll still be here, Evie, won't you?"

"Oh yes, definitely," said Evie.

My own thoughts fixated on why Will's uncle was visiting, apparently on instructions from Will's mother.

Chapter Eleven

"Diane ordered Matt out of the barn this morning! He's hardly slept these last few nights, with the lambs arriving so quickly. Diane's been doing night duties, but it hasn't stopped Matt from turning up in the early hours, so she grabbed the yard brush and threatened to sweep him out with it! His face was a picture! But he took the hint at last. Diane is a good shepherdess and knows when to call the vet if any ewe is in extreme difficulty. So far, we've been lucky." Joe forked up more cottage pie as we all sat round the table in the warm kitchen at suppertime. The dogs sat under the table, waiting hopefully for dropped morsels.

I remembered Mollie's description of Matt's girlfriends in high heels and asked if she would make a good partner for Matt.

"No chance. Diane's a farmer's wife already, although they don't keep sheep anymore," Joe said. "She's also a champion sheep shearer. You must bring Evie over to the sheep sheds to see the new lambs."

"I'd like that. Sorry to change the subject, but do either of you know about the inscription on the obelisk?" asked Evie.

Both Joe and Serena shook their heads. "The Ladies' Bower has been allowed to run wild for decades," said Joe, "certainly since before we arrived. I think William's father and grandfather had plans to restore it but nothing materialised. I don't know who erected it or why it's there."

"It's in the family tree; some members of the family died two hundred years ago, seemingly together at a place near the obelisk."

Joe rubbed his chin while Serena began gathering our plates. I'd tried to do justice to Serena's cooking skills, but hadn't managed more than a few mouthfuls. She raised her eyebrows at me when she took my plate and I mouthed "sorry" at her. She squeezed my shoulder.

"I think I know about that accident," said Joe. "A coach went out of control with some family members in it and it crashed into the old ash tree. They all died and were buried at the chapel. Geoffrey, William's father, oversaw the restoration of the chapel and graveyard and had it re-consecrated, which was fitting as his funeral service was held there. His grave isn't there, although there is a memorial to him. He was cremated."

"Is the chapel easy to get to?" asked Evie. "I tired Clemmie out this afternoon with rootling about in the woods, so I won't go if it's difficult to get to."

"It's a very pleasant walk, especially in the spring and summer, through the fields or the woods. There used to be a proper carriage way that was used by the families down the years but it was ploughed up in the second world war to increase the farm acreage," said Joe.

"It's accessible by road," cut in Serena. "Just head towards Bridgeford, then take the next turning on the right after the farm entrance. It's only a stony track, but it is drivable."

Evie raised her eyebrows at me. "What do you say? Are you up to it? We'll go at your pace, only it sounds interesting and you know my morbid interest in graveyards!"

When we had first met in Halls as First Year University students, and struck up immediate friendship, Evie had persuaded me to accompany her to Highgate Cemetery as part of her first assignment, and we'd visited many old, neglected cemeteries after that.

"When we were at Uni, I dragged Clemmie round a lot of graveyards." Evie regaled us. "Once we were sitting in a very pretty one with spring blossoms on the trees, eating crisps, and then a dog came trotting round the corner where we were sitting with a large bone in its mouth...."

Serena gave a half-horrified laugh. "When Daniel Williamson comes to lunch tomorrow, he'll know much of the estate history. He taught at the Cathedral School and chaired the Local History Society for years," she said.

Evie beamed at the prospect of bombarding the poor man with questions.

"The chapel is older than this house as there was a hamlet and a small manor house near the river in medieval times, but now all you can see in the nettles and brambles are piles of stones opposite the church. There's an old mill on the river built at the same time as the chapel and that's still standing, but be careful of the river. It's in full winter spate. The current is quite rapid and there's still a mill race," said Joe.

"That was the noise we heard when we were on the footpath earlier," I said. "It sounded like a waterfall."

"That was probably the weir," said Joe. "There's a bridge over the river to the other side and you can get to Watcombe through the water meadows, although it will be boggy at this time of year," he added.

We helped load the dishwasher after supper and offered our help tomorrow with lunch preparation. Serena accepted but said it would be best if I avoided food preparation.

Armed with mugs of tea, Evie and I retired to the sitting room again, where Evie stoked up the fire to get a blaze going. As she started studying the family tree scroll again, she remarked we could do with a map of the estate, so I fetched it from the library. Evie pored over it delightedly, noting Harthill House's proximity to the chapel and Mill.

"Looks like there's a boat house as well," she said. "Can you just imagine an Edwardian boating party in punts with wicker picnic hampers?" She was in her element, exclaiming how lucky I was to be here with the wealth of history to embrace. I didn't have the heart to confide my fears to her. Sadly, if my relationship with Will foundered because of the twin attractions of Rafaella and the States, I might never see Harthill House again.

I yawned loudly. "It's hard to stay up late anymore," I apologised. "I'm going to have to leave you and turn in."

She looked up anxiously. "You will stop me if I'm overwhelming you, won't you? You know me when I get the bit between my teeth, I get too single-minded to think about others."

"I'll be fine in the morning. But I'm worried about you giving the Mastermind questioning treatment to Will's Uncle Daniel! I feel sorry for him already and I haven't even met him."

Will must have told his mother about my pregnancy and being here, I thought as I got ready for bed. Did he break the news joyfully, or did he admit to her it was a shock and he wasn't ready for commitment? I assumed that because he lived locally, his mother then phoned Daniel to arrange a meeting with me so he could take stock and report back to her. It made me feel antagonistic towards the man before I'd even met him. I hadn't even thought of giving the news to my parents yet, but for different reasons: I wanted to reach the next baby scan before I felt safe about the pregnancy.

Will had sent lots of photos. Action shots of Will or Hugo or Rafaella on wooded trails, pictures of snow-topped forested ridges and one with a blue helicopter resting in a wide glade. They looked stunning and if we used them on our public website, they would certainly whet the appetites of keen riders. I replied to his email saying I loved the photos and asking if we could use them for promo pictures.

~

Evie woke me the next morning with a rattling tray piled with toast, honey, tea, juice, and boiled eggs in white china eggcups. Unfortunately, the sight and smell of the food on waking drove me into the bathroom urgently and I emerged later hunched in my bathrobe to find that Evie had nearly finished her breakfast and started on mine. She boiled the kettle, and I cradled a cup of ginger tea until I could nibble a piece of cold dry toast.

"I got up early and had a good look round the house," said Evie as she ate my boiled egg. "It's fascinating. I've looked it up, and it's mentioned in Pevsner – he was an architect who went round years ago writing wonderful snippets about England's grand houses and churches - and he says this house is a little gem of architecture, not so large as to be a stately home, but given the dimensions to be a very comfortable and spacious family home. All the rooms seem to have been put to good use, although the North Wing is neglected and there are lots of unused rooms in the South Wing."

"I think Joe said that in Trust meetings, the fabric of the house and wings had to be inspected professionally at least once a year," I remembered. "I assume the North Wing is too costly to restore it to its original condition. I haven't explored all the house yet."

"I met Joe, who was getting the fires ready, so I helped him bring in some logs. I think he's really enjoying your stay here, Clem, from what he was saying, and feels optimistic about Will taking up the reins again."

What could I say? Knowing Will's hyperactive personality, I had doubts that running this estate would satisfy his need for pushing boundaries. "Who knows?" I said, and buried my nose in my teacup to ward off further questions.

"Well, as time is getting on, I'll offer my services to Serena in the kitchen, but I'm sure Serena will find something for you to do when you've got yourself ready. I slept very well in the green room despite those nightmares inducing giant roses, although it took me a while to nod off without the background of traffic noise or aircraft or sirens!"

Evie disappeared downstairs while I showered. There were no undesirable figures in the meadow and wood. As I descended the basement stairs, I heard the murmur of conversation. Serena was basting a lamb joint and returning it to the oven, and Evie sat at the table peeling potatoes and carrots. After being given a boisterous welcome by the two dogs, I retreated to the far end of the table. I was already full of nerves at the prospect of meeting an unknown relative of Will's and didn't want nausea to ruin things.

"Evie said you were delicate this morning, so I think it's best you stay away from the kitchen," said Serena, blitzing something in a food mixer. "Joe was sorting out cutlery and china for the dining room, if you might like to give him a hand. It's been a while since he laid a table!" She chuckled as she said this and I saw that rather than feeling put upon, Serena was enjoying the preparation.

The small dining room off the Hall at the front of the house overlooked the drive and the fields nearest to the farm. Joe was lighting the fire in yet another marble fireplace and greeted me. "This room should have warmed up by the time we have lunch," he said and went over to feel the radiator under one of the windows.

"It's quite a small dining room for a large house," I commented.

"There's the larger one in the South Wing which I showed you the other day, "said Joe. "That's big enough to be a ballroom, but we haven't had any demands on its use yet!"

I liked the intimate feeling of this room. The walls were papered in a dark red flock and the heavy curtains at the two sash windows were striped in dark red, green, and yellow. A rug under the table covered the polished floor. Oil paintings of fruits and flowers hung on the two end walls and a mirror hung over the fireplace, reflecting the light from the windows. Joe went to a sideboard behind the door and opened a drawer, revealing white tablecloths and table napkins. We spread one of the linen cloths over the table, and I saw that some napkins had embroidered initials in their corners. "They'll be from another generation, possibly Victorian," Joe said when I showed them to him. "They had time to sit and do things like that, I suppose."

Again, I experienced that feeling of past and present overlapping; that if I walked into the Hall, I would see ladies and gentlemen in Victorian clothes, or the crinolines and knee breeches of an earlier era. We laid the table but Joe was dubious about putting out wine glasses. Neither he nor Serena drank much wine; I certainly couldn't drink any alcohol; Uncle Daniel would be driving, which left Evie. I put my head round the kitchen door to ask if she wanted wine, but Serena had already solved the problem by putting out some bottles of lager and a jug of juice and one of water. Evie was neatly slicing up avocado and arranged them on side plates. Serena added a little chilli sauce and crispy bacon bits on top. I found my mouth watering; after all, I'd only managed a bit of dry toast earlier.

Evie and I went back to the Hall to wait for Daniel. The fire was crackling in the huge grate and we sat on the fender, warming ourselves.

"You'll have to kick me if I monopolise this Uncle Daniel," said Evie. "You know what I'm like and I want to know as much as possible about the history of Harthill House, but he has come to see you!"

"I'll be glad of your questions – I'm suspicious that he's come to spy on me and report back to Will's mother."

Evie raised her eyebrows. "You suspect everything and everyone lately! As if she's got to approve that you are a suitable partner for her son! She's known about you for years. I'm sure that's not the reason. Maybe she feels guilty she's not here herself to make you feel comfortable while Will's away."

"Maybe," I shrugged. There was nothing to stop Roberta Payne-Ashton from living here again now her husband was dead. It was odd that she'd chosen not to live with her husband and influenced Will in his decision to ignore the house and estate.

Crunching gravel outside heralded the approach of an ancient Morris Minor estate car. We went to open the big door to greet him, only to find that Joe was hurrying forward, accompanied by the two excited dogs.

"I'll act as butler today and introduce you," he grinned.

We all stood under the portico while an elderly man slowly unfolded himself from the Morris Minor. As he straightened, I saw that despite his lined face; he carried himself erect. His hair was white and neatly parted and he wore the ubiquitous country apparel of corduroy trousers, a well-worn tweed jacket with leather elbow patches over a green checked open-necked shirt with a paisley cravat round his neck. He looked from me to Evie and although smiling, clearly didn't know which one of us was his nephew's fiancée.

Joe immediately shook his hand and guided him into the warmth. "Good to see you again, Joe," said Daniel Williamson. "How are you and Serena?"

"Both of us are in good health. Thanks, Daniel. And you are looking very well. Now, can I introduce you to Clemency, William's fiancée, and Evie, Clemency's friend who's visiting for the weekend?"

Daniel shook my hand, his grip warm and firm, and he looked

at me for long seconds before releasing my hand. His eyes were pale blue, but clear and friendly. "It is a genuine pleasure to meet you, Clemency," he said. "I hope it's not too long before I see you both here together."

Before I could formulate any answer, he turned to Evie and shook her hand with a friendly greeting. Joe ushered us into the small sitting room to wait for lunch. He offered to get us drinks, and Daniel and Evie accepted lager while I shook my head. Daniel spotted the map still spread out on the coffee table. Under it the Family Tree was out of sight. "Aha, you are acquainting yourselves with the layout of the estate and its environs, I see," he said delightedly and as he was about to plump down on the sofa, he remembered his manners and indicated that we should sit first. I smiled at such gentlemanly conduct one didn't encounter much these days.

"How much of the history of Harthill House do you already know?" he asked, addressing both of us.

"Almost nothing," I answered before Evie jumped in. "Until Will brought me down here, I didn't even know this house existed. I'm still in shock over the size and scale of it." I nearly added that I was still in shock at my pregnancy as well, but refrained.

"So, this is your first visit?" he asked in genuine surprise.

"Yes, Will is always busy rushing round the globe on his bike," I laughed. "And me and the rest of the team in London are kept busy arranging more treks and itineraries. He's never so much as hinted at it."

Daniel looked thoughtful, as if choosing his next words carefully. "He certainly didn't spend much time here in his childhood and youth, I admit. His mother lived in London then and there was so much more to do there. Will spent his summer vacations here with his father, and occasional Christmases – he and Matt Crane were little tearaways then. You have met Matt, I presume?" he asked.

"Yes, and I've watched lambing and visited the farmhouse. It all seems to be running in perfect order here and on the farm. I'm sure Will is more than happy that the management of the estate is in safe hands."

"The Estate Trust oversees everything, but Joe and Serena and Matt are the hard workers here."

Evie sat relaxed, studying the map again and brought out the family tree from underneath it.

Daniel continued to study me, but I didn't feel patronised or intimidated. Possibly he was treading carefully and wondering how to bring up the subject of my pregnancy and our future. Obviously, he didn't know anything about the situation in the States and it wouldn't be fair to lumber him with my overwhelming concerns, although instinctively I felt I could be open with him and he would understand without being judgemental.

Daniel's eye fell on the family tree scroll and his eyes lit up. "Well, I'm glad this still exists," he exclaimed. "It took me a long time to bring it up to my satisfaction and there is still research to do."

"It's fascinating," said Evie, "and we are full of questions. I'm an archivist, so this sort of thing is my bread and butter, like the library full of rare books. For instance......."

Evie never had a chance to finish, as Joe put his head round the door. "Lunch is ready, "he announced. "I just need a little help to carry the stuff through to the dining room."

A strange clanking noise echoed in the hallway, and Joe went to the end wall at the top of the basement stairs and opened a hatch. I hadn't spotted it before and as the clanking increased, a box attached to a pulley appeared, with some covered dishes in it. I laughed in amazement as Joe handed one dish to me and one to Evie.

"This is a little lift called a dumb waiter, very useful when the kitchen is downstairs and the dining room upstairs!" explained Joe to Evie and me.

"It was installed in the 1920s by William's grandfather," said Daniel. "I believe he used to entertain quite often. In those days, hunting and shooting and fishing were pastimes much practised in the country, so guests stayed for weekends with lunches and dinner parties."

When the last of the dishes had been carried into the dining room and placed on the hotplate, we all collected a plate and helped ourselves, insisting that Joe and Serena weren't to wait on us. To my relief, I was hungry and helped myself to a little of the tender-looking lamb, roast potatoes, and selection of green and root vegetables on offer. The others filled their plates and for a while conversation comprised praise for Serena's culinary expertise and murmurs of appreciation, talk of lambing and weather. Daniel put down his knife and fork tidily on his plate and asked me what my impressions of Harthill House were after my initial shock and surprise had worn off.

"I find it hard to relate it to my life," I confessed. "I find it hard to connect Will to this house at all. He's so into pursuing physical challenges trekking all over Europe and this place is the opposite - steeped in history and memories. If he was sitting here with us now, he'd be shovelling this meal in as fast as possible so he could get outside. In a way, he is not so dissimilar to Matt, as Matt spends all his time out and about on the farm."

"Can you feel the history or memories of the past?" Daniel probed.

Despite being conscious of all eyes focussing on me, I was quick to respond. "Oh, yes, when I go into certain rooms or the basement corridor for example where all the cellars and rooms for storing and preparing are, I can see the bustle of the house in its heyday: scullery maids and servants and footmen in their livery. The servants seem to have left strong impressions behind. And in the reception rooms like the hall and drawing room, I can't see men and women in period clothes and wigs and dogs milling round, but I sense their presences."

Joe and Serena looked amazed at each other.

"We must be pretty thick skinned," said Joe. "I don't think either of us has encountered any such presences."

Serena nodded in agreement. "Well, after what Clemency has just described, I might just be casting an eye over my shoulder now and again! Mollie is a good person to ask about 'impressions'. Her family has been around as long as William's forebears." She offered seconds as she spoke.

Evie laughed in delight. "You are a dark horse, Clem. You gave me the impression that you found the place quite intimidating. Although you said you saw someone when we were out for our walk. She went as white as a sheet at one point and said she thought someone was watching from the gate to the woods, didn't you?"

Daniel looked directly at me questioningly and I thought this is my chance to explain about the Twins, who nobody else seemed to see or remark on.

"What did you think you saw?" asked Daniel, and I frowned because it didn't quite fit into my understanding of why he was here: to make sure all was well so he could report to Roberta, Will's mother.

"Well, I keep seeing the same two people. They must live near here, but they don't respond if I call out and, to be honest, they creep me out."

Joe and Serena stopped clearing. "I hope they haven't got any criminal intentions," said Joe. "I'll check all the alarms and security lighting. I'm sorry you feel scared, Clemency. Matt and I will walk round every evening just to check everything. Dr Laidlaw mentioned somebody loitering the other night."

Daniel looked intently at me, but we were both quiet.

"I'll fetch pudding," said Serena. "I hope you'll all find room for apple and blackberry crumble and custard. They're our own apples and blackberries, of course."

Daniel obviously decided it was no use pursuing his agenda any further. As we all helped to gather plates and dishes together to transport to the dumbwaiter, I mentally stored the ridiculous name in my memory to tell Will. *Oh, incidentally, Will, I met your dumb waiter today* ...... Daniel took my elbow gently. "Clemency, I would very much like you to come and visit me in Salisbury before you return to London. I can show you round the Cathedral and we can have tea in the Refectory there. It's a wonderful construction which enhances the architecture."

I sensed another unspoken reason for visiting him, and I readily agreed. "I'll give you my phone number. Come soon. If you find transport difficult, I will come and collect you."

Although puzzled by his insistence, I assured him I would love to visit and see the famous cathedral. Serena appeared bearing a dish from which came glorious aromas of fruit and cinnamon, and I sniffed appreciatively.

Just as Serena was dishing it out and Evie was discussing the family tree with Daniel, Matt appeared in the doorway, looking apologetically sheepish. He was in a heavy duty puffa jacket and beanie hat, his nose red with cold. "Hi everybody, I'm a pest butting in, but I saw Daniel's car outside and just wanted to come and say hello to him before returning to the lambing barns."

He shook Daniel's hand and was introduced to Evie. At our insistence, he was made to sit down and was soon spooning hot crumble and custard down as if he hadn't eaten for a week.

"Only had cheese on toast for my very early lunch, "he said apologetically. "Diane's had to go back home just for today, bit of a family crisis."

"I can come over and give you a hand, lad," said Joe. "Eat up first though."

"If you have time, come and see the lambs," said Matt to Evie and me, and Evie nodded enthusiastically.

Daniel said he would leave before dusk fell, as his old eyes didn't like night driving. Serena insisted that clearing up was easy and to stay and talk with Uncle Daniel so I went down to make tea and coffee before he left and took it up to the small sitting room, where Evie had fed the fire with more logs and she and Daniel were studying the map of the estate.

"It is hand drawn, as you can see, exquisitely done. Look at the care and scale of the house and gardens and estate and I'm certain the person who drew this map is Helene Barnard. She was one of Sir Horace's daughters and later married Henry Wallington. She was a gifted artist and portrait painter and some of her sketchbooks are in the library. You can see that the drive sweeps past the house frontage and carries on through the fields to the chapel and then meets the road to Bridgeford. That part of the drive disappeared under the plough many years ago." Daniel stirred sugar into his black coffee.

"Has anybody been over it with a metal detector? Seeing we know the owner of the estate and one of its trustees is sitting here, it shouldn't be too hard to get permission!"

"I'm sure that's permissible," smiled Daniel. "Although I think it unlikely you will find any Saxon hoards hereabouts!"

"We explored the Ladies' Bower yesterday. It's terribly overgrown now, of course. It looks like a little maze, but there is no Obelisk marked on the map. We found the inscription in the memory of Gyles Payne, his son and Honoria's cousin, carved into it. Look, here are some photos I took."

Evie scrolled through the photos she'd taken yesterday on her digital camera.

"I found all the names in the family tree, but we couldn't figure out how they all died at the same time until Joe reckoned it was a carriage accident."

"According to records, they were killed when the horses spooked and their carriage swung round and hit a tree in the drive – the old ash tree, I believe. It's been aged as over five hundred years old, so it would have been fully grown even in 1809. Gyles and Edmund were killed outright. Bartholomew and the groom crawled away to get help but Bartholomew died before help arrived. Only the groom survived. There's an account in the archives of the Salisbury Courier and there was an obituary to Gyles Payne in The Times. It must have been quite a sensation back then, equivalent to a car pile-up today," said Daniel. "Some stories are sad and some hard to believe. Edwin, Honoria's son, married Doctor Birch's daughter, who attended after the accident, although their two children died at very early ages. Somewhere in the library there is supposed to be a journal written by Honoria, Sir Horace's granddaughter, but I have never tried to look for it. She was the real driving force behind the family and lived to a ripe old age."

"I can't understand why her children inherited. I can see that one by one the male heirs died, but there was still a son of Sir Horace around here. Look, Gerard. He should really have inherited, surely."

"Ah, Gerard, he was the black sheep of the family. He didn't live at Harthill House until after his marriage. When the accident happened, Honoria was left to run the estate as her father James and her Uncle Laurence, who still lived in this house, were elderly by then. James Barnard managed the estate throughout his life, assisted by his daughter and son-in-law. Honoria wasn't going to give up the reins lightly to a profligate uncle, even if his claim was valid. In James' Will he left the estate entailed on the male heirs of his daughter. You should be able to trace that through National Archives or Probate Laws." Daniel expected Evie's next question.

"Yes, I have software from which I can access Wills – it's necessary for my work," said Evie.

"Gerard returned to the fold like a prodigal son after the deaths and tried to contest the Will. He was obviously unsuccessful. Apparently, he had many illegitimate offspring whom he failed to acknowledge."

Evie turned to me. "I told you there were skeletons in the cupboard, didn't I?"

Daniel shrugged. "My energy for research has somewhat waned over the years, I'm afraid," he said smiling. "It would be refreshing for fresh eyes to throw light on the family history, but there are stories which are not comfortable to be out in the open."

He looked at me as he spoke and I shivered unaccountably. Then he glanced out of the windows. "Reluctantly, I must leave you both now before it gets too dark; my old eyes don't like the glare of headlights when I drive at night. There are photo albums in the library going back to the days of early photography. They used to be in one of the long drawers under the bookshelves. They will fascinate you both, I'm sure. I will just go and say goodbye and thank you to Joe and Serena for their hospitality. Will you show me the way, my dear," he addressed me and I accompanied him downstairs. Serena sat with a mug of tea, reading a magazine while the dishwasher hummed in the background.

"Joe is helping Matt," she said as Daniel kissed her cheeks, "but I will pass on your regards and please come again as often as you wish. You know there's no need for a formal invitation."

"Thank you, I also feel it incumbent of me to keep one eye on Clemency in William's absence."

As he wound his scarf round his neck against the cold, he kissed me on the cheeks and repeated his invitation to visit him with more emphasis.

"There is more we can discuss, just you and me, my dear," he said, his eyes crinkling with warmth. "Also, take care when you are out and about on the estate. Maybe go in company so that you take no risks."

I promised I would not forget, and we waved him off as his ancient Morris set off down the drive.

"I am really peeved I have to go back so soon," Evie said, linking arms as we went back inside. "Daniel is a dear and a mine of information and I would dearly love to hunt for Honoria's Journal and any other contemporary sources. You'll have to be my eyes and keep me informed until I get here again. Now, are you very pooped after entertaining or can we go and see the lambs? I'm not a sentimental animal person, but it's not often you see lambs being born!"

"Serena, thank you for that lovely lunch," I said on our way out of the back door, "please don't prepare any supper for us. Evie and I'll come down later and just make some toast and tea."

"Good, there's a TV series which I have been watching. Help yourself to whatever you fancy."

Evie kept a firm grip on my elbow as we made our way through the deepening gloom to the barns. My head was full of Daniel's conversation and I only remembered that I hadn't been fearful of seeing the Twins until we got to the barns.

Chapter Twelve

By the time we'd admired the lambs and Evie had pumped information from Matt about his single status quite flagrantly, I was beginning to tire. I was cross about feeling so feeble, especially as my lifestyle was normally active. I hoped I wouldn't feel like this throughout my pregnancy. Having read about what other women achieved while pregnant, sometimes doing risky activities, I was determined not to let nausea rule my life. Instead, I sat on a hay bale cuddling a lamb while Evie inspected nearly all the pens. Eventually she did extricate herself from the lifecycle of the ewes' gestation period and we emerged into a cold, dark evening. We gazed at the spectacle of constellations and moon so bright in the heavens.

"Matt's a sweetie," she remarked as we made our way back to the house.

"So I observed," I said sarcastically. "I wondered if you were more interested in him than the lambs!"

"Oh, he's not my type," she laughed. "But I can't believe he hasn't been snapped up already!"

"Mollie said girls round here were frightened off by real animals and the stuff that comes out of them!"

Later, after tea and toast in the kitchen, we stoked up the fire in the small sitting room, which looked at its cosiest when the lamps were lit, curtains drawn and burning logs crackling cheerfully. The dogs would have been happy in here, ensconced by the fire, but Joe had taken them upstairs after being let out for their evening 'performances'.

I would have been content to idly watch TV and chat to Evie, but she had other ideas. She disappeared, and I settled back comfortably with my feet up on the sofa, feeling pleasantly drowsy while a game show droned away on the TV. I tried to think when it would be convenient to visit Uncle Daniel. If I left it too long, he might get the impression that I had no intention of seeing him again, although I'd only been here a few days.

Evie returned carrying a couple of large flat tomes. "Photo albums!" she announced triumphantly. "I did have a quick scan of the shelves to see if Honoria's Journal stood out amongst all the other publications, but it was rather chilly in there. You'll have to search after I've gone but get togged up in case you freeze to death. Budge up then, and we'll have a look at your child's ancient ancestors."

The photographs in the album Evie opened were a perfect record of family and social life after the mid-1850s. Many depicted groups of people standing stiffly to attention, as the camera needed several minutes of exposure. Gentlemen wore bowler hats, and all carried walking canes. The older ladies were dressed in an assortment of fashions. One lady wore a mob cap, lace collar and the full skirts of the crinoline fashion, although the other females wore the high collars and tight-fitting buttoned blouses and less full skirts of a later era. Without names identifying them, we had no idea who they were. There were many photos depicting the Hunt Meet in front of the house with men and women on horseback, dogs milling around, and servants with trays of glasses filled with sherry or port. Photos of livestock were abundant too – great bulls with proud handlers, children with small ponies and always dogs.

"I wish we could name a few people. They must nearly all be in the family tree and the same faces keep appearing," said Evie. "With a good guess I bet I could identify Honoria by the number of appearances she makes." She quietly turned pages while I looked at the next album. The same country activities such as riding were depicted as were the inevitable hunts and shooting parties and picnics. A large, faded photo which filled the page made me sit up. It was another family scene in the easily recognisable gardens. A cloth-covered table was set in the shade of the cedar tree still standing today. It was laden with all the paraphernalia required for a tea party: tiered cake stands, teapots, jugs, and plates. Several people sat round the table looking towards the camera and this time names were written in spidery black ink beneath the picture.

"Bingo," I said, nudging Evie. Together we read the names identifying each of the persons present.

A stern-faced lady, her face lined by age, sat to the left. She wore a black dress edged with lace at the neck and cuffs and a black bonnet edged with lace. The name underneath read: Honoria. We looked at each other, and then Evie dived for the family tree.

"Honoria died in 1866, aged 98! This photograph must have been taken just before she died. She looks formidable, don't you think? We should be able to identify her features in other photos, but that period is early for photography," said Evie.

The next person on Honoria's left behind the table was an elderly gentleman wearing a dark jacket, waistcoat, and a white stock round his neck. A bowler hat lay on the table next to him.

His white beard and moustache covered half of his face. "Edwin," I said.

"Honoria's son, born in 1790, so he's not young in this photo either," said Evie.

Next to Edwin sat another elderly lady, hatless with white hair piled up in a curled topknot. A shawl was draped round her ample shoulders and her mouth curved in a slight smile. "Mary," I dutifully read.

"Edwin's wife. They certainly lived a long life," said Evie, referring to the Family Tree again. A man with a dark beard and whiskers sat next to Mary with a cigar lifted in acknowledgement of the camera. "Samuel."

"That's Edwin and Mary's son. According to the family tree, he had a twin called Julius, who apparently died in a fight in 1832."

"This lady next to him is the only one with a smiley face," I said, looking at her broad face and light hair. She wore a high-necked flowered dress or blouse and she was half turned towards the younger woman on her left, towards the end of the table.

"That's Sarah Somerset, who married Samuel," Evie read out. Glancing at the photo and then back to the family tree, she announced that the young woman was Maud, Samuel, and Sarah's daughter. Next to her, at the far end of the table opposite Honoria, was a large lady in a wide-brimmed hat decorated with ribbons. Her face was in shadow, but the name underneath read Lily.

"That must be Gerard's wife and behind her are her sons Wilfred and George, who look like they haven't been invited to tea!" laughed Evie.

"Who is the young man sitting on the grass in front of the table?" I asked.

"Johannes," Evie said. The youth was light-haired and despite the age of the photograph, there was a distinct resemblance to Will and Matt.

Evie was scanning the family tree. "No sign of a Johannes," she said. "There's a Johannes in the tree born in 1807 illegitimately to Edwin, but it can't be him because of the age. But look, Clemmie, Maud is Will's paternal great-great grandmother. She married a Joshua Ashton after this photo, adding it to the family name. Honoria is his five times great grandmother. I wonder if he has seen these photos?"

"Probably," I said as I flicked to the back of the album at more modern photos labelled in neat handwriting. "There are lots here of his grandfather and other people. Were there other albums in the drawer?"

"Yes, but I was only interested in the older ones. You have plenty of time to peruse the others."

She turned the pages of the one she held and stopped and laughed.

"You remember Uncle Daniel talking about the profligate son Gerard? Well, here's another one of his twin sons. They lived until they were a hundred years old and still didn't inherit! Bet they were mad, judging by their expressions! They look like something out of a Thomas Hardy book–Far from the Madding Crowd, perhaps?"

When she mentioned Thomas Hardy, an icy chill crawled down my spine and the hairs on my arms stood up.

She turned the album round to show me the sepia toned image, and I clutched my chest as I thought my heart would jump out of my throat. There staring out at me were my stalking twins–dressed in their smocks, lower legs bound with strips and buttoned gaiters, and wearing boots, with straw hats set back on their heads. Each carried a crook, and each glared at the camera with that familiar, glowering expression I dreaded.

"George and Wilfred," said Evie, and my heart sank. Then she saw my face.

"What's up, Clemmie? You've gone pale! Do you feel sick?"

The Shadow Watchers

"No, no, it's just seeing that photo..." I put my hand up to my head. I mustn't faint again. It was time to unburden myself. I wasn't hallucinating; or suffering from pregnancy hormones or going mad. The evidence was in front of me. I was being stalked – by ghostly beings who had died a century ago.

"You know when we were out yesterday and I saw something or somebody?" Evie nodded. "I keep seeing these two," I said quietly, "right from the first day I was here. I thought they were quaintly dressed farm workers, just like you say, like characters from a Thomas Hardy novel. But they keep popping up when I'm out. I've seen them when I've been with Joe and with you. Neither of you saw them, and I thought my hormones were playing tricks on me. But they really frighten me. It's as if they want to harm me. Joe and Matt have said they don't employ farm workers. Remember, I mentioned them at lunch? Clearly, Joe and Serena have never encountered them. You were with me when I saw them, but you saw nothing. But I'm not imagining them. I could have described them exactly before seeing this photo."

I could tell Evie was at a loss for what to say. She knew me too well to laugh at me. Instead, she squeezed my arm, and I breathed out slowly. Unburdening myself was the first step to regaining control. What I could do about the Twins was another problem.

"Perhaps I need an exorcist," I laughed shakily. It broke the tension between us and Evie said, "Well, you were expounding to Uncle Daniel how you saw presences here, so I'm not doubting you. As for them harming you, you can forget that silly nonsense. That's only for B-rated horror movies. I'll make you a mug of hot chocolate and a hot water bottle and you can relax in bed," she continued. "Phone Will. Be normal. Don't let two silly old ghosts stop you from doing normal things."

This was Evie, at her most pragmatic self. She closed the albums decisively and stood up to make my promised hot chocolate.

"I was going to suggest we drive down to the chapel tomorrow and have a rootle round the gravestones and then have some lunch out. But if you'd rather not..."

"I'll come, Evie. Remember, I was your backup on your haunts round London's cemeteries! Very morbid, but quite satisfying, somehow. Only don't show me George and Wilfred's gravestone unless I'm carrying a silver dagger!"

To tell the truth, it would be macabre going round a churchyard where we might see some of the names on gravestones of the people in the photos we'd just been looking at, but as Evie's stay was so short, I would help her satisfy her curiosity. I went to bed with mixed feelings: relief that my imagination wasn't running riot and foreboding that every time I stepped out of doors I would be confronted by the apparition of 'real life' unfriendly departed spirits. I couldn't stay indoors all the time I was here, so I might just as well return to London and away from the Twins. Why were they stalking me, anyway? The family had lived here continuously from the early eighteenth century and certainly in the Twins' lifetime. Where had they lived on the estate? Gerard was in his sixties when the twins had been born and if he had tried to contest the Will in which his brother James had stipulated that the estate go to his own daughter Honoria's male heirs, he was bound to be resentful.

It was a relief to open Will's email and look at the photos he'd attached. He and Hugo had been flown to the residence of Rafaella's parents in New Hampshire. There were photos of an old colonial style residence with a verandah supported by wooden white painted posts and surrounded by tall firs. The lawn was white with snow. He was effusive in his descriptions and enthusiasm.

> There are so many trails and National Parks around here, Clem. We could trek all year round quite happily. Raf's parents are fun and entertaining us in style. Tomorrow we are going up some forest trails so expect more pics. Hugo's forwarded them on to the team as well. Don't forget you are meant to rest, Clem, love. Bye Will xxx.

'Fun parents!' In my mind, I could see my prim and proper mother and conventional father. How nice it must be to have 'fun' parents!' But by being led further into the heart of East Coast terrain, Will was succumbing to the appeal of the place and the people. In my heart, I knew that even if he returned from the States and resumed trekking in Europe again, he would be changed. His email could have been copied to his friends as there was nothing personal in it; even the closing kisses would not have looked out of place in a shared message.

I answered his email, telling him about Uncle Daniel's visit and spending the evening looking through old family photo albums. Boring to Will, but he would be happy that such mundane activities were keeping me occupied. When he came home, I would ask him why his mother had sent Uncle Daniel to check up on me.

Chapter Thirteen

Evie's mind ran ahead of her the next morning, in contrast to my own, sluggish after the usual horrible morning ritual. She had been up early and braved the chill of the library. "There are some fabulously rare books in there and Will has some seriously talented ancestors, but no sign of any journal. I've left the photo albums in the small sitting room, but I rolled up the map so we can refer to it down by the chapel. I'll take good care of it. I know it is the original map," she added when she saw my worried face. "It's such a pity the old driveway has vanished – it must have been a pretty ride or walk through the fields, especially in summer. Do you think Joe's got a metal detector?"

Monotonous grey clouds stretched to the horizon. We looked with more interest at the old ash tree, which had been the scene of the accident two hundred years ago as we drove past. Even in winter, stripped of greenery, it was huge and gnarled; several twisted trunks making one considerable girth, with heavy boughs weighing it down. "I can see why the crash was fatal," Evie remarked. "It's a big tree to smash into."

An icy shiver ran through me.

Smoke rose from the mock Elizabethan twisted chimney stack when we passed Mollie's lodge cottage, and the snowdrops under her hedges brightened the dull day. Matt's tractor lumbered up the farm drive and Evie commented on his single status again.

I laughed. "I'm sure you wouldn't mind getting your hands dirty if you are that keen!"

"I'm a city girl and he's not my type," she grinned. I looked at her, curious to know what 'type' she preferred. In all the years we'd known each other, she'd never been in a relationship and I'd just accepted that she was a dedicated career woman.

The road to the old chapel appeared on a bend further down on the right and it ran down a steep incline, studded with muddy potholes, littered with dead leaves and small branches, and bounded on either side by bushes and trees. A broken-down wall appeared on the left, ending in a mound of bricks and nettles and shrubs, and opposite, low walls enclosed a small church and graveyard.

"What a pretty little chapel," I said, looking up at the gabled roof. There was no steeple or tower, just a stone cross on the roof above the arched window in the west wall. The walls were built of flint and stone in a chequered pattern, all the windows were boarded and a wrought iron grille shut off the entrance to the porch, presumably against vandalism.

Evie parked the car against the wall and climbed out, but instead of opening the gate into the church grounds, she strode over the road to where the wall ended in the mound of rubble and brambles. She had the map partially unrolled. "These must be the ruins of the old manor which stood here before Harthill House was built. Look, it's named Petherick Manor on the map. It must have still been standing when Harthill House was built. Look at the L shaped building drawn." She rolled the map up carefully and put it back in the car, turning her attention to the church.

"What a pity it's all boarded up and locked," she said, getting out her camera, "but it's inevitable nowadays. That front porch looks like a Victorian addition."

"The Chapel of St Mary the Virgin," I read from a weathered wooden board on the wall of the porch.

We walked round the little chapel, peering through the wrought iron grille into the porch. The entrance door to the chapel was quite substantial and quite probably as old as the original building. Above the boarded window on the west wall, Evie spotted a date: MDCLXV. "1665", she murmured.

Surprisingly, the grass around the old gravestones and memorials had been kept manicured, so it was easy to move around. The ones nearest to the little church were the oldest, and Evie wasted no time in hunkering down and rubbing at the eroded inscriptions. She soon had a small scraper in her hand and delicately removed moss. "This one is dated 1675 in Roman numerals, and the name Edward Petherick. I bet he lived in the Manor across the road."

I ran back to the car and spread the old map carefully on the seat so it wouldn't get damp. The church was drawn exactly as it looked now minus its porch and across the lane, the outline of the house built in an L shape was drawn. A garden had been marked, divided into areas with tiny drawings of fruit trees at the far end near the river, which ran at the end of the property. Further down the lane where the river was much broader, another building had been drawn, marked The Mill with a bridge crossing the river at a narrow point and along the bank facing the river a sketch of a building labelled The Boathouse had been made. I rolled the map up again and returned to Evie, busy deciphering inscriptions on headstones.

"It must have been a substantial manor house to support a church. I expect Will's Uncle Daniel knows all the dates and who is buried here. Maybe there's a vault in the church commemorating the families who lived here before Sir Horace built Harthill House. We should have asked about keys before we set out. Still,

The Shadow Watchers

it's more exciting discovering for ourselves, isn't it?" Evie said cheerfully.

Exciting! On a grey chilly day like today with the clouds pressing down, I could not think of a more depressing place to be. A keen wind blew down the lane and I moved into the lee of the church. Dark yews bordered the churchyard and there were catkins on the naked branches of smaller trees. I walked through the marked plots bordered with snowdrops and early primroses that were bravely proclaiming new life in wintery conditions. I passed newer gravestones on which the words were easier to make out and read: "Henrietta Payne-Ashton Born 1879. Taken Into the Arms of Jesus 1882."

I groaned. I really didn't want to be reminded of the perils of childbirth and childhood illnesses that carried away so many long ago. I could hear Evie over by a stone tabletop tomb.

"Come and see, Clemmie. This is where Gyles Payne, his son and cousin are interred with the date they died, 8th April 1809, on it. It's in pretty good condition, considering its age. I'm surprised Honoria isn't here too...... oh yes, she is, look, her name is at the bottom, Born 1768 and died in December 1866. She lived an awful long time as a widow." She took several photographs from different angles.

Evie's voice faded as she bent over other headstones and I drifted over to the hazel and hawthorns and slender silver birches at the boundary wall, where the catkins stirred in the cold breeze. The hazels had grown close together and formed a bower of twisted branches overrun with dark ivy and Traveller's Joy, and the grass was unkempt here. I didn't see the stone angel until it loomed out of the shadows. It was life size, dark with age, and covered in places with grey and yellow lichen. The angel's wings spread out protectively on either side. Once, it must have been the most imposing memorial in the little churchyard. I looked up at the finely chiselled features; the face bore an expression of sadness and compassion. I laid my hand gently on a wing. My boots scraped against the base and then I saw that the angel's arms stretched down; its hands resting on the heads of two small child-like figures.

I called out to Evie, who was leaning over another headstone. "Look at this angel. It's hidden away under the branches, but it's rather lovely. Come and take a photo."

Evie agreed with me on its beauty and took photos from different angles. She ran her hands over the surfaces and angles to see if she could detect any inscription, and then knelt. "It has feet," she exclaimed, scraping at the moss and ivy at the base. She exposed the hem of the statue's long draped garment and peeping beneath it were the angel's feet, raised up on its toes. She scraped at more undergrowth and uncovered a cushion shaped stone on which the feet rested. "It's a perfect," she murmured. "It needs some attention restoring it. Perhaps I can bring some kit with me on one of my next visits."

A moment later she exclaimed again and there on the fully exposed cushion an inscription was incised into the stone and once she had scraped the earth and moss and lichens away, I knelt with her to read:

<blockquote>
Here lie the mortal remains of
Frances, beloved wife of Edwin Barnard,
Aged eighteen years.
Loving daughter to Thomas Birch, Esq and his Wife Elizabeth.
Taken suddenly from this Earth on 14th February
In the Year of Our Lord 1812.
Also, her beloved sons Frederick Thomas
Departed from Earthly Life aged nine weeks 1811.
And Robert Edwin, aged three months 1812.
May Our Lord Jesus Christ and Mary His Virgin Mother ease her
Great Grief.
</blockquote>

Evie sat back on her heels and blew out her cheeks. I hiccupped as tears welled up and I stumbled to my feet. A great weight of grief and sadness pressed in on my chest.

"Evie caught up with me. "I'm so sorry, Clemmie, I should have realised what an effect all this would have on you."

"We weren't to know what the inscription read." I blew my nose fiercely. "To imagine this poor girl losing two babies in two years and she was only eighteen. The inscription reads she was 'taken suddenly'. Do you think she was ill after her last baby was born, or did she take her own life? 'Her Great Grief.' I just have an awful feeling that she couldn't bear to live without her children." I scrubbed my face with a tissue and inhaled deeply.

"The Church could refuse to bury a poor soul in consecrated ground if they considered a person had taken their own life. This angel is right on the edge of the churchyard, so perhaps it couldn't be proved that she took her own life. Let's call it a day here. I've got some good photos and inscriptions to match names in the family tree. Let's go and get warmed up."

We gratefully got in the car out of the chill wind. Turning on the ignition, Evie cursed. "Damn, I can't turn the car round here. Look how narrow it is. I'm not going to even try to reverse up this rutted track!"

She peered out of the windows, assessing the width of the track. I got out of the car.

"I'll see if you can turn round further on," I said, pulling my bobble hat firmly down.

"We'll both go," said Evie. "We can have a look at the Mill and the boathouse."

She linked her arm through mine and we made slippery progress down the potholed track, strewn with winter debris.

Round a corner obstructed by leaning tree trunks, the river came into view and ahead the track levelled across a bridge wide enough to allow a vehicle to cross, before broadening into a stony forecourt in front of the Mill.

"This is obviously the mill. Look at the fixings where the millwheel used to be."

I went over to the low wall of the bridge. Beneath, a narrow strip of water flowed rapidly.

"That must be the Mill Race: look how straight it is and how fast the current," observed Evie, leaning over. She turned to look up at the front of the Mill. "There's a date over the door here, 1665 again and initials EP underneath. Edward Petherick again. The mill looks in a good structural state for its age." We walked past the building to where a patch of grass ran down to a stretch of river with a wood full of broken limbed trees on the other bank.

"Where is the boathouse?" I said, looking around.

We crossed over from the Mill and although there was a muddy track leading along the riverbank, there was no sign of the boathouse, until Evie spotted a horseshoe shaped indentation in the bank which looked man made. "It might have been pulled down or just collapsed with under use. It looks too perilously close to the river to start poking around. Although winter is a good time to explore because weeds and nettles haven't grown yet."

She started kicking at the vegetation with her boot and soon uncovered rotten planks of wood. "Aha, I was right! We'll have to come back when it's drier and explore more!"

The wide river from this bank was greenish grey and sombre in dull daylight. It ran swiftly and silently as it slid over the weir, churning noisy white foam at the bottom. A sudden shiver made me turn back to retrace our steps to the car, and a wagtail ran along the track in front of me, his tail bobbing animatedly, then the melodious song of a robin came from the woods. It was good to see and hear signs of life after the sad markers in the churchyard. I called to Evie to say I was going back to the car.

"Just coming," she replied.

As I started back again, a small bedraggled white dog shot out of the bushes and stopped on the riverbank some yards from Evie. It ran backwards and forwards, whining and shivering violently.

It's lost. "Here boy, good dog," I called softly, walking slowly towards it. Evie was still peering in the undergrowth. The little terrier ignored me and continued to pace. I stepped closer. The bank was steep here and the river deep. I bent forward, holding my hand towards it and slipped on the muddy edge. I had no time to call out and the icy water took my breath away as I floundered waist deep. The little dog had vanished. Had it fallen in too? I found my voice as I tried and failed to haul myself out. Evie arrived at a run.

"Christ, what happened?" she yelped as she stretched her arms out and helped drag me out. Behind her in the shadow of the trees, the Twins lurked, leering.

"What on earth happened?" she repeated as she helped me towards the car. My trousers and half my jacket streamed water and my boots needed emptying. There was a doubt screaming through my mind. Had the Twins manufactured the dog?

"Did you see a little white dog on the riverbank?" I asked, trying not to let my teeth chatter.

"Dog? There is no dog, Clemmie. Let's get you in the car."

"I'm going to soak your car seat," I said.

"There's an old blanket in the boot. Wrap it round you and I'll get you back to the house."

"Evie, please don't say anything to Serena and Joe. Just smuggle me in and I'll get changed. I feel such a fool."

Evie looked at me oddly. We arrived at the front of the house and Evie slipped out of the car to try the front door. I didn't want to risk bumping into Joe or Serena by the kitchen if I went in the back door. I gusted a sigh of relief when she gave me the thumbs up.

We crept up the servants' staircase, and I tried not to drip.

"We're like two naughty schoolgirls creeping in after lights out," Evie quipped.

I dumped my wet clothes in the bath and warmed up under the shower. Back in my bedroom, I pulled on a change of clothes just as Evie and Serena arrived at my door.

"I was just coming to see if you were back. There's soup ready if you are."

"We're on the way," I said and hoped Serena wouldn't discover my wet things in the bathroom. I'd put them in the washing machine later.

"So, what really happened?" Evie persisted.

"There was a little dog shivering on the bank. I thought it was lost and slipped trying to catch it."

"I didn't see any dog. Where did it go when you fell in?"

"I don't know. It all happened so suddenly. All I remember is seeing a distressed dog, the leering Twins and then slipping into the river." I shivered. "What significance does a dog have linked to the Twins? What makes it even worse is that you didn't see either."

"You need some soup down you. Let's go," said Evie.

After a few spoonfuls, I started to feel better. What happened to me at the river was like being caught up in a dream over which I had no control. In between the flow of conversation, I worried in case my cold dip had harmed the baby. *How would I know? I must ring Dr Laidlaw. This was what the Twins contrived: to harm me.*

As we cleared away, Matt arrived.

"I've just been listening to the weather forecast, Evie. Snow blizzards and high winds have hit the west and heading this way. I wasn't sure whether you were going today."

"I was going to stay till tomorrow, but if you're sure, I'd better collect my stuff and leave now."

I went upstairs with Evie and sat on her bed while she threw her stuff into her bag. "I'm still worried about your dog episode," she said. "Are you sure there was a dog?"

I didn't want to lie to Evie and sighed. "I'm beginning to doubt the whole episode, but the Twins were there, Evie. I saw them as you were pulling me out. They wanted me in the river. The baby..."

"Tosh and rot," Evie said fiercely. "But do you feel ok? I don't suppose the baby would notice a dunking."

"I'm going to call Dr Laidlaw. If the Twins are trying to harm me...." I left the rest of my fears unspoken.

"No, you mustn't dwell on that," Evie said firmly. "I wish I didn't have to go. Don't wander about alone outdoors."

She did believe in the Twins' malice.

As Evie swung her bag into the back of her car, the first flakes of snow swirled down, delicately, fast, silently. Joe and Matt appeared from the direction of the farm and so she had quite a send-off. She squeezed my arm and said she'd call me as soon as she got home.

Joe squinted up at the sky through the increasing snowflakes. "It's coming from the northwest, so you should keep ahead of it on your drive back."

"Mustn't lose my sense of direction, then," Evie said, quirking an eyebrow. "I'll miss you all."

She noisily revved the car, grinning, and shot off in a shower of gravel in an increasing blizzard.

We all stood waving until the car disappeared round the bend in the drive. "I'm putting the kettle on," said Serena, rubbing her arms. "Let's warm up in the kitchen."

Matt followed us inside. "We haven't had any significant snowfall for a few years. Looks like mothers and babies will be keeping warm in the barns for a bit longer."

"I'll light the fire in the sitting room and then I'll take the dogs for a bit of exercise," said Joe.

Serena refused my offer of help, telling me to relax, as she knew that Evie had been dragging me around the estate exploring.

"She's fascinated by the history of the house and the estate," I explained. "I think she'd like to compile some sort of written history besides the Family Tree that Uncle Daniel produced. We had to look at all the gravestones by the chapel. There was a rather lovely angel commemorating one of Will's ancestors."

"Joe maintains the churchyard in the summer. He doesn't like it to look overgrown and neglected."

I went up to the sitting room where the fire sent out comforting heat. I called Dr Laidlaw and reluctantly admitted that I'd stumbled into the river, but I didn't want to burden Joe and Serena with my worry. "As it happens, I am in Bridgeford at the moment, so it will be no problem to call in, my dear," he said in a cheerful tone.

He arrived shortly afterwards, admitted by a surprised Serena, but after he'd taken all my vital signs and listened to the foetal heartbeat, he reassured me all was well. It was a relief knowing he was he was so readily available.

The family tree was still laid out and the photo albums, and I was glad I'd remembered to remove the old map from Evie's car. After finding the angel and its heartbreaking inscription, I was reluctant to immerse myself in history again, but I skimmed along the lines until I alighted on Frances's name. Married at sixteen, dead at eighteen. My heart went out to her, even though she had lain silently under the stone angel with her two babies for two centuries.

From the window I watched snow swirling in the rising wind outside before pulling the shutters across. Already the field in front of the Ladies' Bower was white. A fox emerged from the wood, sniffed around, then returned to the shelter of the trees. In my preoccupation, it was a few moments before registering the two figures standing stock still and oblivious to the weather. I jumped back in alarm and quickly slammed the shutters against both windows and drew the curtains. They were always outside, but with an imagination in overdrive, the thought of those two resentful ghosts drifting through walls or windows panicked me.

If I stay much longer, I'll be a prisoner, afraid to go outside in case I see the Twins. Why am I the only person who sees them? Why are they targeting only me? Stupid! Ghosts don't 'target' people. If the snow didn't impede transport, I'd ask Joe for a lift into Salisbury in the next few days and talk to Daniel. He had raised the subject of ghostly presences calmly at lunch.

When my phone rang, I jumped. Expecting it to be Evie and hoping she wasn't stuck in a snowdrift, I lifted it to my ear without checking caller display.

"Clemmie? How are you? I hear it's snowing out there. We've had fresh snowfall overnight and we're having a change from biking and trying snowboarding in a little while." Will's voice sounded very near and happy.

"Will! Have you got news when you're coming home?"

"Not yet, but I have some terrific news. I had to phone Serena first to get her approval so don't be upset that she's the first to know...." My thoughts were tumbling around again; first to know what?

"Rafaella wants to bring her team to the UK to meet all our teams. She thinks it will be good bonding for all of us instead of crouching around a screen all the time and it makes sense to know each other better so that we'll all be one team."

My thoughts stilled as I listened incredulously. "Do Kim and the rest of our team know yet?" I asked.

"I've just emailed our team and I can hear replies pinging in as we speak! Hugo is flying back in a couple of days and he thinks it's a terrific idea."

"When will all this happen, Will? I'd better come up to London to meet you."

"No need, honey," said Will, and my hackles rose. He had never in all our time together called me 'honey'! *That's Rafaella's influence over him.* I bristled, but then his implication hit me. No need for me to be included in this meeting. I was going to be sidelined. I no longer fitted into his plans. I was so consumed by my thoughts I didn't take in any of his next words and had to stop him and make him repeat them.

"No need for you to come to London, Clem, because we are all coming to you! That's why I had to phone Serena first; it'll take a bit of organisation to fit us all in Harthill, but it's ideal for us all to get together. Rafaella insists on covering some of the catering costs, as it's too much to ask Serena to cater for all of us for a weekend. Isn't it amazing?"

This was the Will I knew, buoyed up with enthusiasm for a new venture. "I can't take it all in, Will," I said faintly. "When is all this happening? Serena can't be expected to transform this place into a hotel overnight. And although she's a first-rate cook, it'll be too much for her."

"Precisely, so we've told Serena to find a reputable local catering company who can come in for the weekend and take over. Serena will get involved, of course. She won't be able to help herself, but she won't have the burden of cooking. And you mustn't get involved in any lifting and carrying either and undo all the rest you've been having."

"Well, thanks," I said, still bridling. "Very thoughtful of you both."

"Come on, Clemmie, chill out! Our team in London is up for it. It'll be a fantastic opportunity to all get together."

"Are you flying home with Hugo, then?" I asked hopefully.

"No, I'll stay out here until Serena's got firm dates for a caterer. We can research more routes and then we'll all fly out together. Rafaella is covering the cost of all her team's flights and contributing to the catering, so you mustn't worry that all our profits will be swallowed up in a fun weekend."

"Fun weekend," I echoed. It was just dawning on me that I

wouldn't see Will for maybe another fortnight and he would have Rafaella all to himself without Hugo as chaperone.

"Got to go now, Clemmie. Our transport has just arrived. Keep in touch about dates and so on and to confirm the caterers as soon as possible. I know Serena and Joe will take it all in their stride!"

I'm taking a little longer to absorb it.

So Rafaella and I would soon be meeting in person. Up to now she was a two-dimensional figure on a screen which displayed her physical presence remotely. Soon I would have to confront my rival face to face and right now my confidence was at a low ebb. *If Will remains alone with Rafaella for much longer, will he be able to resist the full force of her overtly sexual magnetism? Why shouldn't I trust him? We are engaged and there's a baby on the way. I should trust him. But I don't trust Rafaella.*

I ran down the stairs to the kitchen. Serena was talking animatedly to Joe as she tipped pasta into a steaming pot on the Aga. Joe was still in his outdoor gear, but by the grins on their faces, they were obviously not aghast at the news.

"I'm so sorry Will has lumbered you with his bombshell announcement. How do you both feel about it?"

"At first, I was cross that William refused to let me do the catering, but now I see that it would have been a bit too much to do it all single-handed. Although I could have got some girls in from the village, I suppose..." Serena tailed off as she gazed into the middle distance.

"No, love, you heard what William said, that he would bear the expenses. You're going to source a reputable catering firm which may take longer than you think. And sort out where everybody is going to sleep!" said Joe. He grinned at me. "We go from pottering around doing our normal mundane jobs to being hosts at an International Conference!"

"Yes, I will need your help with numbers, Clemency, to sort out boys and girls and those who can share rooms. Once I have actual numbers, I can get organised. First, I need to ask you if you can bear to eat a carbonara tonight, something I can rustle up quickly and then get down to business."

My uneasiness at giving Joe and Serena a lot of work began to recede. Earlier, I'd felt like curling up and taking to my bed, but Will's shock announcement galvanised me from melancholy and I was glad to feel useful again.

While Joe loaded the dishwasher after supper, Serena fetched her notepad and we sat down. I hoped I'd remember all the names of Rafaella's team. I hadn't been feeling my best when she'd introduced them all.

"These are the two teams: Will and me, Kim Lee, Hugo Young, Ben Layton and Andy Frampton, Rafaella Benotti, Jimmy Jordan, Ruby Romanescu, then Sam Levy and Dunc Downing."

Serena jotted the names down in two columns, male and female.

"Now we must work out how many usable rooms we have. Most of your guests will have to share," said Serena, almost apologetically.

"There are two bedrooms and a box room with working radiators and a usable bathroom in the South Wing," said Joe."

"Clemency will keep her room, of course, and can I assume William will be in there as well?"

I stalled. "Well, it would be natural, but as I'm early to bed and a restless sleeper, these days Will would probably burn the midnight oil and he's always an early riser."

"We'll leave him out for the minute. Is Rafaella Benotti the leader of the American team?" I nodded, and she wrote Master Bedroom next to her name. It had never been used since Will's father had been alive, but it was next to Evie's room. Which reminded me of Evie. "I'd like to invite Evie back again for that weekend when we have definite dates. As an historian, she might be able to entertain our guests with a potted history."

"The other two ladies, Kim Lee and Ruby Romanescu, can share the Yellow Bedroom. It has an ensuite shower and loo in there and William can use the Orchid Room at the top of the stairs; there are no facilities in there so he will have to use your bathroom."

Despite the size of the main block, the reason there were so few bedrooms on this floor was because of the Hall taking up the height of two floors. The Yellow bedroom was the only one facing the front of the house.

"Now we have six men to sort out," said Serena. "As Joe pointed out, there are two bedrooms in the south wing that are habitable if we have two in each."

"Two men could go in the nursery," said Joe from the Aga. "There are mattresses in the junk room and then the others would go into the South Wing."

"Ben and Andy can go into the nursery," I said. I was sure they wouldn't object to sleeping on mattresses on the floor. Hopefully, they wouldn't sense any atmosphere.

"It's only for a weekend and once we get heating on, everyone will be fine." She sat back. "That didn't take long to sort out. The next mission is to find a reputable caterer. I'm still certain I could cope with the meals...."

"No!" Joe and I said in unison.

"Will said the catering costs would be taken care of. You might manage one main meal and then get bogged down." I said sympathetically, understanding her feeling of being sidelined. Serena nodded and sighed acquiescence. "I suppose so. Just feels strange handing over to strangers."

"I'll spend the morning with Mollie and we'll start a spring clean rota and sort out bedding. If something smells musty, I'll send it to the laundry. The sooner the house is all prepared, the better I'll feel!"

""I think everybody will be blown away spending a weekend

at a proper country house. They'll love it all." I said. "Where did everyone sleep when the house was first built?" I asked. "Looking at the family tree, Sir Horace appeared to have a large family."

"There were rooms where our flat is and the junk room and study on the top floor is large. Sir Horace had the two wings built soon after the main block was finished to house his growing family and their spouses," said Joe.

"You mustn't even think about helping with cleaning. I'll feel easier in my mind because I'd never forgive myself if something went wrong," said Serena. I shrugged. There would be plenty of things for me to do. Serena turned the page in her notepad. "Now to find a caterer."

"We can look up local ones on my laptop," I offered. "Will can't commit to a date for travelling until we've got that sorted."

"Did William say he wanted the main dining room available?" Joe asked. "Getting a dozen or so people round the table in the small dining room will be a bit of a squash. The only thing is that it's not been used for years either, so that will need a good going over as well."

"Oh, I'm sure Will would want to include both of you in any dining arrangements. With catering staff on hand, you'll be able to enjoy being waited on for a change." Serena looked doubtful, but I wanted to make sure that they were included. "It would be good if Matt joined us for the evening meals and got to meet everybody. He must get lonely being so busy around the farm."

The list of local caterers wasn't long, and we spent some time considering their menus on my laptop. Just as my eyelids were drooping, we arrived at one caterer we both favoured and decided to contact him in the morning.

Rafaella had stated she would help with catering costs, but as Tough Treks operated on a tight margin and had to build in outlays for emergency measures and unforeseen expenses, I was determined to keep costs reasonable. She had covered Will's and

Hugo's trip to the States and judging by the helicopter trip and travel to her parents' home; she was obviously wealthier than any of us. Perhaps after seeing her parental home, Will had judged that Harthill House was not such a millstone round his neck and might be an advantage in long-term committal to our joint business venture.

Yawning, I got ready for bed. It had been a long day, emotional and traumatic. I'd missed a call from Evie, but she'd texted to say she was home with no mishaps and there was no snow in London. I'd phone her in the morning and persuade her to come down again and consort with mad cyclists.

I walk past the maze in the Ladies' Bower. Snowdrops nod at me as I brush past them. The path is wet, but the gardeners have swept up the dead wet leaves and there are no puddles, although the sky is heavy with unwept rain. That is how I feel, drowning in my unwept tears, yet I have shed enough to sweep away my reason. I carry on downhill until at last I see the sombre grey of the swollen river before me. The door to the Mill House is open, but there is no one around and I cross to the boathouse. The rowing boat inside rides high in the water and the river laps over the bank in its winter flood. Behind me, I hear twigs snap and turn to look. The Twins are coming towards me from the Mill and my breath catches in my throat. I have nowhere to hide and no one to help me. I turn and run as best I can along the narrow path bordering the river. It is slippery with mud, and twigs and branches lay across the path. I am hampered by my skirts, which are long and heavy and getting heavier with the mud and river water flooding over the path. I look down in puzzlement, and see my belly, swollen beneath the heavy material, and I have on dainty shoes, certainly not fit for outdoor use and they are soon sodden. I run on trying to escape the Twins who I can hear behind me and suddenly I am floundering in icy water, which seeps into my clothes and makes me gasp in shock. I am in the river and it is rising around me and my clothes are dragging me down. The Twins stand a few paces from me on the bank and I can see triumphant smiles on their cruel faces. I stretch out my arms to them, silently imploring for help. I cannot speak as the cold water robs me of my voice. They lift their crooks and I try to reach out, but instead they try to push me deeper into the swirling torrent; their smiles widening to reveal black and broken teeth. I call out at last, but there is no one to help me.

I woke, fear and dread pinning me to the mattress, paralysed with terror as the memory of the vivid nightmare lingered. My limbs felt so heavy, my breathing ragged and my heartbeat rapid. I willed myself to move and with a huge effort, I managed to haul myself into a sitting position and switched on the bedside lamp. The room was quiet; the curtains closed. Despite the chilly temperature, my throat was dry, and I gulped at a glass of water with a shaking hand. Then I pushed back the bedclothes to inspect my legs, half expecting them to be soaking wet, but of course, they were bone dry and clad in pyjamas. Why did I dream I was wearing a skirt or dress of heavy material? I rarely wore one or the other except on special occasions. Then I remembered the ridiculously flimsy slipper-like shoes completely unsuitable for outdoor wear. It was as if I was dressed in period garments. The boathouse in my nightmare was real, as was the boat inside. Evie and I found a little trace of it this morning at the riverbank, just some rotting planks. And in my dream, the Ladies' Bower had been well cared for with trimmed hedges and neat pathways. The memory of the Twins grinning horribly at me, forcing me deeper into the water, made me drag myself out of bed and into the bathroom next door as nausea overtook me.

Eventually, I ran water into the washbasin and rinsed my face. In the mirror, I looked as bad as I felt. I crawled back into bed, trying to dispel the horror of the nightmare. Evie wasn't next door and Serena and Joe were on the top floor in their flat. The memory of feeling completely alone struggling in the river lingered. I switched on the little radio that Serena had lent me and soft late-night music soothed the atmosphere. I wrapped my bath robe tightly round me and sat in bed, trying to force my brain to dismiss the images. After seeing the photographs in the album, the visit to the churchyard filled with so many gravestones, and the dark green river running silently past the mill, coupled with the strange episode of the little dog on the riverbank had all culminated in a vivid nightmare. The Twins had been there, gloating, as I floundered in the river. I couldn't bring myself to go downstairs and make a mug of hot chocolate in the warm kitchen, so I plugged in the kettle and brewed a chamomile tea instead. In the nightmare, my stomach was swollen in advanced pregnancy, but there wasn't much evidence of roundness yet.

Not only was I seeing the Twins in the daytime, now they were invading my sleep as well. If I phoned Will, he would just write off my nightmare as imagination in overdrive. He had no idea who or what the Twins were. Despite the hour, I called Evie, who answered almost immediately.

I told her I'd had a horrible dream about falling in the river and couldn't get back to sleep, so I was bothering her instead. She laughed and said she wasn't surprised after my traumatic morning, so phoning her in the middle of the night was punishment for subjecting me to the horrors of the churchyard! As usual, her cheerful tone helped to dispel the chill memory hanging over me, and I told her about the upcoming weekend where our two teams would meet. "Wow!" said Evie. "You and Will are going to be the perfect host and hostess!"

"I'd better get a posh frock," I sighed. "When we get the dates fixed, will you try to come down here again? You could give a talk on the history of the house to impress the guests!"

Evie gave a snort and said she didn't need an excuse to visit again. Then she yawned loudly and said tartly that some people had to work in the morning and we finished the call.

Talking about posh frocks helped me to decide that I needed a spot of retail therapy and that would be the perfect reason to meet up with Uncle Daniel.

∼

A fairytale white wonderland greeted me when I pulled back the shutters next morning. Snow had fallen silently, thickly carpeting the ground and tops of fences, bushes and branches of trees. The contrast between the white and the dark shadows in the woods was stark.

Through the middle of the meadow imprints of where the cows had trudged lay like a dark stream amidst the white and even as I drank it all in the herd appeared from the left trudging through the same imprints on their way back to the lower meadow after being milked. That they were black and white fitted perfectly into the scene and I took photos. The stillness was broken by the sound of a tractor; its loader filled with hay, churning up the pristine snow as it followed the cows. A muffled-up Matt sat in the cab. The very simplicity of this rural scene made me question my episode on the riverbank yesterday with the mysterious episode of the little dog and The Twins.

Chapter Fourteen

Joe invited me out with the dogs. We didn't need to go far as the dogs careered round, barking, rolling, and pushing their noses into the snow. We threw snowballs for them and they leapt and twisted and sneezed as the powdery snow got up their noses and into their eyes. The sun was well risen now and everything looked pristine, and I felt safe in Joe's company. I had never seen the Twins in the gardens, but I couldn't take that fact for granted, and I hoped Joe didn't notice my nervous glances around.

Back indoors, I went upstairs after shedding my gear. Mollie was just leaving my room dragging the Hoover.

"'Morning, my lovely," she said, appraising me with those eyes that seemed to see right through you. "Your room's had a quick visit today because Serena has told me of William arriving with a load of Yanks, so I've got me work cut out for the next few days... not that I mind...I like to get me hands dirty doing a spot of deep cleaning now and again!"

"Not only Yanks, Mollie, but my team from London are also invading!"

"Lord save us, Yanks and posh Londoners, not that you're posh, my lovely," Mollie said, rolling her eyes, and I laughed.

"None of my team is remotely posh, Mollie. We all struggle to make ends meet in a very expensive city. I hope all the extra work isn't going to be too much for you," I said anxiously, but she frowned fiercely and looked affronted.

"Bit o' hard work never does anyone any harm," she said, trundling down the passage with her Hoover and bag of cleaning equipment. "I'll be that pleased to see young William again. It'll all be worth it!"

"I've had a chat on the phone with Brian Chadwick, the caterer we favoured, and he's more than happy to cook what we want," Serena announced in the kitchen. "His produce is all locally sourced; he caters for all dietary needs and he has a bank of serving staff. He's keen to keep costs down as much as he can and I liked the sound of him on the phone. He's coming out this afternoon to meet us and discuss the menus. I told him about the snow, but he says he's got a four-wheel drive so he'll do his best to get here."

"Brilliant," I said. "If he's amenable to take the job on, it means we can give Will some definite time scale then."

There was a full table at lunchtime, as Serena insisted Mollie stayed after 'doing battle' with extra cleaning.

"My Matthew just happened to pop his head round the door as we were dishing up!" commented Mollie. "He's got a nose as keen as his dog!" Matt nodded to me and grinned as he tore off a hefty bit of bread and dipped it into his soup.

"I suppose you are both up to speed about what's happening?" I said.

"It'll be good to see the old house coming alive again," said Mollie. "There's always been a family here until recent times, that is. 'Bout time, the old ghosts were stirred up with a bit of company."

The Shadow Watchers

I stared at her. Did she sense the presences in the house? Did she also see the Twins outside? Before I could formulate a question, Serena jumped in.

"Nonsense, Mollie," she said in a prim voice. "I hope you won't be scaring all the visitors with talk like that."

Mollie just smiled enigmatically, looking like a mischievous imp.

After we'd all eaten. Joe made a large pot of tea and Mollie insisted he put in extra tea bags. "It'll be like treacle, Mollie," he said, and when he poured a cup out, it did indeed resemble the colour of treacle. I hastily declined a cup, as the sight of it made me feel queasy. "That'll keep me going," Mollie said after downing two cups and made her way out of the kitchen to finish her work.

"Brian Chadwick will be here about three," said Serena, glancing up at the clock. "Let's hope the roads are ok for him."

I put on a padded jacket and took myself off to the library before Brian Chadwick's arrival. Primarily, my quest was to find Honoria Payne-Barnard's diary for Evie. The light of the snow cast brightness round the silent room and dispelled the shadows, but not the chilliness. There was a sort of order to the shelving and I searched for local history books before pulling open the long drawers under the bookshelves again. After years of listening to Evie expounding on her detective approach to finding historical items, I was soon immersed in the contents of the drawers. There was nothing but old maps in the drawer where I had found the layout of the estate. The bottom drawer yielded large hard bound books full of delicate watercolours of local birds, and then some with exotic plumage. They were all signed Laurence Barnard, and the dates varied from 1760 to 1800. Another contained flora, in exquisite colours, from different continents and all signed and dated in the same hand. In another pile, I opened a book full of animal and bird sketches. These were all in pen and ink but very realistic. The signatures at the foot of these sketches bore the name of Joan Barnard. Laurence's wife. What a talent the pair had. I did a quick search on my phone to see if they'd had any public recognition. There were several entries which I saved for later to look into.

A set of fragile sketchbooks were filled with realistic sketches of the heads of men, women, children and babies, some in pen and ink, some in charcoal and some in watercolour. One set of sketches was similar to the quartet of small oval portraits on my bedroom wall. They bore the name Frances and was signed HW. She looked so young and defenceless and so unaware of her fate. Turning the pages, I came upon the sketches of her babies, Freddie and Bertie, both asleep with chubby cheeks and snub little noses. Helene had drawn a delicate tracery of eyelashes on one of the slumbering children and it was hard to believe they died in infancy.

The doorbell sounded, accompanied by loud barking. In the Great Hall, Brian Chadwick was admiring the moulded ceiling, the stucco swags and the fireplace until Serena introduced me.

"This hall would be a grand place to hold a dinner," he said in an Irish accent. "A long table, white tablecloths, candles, wee flower arrangements at intervals along the table, glasses sparkling in the firelight..." Serena and I looked at each other with raised eyebrows. Neither of us had thought of holding a meal in here, but it would be perfect for the two dinner settings. The small dining room would be too squashed and the main dining room in the South Wing was a long way from the kitchen and the difficulty transporting dishes.

For a person of small stature, he was very commanding, but likeably so. I warmed to his affable personality. When he was shown around, he dismissed the drawbacks of a basement kitchen and charmed Serena into accepting his menu suggestions with cheeky Irish humour. He informed us of what he would bring, plus the number of helpers and a firm costing, and we set the date for the weekend after next.

"It'll be a pleasure to work in such grand surroundings," he said as he packed up his laptop. "I'll be in touch very soon, ladies!"

I sent off an email to Will and copied it to Kim and Rafaella about confirmed dates. The 'Big Bash Weekend' was up and running!

After supper, I settled into the sitting room where Joe, bless him, had lit the fire and it was burning merrily. I threw my jacket on the chair and saw the small sketch book sticking out of the pocket where I'd put it earlier. Helene Wallington, daughter of Sir Horace, certainly had a superb gift for capturing the essence of her subjects. I was able to match sketches to the names in the family tree, comparing them with the old photos After a few blank pages, there was another group of sketches, confidently executed. On one page facing each other, she'd drawn a man and a woman, half in profile. The man had long straggly hair and a frowning countenance with craggy eyebrows over deep-set eyes that looked ominously familiar to me. The sketch alongside showed a young woman with her head at a coquettish angle, looking over her shoulder. Her long hair hung loosely round her shoulders. Underneath, Helene had written 'Gerard and Lily 1814'. Gerard, who, as the youngest son of Sir Horace, should by rights have inherited Harthill House and had been deprived by a line of succession from his elder brother James. Had Gerard passed his grievances on to his twin sons so that their bitterness survived? Instinctively, I was sure the Twins knew I carried the next heir to Harthill House and resented it. To use an old-fashioned word, it was a preposterous assumption! Ghosts could not 'resent'. There was no title. Will's family weren't aristocrats. There was just an archaic custom that the house and estate passed down the male line.

Will, at the end of that male line, was blissfully unaware of all this and my struggle to comprehend a threat from beyond the grave. Since I'd had my pregnancy confirmed, I had seen Will only once fleetingly.

Chapter Fifteen

For crying out loud, when is all this going to pass?
I gripped the loo after another bad bout. There was a knock at the bathroom door, which made me jump while I brushed my teeth. Mollie entered the bathroom. "I could hear you in there, my duck, and come t' see if you be all right."

I sat on the side of the bath with my arms over my stomach. I shivered slightly as I had rushed in here before I could put my bathrobe on. Mollie took in the situation, disappeared, and returned, holding up the robe. She held it open, and I pushed my arms into it. My mouth was returning to normal now. "I thought it was all over. I've felt really well the last couple of days."

Mollie fastened the belt loosely round me and reached up to push the sticky hair off my face with fingers roughened by decades of hard work. She was very gentle, and I wanted to weep.

"I'll run a nice bath for you and you can warm up in there. How many weeks gone are you?"

I struggled to count. "I must be about 14 weeks now; I haven't really been counting lately. I thought the sickness would be getting less by now."

"Ah, that's never written in stone. All lasses are affected differently depending on hormones."

"Do you think sheep and cows have morning sickness, Mollie?" I knew it was a stupid question, but my brain wasn't functioning yet.

She shouted with laughter. "I'm sure they don't give any signs of morning sickness, but who knows what goes on in their tiny brains?" She added some rose scented bath essence to the running water. You have a nice soak and then come down and have a cup of real ginger tea. Have a ginger biscuit with it and you'll be as right as rain."

I thanked her and stepped into the bath after she left. Later, warmed up and feeling much better, I obeyed Mollie's instructions and went down to the kitchen, found some fresh ginger in the fridge, and put tiny slices in a mug of hot water. It smelt aromatic and warming and I nibbled a ginger biscuit.

The back door slammed shut and Matt entered. He looked tidier in jeans and a parka rather than boots and overalls. "Has it snowed again?" I asked as he found a mug and spooned instant coffee into it after greeting me and giving me his big smile. Even in his likeness to Will, I'd decided that Matt smiled more often than Will.

"No, but it's chilly out there," he said, adding milk and sugar. "I'm waiting for Joe; we're going into Salisbury to the bank. Two of us must sign when we draw money from the Estate account."

I jumped at the opportunity which had suddenly presented itself. "Do you think I can come too? I need to find something to wear for the big weekend. I only brought jeans and jumpers with me. I never thought I'd be entertaining! It'll be a sort of celebration and a meeting of minds after our merger. Don't think you are excluded either, I'm inviting you to the dinners on Friday night and Saturday night and Sunday lunch if you can manage it. The New Yorkers fly back on the Sunday night. I've managed to persuade Joe and Serena to join in as well because the caterers will do all preparation, cooking and washing up. I'm a bit nervous of meeting the New Yorkers because they all seemed to be so super confidant and shiny toothed when we first linked up via Skype and I felt awful and looked it too!"

"Well, I think you look a lot better than when you first arrived, although you're looking peaky this morning if you ask me!"

"Thank you," I flashed a sarcastic smile at him, nearly adding that he should have seen me first thing this morning. "What time are you leaving? I'll go and get ready. You needn't wait for me when you come back either; I'll get a taxi back as I don't know what I'm looking for!"

"Well, if you're sure you're ok. I don't want to get into trouble with Serena for dragging you out," said Matt doubtfully.

"I'm stronger than I look," I said firmly and went upstairs. My tummy was quiet now and seemingly settled. As I found my bag and checked my bank cards were all there, I suddenly remembered Uncle Daniel's invitation. If we left shortly, I would have time to find a dress and some shoes and meet Daniel for tea. I'd stored his number on my phone and as it rang, I hoped he wouldn't be out. He answered straight away, delighted to hear from me and we arranged to meet at the Refectory Entrance in Salisbury Cathedral at 2.30pm. He listened when I said I was getting a lift into Salisbury and insisted that he would drive me home after our tea together.

Naturally, I hadn't heard anything from Will, and somehow the disappointment was becoming less. My mind slid away from how we would act together when he eventually turned up.

Joe and Matt were waiting in the kitchen when I went back downstairs. Serena and Mollie were sorting out bedding and he'd told her not to expect me in for lunch.

"I'm meeting Uncle Daniel for tea and he said he would drive me back later, so you don't need to worry about me." I said, winding a scarf round my neck and donning gloves.

As I sat with Joe and Matt in Joe's Land Rover listening to their conversation, I felt more cheerful than I had for weeks. We didn't bounce around too much, for which I was grateful. It was good to get out of the house. I was growing to love Harthill House and there were places I wanted to explore, but not having my own transport meant I was a virtual prisoner. I recalled the night Will left me in my bedroom to fly back to New York and I had tried the door, half expecting it to have been locked. *That's what happens after reading too many Bronte sisters' novels.*

Although snow powdered the fields and slush lined the road, the road itself was clear and I watched the countryside slipping by with farms and cottages and stands of trees on small hilltops and here and there on my left, glimpses of the same river that flowed past Harthill House. The main road leading into Salisbury was less picturesque, lined with retail outlets and factories and car sales showrooms. Matt pointed out the spire of Salisbury Cathedral as it soared gracefully over the city. Joe parked in a central car park and he and Matt interrupted each other as they explained that the centre of the city was not large; there were a couple of largish department stores and lots of shoe shops. "Don't stay on your feet too long," warned Joe. "You don't want to overstretch yourself."

"There are coffee shops practically on every corner if you need to sit for a bit," added Matt.

"And if you feel you need to come home at any time, ring me and we'll pick you up straight away," said Joe, holding up his phone. It was like having two kind, generous brothers, and I hugged each of them spontaneously.

Matt had rested his hand on my arm, and I gripped it instinctively to thank him and Joe. As his warm fingers closed over mine,

I felt a spark fly up my arm. Perhaps Matt felt it too as he suddenly released his clasp.

"I'll be fine," I reassured them. "It's quite exciting to be exploring somewhere that hasn't got gravestones in it. Evie's favourite places to visit!" I added, seeing their alarmed expressions. Finally, they walked away, Matt turning and giving a smile in farewell. I wished I could have had his company around town.

Following their instructions, I found myself facing a large square lined with trees and an assortment of shops and cafes and pubs, all crowned with pleasing medieval roof shapes. I spotted a department store across the road and started there. It was hot and crowded and the women's department on several levels was frustrating. I didn't want flimsy party frocks left over from Christmas and New Year or garish multi-patterned jump suits or wedding outfits. I headed for the exit but got lost and found myself in the baby and child section. Reluctantly, I was drawn to the newborn section and darling outfits that would soften the heart of any shopper. Ignoring my head telling me it was too early to start buying anything, I chose a pale lemon-yellow Babygro with a grey elephant logo and a matching jacket and hat. I stopped at the soft toys and picked up a large and extremely soft rabbit with floppy ears which I immediately named Flops. I paid for them quickly before I could change my mind, and I was smiling as I exited the store and chose a cafe at random for a rest. Joe phoned.

"We are finished in Salisbury now, Clemency. Are you ok staying on to meet Daniel? We can give you a lift home now if you're not up to it."

"Thanks, Joe. I've stopped for a breather right now. I'm feeling fine and looking forward to seeing Daniel again."

After looking in a couple more shops, I was beginning to feel despondent and decided to make my way to the Cathedral early to look around it. I spotted a second-hand dress agency with a vintage green velvet dress in the window. On impulse, I went in and asked to try it on, hoping it didn't smell and would fit. It had long sleeves and puffed shoulders and a flattering low square neck. I loved its quirkiness and bought it at a fraction of the cost of one purchased from a London boutique after the assistant assured me all garments were dry cleaned before displaying. Half an hour later and with a new pair of black moderately high-heeled shoes and tights added to my bags, I entered the Cathedral Close.

The sudden sense of peace and tranquillity was apparent as soon as I stepped through the ancient, gated arch into The Close. Buildings from medieval to Georgian lined the wide enclosed area. Even in winter, the trees were dramatic in their wintry forms, and daffodils nodded in the sheltered spaces and in large wooden planters. I had to tip my head back to gaze up to the top of the soaring spire of the Cathedral. I took several photos of the houses and the cathedral to send to Evie. Even on a cold afternoon there were the inevitable tourists and school parties around the cathedral and I imagined it must be a very pretty place to sit on the grass in the summer and just absorb the peacefulness.

Uncle Daniel was waiting just inside the main entrance, out of the cold wind gusting about the cathedral edifice. He kissed me gently on the cheeks and took my arm. "You look a lot better than a few days ago, my dear," he said, inspecting my features.

"I'm feeling well today, although I am gasping for a cup of tea and a sit down!"

"Let's find a table and order some tea and cake and you can tell me what you've been up to," he said, He guided me through a gift shop and along one side of an astounding medieval cloister then into a busy, brightly lit cafe. I stopped dead and gasped when I spotted the glass roof and the view of the graceful spire rising hundreds of feet above us.

"Spectacular, isn't it?" said Daniel proudly. "It looks even better when lit up with floodlights. Here we are, now sit and gaze upwards while I order!" He went off to the counter and returned with a tray with teapot, milk, cups and saucers and sugar. "I've ordered a traditional afternoon tea, so you can choose what you like."

I suddenly felt tongue tied in his company. I couldn't talk about Cathedral architecture and weather till it was time to go home; on the other hand, I didn't feel capable of suddenly launching into the fears that bothered me. I was saved from trying to open a conversation by the arrival of a traditional cake stand filled with tiny sandwiches, finger size slices of quiche and a selection of cakes: bite size profiteroles, mini jam sponges, tiny scones with pots of jam and cream and pink macaron biscuits. My stomach rumbled and while Daniel poured the tea, I filled my plate with dainties. Daniel chose a couple of things, saying that my need was greater.

At last, I wiped my lips and sat back. "That was delicious! I thought I would only manage a couple of things, but because they were so small, I'm afraid I must have eaten far more than my share!"

"It's wonderful to see you enjoying yourself. I must admit I was a little concerned about how peaky you looked at lunch the other day and here you are a couple of days later, looking very much better."

"I'm still suffering from bouts of sickness, but I seem to be able to cope better," I assured him. "In normal life, I'm quite healthy, so all this has had the effect of knocking me sideways."

"Are you planning to stay at Harthill House much longer? I think you said you were looking forward to returning to London for the next scan."

"Oh, that plan has changed considerably," I broke in, and a faint frown showed on Daniel's face. "I mean, I still have to return for the scan, but in the meantime, Will has arranged that the trek team from New York and our trek team in London all meet up together at Harthill House for a grand weekend!"

"Has William returned? That explains your brighter face," Daniel said.

"No, he's still in New York. I do miss him though.... Serena and I have been busy finding a caterer for the weekend. Serena wanted to do all the cooking but Will put his foot down and after we'd gone through menus, it would have been too exhausting for her alone. I wouldn't be any good near cooking smells, which is a nuisance. I hope it changes soon. I hate being like a wishy-washy invalid from some Victorian novella. Serena and Mollie are sorting bedrooms and I feel guilty giving them so much extra work and not helping."

Suddenly, it seemed natural and effortless to talk to Daniel, who wasn't even a relative. Perhaps that was why, as there were no emotional ties to get in the way. Besides, he had such a quiet, unassuming manner about him that I felt very safe in his presence. "Would you like to come, Daniel?" I asked suddenly. "I've invited Evie as well and asked her to give a talk on the history of Harthill House, but in fact, you probably have much more knowledge."

Daniel looked taken aback and faintly alarmed. "You don't want an antediluvian creature like me cramping the style of all you young things," he laughed. "And from the impression I had of Evie, even after our very brief conversations, she seems very capable of holding an audience. I have given many lectures on local history so that wouldn't be a problem, but I do like my solitude these days. But thank you for the kindness of inviting me."

"When did you last see William?" I asked as I eyed the last tiny profiterole.

"Probably last year. If one of his trips coincides with a Trustees' meeting, he cannot always attend."

I felt disloyal to Will, as I had a fleeting thought that the date of his trips might not be accidental.

"Do you know why he hasn't spoken about his home to me or why he seems to take little interest in the place?"

"Ah, my dear, you will have to ask him that yourself. It's not for me to surmise on his reasons," said Daniel. "He lived in London with his mother from an early age, so I can only assume his attachment to Harthill House was not strong, even though his father remained there. Are you getting used to rattling round the place?" he asked guilelessly as he reached for the last profiterole. "Do you still sense presences from the past?"

"Yes, but the ones inside don't pose a threat to me," I said, then as heat flooded through me, now was the time to confess to Daniel; the reason I had asked to meet him. In the calm surroundings of this spiritual setting, the sense of menace I'd experienced emanating from the Twins' presence seemed more manageable and explainable. As Daniel raised his eyebrows enquiringly, I took a deep breath, held my stomach in an unconsciously protective gesture and let go of my fears.

"I have been seeing the same two people appearing from time to time, always out in the open." Daniel's pale eyes never left my face, nor did he blink or register disbelief or scorn. Fortified by his calm attentiveness, I ploughed on, eager to relieve myself of my fears. "I thought I was imagining things, or it was my hormones and even that I was becoming mentally unhinged by all that's happened to me in the past couple of weeks. I took a photo of them on my phone - two men—standing looking at my window. I thought they were farm workers even though they were dressed oddly for this day and age. When I've looked out any of the windows in the house, they always seem to be standing looking at that particular window as if they know where I am." I shivered involuntarily and Daniel refilled my cup. "Joe said they didn't have farm workers and said he'd keep an eye out for them. Then Evie found an old photo album, and we were able to identify some of the people named in your Family Tree."

I hesitated, then took a gulp of the lukewarm tea. "I turned a page and there they were – the two men I'd seen and nobody else had. I call them the Twins and they are identical to the twins in the photo album- George and Wilfred Barnard, sons of Gerard Barnard" I gazed down at my empty cup, so I missed the involuntary look of fear that crossed Daniel's face. "Even Evie believes me now. But even so, she doesn't understand that when I see them, they seem to know exactly who I am and I can feel their hatred. Perhaps I am slightly mad."

I raised my eyes to Daniel's and read the steady, kindly expression in them.

"I believe they are haunting me because I'm carrying an heir to the estate. When we studied the family tree, Evie thought it was odd that the estate didn't go to the youngest son Gerard, as in those days daughters weren't entitled to inherit. Tell me I'm wrong, Daniel."

He took my hand in his and pressed it firmly. "I think you are a perfectly sane young woman capable of analysing events in your life. You assume it's all in your mind because your body is going through an upheaval. You have a gift of second sight, I believe, seeing what others can't. I have never seen any physical manifestations at Harthill House, but I believe others may have done."

"Oh, who, perhaps I can talk to them?" It would be a relief to compare stories and laugh them off.

Daniel looked decidedly cagey. "I'm not sure, maybe Mollie. And William's mother sensed something out of the ordinary, but I can't speak for her. George and Wilfred were indeed sons of Gerard Barnard and as far as I could tell, while doing my research for the family tree, they never left the estate throughout their lives. Perhaps you can sense their trapped spirits. Now, my dear, I'm going to give you some old-fashioned advice and then I'll take you home. If you feel threatened by these manifestations, then I strongly advise that you do not wander about on the estate on your own. I don't want to alarm you unnecessarily," he said, resting his hand on my forearm. "I want you to be sensible. If you are wandering about by yourself and suddenly be confronted by something you cannot explain away, then you may act rashly and put yourself and your baby in danger. Can you see my reasoning?"

"Yes," I said shakily, because Daniel had confirmed my fears. "But Serena and Joe will wonder why I suddenly don't want to go outside. I quite enjoy taking Jasper and Bess for little runs."

"Keep to the gardens if you need exercise and fresh air, but don't wander further afield alone. If you tell them you've got an irrational fear of falling, they will understand. You have fainted before, so I'm sure they'll find a way to accompany you. Rope Matt in as well; he is a rock steady young man. When William returns, he can accompany you. Also, when your weekend with your colleagues comes to an end, please go back to London with them. You need a few weeks of doing normal things in a normal environment surrounded by people you know and not languishing in the country, prey to your fears."

It all made sense, and I could see the logic behind Daniel's words. What was the point of staying at Harthill House if I was afraid of the Twins? If I returned to London, maybe the nightmares would stop as well. I needed to be busy again and not in fear of looking over my shoulder. I looked upwards to gaze at the majestic spire and was surprised that the sky had darkened, the spire impressively lit up by angled floodlights filling me with renewed optimism, and the cafe was slowly emptying of diners.

"I think I would like to go home soon; I've missed Tough Treks and keeping busy. It's not physical work, so I'm sure Dr Laidlaw will agree. I'll arrange it after the big weekend and return with Will and the rest of my team."

Gradually, I felt the dark cloud hanging over my head beginning to shift a little and rays of hope glimmer just as the light illumined the spire above me.

"Are you ready to leave now?" Daniel asked. I nodded, gathering my coat and bags, then had to ask him where the cloakroom was. My mind started working overtime again. I'd unburdened myself to Daniel and, understandably, the only logical advice he could give me was to leave the place and return home. It was true that in the short time I'd been at Harthill House I'd rested as advised, been genuinely cared for and, despite my recurring sickness bouts, I was feeling stronger. I'd told him nothing of my other fear: namely that there was an emotional distance between Will and me that was now maybe far beyond my control and I didn't want to burden this wonderfully kind man with more of my emotional baggage. I shrugged on my coat and scarf in the loos and picked up my bags. It might have been growing dark, but it was not late and as we emerged from the entrance, I was surprised to find that the Cathedral Close was still busy with people and traffic on the road on the other side of the green and chattering school children on their way home. The sky was clear with a bitter wind stirring up dead leaves in little vortexes and snow still lay piled up against the walls which surrounded the Cathedral Green.

"My little house is just across the green where my car is parked," Daniel said, offering me his arm and taking my bags in a true gentlemanly gesture. "As it is not too late, I'll show you around. It won't take very long; as long as I have shelves for my books and music, I am content."

His house was truly compact, tucked into an angle between two very grand Georgian mansions. "One day when it is warmer, I'll conduct you on a personal tour of the Cathedral Close and show you our little gems of architecture," he said as he ushered me through a gate into a tiny garden which contained planters filled with winter pansies and small shrubs. A security light flared, and we faced a solid door with a brass knocker. A wooden plaque on the wall bore the name Martin Cottage and an image of the little bird was painted beneath the name. Inside was a vestibule only just big enough to hang up coats. A staircase faced the front door and to the left was a small sitting room. Lamps came on in the sitting room as he pressed the wall switch. The wall opposite the window was lined with bookshelves, and facing the doorway was a small fireplace, an armchair and an occasional table beside it, and a small sofa opposite. On the table lay an open book and a pair of spectacles. Every available wall space was filled with prints and watercolours. Daniel reached across a desk laden with more books and papers and a reading lamp to swish shut the curtains. It was a warm, cosy room and I could readily see Daniel reading and listening to his music.

"The kitchen, such as it is, is through here," he said, indicating another door off the vestibule. It was indeed miniscule, but I was surprised by the modern units and immaculate white cooker. A pair of bright yellow curtains framed the window and a red kettle and toaster brightened a worktop. "Through there is a little conservatory, where I've got a fridge-freezer and a washing machine and a wicker chair where I can sit in the sun. It opens onto a charming garden which is south facing, so I enjoy pottering when the weather is clement. Upstairs is my bedroom and a little bathroom, which is hardly big enough to swing the proverbial cat. But I'm exceedingly lucky to have this cottage, as most properties in the Close which aren't owned or leased by the Cathedral are way out of my price bracket. When I retired from teaching at the Cathedral School, this cottage unexpectedly came on the market and I managed to scrape enough together to purchase it."

"It's lovely, Daniel, and so cosy!" I said. I wanted to ask if his wife had lived here too, but then I remembered she had died many years ago.

"When Will returns, you must both come and have tea. William might not be interested in the guided tour of the Close, but I promise you that you won't be disappointed. Now we must make tracks. I fear a frost may occur tonight and it's essential I deliver you safely back."

"Of course, thank you for the marvellous tea, Daniel and I love your cottage; it has a very peaceful atmosphere."

"If you need a haven to seek, then look no further!" Daniel wrapped an old school scarf round his neck, jammed a much-worn fedora style hat on his head and ushered me out. His car was parked on the grounds of the large mansion next door as there was ample room. He drove sedately out of Salisbury as traffic was building up and soon we were on the winding road leading to Harthill and Bridgeford. He offered little conversation as he concentrated on the road. The headlights lit up the dirty snow piled up on the roadsides and under hedges, but the surface of the road was clear. He slowed and pulled in for oncoming vehicles. "I've lost a good few wing mirrors to crazy drivers hogging this road," he said, and in hardly any time at all, he was indicating right to turn up the drive to Harthill House. Mollie's cottage windows glowed as we passed, and although the lime trees were bare of leaves, they seemed to crowd over the car as we made our way up the drive. Something in the way Daniel gripped the steering wheel made me look at his face in the dim glow of the dashboard lights and headlights. His chin was set firmly, but he turned and smiled at my enquiring look. "Almost home," he said, and I peered out of the windscreen into the darkness. The huge old ash loomed in the headlights. I screamed as two figures seemed to jump out of the darkness right in front of the car. Instinctively, Daniel braked, and then the figures were gone. I craned round to look out of the back window, but everything was swallowed up in darkness. Daniel drove on, speeding up a little. "Was it the Twins?" he asked.

"Didn't you see them?" I gasped, my heart still thudding. "You seemed to run straight into them!"

"If only I could run over them, then you would have nothing to be fearful about ever again," said Daniel grimly as we passed the last stand of tall beeches, rounded the last graceful curve of the drive and the house came into view. The portico was lit and light flooded over the gravel as Daniel brought the car to a stop. "No, I didn't see them, but it seems the old ash tree is one of their favourite haunts, if you can forgive the pun, so I was half expecting a visitation."

I shakily gathered up my purchases again and opened the door. "Will you come in for a cup of tea?" I offered, but he shook his head.

"I won't come in, my dear, in case the road turns icy. I hope you remember my words about taking care and returning to London at your earliest opportunity. I wish I could take away your fearfulness, but I am sure all will be resolved in good time. Give my best wishes to Joe and Serena and your good friend Evie." He helped me out of his car and took my bags to the door. As I rang the bell, he kissed me on both cheeks. "Ring me anytime you want to talk, anytime," he emphasised.

"Will you be alright going back down the drive?" I asked anxiously. "Oh perfectly," he grinned. "I am of no interest to them."

Just as Joe reached the door, he swung the car round, raised his hand in an encouraging wave, and disappeared into the night.

Joe watched the red taillights fade and disappear. "He was worried about icy roads, so he sends his best wishes to you and Serena."

"I could have collected you if he was worried," he grumbled, carrying my bags into the hall. As he looked at me, he frowned. "Good, grief, girl, you look as if you've seen a ghost!" he exclaimed.

I put my hand involuntarily up to my face. "It must be the wind. It's icy out there. I'm fine really Joe." How would he react if I told him I had seen not one but two ghosts?

"Come down to the kitchen and warm up. I'll take these bags up to your room. You obviously found some shops you liked?"

I really wanted to go up to my room or sit in front of a roaring fire in the sitting room, but I went downstairs to greet Serena. I declined supper describing the mammoth tea I'd consumed. I made a mug of mint tea and gradually I felt my body thawing. Describing my afternoon shopping and the wonders of the Cathedral was better therapy than brooding about events alone in my room.

"Did you manage to get back to William?" Serena asked, and I looked blankly at her. "He wanted to know if we've finalised arrangements so flights can be booked. He phoned us here because he couldn't get hold of you."

I looked around for my bag, but Joe must have taken it upstairs with my other purchases. I hadn't looked at it all afternoon. "I told him we'd found a very amenable caterer and agreed menus and all we had to do now was get rooms ready. He seemed very relieved and thanked us for moving so quickly. He said he could now arrange for Rafaella and her team to fly over."

"I must have had my phone switched off," I said. "I'll just go upstairs and see if I can ring him back."

I ran up the stairs and rummaged in my tote until I found my phone. Sure enough, there had been a couple of missed calls from Will. I pressed call, hoping he would be around to answer. His phone went straight to his messaging service. I left him a message, a little garbled, and thought for a moment, fingers drumming on my lips. I found Kim's private number and called her. She'd had a Skype message from Will. Hugo was flying back now. She affirmed all arrangements were in place and Ruby was going ahead booking flights. She said she was so looking forward to seeing me again and they were all agog about the size of Will's ancestral home!

I dashed to the bathroom and then sank onto my bed, my brain whirling. Was Will flying over with Rafaella after all? It must be so, because Kim had only confirmed that Hugo was flying back. How on earth was I to cope with all the teams arriving on the doorstep of Harthill House and having to meet and greet my long absent fiancé in front of all of them like some medieval lady of the manor greeting her long absent lord? (*and his mistress?*) Even if he arrived before the others, how would we react? While I desperately longed for a 'kiss and make up' scenario, deep down, I felt we would be reserved, especially Will.

Should I scream and shout at him and make a scene like the wronged wife? Except I wasn't his wife, and I had no proof that I had even been wronged. His phone calls while he'd been away had been all about the excursions he'd done with Rafaella and Hugo and her team. He never bothered to have personal chats or the silly conversations we used to have. I didn't want to be wrong-footed on his arrival, and I would have to have all my senses keenly tuned. My mind was so clogged up dealing with sickness and facing the threat of running into apparitions who seemed to be targeting me. What had Uncle Daniel said? 'You have second sight.' What good would that do me? If only I could get some reassurance about the future for me and my unborn child…… I stood up like a horse ready to bolt from unexpected danger, but I took several deep breaths and sought the company of Joe and Serena and normal conversations instead.

Chapter Sixteen

"Hi babe, *I've got an apology to make to you.*" Will said on the phone much later that night. He sounded so sheepish that all my senses went on high alert. *Babe? Is that his favourite word of endearment for Rafaella?* "I haven't kept in touch with you enough lately; while I've been out enjoying myself, you've been spewing your guts up."

"God, thanks, Will. You sure know how to flatter a girl," I said caustically.

He laughed, and all pretence of eating humble pie vanished. "Rafaella's booked all her team's flights now. She thought they'd enjoy a few days in the UK sightseeing, so they're coming over next Tuesday."

"Are you flying with them?" I asked, holding my breath.

"I thought about it because they want me to be their escort on their tour of hot spots," he admitted. "But I thought I'd better fly sooner, so I'll be over in a couple of days when I can get a flight. I'll let you know." He sounded condescending, as if he was making a big sacrifice, flying back sooner.

I expelled my breath gustily as relief flooded through me.

"Will they all be coming here straight away?" I asked, thinking about more meals to cater for and soaring costs.

"No, they'll be doing the usual touristy stuff when they arrive, you know, the Tower of London, the Palace, Harrods or Selfridges, Hampton Court, so they'll be staying in London. Then they want to see Windsor Castle and Shakespeare's Stratford and Bath, so that will take up the next day. Then It'll be Avebury and Stonehenge and Salisbury and then on to Harthill House."

"That will be exciting for them. They do have a very generous boss, Will. Is Rafaella covering all this, or is some of it coming out of our profits?"

"Now, now, that's not like you, Clem. It's a fantastic opportunity and makes for better bonding."

"Well, I'm thinking our profits will disappear if we fund team holidays to the US and bear the cost of finding temps in the meantime." I didn't mean to sound so chippy, but it sounded as if Will's loyalty had transferred to his adopted team in New York.

"Rafaella's father, brother Franco and a temp are covering their office while they're all away."

"I'll arrange with Kim to set up an out of office message system while they're here. I'm longing to see you before everybody arrives, Will."

"Of course, you'll see me, Clem. I'll drive down to Wiltshire after looking in on our team and then go back to meet their flight." *Another fleeting visit.*

"I can't wait to see you, love. It seems a long time ago since you abandoned me here."

Will tutted. "Clem!" he protested.

"It's true!"

There was a minimal pause. "Well, I'll let you know when I arrive. Don't worry."

We had wished each other a rather formal goodnight. I'd put Will in a corner and I was cross with myself. *Was Rafaella there beside him, listening?* Flops the bunny looked as forlorn as me sitting lopsidedly on the chair and I picked him up for a cuddle.

∽

The next morning, I appeared downstairs after a night spent tossing and turning and a spell in the bathroom earlier.

"You look pasty faced, ginger tea on its way, my dear," said Serena. She had a large basket full of cleaning materials. "Mollie and I are tackling the bedrooms in the south wing this morning."

I opened my mouth to offer help, as the last thing I needed was to waste a day moodily dwelling on my prospects.

"When you are feeling up to it, I wonder if you'd mind going over all the rooms and make a list of towels and toiletries needed.

I sipped my tea gratefully. Mollie arrived with a headscarf tied round her wiry hair, in a 1940s turban style, and Serena and I both laughed. Mollie pretended to be affronted, but she struck a pose with her long-handled duster, and I took a photo of her on my phone. I showed it to her.

"Lord bless us!" she said, clasping her bosom. "All this tech... electrical stuff is too much for me! I haven't even got one of them there phones, although Matthew keeps telling me I ought to have one in case of emergencies. 'I'll keep me old-fashioned one with wires attached, thank you,' I told him."

"I'd print it out for you, Mollie, if we had a printer."

"We have, we have computers and a fax and a printer in the office down at the stables," said Serena. "You're more than welcome to go in and have a look and use any equipment you need. Joe tries to do a few hours of admin each week."

"I'm learning more and more each day; I must go and investigate!"

Before telling them of Will's return, I'd wait till he gave me a definite date. Serena and Mollie left to get on with the cleaning,

Evie was working from home when I called her. "Can you rootle through my wardrobe? I need something decent for Friday night's dinner when everybody turns up. You'll need something besides jeans as well." She grumbled a bit about dressing up but agreed amiably to dig out some decent tops and trousers for me.

"Have you searched for Honoria's Journal yet?" she asked.

"Evie, getting ready for the Big Bash has rather taken over our lives, but I'll have another exploration when I can to keep you happy! It's not that important, anyway."

I felt like the chatelaine as I mounted the stairs on my way to inspect the rooms. I started on the first floor, where the main bedrooms were. Joe had only partially opened doors when he'd shown me around, announcing 'another bedroom', so apart from the Green Bedroom where Evie had slept, I hadn't fully investigated the others. I went straight to the master bedroom where Rafaella would sleep. It was a larger room than mine, with two long sash windows. The walls were lined with thick creamy wallpaper embossed with clusters of delicate apple blossom on which small birds perched. The focal point of the room was the four-poster bed. The hanging drapes, gathered by silken cords, were a deep cream with soft green edgings and the long curtains at the sash windows were of the same material and the room reflected the light streaming in. The deep piled carpet was cream and rugs lay on either side of the bed. Two round bedside tables bore cream shaded lamps and the same heavy material draped the tables. There was a tall chest of drawers on the wall to the left and fitted cupboards behind the door. Between the windows was a small rosewood bureau on which stood a pair of Dresden candlesticks and a small vase. Headed cards and notepaper lay in the carved pigeonholes, but all the drawers were empty. An armchair was positioned by one window and a small cushion topped ottoman lay at the foot of the bed. Surely Rafaella was bound to be impressed, including the modern en-suite bathroom.

Reluctantly, I started up the stairs to the top floor where the nursery was situated. I hadn't been up there since I'd heard the cries of an infant, and my feet faltered as I heard scraping noises. "Who's there?" I called, sounding braver than I felt, and Joe's head popped round the door to the nursery.

"Hi, Clemency, have you come to look?" he said, holding the door wide. The bare nursery was in a state of transition. The windows were wide open, admitting chilly air. A large pot of magnolia paint lay on a newspaper covered table with a tray and a roller resting on it. "I thought it could do with sprucing up; there haven't been any occupants since William was a baby, apparently! I've just finished- does it look a bit brighter to you?"

Joe had made a good job, despite the rush, and he'd left the delightful frieze of animals intact. "There's a large rug in the junk room which I'll bring in when I've given the floor boards a scrub and a polish, and when the windows are clean, Serena can put up some curtains. There are sets in the junk room. Matt can help me with bed frames and mattresses. If Mollie can give the bathroom a good going over when it's finished in here, I'll decide if it needs a coat in there as well. Don't worry about us finishing on time. There's still over a week to go yet."

He nodded towards a door next to a window and I had a look in. It was a functional bathroom with a white painted chair and an old-fashioned wooden towel holder. The floor and windowsill were covered in dead flies. There was no radiator in here, so I hoped Ben and Andy wouldn't freeze in it.

"It seems an awful lot of hard work," I said, "But I'm sure Will's going to be very grateful. I've told him you are all pulling the stops out."

"It'll be good to see the old house full of people. It was built for family and entertaining."

"Have you seen the junk room yet?" Joe said. "Prepare to be amazed! There are generations' worth of stuff in there. Just go a couple of doors down the passage while I finish here. It's quick drying paint with not much smell so there shouldn't be any lingering odours! And my stomach's telling me it's lunchtime!"

I stepped out of the nursery and wandered down the corridor. The next door opened on to a small bedroom. Thin cotton floral curtains were closed over a tiny window and drawing them back, I saw the small single bed frame, a nightstand, a utilitarian chest of drawers and plain wooden chair. The bed was unmade, but on the wall above the brass bedstead was a large crucifix. Joe must have heard me and came in behind me.

"This is the nanny's bedroom," he said. "I'd forgotten about it! I don't think there's been a nanny since Mr Geoffrey was a baby. I'll mention it to Serena for a spot of sprucing and that makes another available bedroom."

He went out again. This room had the same effect on me as the nursery. I could feel hairs on my arms standing up. Next door to the nanny's room was the junk room, as described by Joe. A little light entered through the far window which was obscured by piled up chairs, boxes and chests, mattresses wrapped in plastic sheeting and bed frames, antique occasional tables, lamp standards and lampshades, a large old-fashioned pram and various cardboard boxes and black bags containing who knew what and rolled-up carpets stood upright against a wall. It was like an antique emporium with absolutely no order, and I was glad I didn't have to look for anything in there. Opposite the junk room was another door, which was locked.

Joe appeared out of the nursery, waving his phone. "Lunch is ready!" he said and made off down the stairs, before I could ask him about it. I stopped off at my room to freshen up and check for messages. There were none.

Matt and Mollie were already at the table in the warm kitchen. I was just in time to hand round bowls of soup as Serena ladled it out of the pan on the Aga.

"There was a locked door on the top floor," I said. "Is it another bedroom we could use?"

"That be Mr Geoffrey's study," said Mollie in a tone which implied it was none of my business.

"So nobody is allowed in there?" I asked as the thought occurred to me that Honoria's Journal might be in it.

"Of course you can go in, Clemency, the key is on the board outside," said Serena from the Aga, turning and frowning at Mollie.

"Well, there be no need for anyone to go in now," said Mollie defensively, meeting Serena's eyes.

"I just thought if it was an extra bedroom, we could use it as a standby. Evie is definitely coming next weekend. I might ask her to give a talk on the house's history, if any of the guests are interested," I explained, keen to placate Mollie's belligerence. It had the opposite effect.

"What does she know about the history, she were only here for a couple of days!" she retorted to everyone's amazement.

"Nan!" said Matt, shocked, putting his hand on her arm, which she moved impatiently.

"Well, I were only speaking my mind. I've been here longer than all of you, and I could tell you a fact or two about the history," grumbled Mollie.

"I didn't mean to upset you, Mollie. Evie is an historian, so she'll focus on the architecture and period it was built," I gushed in a bid to mollify her. "She'll blind everyone with facts about architectural pediments and decorative swags and so on, but if you have interesting stories about the people who lived here, I'm sure the guests will be fascinated."

Mollie sniffed, but relaxed and poured more tea into her mug from the big teapot on the table.

"I'd like to hear your stories as well," I said, hoping she could shed light on the many sightings of the Twins.

"You be welcome to my little house anytime you like," said Mollie, looking more amenable now.

"The old nanny's room next to the nursery could be spruced up for use as well," said Joe to Serena.

Mollie opened her mouth, but before she could utter, Matt got up from the table.

"Well, I'll be getting back now. Thanks for lunch, Serena; I wasn't expecting soup, honestly!" He said this with such a cheeky grin that Serena swiped at him with a tea towel.

"Can I walk with you to the barns to see the lambs again?" I asked. It would be a good opportunity to get some fresh air and in company, as Uncle Daniel had advised.

The afternoon was bright, with long shadows cast by the trees and only the sound of noisy rooks filled the still air as we tramped towards the farm.

"I hope Nan didn't upset you at lunch," Matt said, as we paddled in the disinfectant baths outside the barn. "I think she feels she is the only link between the house and its past, especially in the absence of any family."

"It's natural that she feels so possessive then, and she is looking after the house as well. Is Mollie related to the Payne–Ashtons?" I asked curiously. It would explain the similarity in appearances between Matt and Will, and it was odd that no one had mentioned the likeness.

"I can't remember her maiden name before she married into the Crane family, although her family lived around here, too. When I was younger and Mum and Dad were alive, she was always going on about the Cranes living here before this house was built, but as far as I know they were either agricultural workers on the land or servants of the Pethericks in the old manor house by the river before Harthill was built. Her stories about past residents went over my head; I was more interested in my present and future than obsessing about the past."

I laughed at his remark. "That sounds very much like a Will remark! I really would like to hear your nan's stories, but I wouldn't admit that you aren't interested in history in front of Evie if I were you! She gets carried away explaining historical facts and figures and can't understand why people get bored!"

Matt pulled the heavy door shut behind us and the warm smell of animals, ammonia, and straw assailed my nostrils. He laughed as I wrinkled my nose.

"It is time for a muck out! Seriously though, please don't mention about Evie doing research to Nan. She might feel threatened that she'll be of no use anymore."

The soft heads of curious lambs were irresistible as I leaned over a partition to scratch them. "I hope Mollie isn't threatened by my presence. Does she think we'll retire her if we come to live here? I'm not even sure whether Will and I will settle here; after all I only came to know of its existence not long ago myself!"

In Mollie's eyes, I was the future lady of the manor and might choose to dispense of her services and I couldn't give her any assurances because my future was more uncertain than hers. While Mollie had never said or done anything to make me feel unwelcome, I sensed she kept a wary eye on me, as if either assessing me as a friend or a foe, and hadn't quite made up her mind yet.

"Nan will keep going until she drops," remarked Matt. "She's tough and likes to be busy."

"She's a marvel. I won't keep you long, Matt; you'll want to get on with all your jobs. The lambs soon grow, don't they?" I laughed as I watched their high-spirited leaps and jumps.

"The weather forecasts no more snow, but if the temperature remains below zero, I'll hold them in longer."

"Matt, you will come to our weekend do, won't you? We're all the same age and it seems a bit mean if you are kicking your heels on your own while we're all partying! And you'll be able to catch up with Will..."

Matt looked doubtful, and then looked at me with his friendly blue eyes and grinned. "I actually can't think of a reason to refuse your offer, Clemency. I thought you'd be holding lots of business meetings."

"I hope not. According to Will, the American leader of her team thought it would be good to meet up seeing as we'll be working so closely with them. You don't need to be there all day, just come to the evening meals on Friday and Saturday and Sunday lunch. The menus we've put together with the caterer are very impressive!"

"Right, that's decided me! You know my appetite well!"

His acceptance made me happier than I'd reason to be. We both stood there grinning at each other like idiots. Then he looked at his watch and pulled a face.

"Milking time soon, so I've got to get the sheds ready for the ladies. They also like dinner on the table in front of them!"

"I wish I could help," I said.

Matt looked down at me with a raised eyebrow. "I'll remember that offer for the future!"

With a pang, I realised I'd have to walk home alone as dusk fell. Pride prevented me from asking Matt to escort me, but Daniel's words resounded in my ears.

It was only a short distance back to the house. Boldly, I set off along the track, through the farm gate and along the path lined with laurel hedges that led to the house. A hush had descended as the sun sank behind the ridge crowned by the tree ringed hill fort to the west, which I'd discovered was called Hoddenbury Rings. There was no wind, and the rooks had fallen silent. I shivered and pulled my jacket round me closer, humming tunelessly. On the last stretch, hurrying, out of the corner of my eye, I glimpsed movement. A shadow, darker than the hedge, moved as if to intercept me. The shadow becomes two shapes. If the shapes appeared in front of me, I would be trapped between the high hedges.

Breaking into a panicked run, I stumbled and fell heavily on one knee. I scrabbled to my feet and looked round wildly. *Where are they? Should I run back to the barn and Matt? Oh God, what if I run into them? Stupid idiot, they are not solid, they can't physically touch me!* The shapes were behind me and I recognised them as the Twins. Whether they transmitted fear or it was my paranoia, whichever it was driving me forward. Blood seeped through the knee of my trousers and the material stuck painfully to the wound as I scrambled for the steps, hurling myself down the uneven stone treads and falling painfully on my knees again at the bottom. I couldn't hold back the dry sobs as I prayed that the back door was open. It was. Glancing back in total fear, the courtyard lit up in a blaze of security light: silent and empty. Slamming the door behind me, it took all my evaporating control to get upstairs to my bathroom before I violently threw up. My trousers were ripped and there was a large bleeding graze on my knee. I dabbed at it with toilet paper. My shaking subsided and as I held my hands under the hot flow of water from the tap, panic subsided to be replaced by embarrassment. There was a small cabinet on the wall and, fortunately, inside was antiseptic cream and a box of plasters.

Back in the bedroom, I discarded my jacket and climbed under the duvet, shivering. I was sure I could hear the mocking cry of a magpie outside. Trying to stem tears of frustration at my fear, I just felt a complete fool.

There was a light knock on the door. "Come in," I called in manufactured assurance.

"It's only me, Clemency. Joe thought he heard the door bang a while ago."

"Yes, that was me," I said, disentangling myself from the duvet wrapped around me. "I could hardly get to the bathroom in time."

"I think another visit from Dr Laidlaw wouldn't do any harm," she said tactfully. "You still look peaky. We don't want you missing out on all the fun of seeing your colleagues, and it will be quite hectic until then." She added.

I shrugged. Dr Laidlaw couldn't take my fear away, but if it was stressing the baby, then I had to get away from here as soon as the big weekend was over. Serena smoothed down the covers and told me she was going to bring up a tray and I had to try to get something down me. I wasn't up to protesting; the fight had gone out of me and my fear replaced with mortifying embarrassment. Tomorrow, I'd take a deep breath and start again.

～

Dr Laidlaw reassured me that the baby's heartbeat was steady and so was my blood pressure when he examined me next morning. The frosts and blue skies had been replaced by clouds and rain in the night and Dr Laidlaw cheerfully informed me it was a lot milder than of late.

"Unfortunately, some expectant mothers can experience morning sickness a long way into pregnancy; in others it passes quickly," he said, packing away his equipment. "We can only hope it will improve soon. Keep as active as you can with plenty of fresh air, good sensible eating, and rest. Old-fashioned advice from an old-fashioned general practitioner, I know, but tried and tested advice. The worst thing you can do is over worry as it will affect both your mental and physical state and we don't want a stressed baby!"

"I know," I sighed, "but it's hard not to worry because there are a lot of ifs and buts in my life at present. But when Will returns, a lot of my anxiety may disappear."

"That's the ticket. When you go for your next scan soon, you'll both be happier."

I thanked him and walked with him to the front door and waved as he ran through the downpour to his car. He was of the same generation as Daniel and possessed the same old-world charm and courtesy.

"I've just got to put up with these ups and downs for the time being," I said to Serena later. "I feel ok today and the baby's heartbeat is steady. Do you want me to do some more checks today?"

Serena was just about to embark on another cleaning mission. "Mollie says she is coming to help wash up, even though I've told her Mr Chadwick has staff," she said, picking up her box of cleaning materials.

"She needs to feel wanted," I said, remembering her outburst yesterday and Matt's remarks. "It's best not to try to stop her."

"And Joe and I have decided that we'll be Brian Chadwick's helpers, too. I wouldn't feel comfortable wining and dining without giving some assistance and we know where everything is. Joe can play being the butler when your friends arrive. Your American friends will love that! Oh, and the study is certainly not sacrosanct. It's locked because some of Mr Geoffrey's estate documents were kept in there. The key is on the board outside in the passage if you want to nose around. You're part of the family now. And we're going to fix up the single bedroom in the South Wing as well, in case Mr Chadwick wants to spend the weekend on the premises. It's a good feeling opening and airing all these rooms; they've been shut up and gathering dust for too long."

With that, Serena placed her mug in the dishwasher, picked up her rubber gloves and sallied forth with her dusters again.

The keys hanging on the vintage keyboard were antiquities in themselves, with ornately styled bow ends. Thankfully, the labels above all the hooks were handcrafted in clear Victorian copperplate writing. The top floor room keys were all at the top of the board, so it was quite easy to pick off the one for the study and I hurried up to the top floor. Joe was in the nursery, sandpapering the windowsill to prepare for painting.

"Good morning, Joe, I'm just poking about up here, so if you hear noises, it's only me," I said from the doorway. Joe lifted his hand in greeting. "Have a good rummage," he said and carried on rubbing. Quietly, I inserted the key and opened the door with trepidation. Irrationally, I thought I was about to disturb the occupant of the study. I closed the door behind me and inserted the key in the inside lock. It was not a brightly lit room; the arched window was at floor level because this room was at the centre of the house over the portico and the cubed shaped Hall below. A desk faced the window with a desk lamp and two chairs with cushions on them. The desktop was empty apart from a mounted blotting paper sheet, much used, a mug full of pencils and pens and a tarnished brass ashtray. The wall on the left of the room held a couple of shelves and I moved closer to see the titles of the books haphazardly arranged on them. Most of them were on estate management, accountancy, and farming methods. Nothing of interest there. A lumpy looking sofa filled the wall on the right and a small, framed oil painting of a smiling woman hung alongside a large-scale modern map of the estate above the sofa. The woman in the portrait wore a cloche hat and collared 1930s style dress with dark curls springing from under the hat. A small dachshund with bright eyes sat on her lap, and she held a cigarette holder aloft in the other hand Another look through the photo albums might reveal who it was but I had an inkling it might be Geoffrey's mother, and therefore Will's grandmother.

All the drawers of the filing cabinet were empty. Presumably, the house deeds and accounts were in the hands of the family solicitors and accountants and used when the Estate Trustees met during the year. I don't know quite what I had expected, but I was vaguely disappointed by its functional appearance. It wasn't as sacrosanct as Mollie had implied.

I pulled open the desk drawers one by one. The top one held writing paper, envelopes, paper clips, and a clumpy early pocket calculator. On the other side, one drawer revealed a large desk diary for the year 1973. Flicking through the pages only revealed functional entries such as *'Meet Henry 12.30 White Hart'*, *'Quarterly Returns due'*, *'Vet to check herd,'* *'car to garage'*, *'arrange drinks and snacks for Meet'*. An entry in early September read *'Harvest all in, hallelujah! Non-stop rain for weeks afterwards!'* So much history in this house, yet routine activities prevailed. Then one entry at the end of September grabbed my attention. *'Terrible day- Roberta in hospital- baby could not be saved.'* Such a simple entry imbued with such terrible starkness. It was some years before Will's birth, and he had certainly never mentioned any brothers or sisters that had died. Perhaps Roberta had miscarried and so had never revealed this to her surviving son. I quickly scanned the rest of the pages, but apart from an entry in November reading: "*Shoot going ahead, but heart not in it, nevertheless must play the host.*" Poor Geoffrey obviously had taken the loss of the baby quite badly. And then after a last entry reading *'Christmas with the Forbes' in Devon'*, there was nothing else. I quickly returned the diary and closed the drawer. The other drawers held nothing of interest: more farming magazines, a conservation society quarterly magazine, a couple of photocopied pictures of prize cattle. There didn't seem to be much evidence of Geoffrey's work as far as I could see. I didn't know if he was involved in any other work apart from the upkeep of the house and estate. Somehow, this floor of the house was imbued with a legacy of sorrow.

There was no sign of anything that looked like an ancient journal. My eye fell on a tan leather satchel hanging on the back of the door. It was worn and scratched and obviously much used. I inserted the key in the door to lock it, then reached behind the door and lifted the satchel off the hook. Will might like it as a memento of his father. It was surprisingly heavy and not an object I could hide if I ran into someone. But who would care? Only Mollie would say I was snooping! It didn't have Geoffrey's name emblazoned on it so nobody would give it a second look. Nevertheless, I clumsily scrabbled at the keyhole, pocketed the key and went to my room. *I feel like a naughty child who's just stolen cakes from the kitchen when expressly forbidden from touching them.* A memory of my mother popped into in my mind, standing with hands on hips with a look of outrage on her face. "You've eaten some fairy cakes without my permission." She glares at me and my brother, who is standing nonchalantly leaning against the stairs, shrugs. I feel a flush rising from my neck to my cheeks. Tom had given one to me and I'd eaten it innocently. "You're a naughty child," Mum had cried, "stealing without asking! No tea for you tonight!" I start up the stairs and remember the shock of the stinging slaps on my legs as I go. Tom smirks and says nothing.

I pushed the satchel to the back of the upper shelf in the wardrobe and covered it with one of the spare blankets. After lunch, I'd have a quick look inside, but for now, I didn't want Mollie to know I had it in my possession. She could easily pop her head round the door to check on the room in my absence, and I was certain she always had a quick snoop amongst anything I left lying around.

At the bottom of the staircase, I heard the front doorbell ring and the loud barking response of the dogs as they rushed up from the basement. They streamed past me and I followed, still limping from yesterday's tumble, shushing them and, making them sit as I'd seen Joe do, I opened the door.

"Hugo!" I squeaked as he grinned and held his arms wide. The dogs forgot their training and rushed out, milling around us, tails waving like pennants. I looked over Hugo's shoulder to his car. No sign of Will. "Where's Will?"

"He's on the next flight and will be with you tomorrow. Can you put up with me for a couple of hours?"

"Yes, absolutely! Oh, it's so lovely to see a familiar face, Hugo.

Come in and met the others. I expect there'll be enough lunch for you; Serena always makes enough for a rugby team!"

Hugo inspected me carefully. "How are you, Clem? I couldn't wait for next weekend before seeing how you are. It's been quiet without you and you should have been in the States as well. You're still looking pale and thin, though."

"I'm well enough, Hugo. Serena and Joe are mothering me, but I'm still having bad bouts of nausea, so whatever I eat doesn't seem to fatten me up! I'm seeing a local doctor here who's keeping me under observation and he's satisfied that me and the baby are fine."

Hugo wrapped his arm round my shoulder, and I led him through the hall and passage to the basement stairs. He whistled in amazement at the alcoves filled with busts, the overhead chandelier, and the sweep of the polished staircase. "This place never fails to impress," he said. "I have been here before, you know, when Will and I were just starting out and his father was delightful, always so pleased to see his son. I didn't know you knew nothing about the place until Kim mentioned it when you told her you were coming here. Just think, you can be a real-life Lady of the Manor now!"

"I can't understand why Will never talked about it," I admitted. "I'm getting used to it now, but there are still rooms I haven't been in yet, not to mention the stable block and the great outdoors! Let's see if there's some lunch left and then you'll have to fill me in on your opinion of the States."

Hugo nodded, but with an almost imperceptible pause, which I latched onto suspiciously.

Serena, Joe, and Matt were in the kitchen, as I'd expected. After introductions, Hugo was seated and bowls of soup placed before us. "Airline food always tastes synthetic, so it's good to eat something which tastes real!" he said.

"Hugo's been on the same trip as Will, and Will's arriving tomorrow," I said.

There was a chorus of approval. "About time," said Matt, and then started questioning Hugo. Soon we were all listening to his descriptions of the winter snows, forest trails, stunning scenery, and, of course, New York, passing his phone round so that we could scroll through some of his photos. I was relieved to see that the photos of Will and Rafaella on their bikes looked like ordinary expedition poses for the camera.

Matt suddenly jumped up to leave and, shaking Hugo's hand, said he would see him again next week. Serena left with Joe, so Hugo and I had the kitchen to ourselves. Hugo drank his coffee black and sugarless, while I added a little honey to my tea.

"Kim has been so thoughtful just keeping in touch and hoping I'm ok, but I wonder if I'm being excluded so as not to stress me."

Hugo opened his mouth to approve of that decision, but I anticipated his comments. "And d'you know what, Hugo, the longer I'm here, the less I'm worrying about work. Kim is just as capable as I am, if not more so, and nothing terrible has happened in my absence!"

"Sensible girl," he said. "You have the knack of delegating workloads instead of monopolising them yourself, so it is natural for everyone to carry on. Anyway, when you're feeling up to it, you'll be welcomed back with open arms!"

"I'm managing to fill my time here, especially now preparing for next weekend, but I can't rattle around here forever. I'm coming back to London after the big weekend. The structure of the two teams will need careful monitoring. I don't want any of our team thinking they might lose their jobs and I'm sure Rafaella feels the same about her team."

"Rafaella, yes," said Hugo cryptically, and I looked at him, eyebrows raised. Hugo shifted uncomfortably, and my heart plummeted.

"Rafaella is a Tour de force," Hugo began slowly, searching for the right words. "She is everything you'd expect from someone running a successful business and she is ambitious, has family backing, challenges every aspect and sets her team challenges of what can be achieved."

So far, Hugo was not revealing any thoughts about a personal relationship between Will and Rafaella. I wouldn't expect him to be disloyal about his good mate, but was he subtly preparing me?

"Are you suggesting she might walk all over us to achieve her aims?" I asked. "Or more to the point, do you think Will is in her thrall and might let her walk all over him, to our detriment? She is very attractive," I added, fishing for clues.

Hugo puffed out his cheeks. "You're not wrong there! But she is not underhand; she's a very direct person and is very clear about the aim of Trekkers International; that is to introduce new clientele, in her words, to the 'awesome' beauty of her region. We've got to be on top of our game and make our European trips sound as exciting as hers. In that way, she'll respect our knowledge as Will and I without a doubt respect hers, and all our teams will keep their jobs."

I felt a stirring of renewed energy and desire to get back amongst our team and keep them inspired.

"And is Will eating out of Rafaella's hand?" I threw the question at Hugo. He blinked at me, put his hand on my arm as if in reassurance, shrugged and chuckled.

"Rafaella can make anyone eat out of her hand, including me! She has a knack of charming everyone, male and female. But neither of us would sell out our team to her for the sake of a few crumbs of feminine wiles! I think the gathering next weekend will put us on the right track. Rafaella's team are a good bunch of kids, as enthusiastic and eager to set their pitch as ours are and I'm certain we'll all get along fine. And Will hasn't forgotten about you if that's what's worrying you!"

Hugo had read the meaning behind my questioning, and it reassured me a little. He showed signs of getting up and I knew I'd get no more out of him by probing too deeply. While he went to the bathroom, I went over his words. If Rafaella had charmed her way into Will's affection, then my way of winning him back was to stage a charm offensive on my part. Instead of giving him the third degree, which deep down I knew would have him backing off, I had to swallow my pride and go on a charm offensive of my own! Hugo had done me a favour after all; when Will returned, there was to be no showdown or reproachful moaning about leaving me all alone. Evie would throw her hands up in horror if she thought I would gladly sacrifice feminist principals for feminine wiles!

Chapter Seventeen

My phone pinged. It was a text from Will, brief as usual:

> Driving up after flight, be with you at 2pm. XXX

In my room, I piled my hair up, brushed it out, made a loose ponytail, brushed it out and just let it fall in its usual curly way around my face. I applied a little tinted moisturiser. Hugo was right. I was too pale. The eyeliner and lipstick were wiped off impatiently when I saw my demented expression. Eventually I just pulled on my boots and jacket, stuffed my hair into a bobble hat and set off down the drive. I wanted to greet Will privately, without Serena and Joe's presence. Despite my convictions of yesterday, I was a complete bundle of nerves. The afternoon was mild and sunny with just the faintest of breezes to stir the dead leaves under the trees, still wet from rain and melted snow. Some of the cattle in the field on my right lifted heads and stared, ruminating slowly. Matt had put hay in the feeders after releasing them from the barn. "There's not a lot of nutrients in the grass at this time of year," he'd explained. "I'll probably have to bring them in again."

As I neared the old ash, I heard a vehicle approaching. A jackdaw flew silently down from a high bough, followed by another; there must be a nest somewhere in this great tree.

When the Twins suddenly materialised from behind the trunk to stand in the drive only a stone's throw away from me, I stumbled to a halt. The shock was as great as if I'd walked into a brick wall. Trembling, half of me wanted to give them a good whack with something hard, but the other half was desperate to flee.

Will's old Range Rover appeared round the curve of the drive. I could see his face through the windscreen, his eyes shielded by sunglasses. The Twins turned their insolent gaze from me to face the Range Rover. As if released from their power, my body sagged with relief. The Twins were directly in Will's path. He'd drive through them just as Uncle Daniel had the other night. I heard a tchack, tchack from the jackdaws in the ash. Everything slowed down. Where did the mist come from? It obscured the Twins and Will and the trunk of the ash. Then the Rover shot out of the mist. It gathered speed and came hurtling towards me, bumping over the grass verge erratically. Instinct took over as I threw myself sideways out of its path. A searing pain ripped through my hand, making me scream. My hand was impaled on the barbed wire fence. The car skidded to a halt close enough to shower me in a flurry of churned up clods of grass and mud. Will threw himself out of the car.

"Christ, what the hell happened? Are you alright, Clem? Oh, my god, you're bleeding!"

He gripped my hand and gently prised it off the barbs. Blood trickled down, and I sank down. Will's arms were round me as we rocked together on our knees, the wet grass soaking into our jeans. Whimpering in pain and shock, I held out my damaged hand.

There was blood dripping everywhere, and I let go of Will to reach into my jacket pocket where there were some tissues. Will took them from me wordlessly and wrapped them round my hand, pressing gently to stem the bleeding. I winced. Then he was kissing me, my eyes, my tears, my lips, and I responded, leaning into him to stop my shivering, letting his familiar warmth envelop me.

"We've got to get your hand seen to Clem. Come on, can you walk? No other damage?" He raised me to my feet and lifted me onto the passenger seat. "What the hell happened? I caught sight of you walking and then, I don't know, there was a kind of mist in front of the car and then I was heading straight for you! It wasn't the sun; it's gone behind the trees now! I'm sorry; I'm so sorry, my darling. I gave you such a fright. Christ, I gave myself a fright. I must get the brakes looked at; it was as if I had no control at all."

All the time he was gabbling, reassuring me, reassuring himself; trying to explain it all logically. How could I tell him it was the Twins? There was something about this ash tree and the Twins presence there. They'd been at the same spot when Uncle Daniel had driven me home. The ash tree had been the cause of death of Will's ancestors two centuries ago. *Were the Twins drawn to the energy around that timeless patch of ground where violent death had occurred?*

Will drove at breakneck speed and braked in a flurry of gravel by the portico. He ran to the door and pressed the doorbell several times before coming back to help me out of the car. My hand was throbbing, and the tissue had turned red and sticky. Joe appeared, his face split into a huge grin as he pulled open the heavy door and the dogs spilled out, circling us, sniffing the car, trying to sniff my hand. When Joe saw our faces and me cradling my bloody hand, he leapt forward to take my other arm and we crossed the threshold into the hall, a welcoming fire in the hearth.

"What happened?" he asked as he steered us towards the stairs down to the kitchen. "Serena," he called, and she came to the foot of the stairs, drawn by the urgency in his voice.

The tissue had stuck in places and Serena examined the several wounds where the barbed wire had pierced and torn the skin.

"I'm reluctant to touch this," she said at last. "I can see the skin is torn raggedly and you'll probably need stitches." She saw me wincing and said, "I'm sorry, but I think you ought to go to A&E. They'll examine your hand properly and you might get away with steri strips. But first, you need a cup of hot sweet tea for the shock." Joe had already boiled the water, and a mug appeared in front of me.

"I'll get the Discovery out," said Joe, donning a jacket. He clapped Will on the back on his way out. "Some homecoming, eh, Will? I'll see you out front."

I sipped my tea gratefully, and the warmth and sweetness quelled my trembling.

"That's good." I'd said very little since the incident. I looked up at Will, who was pacing as he held his mug forgotten in his hand. "I can't explain it. The drive's not icy or greasy with mud. Did you see the mist, Clem? I must have got disorientated by it. I'll get Matt to check the brakes and steering first. He's good with mechanics. I am so sorry." He knelt beside my chair and I stroked his hair.

"It wasn't your fault, honestly," I whispered. "I saw the mist as well. It just appeared."

"It looked like I was deliberately trying to mow her down," he said wildly to Serena, who glanced at me, shocked.

"Well, luckily you didn't," I said, trying to joke. On another level, I was telling myself that Will needed to be told the truth. Matt would find nothing wrong with the car; I was convinced of that.

Serena helped me to my feet. "Joe will be waiting for you now.

I hope you won't have too long to wait before you're seen at the hospital." She gave me a towel to wrap round my bloody hand and kissed me on the cheek.

On the way to the hospital, Will tried to explain again to Joe what had happened. "It gets more bizarre the more I try to make sense of it," he said, his arm wrapped firmly round me in the back of Joe's Land Rover Discovery.

∼

We returned to Harthill House by taxi. Joe had dropped us at the entrance to A&E and Will had sent him home as there was no knowing how long I'd have to wait to be seen. The triage nurse assessed my hand and ruled out soft tissue damage. He said I was lucky that the department was not overly busy. "Wait till the pubs and clubs pour out tonight. There'll be all sorts of alcohol and drug related injuries!" he had said gloomily.

I was stitched up in no time, my hand bandaged, paracetamol prescribed for the pain and tetanus injection recommended. Fortunately, I'd had the full set in the last three years in case I went on a trek and I declined the paracetamol because I was pregnant. This caused a stir. The nurse was about to send me to gynaecology, but went to make a quick phone call and after a surprisingly short wait, a midwife appeared and listened to the foetal heartbeat using a handheld ultrasound device.

"Baby's heartbeat is good and strong, "she announced in a lilting Irish accent.

"That's amazing," Will said. He stared at me with a dazed expression, listening to the rapid whooshing noise. "Just listen to that heartbeat!"

Tears filled my eyes. Will squeezed my good hand.

"When is your next scan?" the nurse asked.

"I've got an appointment at a London hospital in a few weeks," I said. I'm only in Wiltshire for a short time."

"Try to bring it forward, then, and if you experience any pain or blood loss, come back at once."

Will shifted uncomfortably in the chair. I could see that the episode in the drive had diverted his attention from the baby, and now he was uncomfortably aware of what may have happened to me and our unborn child.

"But now you are good to go," the nurse smiled, "take care."

Once again, I sat with Will's arm wrapped around me in the back of the taxi on the way back to Harthill House.

"I can't believe I nearly ran over you!" he said. "I could have nearly killed you and the baby."

I snuggled into him. In a grim twist, the accident had forced him to acknowledge my pregnancy. Fears and anxiety about any hold Rafaella had on Will had dissipated when we'd listened to our baby's heartbeat.

"Hugo came to see me yesterday," I said, trying to ignore my throbbing hand.

"What?" said Will, craning round and staring at me.

"It was lovely to see him. He said he'd missed me; well, you'd all missed me so I think he came to cheer me up. And he cheered me up because he told me you were practically right behind him!"

Will gave a sheepish chuckle. "He's a good wing man. In fact, he gave me a bollocking when I said I was flying over with Raf and her team. Said I was putting myself before you and all that rot!"

"Oh, Will," I squeezed him, determined not to let my disappointment ruin our rekindled closeness. "Serena fed him up, and we saw his photos. He's looking forward to us all getting together, and he cares a lot about getting this venture right. He made me feel quite optimistic about the future."

"It is going to be quite exciting and you'll be part of it as well."

It was close to eight o'clock when the taxi pulled up outside Harthill. I could hear the dogs barking, and Joe soon had the door open. He gave me a gentle hug before I could enter. "Glad to see you on your feet. Serena and I wondered if they'd keep you in overnight to check on the baby," he said, leading the way. All I wanted to do was lie down, but Will said I had to have a hot drink and something to eat.

"I'm starving," he said. "I hope Serena has saved some supper. And a whisky wouldn't go amiss either!"

While Serena piled beef casserole onto Will's plate, and he helped himself to a large measure of whisky, I opted for a poached egg on toast and a mug of hot chocolate.

"Comfort food," said Serena, but at least you're eating!"

"Matt gave your car a quick check and said he couldn't see any damage to brakes, steering or the engine, as far as he could tell. He said it would be best to take it to the garage in Bridgeford, where they'll run diagnostic tests," said Joe.

"I'll give them a bell in the morning and book it in," said Will. "I'll need it to get up to London on Tuesday, pick up the minibus and meet the New York team."

He looked apologetically at me as he spoke. Exhaustion washed over me.

"I think I'll go up now," I said.

Will sprang up and together we went up the two lots of stairs. As I wearily collapsed onto the bed, he drew the curtains, switched on the bedside lamps, and knelt to pull my boots off.

"I'll worry about how to manage a shower tomorrow." I said and left him to visit the bathroom next door.

When I got back, Will wasn't there, and my heart quailed. Before I could assemble my thoughts, he reappeared with his overnight bag.

"Left it in the car," he grinned, then gathered me up in a tight embrace. "I've been so taken up with events on the other side of the pond; I'd forgotten how cuddly you are. Except that you've got bony. You need to eat more, girl!"

"I'm sure I will once what goes down stays down," I said tartly.

Will said nothing, but slowly he helped me undress. He ran his warm hands over my belly, where there might be a slight roundness. He kissed it softly, and I shivered, not from cold. He threw back the duvet and lifted me into bed. I looked at him in anguish. *This is where he's going to kiss me on the forehead and leave me,* I thought wildly.

Instead, he hastily undressed and left everything in a heap on the floor and slid into bed beside me. His arm went round my shoulders, and we lay close, breathing in each other while his familiar smell enveloped me and I drew him closer. His hand stroked my face and hair and he looked into my eyes. "Hello, you," he said, and kissed me. I pulled him to me until we were staring into each other's eyes.

"Will it be safe?" he asked earnestly." I don't want to risk any harm."

I kissed him longingly and deeply. "Slow and gentle," I said, and kissed him again.

I woke later feeling warm and relaxed and stupidly happy. I turned and Will was facing me, asleep and lightly snoring. I stroked his face and in response, his arm went around me and drew me closer.

The rattle of china woke me again and this time it was daylight, the curtains drawn back to reveal an ice-blue sky, and Will placed a tray on the bed beside me.

"And I've got a plastic bag and elastic band to keep your hand dry in the shower!" he announced, holding it out.

I stretched and hauled myself up on the pillows and felt ridiculously happy. I even tucked into the toast and honey Will had brought and sipped cautiously at the tea.

"I think you can rest in bed after your restless night," Will said with a straight face. "I'm afraid I can't join you even though you've worn me out...." He dodged the pillow I threw at him. "I'm having another look at the car with Matt."

"I feel very lazy. I might just stay here and recover," I said, stretching again. Reluctantly, my bubble of languor was fading. "I don't think the garage will find anything wrong with your car, Will," I began, and he raised his eyebrows.

"Do you think I drove at you deliberately? Have you got a humongous life insurance I can claim?"

"No, silly, it's just that you said Matt didn't spot anything obvious..." I braced myself to tell him what really had happened, but Will's phone pinged.

"It's Matt," he said, reading the screen. "He's downstairs waiting for me. Apparently, he's managed to get one of the mechanics at the garage who's a mate of his to look at the car without booking it in first."

"Ok," I said, then leaned forward as Will kissed me on the lips.

"Bye, Honey Chops, I'll see you later." He winked and closed the door behind him.

"Honey Chops," I said aloud to the door. "Another Americanism..."

I got out of bed. My bubble of happiness was replaced with the reality of having to explain what had happened in the drive and my other sightings of the Twins. Instinctively, I knew Will would adamantly pour scorn on all my explanations.

Serena was in the kitchen when I went down after a successful shower, using the plastic bag over my hand. "I'm afraid I've left the tray in the bedroom."

"Not to worry, I'll fetch it later. At least you've got some colour in your cheeks this morning."

Mollie bustled into the kitchen and took down a mug. Seeing my bound hand, she exclaimed.

"My dear Good Lord, now what have you been up to?"

I gave her the briefest of explanations.

"Clemency says it happened near the old ash and there was no ice or even puddles. William says it's a mystery. That's why he's having his car checked," Serena added. Mollie's eyes flicked frowningly on to mine and the expression in them was momentarily calculating before she looked away and gave her habitual sniff.

"So young master is back then?" she said, changing the subject. "I hope 'e stays around long enough to see his old Nanny. That's what he used to call me when he were a toddler running around with my Matthew," she said. She and Serena left the kitchen together to seek out more cleaning.

There was a dark stain on my dressing and I hoped the wounds hadn't re-opened. When I told Will about the Twins, he might never want to see Harthill House again.

Chapter Eighteen

Will

Will drove into Bridgeford, followed by Matt in his pickup, in case he had to leave the Range Rover at the garage. His thoughts were whirling around his head. As he'd driven up to Wiltshire yesterday, he couldn't shake off his regret leaving New York. Hugo's outburst in the hotel room before he'd left to catch his flight had left him feeling annoyance at his best mate's interference and then guilt. Hugo had spoken the truth; he had put Clemmie and the baby on the back burner while he pursued his interests. He'd been truly caught up in Rafaella's irresistible allure: Nothing sexual had happened between him and Rafaella, but he was convinced she wouldn't rebuff him if he came on to her.

Yesterday's episode replayed in his mind. When he'd caught sight of Clemmie striding down the drive yesterday, a bobble hat pulled down practically over her eyes, he'd laughed out loud. Clemmie looked slimmer and pale, but even at a distance he could see her chin raised, and his heart had leapt at her innate ability to defy all the complexities in her life to be with him.

And then something had obscured his vision. Clemmie had disappeared, and he'd struggled to keep the Range Rover in a straight line. He'd been horrified at seeing her on the ground in front of the car. After that, instinct had taken over. All he'd wanted to do was to gather her to him and never let go.

In the hospital, listening incredulously to those strong heartbeats of their baby had turned his insides to jelly. Christ, he'd nearly mowed her down! Shame overcame him as he realised how close he'd been tempted to betray Clemency.

He wasn't a praying man, but the words "Thank God for making me come to my senses." Escaped from his lips.

He glanced right and left as the landscape re-established itself in his memory. On his left, beyond the ploughed fields and grassy meadows, flanks of wooded ridges separated the valley from the edges of the New Forest. On the right, across the fields and water meadows. Was the river, bordered by osiers, alders, aspens, elder and the taller beeches and sycamores, all bare now but luxuriant in summer months. As a lad, he'd caught trout in the little cuts that helped drain the water meadows, cropped by their sheep in summer.

It was the familiarity of this landscape that had made him eager to explore further afield. As he grew older, school studies, then university had limited his time spent at his father's house. He'd deliberately forgotten the old to embrace the new and exciting. Maybe it was time to address the issue he had with Harthill.

Chapter Nineteen

Joe was in the Hall with a bundle of post in his hand.

"Good morning, Clemency, how are you today?"

"I'm fine," I assured him. "Are Will and Matt still having the car checked?"

"Yes, I saw Matt earlier. He doesn't think there's anything wrong with it, but best to make sure. From what Matt says, he thinks Will hopes there's a fault, otherwise there's no explanation for the mishap."

I frowned. "He mustn't keep blaming himself." Will had to be told today about the Twins, even though he'd think I was mad, because I had no proof other than the old photos in the albums, which Will would naturally say I had seen before 'imagining' the Twins. Nobody else had seen them. Only Uncle Daniel believed me; could he convince Will that I wasn't delusional? The obvious answer was to drag Will to see Uncle Daniel, but there wasn't any time before Will left again to pick up the New Yorkers from Heathrow and take them on their guided tour.

I turned to go upstairs, but Joe called me back. "There's a letter for you, Clemency."

He handed me a long white envelope with my name and address handwritten in bold black italic strokes. I looked at the unfamiliar stamp. It was French, as was the postmark. I took it into the sitting room, where, thanks to Joe, a fire crackled merrily.

There was a faint perfume attached to the letter, and I opened it carefully. One sheet of paper was inside, written in the same confident strokes as on the envelope. The address heading the notepaper was printed. I read:

> My Dear Clemency,
>
> I was so thrilled when Will told me the news of your pregnancy, and then desperately worried when he informed me of your stay in hospital. What a shock it must have been for you both to learn about the baby and be threatened with losing it at the same time.
>
> However, I hear you are now in the care of the admirable Serena and Joe. They are truly trustworthy and loyal keepers of Harthill House in our absence, so I have every confidence in their care of you.
>
> I am planning to visit the UK soon and hope to meet up with you and Will. I will let him know by phone of my arrival. I understand he is in the field on his 'Action Man' endeavours, so don't be alarmed if this baby does not stop him doing what he loves! I know he cares deeply about you.
>
> Please take every care of yourself in every respect, especially when you must be experiencing both elation and fear at the same time. I am greatly looking forward to meeting you.
>
> My very best wishes,

Roberta

The letter was dated a few days ago, so she could be arriving any day now. What with Will's arrival, the imminent gathering and now meeting his mother, everything was suddenly speeding up. I reread Roberta's letter. She'd heard from Will about the pregnancy and she hadn't told me to leave Harthill House at the earliest opportunity, as Uncle Daniel had advised. Had he been in touch with her since she'd written the letter? The phrase 'elation and fear' were so appropriate for my condition and my reactions when the Twins appeared.

I heard a commotion: the dogs barking, doors banging. *Will's back. No more stalling. I've got to tell him my version of what happened and it's up to him whether he believes me.*

Will barged into the sitting room; his expression was a mixture of frustration and incomprehension.

"There is nothing wrong with your car," I asserted, before he could get any words out.

He flung himself on the sofa. "I don't understand - we drove round for miles and couldn't hear any strange noises or feel any steering faults."

"I need to show you something," I said, holding out my hand. "Do you want some coffee first?"

"No thanks. Matt and I stopped at the Red Lion for coffee on the way back. What do you want to show me?"

He looked calmer now. The photo albums, book of sketches and family tree scroll were all as I'd left them. Will wandered round, picking up framed photos one after the other. "I remember Ma letter writing in here when she came to stay, sitting at the little bureau. I'm glad her paintings are still up on the walls. We should go to her studio near Paris some time, she's very talented."

I took the letter out of my pocket. "This arrived from her," I said, handing it to Will and he read it in silence.

"She must have written it right after I phoned her. I suppose I was worried and needed some reassurance. It was all a shock and a bit of a blur afterwards, wasn't it? And I wasn't sure how to handle the news - or you. I've been like a spoilt brat the way I've behaved towards you. I'm sorry, Clem."

I wrapped my arms round his stiff body and after a while; he sagged against me and we held each other silently for a few minutes.

"Your mother might be arriving any time now," I said as we collapsed on the sofa together.

"Not great timing, then. I have to be off soon to organise the New Yorkers."

"If she comes while you're gone, I'm sure I can cope on my own!" I said, although I hoped I didn't have to. "She's familiar with this house and can tell me all about you! And Serena and Joe will look after us both. She says she will ring you when she flies over, so you'll have some warning."

Will got up to throw another log onto the fire and glanced down at all the items documenting the life of his ancestors down the centuries.

"What did you want to show me?" he asked, looking at the family tree like it was some form of dreaded homework.

I took a deep breath. "I've been looking at all this relating to your family because you brought me here to this great house, of which you'd told me nothing. So, you can imagine it was another shock on top of the reason for being here. Added to that, you then went and left me to flounder around somewhat. If Serena and Joe hadn't taken me under their wings, I'm not sure what I would have done. Evie being here helped, and now I've met your Uncle Daniel and Dr Laidlaw. I feel more at home here."

Will opened his mouth, either to explain or defend himself. I needed to carry on, so I put my finger gently on his lips. "It's a lovely house, Will. I'm getting used to it now and I have so many ideas in my head about how it could come alive again. Evie's been a great help with the family tree, and your Uncle Daniel, who set it all out. I've met him twice now, and he is such a good and gentle man." I paused and Will looked enquiringly at me, eyebrows raised, waiting.

"I can sense the history of the house in many of the rooms – the basement with all its special rooms for various domestic activities has a definite atmosphere of the past – I can see footmen and servants in big skirts and aprons and caps bustling around. And the top floor where the nursery is spooks me out."

Will laughed. "You've been listening to Mollie's stories, haven't you? She used to try to scare Matt and me with her stories of ghostly ancestors prowling the corridors and woods, but my father would tell her not to, although now I come to think of it, my mother had strange feelings about the place. I think that's why she left in the end, because she said she was always looking over her shoulder."

So Roberta had given her son a hint why she left. I ploughed on.

"Promise you'll listen to me now without laughing, please Will, because I've found out something which is scaring me half to death!" I drew a breath as he quirked his eyebrows at me and tried to compose his face in a seriously attentive expression which threw me, and I playfully punched his arm.

"Stop it! There is nothing wrong with the Range Rover because I know the reason it went out of control."

His mouth gaped open. "What....?" he began, but I jumped in.

"I can see the ghosts in the basement corridor and they're harmless. But I've had several encounters with what you might call malevolent spirits. They only appear to me as far as I know and only when I'm outside. I'm safe in the house. I think their purpose is to harm me."

Will's expression was turning from 'let's listen to this harmless rubbish' to frowning scepticism. I ignored his expression and ploughed on.

"They've appeared when I've been with either Evie, Matt, or Joe. I described them to Joe and Serena and they aren't farmworkers. I thought they were walkers, then stalkers, because they turn up in all the places I happen to be outside. Your uncle guessed and believed me. I described them to Evie, and she turned to the family tree for clues. When I was near the ash tree yesterday, they suddenly appeared, standing between me and you in the Rover. They looked at me and then turned to you. That's when you lost control and came careering towards me. They wanted you to mow me down. Somehow, they controlled the situation."

"Clemmie, I'm sorry. This has got to be the biggest load of bunkum I've ever heard. Evil spirits controlling my car? Come on, you've been watching too many haunted house programmes." Will could hardly contain his scepticism. I wasn't angry with him. To anyone rational, it was just too improbable.

"You saw the mist yesterday. I did too. It obscured your vision, and it disorientated you. I described my apparitions to Evie and Uncle Daniel. When I first saw them, they were in the field by the Ladies' Bower, looking up at my window. I laughed too; they are dressed weirdly: smocks, straw hats, shepherds' crooks, old boots, and legs bound in cloth like gaiters. Just like they'd been kitted out by a period drama costume department. I didn't laugh at their faces, though. Even from that distance, their faces made me shiver, they looked so threateningly at me. I even took a photo with my phone, but when I looked at it, they weren't in it."

Will was beginning to look uncomfortable now. He stood up and began pacing, prodding the logs with a poker, making them blaze up.

"Evie found the old photo albums, and we were trying to match up photos with the family tree going back to the nineteenth century. Then we came to one particular photo, and I nearly passed out. Look, this is what I want to show you." I opened the photo album at the appropriate page and Will reluctantly looked sideways at the photograph I was pointing to. Even now, goose bumps rose on my arms as I forced myself to look at the sneering, menacing expressions on the Twins' faces.

"These are what I call the Twins. They always appear together, always dressed like this."

"Well, that explains everything," Will exclaimed loudly, as if he'd just found a solution to a nasty problem. "You saw this photo, and it made you feel creepy, so of course they keep popping up in front of you. It's your mind playing tricks, like hallucinations in the desert!"

"No Will, I was seeing the Twins long before I saw this photograph, I swear it. That's why I nearly fainted. I was just as incredulous as you. They've also been in my dreams, well, nightmares, and they're always threatening me. I think they want to harm me and the baby." I was cradling my stomach as I spoke.

Will sat down again. "Perhaps pregnancy affects your mind as well as your hormones. Would it help to speak to someone about it?"

"Like a psychiatrist, you mean?" I asked. I was icy calm now. "You think I need locking up in a Victorian asylum, out of sight and out of mind? I know it takes a lot to believe someone who professes to see ghosts. I would have poured scorn on anyone as well before now. When I described them to your Uncle Daniel, he knew exactly who I was talking about. He advised me not to go out alone unless I was with someone. What happened yesterday was the second time anything physical has happened near me when they appear. I know who they are, Will. Here they are in the family tree: George and Wilfred Barnard. They were born in 1812, which explains their rustic clothing. Their father was Gerard, the youngest son of Sir Horace Barnard. After a series of accidents, he should have been the direct heir to Harthill House and, of course, his sons and their descendants. But he didn't inherit, and neither did his sons. I don't know the whole story yet but I think the Twins have been haunting the place down the centuries and looking for revenge."

There was silence except for the crackling logs on the fire.

"I don't know what to say," said Will at last. "I never took much interest in this place, as you know, especially after we moved to London. I've never seen this family tree or the photograph album of all these forgotten relatives."

"You said yourself that your mother was always looking over her shoulder," I said gently. "I think we should ask her when she comes over." Will half nodded, just as we were interrupted by a knock on the door. It was Joe asking if we'd like some lunch, as it was ready downstairs. Looking like a man who'd just received a reprieve, Will sprang up and helping me up, firmly guided me away from the historical memorabilia in the sitting room.

Unfortunately for Will, he couldn't escape Joe's probing about the Range Rover during lunch. Will's eyes swung from mine to Joe's as if he wanted me to intervene, but at this stage there was nothing I could say to explain it all away.

"I went down the drive and had a look," said Joe, wiping round his bowl with a hunk of bread. "Do you think your foot accidentally got stuck on the accelerator? Only it looked to me as if the car suddenly picked up speed, judging by the amount of grass and mud it took with it before stopping."

"I don't know, I don't know," Will said. "I suppose I could have hit the gas instead of the brakes when I spotted Clem."

"Anyway, what's done is in the past now. I'm alright and so is the car, so we'll just forget about it now. There's a busy week ahead of us." I spoke quietly but forcefully, gripping Will's hand as I spoke. "Shall we take the dogs out for a little walk?" I smiled at Serena and Joe.

"Those dogs would go out any time even if they've just come in!" said Serena, gathering plates and bowls.

Will's phone bleeped. He looked at the caller display and went out into the basement corridor. He walked right up to the far end near the old laundry room and I could hear his quiet voice. It wasn't a long call, and he strode back down the corridor. "That was Rafaella. She and her team will be departing later this evening their time and landing around 8am our time tomorrow morning at Heathrow. I'll just call Kim and make sure transport is arranged."

While Will was talking to Kim, I put my head round the kitchen door. "Looks like all systems go; our guests will all be arriving Friday as planned."

"Oh, I nearly forgot. Brian Chadwick is arriving on Thursday to start preparations ahead of his team, who'll arrive on Friday. It's a good thing we got that little room in the wing ready for him," said Serena.

"You've got it all under control, Serena. And I hope it means you won't be running around with the catering team all the time," said Will seriously.

"You know Serena, she will be around to make sure everything IS under control," added Joe, who was also putting his boots on.

"I think I'll have to leave this evening if I'm to meet them early tomorrow, said Will apologetically.

Pushing my feet into my boots masked my sudden look of sadness.

"Yes, I suppose so," I said, smiling up at him. I wanted to avoid any more displays of self-pity. "But let's take the dogs out first. Look at them; they've been waiting at the door all the time you were on the phone!"

Jasper and Bess were standing with their noses pressed to the back door, tails beating in a wild rhythm.

They disappeared in a scrabble of claws as Will opened the door and we followed them up the steps out of the courtyard. As we crossed the track leading to the farm, Matt appeared, driving a tractor and trailer laden with the mucking out from the sheep barns. He waved and disappeared over a little rise in the meadow.

The afternoon was mild and a little misty after the sunny morning and moisture clung to the bare branches of trees and shrubs.

"We won't go far if I've got to leave later," said Will, grabbing my good hand. "I seem to be always upping sticks and leaving you lately. Well, I'll be seeing you again soon," he said, swinging my arm and leaning down to kiss me.

"You seemed reluctant to bring up the subject of the Twins when Joe asked about the accident," I said.

"I had no intention of bringing them up, even though I really didn't know how to answer Joe's questions. I need to get my head around your 'ghosts' first."

The tall grey shape of the obelisk loomed out of the misty woods. The dogs were snuffling just ahead of us. "Do you remember the obelisk?" I asked Will as he gazed at it. "Evie and I discovered it, and she found the inscription on it."

"I never knew there was an inscription on it. I tried to scale it when I was a kid, see the horizontal bands around it? That stone is pretty rough, and I always ended up skinning my arms and shins sliding down."

We passed through the network of overgrown hedges which had bordered the Ladies' Bower. Will silently read the inscription through the scraped away layers of moss.

"Apparently, the coach carrying all those people crashed into the old ash tree," I said. "Evie looked up the details from the local paper, which is all online now."

Will jerked his head up sharply. I knew he had made the connection between the accidents; one occurring two hundred years ago and a much smaller incident yesterday, but would it bring him any closer to accepting my theory?

The Shadow Watchers

The silence of the woods pressed in on me; no wind disturbed the trees, no noisy rooks calling to each other. The mist covered everything in droplets of moisture. I looked round. "Where are the dogs?" I said and Will called them. Bess, the more obedient of the two, returned to us, panting, with her coat covered in dead leaves and mud. She turned to go back to Jasper, so we followed. He was only a short distance away, snuffling down a hole and scraping at it with his front paws.

"Come away, boy," said Will as we continued down towards the river. Will led us down a narrow path at right angles to the main track. "Good, it's still here," he said. "I thought it might be overgrown by now. It's a shorter route down to the river."

"Evie drove me down to the chapel, and we saw the old mill. We didn't stay long, as I wasn't feeling too good." I didn't tell him about our scrabbling about in the little churchyard and how I'd been overcome at the sight of the angel memorial to a tragic young mother.

The track led steeply downhill and Will led the way down the narrow path while the dogs streamed ahead, barking at nothing and each other. We could see the tangle of bushes and small trees on the opposite bank of the river, which slid silently towards the weir. It was almost twilight down here and the thought of seeing the Twins unnerved me, even with Will to 'protect' me.

"Was a boathouse standing when you were young?" I asked.

"There was no sign of it. I remember poking about where it stood, but never found anything apart from bits of broken crockery. We can go past it this way and then get back on the track above the Mill."

The path along the river looked perilously near the water and suddenly the memory of my nightmare the other night when I'd dreamt the Twins trying to push me into the water turned my legs to jelly.

"Will, I'm sorry, but can we go back? Sometimes fatigue just sweeps over me and makes me feel wimpy."

"Come on then, Wimp," said Will, amused. "Give me your good hand and I'll pull you back up the path. It is getting dark anyway. I was carried away, revisiting all my childhood haunts."

As we turned once again onto the main path and the gate loomed ahead of us, Will's phone rang. He whipped it out of his back pocket and looked at the caller display. "Ma," he said, putting it to his ear. "Tomorrow?" he said, pulling a face at me. "I've got to meet our colleagues from New York at Heathrow tomorrow morning, Ma."

He listened; his other arm draped across my shoulders. "What time does your plane land?" While he listened, he looked at me, chewing his lip and then looked at his watch as if calculating.

"We'll do our best, ma. Tell you what; if you ring me again when you get to your hotel, I'll arrange something then. No, don't be sorry, Ma, we'll make it work out. Don't worry. Have a safe journey and we'll both be there. Yes, she's with me now... yes, she is feeling a lot better. Love you too, Ma, Bye."

Will pulled a face. "Well, that's complicated things! Ma's flying in from France tomorrow morning. She says she has meetings with gallery owners about her new exhibition and thought it would be a good idea to meet up in London rather than come down here. Timing's not great, but she 'so wants to meet you', she says. But it means that you'll be coming back to London with me tonight. It'll be silly to make the journey up on your own tomorrow to see Ma."

Chapter Twenty

It was past eight o'clock in the morning; we were waiting in Arrivals at Terminal 3 and I was not feeling my best. I desperately tried to hide my discomfort from Will because he was twitchy, looking at the arrivals screen and glancing at his watch. I knew his nervousness stemmed from the fact that he was coming face to face with Rafaella in a few minutes with his washed-out fiancée hanging on to his arm. I had sussed out the location of the nearest loo and had been nibbling on a ginger biscuit as a preventative measure.

As soon as we'd started off last night, I regretted not packing something smarter for meeting up with Will's mother. I could feel preoccupation emanating from Will as we drove. I would have liked to have stayed at my flat and shared a cosy evening with Evie, but an early start for Heathrow would have been too awkward from there. As well as physically feeling pale and nauseous, it was clear that I was turning into a country bumpkin, having forgotten the few items of cosmetics that I had brought to Wiltshire. I'd literally thrown a few things in a backpack and returned the family tree scroll and photo albums to the library. Serena had insisted on changing the dressing on my hand as blood had seeped through. Luckily, the wounds were not angry looking and after covering them with lint and a clean bandage, she declared herself satisfied.

In bed the previous night, we'd talked about the itinerary and the meeting with his mother which, "frankly, I could have done without. She could have come almost any other time, but I suppose she has a busy schedule as well," Will had sighed. We decided last night that as soon as we'd heard from Roberta and hopefully meeting her before the day was out, I would get a tube or taxi back to my old flat and spend the night there. The next day, I'd get the train to Salisbury and arrange for Joe to collect me. Then I would be at Harthill House to make sure all the preparations were in place, while Will continued the mini tour. I was really looking forward to going back to the flat and catching up with Evie.

My night had been restless thinking about meeting Rafaella and meeting Roberta. Will also tossed and turned beside me. Will had witnessed my discomfort when I'd disappeared into the bathroom as soon as the alarm went off before six am. On the plus side, the hired minibus arrived exactly on time to collect us, and the driver, who introduced himself as Mick, was young, cheerful, and smart in white shirt, tie, and black trousers. At the airport, Will had found coffee and croissants, but I could only face occasional sips of water.

"Are you ok?" asked Will as I practised deep breaths through my nose and out through my mouth while we waited with crowds of people. I wished I could sit down, but I didn't want to spoil greeting our colleagues who'd probably be tired from traveling overnight.

The flight had landed some time ago, and the baggage was coming through, so they'd all be streaming through arrivals any minute. Mick had prepared a large card with Rafaella's name on it.

"Rafaella will recognise you straightaway, after all the time you've spent there!" I joked, but Will just looked doubtfully at me.

There was no time now for a loo visit and I rubbed my cheeks to bring some colour into them.

"There they are," said Will, stretching up and waving.

Rafaella was instantly recognisable. Even after a night flight, her glossy hair was neatly tied back and her dark eyes were alert and shining. She wore a body-hugging leather jacket and black leggings, boots, and a brightly patterned silk scarf around her shoulders. An oversize bag hung from her shoulder. She looked like a movie star and I half expected a phalanx of paparazzi to appear with cameras. Beside her and behind her was the rest of the team, familiar from our Skype conversations. One of them was wheeling a large baggage trolley filled with their combined luggage.

Rafaella spotted us. Correction spotted Will and lifted her hand in a graceful acknowledgement. Had she clocked that the pale mousey woman next to Will was me?

There was a tug at my elbow and I turned to see Kim, out of breath, with a huge smile on her face.

"Kim!" I said delightedly and hugged her, feeling better with her familiar presence to help dispel my nerves.

"I had to make sure Will had arrived, and the minibus. I couldn't bear it if Rafaella had to stand around waiting because of a mixup! I didn't know you'd be coming..." She didn't have time to finish as Rafaella and her colleagues emerged through the barriers at last and Will hurried off to greet them. As we followed him, I was still holding on to Kim's arm affectionately. I saw Will stop and self-consciously kiss her on both cheeks. He repeated the gesture with Ruby and shook hands energetically with the guys. If he was surprised to see Kim's sudden appearance, he didn't show it and we went through the process of introductions. Rafaella rested her hand lightly on my arm and gave me air kisses and then looked hard at me.

"Thank you so much for meeting us, Clemency, but you look exhausted. I hope all is well with your pregnancy?"

There was the briefest of pauses as all eyes focussed on me before excited chatter broke out again.

"Thanks for your concern, Rafaella. I'm fine and it's lovely to see you all in person instead of on screen. I hope you all had a good flight?" I was determined to sound friendly and professional instead of acting pale and fluttery. Rafaella's remark was not a tactful one to make at our first meeting.

I turned my attention to the others in Rafaella's party, as colour now suffused my cheeks. Ruby was small, with a mass of reddish blonde curls and brown eyes. She embraced me and greeted me in an Eastern European accent.

"Hi, Clemency, I'm so glad to get to meet you. I'm just so excited about this trip!"

Dunc Downing looked barely out of school, tall and loose-limbed, with a fresh-faced complexion and masses of freckles. His copper hair stood up straight from his forehead, but his laugh was infectious.

Sam Levy was tall, dark, and handsome; whip thin, with a serious expression and looking extremely fit, as he had to be on Rafaella's team.

Will had told us that Jimmy Jordan was Rafaella's second trek captain. I noticed his white teeth gleaming in the widest grin I'd ever seen. His dark head was shaved and shone in the overhead lights. Kim and I glanced at each other. They seemed to be a happy and lively bunch, and I knew we would all get along fine.

Will looked at his watch. He pulled out his phone and spoke briefly on it. I noticed he stood close to Rafaella while I had to work my way to stand beside him.

"If we make our way to the entrance, Mick will be waiting in the pickup area with the minibus to take you all to your first stop, your hotel, so we'd better keep moving. I'm sure you'll all want to freshen up before the next stop on our whirlwind tour."

Kim had chosen a small but well-equipped hotel in Bloomsbury and as they were being transported around by Mick, it meant they weren't subject to public transport, although they all seemed disappointed at not taking a tube somewhere. We waited in the lounge of the hotel while they went to their rooms and I'd persuaded Kim to stay with us to accompany them to the Tower in the event of Will and I rushing off to see his mother. After a very short fifteen minutes or so they all reappeared, still remarkably cheerful after their flight and keen to see the sights. Coffee and soft drinks and tea were ordered, and plates of assorted biscuits appeared. Jimmy was delighted with the size of the biscuits. "These are no cookies," he chortled. "Definitely daintily British!"

∼

My phone rang as I sat in the hotel lounge later that afternoon with a pot of mint tea on a small table beside me and the hum of traffic in the background.

"Can you get to The Laburnum Mews Hotel in Mayfair for six o'clock?" Will asked. "Ma has booked us in for dinner and will meet us in reception. Take a taxi, Clem, as I'm not sure where the nearest tube station is. Mick is going to drive me there after dropping everybody in the West End."

The Laburnum Mews Hotel was tucked away from the main streets at the end of a secluded cul-de-sac. It looked like a large French Maison with its black wooden louvred shutters and iron railings enclosing the frontage behind which bay trees stood in elegant planters. Four steps led up to the canopied entrance, and it automatically opened as I approached. Nervously, I raked my hair and hoped I didn't appear as pale as I felt. A doorman greeted me once inside the reception area, carpeted in a dark red floral pattern and lit by small table lamps, giving an ambient atmosphere. The reception desk itself was discreetly tucked behind potted plants and a display of early tulips.

"I'm here to meet...Mrs Payne-Ashton," I informed the receptionist, nearly blurting out 'Will's mother' by accident. "I'm Clemency Wyatt."

"Good evening, Ms Wyatt, Mrs Payne-Ashton is expecting you and Marius will take you up to her room." The doorman led me up a short flight of carpeted staircase to the next floor and tapped on one of the white doors with gilt-edged panels. It flew open almost immediately, as if Roberta had been waiting for the knock.

"Clemency, my dear, how lovely to meet you at last." She grasped my arm and drew me gently into the room, then turned back. "Thank you, Marius," she said, pushing something into the doorman's hand and closed the door.

"I thought it much more private to meet in my room. As you can see, the hotel is quite small and it's easy to overhear other conversations. I have been coming here for years; it's very homely and discreet and I've got to know the staff quite well, although not all stay very long."

She indicated a pair of armchairs. It wasn't a large room, and the furnishings were period. On the way over in the taxi, my thoughts had mulled over the person who was Will's mother. I knew very little about her, if truth be told. I would have recognised her in person from the portrait which hung in Harthill House, which depicted a fair headed woman with shoulder length hair pinned back at the sides by little curvy tortoiseshell combs, pleasant faced and blue eyed, which Will had inherited. She appeared strong willed: hadn't she upped sticks and deserted her husband, taking her baby with her, first to London and then when Will went to university, moving to France? Her actions seemed controlled, removing Will from his father and by words and deeds, influencing him against his home and possibly his father. So, understandably, I was filled with trepidation about our meeting.

I sat in one chair with Roberta opposite me. The years between her portrait sitting and the present sat lightly on her. Her hair was still soft and fair. She quietly appraised me, calmly and benignly, and I felt some tension slipping from me.

"I'm so pleased to meet you after all this time," she said. "You and Will have been together for such a long time and I feel dreadful that we haven't met before. He tells me all about you, so I feel I know you better than you know me. How are you feeling, my dear? Will said you've been having a horrid time so far."

I assured her that the worst was over. "I'm just taking one day at a time," I replied. "One day I'm good, the next I'm not!"

"What have you done to your hand?" she asked, staring at the dressing. I'd unwrapped the gauze earlier and inspected the damage. The messy wounds were healing but still sore and unsightly so I'd found a pharmacy, bought new dressing and tape which I'd applied clumsily with my good hand and then splashed out on a lipstick which I'd rubbed sparingly onto my cheeks.

I shrugged. "Oh, just a little argument with some barbed wire while I was walking," I answered, not untruthfully.

"Can I offer you a drink?" she asked, indicating a surface on which stood the usual kettle, and drinks paraphernalia laid on by hotels. "I like the convenience of these resources, even though my stay is all too brief. I won't offer you alcohol; we'll wait for Will to arrive and go to the dining room. I quite like a G &T about this time..."

Uncle Daniel was the link between us. "I've met Will's Uncle Daniel twice already since I've been at Harthill House. He is a keen historian, isn't he? I've been looking at the Family Tree scroll he created. It's been a help because I did not know Will owned such a big house. I think that was shock number two after the baby: nothing prepared me for its size and age when he drove me to Wiltshire to rest."

"It's a thorn in his side, I admit," said Roberta. "He would sell up if it wasn't for the stipulation in every will that the house and land be passed down to the next heir." She got up suddenly and busied herself pouring herself a G&T before sitting down again, turning the glass in her hands.

"Daniel is a good friend, as well as being my brother-in-law. He keeps me informed of the meetings of the trustees, even though all the minutes and actions of the meetings are emailed to me if I'm unable to attend in person. Even if Will attended, he never tells me what's transpired! To be fair, I haven't instilled in Will a love or loyalty to the family seat. Geoffrey did his best when Will stayed in vacations and they both loved the countryside around and the shooting and fishing. I think that's where Will developed his passion for exploration."

"What about you?" I asked tentatively as Roberta sipped from her glass. "Were you lonely there? I thought I'd be lonely when I first arrived; I was daunted by the size and the weight of history, but it is a lovely house. I feel silly mentioning it, but I have seen ghostly servants bustling about their duties as if the house was still in the nineteenth century. Uncle Daniel understood. He was interested when I mentioned ghosts or spirits or whatever you want to call them..."

Roberta stopped fiddling with her glass and narrowed her eyes at me.

It was so bizarre to be sitting in a bijou hotel having a cosy tête-à-tête with my prospective mother-in-law. While we should have been chatting about babygrows and finding out the sex of the foetus, I was chattering about ghosts.

"It does sound so ridiculous discussing ghosts – but where have you come across them?"

"The presences indoors are harmless; they aren't aware of our presence at all. But when I'm outdoors, I've seen figures in the woods and round the estate. I thought they were farmworkers at first, but Joe insists none are employed on the estate. I told Will, but he thinks my hormones are affecting my sanity."

"You've told Will?" She barked so fiercely that I recoiled.

"Yes, I had to. There was an incident with the Range Rover a couple of days ago and I knew it wasn't his fault."

Roberta insisted I told her about the accident and when I'd finished, she took a long sip of her G&T and sighed.

"I firmly believed that there was something evil around that place, but I never told William or Geoffrey. Like you, I doubted anyone would have believed me. And Daniel was living in Salisbury then," she stared off into the distance.

"I know who they are," I said, feeling a familiar pang of fear when she said evil spirits. "They're the Twins, George and Wilfred Barnard, born in the year 1812, the twin sons of Gerard Barnard: I've seen their photograph in an old family album......"

At that moment as Roberta looked aghast at me; there was a knock on the door. Swiftly, Roberta appeared to mentally shake herself. "William," she announced, standing up and draining her glass. "Let's not talk about it while he's here," she pleaded and headed for the door.

While I waited for Will, I wasn't sure whether I was relieved I'd divulged all to Roberta and convinced there were still a lot of unspoken words to come.

Will hugged his mother in the little entrance hall to the room. "Sorry I'm late, Ma," he said. "It took longer to get back from The Tower than we'd counted on once we'd rounded everyone up."

He hugged me, looking quizzically at my face. I wouldn't have minded a fortifying slug of G&T after my conversation with Roberta.

She chivvied us up and took us down to the dining room. For a modest hotel, the dining room took up half the area of the ground floor. It was obviously a favoured place as we threaded our way to a table guided by an attentive waiter. The food was good, not pretentious, and despite still feeling tense after our conversation, I was quite hungry. Roberta ordered house red wine, and I noticed that as soon as her glass was filled, she took rapid sips. *Was it because I'd raised the subject of malevolent beings? Had she turned to drink because of her experiences? Would I turn into an alcoholic after my experiences?*

Will didn't notice any tension and regaled us with the reactions of Rafaella's team to their historic tour.

"You wouldn't think they'd just got off a plane. They haven't stopped all day. After I've seen you into a taxi home, Clem, I'll go back to their hotel and make sure they're ok and geared up for another packed day tomorrow."

We steered round various subjects throughout the meal, but I could tell that Roberta was only paying scant attention. As we ordered tea for me and coffees for Roberta and Will at the end of the meal, she threw both of us off balance.

"When are you two thinking of getting married?" she said, leaning forward earnestly. "If your baby is to inherit, Will, he will have to be born inside of wedlock, to use an old-fashioned term. I'm sorry to offend your modern outlooks, but the terms of the Will are most definite."

Will looked totally gobsmacked. I was equally dumbfounded. Although marriage had lurked at the back of my mind since the pregnancy had been confirmed, I'd had other problems which took priority. And judging from Will's silence, marriage certainly wasn't high on his to do list either. He looked defensive and my heart quailed a little.

"There's too much going on at the moment, Ma," he said petulantly. "There's plenty of time, isn't there, Clem?"

Oh, how I wished he had taken my hand and announced, 'We'll marry as soon as things have calmed down!' He was frowning slightly, and I had a presentiment that marriage had not yet occurred to him. I still couldn't think of anything to say.

"For Clemency's sake, it would be nice if you married her before she has to take a midwife with her up the aisle or into a register office," Roberta remarked, oblivious to the waves of irritation emanating from Will. He glanced at my stomach. "There's nothing happening at the moment, Ma. She's not going to suddenly inflate like a balloon."

"You'll be surprised how soon Clemency will start to show," said Roberta, attempting to lighten the mood, but Will just glowered.

"Sorry, I need the cloakroom," I said, suddenly rising, almost upsetting my tea and looking round wildly for signs.

"Over there, my dear," Roberta pointed. "Are you all right?"

I nodded and wove through the tables, trying not to knock into backs of chairs and dining customers.

Thankfully, the loos were solid cubicles, and I bolted myself into one and tried not to burst into a frustrated storm of noisy tears. My fears were coming true: Will preferred Rafaella; he had no intentions of marrying me; no more daydreaming of being lady of the manor; I would have to get used to being a single parent.

Despite my misery and suppressed anger, I was conscious that I shouldn't be absent for too long. I pulled out a handful of tissue, blew my nose hard, flushed the loo, emerged from the cubicle and stood in front of the vanity unit. I wasn't usually tearful but since becoming pregnant, any little thing upset me and I was damned if I let either of them see my hurt.

Whatever Roberta had said to her son in my absence had had the desired effect. He stood up when he saw me and took my hand as I defiantly sat down.

"Sorry," I muttered. "Busy day." I knew I hadn't fooled Roberta, who was frowning sympathetically at me.

"It's my turn to apologise. It was insensitive of me to bring up wedding arrangements when you are both so busy organising business deals and party weekends," she said with a raised eyebrow and a hint of sarcasm.

I suppressed a smile at Roberta's acid remark. Will rubbed his thumb over the back of my hand.

"Clemmie and I have some talking to do, Ma. It hasn't been an easy time lately, for either of us, but we won't forget what you say. Just don't get me started on bloody archaic laws!" He glanced at his watch: "I ought to get back to our guests soon and make sure they're settled in; we've got another early start tomorrow."

Roberta tactfully conceded that there would be no more talk of marriage this evening. She kissed us both and said, "Please ring me tomorrow morning, Clemency. We haven't spoken for nearly long enough. I'm in Rodney's Gallery all day arranging my exhibition, so if you have a couple of hours to spare before returning to Wiltshire, I shall be so pleased to see you." She kissed me on both cheeks. "Good night to both of you. Please look after Clemency, Will." She hugged her son but shook him gently after her last sentence.

I promised Roberta I would ring her first thing.

Roberta turned and left us. I could see Will was eager to return to his charges as he kept glancing at his watch as we sat on a squashy sofa waiting for my taxi which the receptionist had ordered.

"I feel guilty leaving them on their own," said Will, looking at his watch yet again.

"Come on, Will, they're not children! I expect they're all more than capable of finding their way around the West End and they know the name and address of their hotel if they get lost. They are a lively bunch, aren't they? I think we'll all have a fun weekend together if there are no hitches."

Will squeezed me closer as I leant on his shoulder. "Between all of you, it will go perfectly, you'll see. Clem, I am sorry for saying such a crass thing about us before. Of course, we're going to be married. Ma just sprang it on us without warning and our concentration is all on getting this merger up and running, isn't it?"

"You are the one concentrating on the business, Will. I am concentrating on keeping this child safe in my womb."

"I promise as soon as there are bookings for US treks and the logistics are in place, we'll start planning. After I come back from New York, we'll go and see your Mum and Dad, shall we? I bet you haven't told them about the baby yet?"

"No, as you say, there's been too much happening," I said although I knew I'd been putting off breaking the news to them because I'd been so worried about losing the baby and on top of that, Will's preoccupation with the States.

"We'll make plans for the wedding and then we can tell them about the baby at the same time. That should render your mother speechless for a few seconds, at least. Not that she'll forgive me for knocking you up out of wedlock!" He grinned mischievously and I couldn't help but laugh at his correct assumption.

"We'll invite them both to Harthill House. Do you think that might push me up a few notches in your mother's estimation of me?"

"I'll have to have a camera ready for her expression when she sees the size of the place," I laughed. I kissed Will lightly. "But I'm holding you to all these promises, Will Payne-Ashton! No backtracking." I stared at him hard and he had the grace to flush slightly.

"I won't let you down again," he said, as he glanced away to look at his watch.

The receptionist approached to tell me that my taxi was waiting, so Will had no time to say any more as he waved me off before loping off toward Bloomsbury. He could easily have phoned the New Yorkers to check on them, but I knew Will well enough by now to know he had to be on hand for them throughout their stay.

As the taxi negotiated traffic, I relished the thought of a hot bath, fluffy dressing gown, my own bed, and Evie's chatter.

~

"Bloody Hell," said Evie succinctly when I'd brought her up to date on events. I'd had a long soak and now lay on the sofa in our flat with a cup of herbal tea while Evie sipped a late-night whisky. "So, seeing the Twins was the probable reason that Roberta ran away from Harthill House," she surmised.

"We didn't get that far because Will turned up, but she looked shocked when I described them and gave them names."

"Well, I've been doing a bit more digging on Will's family tree on our swanky new genealogy software and there's more than a bit of a mystery in there," Evie said, preparing to launch into a full-length history lecture.

I yawned loudly. "What with Rafaella practically telling me I looked like death warmed up when she got off the plane, having to meet my future mother-in-law before Will arrived, Roberta springing the wedding question onto Will who practically blew his top... sorry, I am curious to know, but as I was up before dawn this morning it has been an emotional rollercoaster of a day. I promised Roberta that I'd see her at her gallery before travelling down to Wiltshire, so I'd better go to bed now," I said smothering another yawn. "You can tell me what you've discovered in the family tree when I see you at Harthill."

"Look, if you are meeting Roberta in the morning, I can arrange to take a bit of time off work and we can drive down together in the afternoon. It will be less hassle for you than catching tubes and trains and then waiting to be picked up from Salisbury."

I beamed at Evie. "That would be perfect. I'll ring Serena first thing tomorrow to let her know. I'll be glad for your support. Don't get me wrong, the New York team is all lovely. You will like them too, but Rafaella is in a different league."

"Go and get your beauty sleep then-I'll wake you up before I leave for work tomorrow."

I climbed into my own bed, aware of the hum of traffic and streetlights in contrast to the silence and darkness at Harthill House. *I feel safe here, away from the Twins. Perhaps I should take Roberta's advice and not stay there any longer than necessary. But I love the house.* I cradled my hardly there bump and whispered aloud: "we are going to be alright, you and me. Nobody is going to harm you, and I promise to keep you safe." As I stroked my stomach, I swear I felt a tiny sensation, like the delicate brush of butterfly wings inside me.

Despite being in my old bed, I had a restless night and was dozing when Evie knocked at seven am. She was going into the museum early and return here hopefully by 1pm. It gave me plenty of time to meet Roberta and although feeling queasy I forced myself to eat some toast before phoning Serena first and then Roberta. She answered promptly and I could hear clinks of breakfast china in the background. She insisted on ordering a taxi for me, so I had time to ransack my drawers and wardrobe to search for something other than the fleece hoodies and jeans I had been wearing at Harthill House. I quickly chose a couple of long tunic style tops and leggings which would be less restrictive than my jeans and a tawny silk shirt, which I decided to wear on Friday. I folded them in my small bag with some colourful scarves, ankle boots, and my cosmetic bag and quickly zipped it up. I knew I could not compete with Rafaella in the fashion stakes, but I could at least have a few more options to boost my morale! There were no messages from Will. He would be giving all his attention to his other little team. My phone pinged to let me know the cab was outside. What else would Roberta tell me?

When the cab pulled up outside Rodney's Gallery, a double

fronted shop, both large windows displaying artworks varying from abstract to portraiture, Roberta appeared, paid the driver, then helped me out.

"Welcome," she said as she kissed both cheeks. She seemed lighter in spirit today, maybe because she had met me and got her worry about marriage off her chest. Roberta led me through the airy ground floor space; the walls adorned with framed pictures and easels artfully placed. "Which paintings are yours?" I asked, not wishing to appear to be ignorant. Roberta led me to a side alcove displaying about a dozen rural scenes. "Some are in acrylic as the colours are brighter. I have used gouache as well, but I favour old fashioned water colour best," she said, viewing them critically. "Most of them are around my home in France, and a few of typical English countryside."

"I like them all. The colours seem to glow," I said truthfully.

"Thank you, Clemency, but I haven't brought you here in order for you to make a purchase," she laughed. Come upstairs, I need my morning coffee and I expect you will only have tea or water? Arturo?" she called softly to a young man with a topknot dressed in a black polo necked jumper and black trousers who was tucked discreetly behind a small desk in a corner. As he looked up, she pointed upstairs, and he nodded.

The large room upstairs was a complete contrast to the clean open spaciousness of the gallery below. Several tables filled the space, all covered in the paraphernalia needed to prepare for framing, and the walls were stacked with more frames and pictures, either in bubble wrap or draped in material. Roberta switched on the kettle in the little kitchenette at the back with a window overlooking a surprisingly long garden full of nodding daffodils and small shrubs. We sat in comfortable chairs overlooking the garden and warmed by the radiator under the window.

"So," Roberta said at last. "You have seen the same ghosts that I may have sensed. When you described them, I'm sure I glimpsed them at some point. You have identified them. Are you sure you hadn't seen the photos before your encounters?"

"No, definitely not. I'd seen them on quite a few occasions by the time we found the old family photograph albums. Evie, my friend, was keen to match up any photos to the names in the family tree. When I came across the photo of the twins taken when they were quite old, they were dressed just as I had seen them and it gave me a terrible shock."

"They are evil. You described a near accident in Will's car. The same happened to me when I was driving; they suddenly appeared in front of the windscreen and I had to swerve violently. Not just once, but another time..." she stopped, looking distressed before continuing. "It happened not just to me either. After that, I had no choice but to leave Harthill House because I was living in fear of my life every day." Roberta looked at me with such grief in her eyes I didn't want her to tell me anymore. And she must have seen the look of fear on my face because she abruptly pulled herself together. "So that is why I would advise you not to stay at Harthill House any longer than necessary."

"I'm going back this afternoon because we are hosting our colleagues from New York," I said. "But it will be such a busy weekend I'm not likely to be wandering about outside on my own. They've never appeared inside the house, which makes me think that they never actually lived in the house when they were alive."

Roberta sighed and refilled her coffee cup. She offered me more tea, but I refused. I needed to get back soon to be ready for Evie.

"I must admit, I know little of the history of Harthill House. We had friends who came to stay at weekends and, of course, there was all the administration of the estate and I helped Geoffrey with all that. He spent a lot of time on the family history and estate management and he loved walking about the estate and bird watching and fishing. He'd be out of the house nearly all day in the summer with the dogs and arrive home late for supper very often. He was always totally surprised how the hours had passed. And of course, that was pre mobile phone days so there was no reminding him by text!"

"If only it would be easy to exorcise their spirits," said Roberta suddenly. "I have no knowledge of the practise and wouldn't know if it can be done outdoors. If you know who they are, surely something could be attempted. They can't be allowed to terrorise people and cause actual physical harm forever."

"Evie has a theory that their father was convinced he would inherit. He was Gerard, the youngest son of Sir Horace Barnard, who built Harthill House when he married. I can't remember much of the family tree, but the line of succession continued through a granddaughter and her son and his heirs, which probably made Gerard very angry."

"I haven't given any thought to family trees and lines of succession for years," said Roberta, staring out of the window. The daffodils nodded sociably in the light breeze, and a blackbird sang his heart out on a branch of a budding tree. She shivered and turned again to me. "I know you have to go back, but will you promise me not to stay any longer than necessary?"

I shrugged because a new sensation of stubbornness arose in me. "I don't want them to win," I said defiantly. "They've succeeded in causing distress for too many years. I almost wish I could take them on in a battle of wills, but I know I can't do that. I promise I will be careful, Roberta, and I'll keep in close touch with you."

Roberta stood and folded me into a tight embrace. "You and William are so right for each other and if I was religious, I would pray for your safety. Maybe it's not too late to start! And remind him of wedding bells very frequently. He has inherited his father's lack of awareness of time passing!" She gave a slight laugh and led me downstairs after phoning for a cab.

"I hope your weekend goes happily. So many young people enjoying themselves. It will lift you from this depressing conversation we've just had." She kissed me on both cheeks again and handed me into the waiting cab, remaining on the pavement as we pulled away into the traffic. I turned to wave out of the rear window before the cab turned the corner and she was still there, her arms wrapped round her upper body.

Chapter Twenty-One

Evie was already home making a cheese and tomato sandwich. "Would you like one?" she asked when Clemency came in. "It will be easier if you have a sandwich with me instead of watching me eat on my own."

She tutted when she noticed Clem wavering.

"I've got so used to denying myself sustenance in case it makes me sick, but it makes no difference. I'm sorry I'm a bit late," she said, and Evie suppressed a smile when she saw Clemency eyeing the thick slice of cheese in her sandwich with trepidation. "I did a detour to the office after I'd left Roberta to say hello and reassure them that I'd be greeting them at the door at Harthill and not on my deathbed! Will brought all Rafaella's team round first thing this morning, apparently, before they set off on their sightseeing. According to Kim, they were impressed we ran such a successful business in such tiny premises! Their office in New York is quite grand, Will said."

Once on the way, Evie glanced over to Clemmie as her head sank onto her chest. In sleep she looked less troubled, but Evie noticed the bruised appearance of the skin under her eyes and she still looked too thin. Involuntarily, her left hand crept up to tidy back a stray lock of hair from Clem's face. She and Clemmie had been firm friends for years now; through university, finding jobs and lodgings and then sharing their flat. She'd been attracted to Clemmie at Uni, but Clemmie was straight and Evie recognised Clemmie had no inkling of her feelings. She'd teased Evie mercilessly, calling her big sister, second mother and her favourite title matron. Not once had Evie let Clemmie know her true feelings. Their friendship was too precious. Clemmie had had a couple of disastrous relationships with immature male students and she'd used Evie's willing shoulder to weep on and share cheap plonk to cover her hurt. Then Will had appeared on the scene and Evie had known almost instantly that they were an 'item'. They'd decided on building up their bike trekking business during Clemency's final year using a legacy that Will had been left. They'd even managed to convince a sceptical Evie with their enthusiasm, and Evie had been touched when Clemmie decided to continue sharing with Evie even after her engagement to Will.

"Will's away so much touring and trekking." Clemmie had explained to Evie. "I'd get lonely rattling around his flat and I'd miss you. Will totally understands and accepts it all."

The arrangement worked well and Evie had got used to Will's frequent presence in the flat, although in her heart she was convinced that he took Clemmie for granted. And now.... concentrating on negotiating the slip road on to the A30 to the West, she halted her thoughts for a while as she adjusted to two-way traffic again. Glancing again at Clemmie's sleeping form, she silently cursed Will for his, in her opinion, cavalier attitude towards Clemmie. As far as she was concerned, Will seemed to be unhealthily obsessed with this new venture in the States and although she'd only heard Clemmie's description of Rafaella, her intuition told her Clemmie was right to be fearful of Rafaella's attraction.

"Well, I'll be right beside you for as long as you want me," she said aloud.

"What, were you talking to me, Evie? Sorry, I must have dropped off. Where are we?" Clemency sat up straight, adjusted her seat belt, pushed back her hair and grinned sheepishly at Evie. "I've not been much company while you've been driving. How much further?"

"Not too far to go now. We're on the A30 to Salisbury, so we should get to Harthill House well before dark."

"I'll give Serena a call to let her know we'll be back soon. I still don't know what to call Harthill yet. It's not exactly home, but I feel a responsibility for it. Will said we'd make wedding plans soon, but I really don't think he'll want to live there after we're married and the baby comes along."

Evie pushed her glasses up her nose and refrained from commenting. Clemmie hadn't said anything about fearing the presence of the Twins that seemed to be the number one obstacle to living at Harthill House.

"Concentrate on the weekend first. I'm sure it's going to be a big hit with all the teams," she said. "You and Will are going to be Lord and Lady of the manor in everyone's eyes, so make the most of it!"

"I hope the weather stays fine so that everybody can have a good tramp through the estate – ha - that sounds grand, doesn't it, the estate! Even though there's not much of it left, it sounds very British! I bet Will is keen to drag anyone interested round for a couple of miles, at least. He'll be wishing everyone had bikes, then he would lead them halfway round Wiltshire!"

"And for lazy people who just want to sit by a log fire I can give a potted history of Harthill House if they are interested," said Evie. "In fact, I think you'll find the weekend will go quicker than you realise."

"You must also be careful with Mollie. When I mentioned you

were prepared to talk about the history of the house and estate, she got quite -well- animated, is the only way I can describe her attitude. We all had to placate her."

"OK, fair enough, we can always let people know Mollie knows some interesting family history! The servants of big houses are usually the first to know good gossip! And your pesky ghosts should be lying low with everybody trampling round the grounds!" Evie declared vehemently.

Evie put Radio 4 on to listen to some discussion while Clemency slumped in the passenger seat, chewing her lip. Negotiating the build-up of late afternoon traffic around Salisbury, she sensed Clemency's tension.

"I'm just thinking of what the Twins did when Will passed the ash," Clem answered Evie's enquiring look.

"Right, close your eyes. We're just approaching the gate and I'll put my foot down," Evie said, determinedly.

Obediently Clem closed her eyes as the car swung to the right and Evie sped up the deserted drive, trees standing sentinel, but she made no comment until they crunched onto gravel. "You can open your eyes now, Clem. We're here and no sign of the bastards!"

The dogs had heard the car with a chorus of barking and ran out to greet them as soon as Joe opened the door.

"Welcome back," he said, taking the bags. "Serena is in the kitchen with a brew on, and I'll take your bags upstairs."

The kitchen was warm and bright and filled with the aroma of freshly baked scones. Matt jumped up from the table, hastily swallowing a sizeable lump of scone, and Serena bustled around with mugs and plates.

"Brian Chadwick is coming tomorrow with his kit and caboodle," she said, pouring hot water onto Clemency's chamomile tea bag. "He's bringing a couple of chaps to move furniture around, although Joe will help, of course. He's even bringing a fridge freezer to keep the ready prepared stuff in. It'll be like Piccadilly circus in here. Not that I mind, of course," she added as Clem gave her an anxious look. "I've just finished a mammoth batch of scones, which I'll freeze for the weekend when they've cooled down. If there are any left!" she added, looking pointedly at Matt.

"You wanted my opinion of them, Serena. You know you would have been upset if I'd refused! It's good to see you home again, Clemency, and you too Evie." Matt drained his mug, touching Clemency on the arm on his way out.

"I suppose being a farmer means he doesn't get much of a social life," said Evie, helping Serena pack scones into plastic boxes for freezing.

"There's a popular Young Farmers club that meets in Ringwood down the road towards Bournemouth," said Joe. "He goes to quiz nights and for a drink now and again, but obviously he hasn't met the right one yet!"

Evie had noticed Matt's eyes light up when Clemency entered the kitchen and his affectionate gesture. Interesting, she mused.

Chapter Twenty-Two

When I went upstairs to unpack, Roberta texted me. There were no missed calls from Will.

> I hope your trip to London was not too tiring for you, my dear. We must meet more often and I'm sure when you are back in the City we can arrange some lunches. I feel I ought to apologise on behalf of my idiot son and his outrageous behaviour at dinner. I hope you gave him a piece of your mind! He likes to think he can always have his own way. My fault, I think, for not being stricter in his upbringing! Please take care, Clemency, and I hope your house party goes with a swing! The Americans will adore the old house!

I saw she hadn't apologised for bringing up the M word. Evie had commented on Roberta's decision to leave Harthill House when Will was very young.

"Something terrible did happen," I'd said. "She admitted to having an accident caused by the Twins as well. And she said it happened not just to her... I think she'd open up more if I saw her again soon. If I knew exactly what I had to contend with, it might be possible to overcome their evil."

Now, sitting cross-legged on my bed in a surprisingly warm bedroom because Joe had adjusted thermostats, I pondered Roberta's encounters with the twins. She'd recognised my description of them and hadn't laughed them off as a figment of my imagination. She was very keen that I returned to London as soon as the house party was over. Both she and Daniel had exhorted me to take care. The Twins were a real threat to me. But how could dead twins mount a fight for inheritance from beyond the grave? It made no sense.

Apart from Roberta and Mollie, none of the others had even hinted at seeing spectral figures. Mollie was secretive, hinting then pulling back. And she'd left me alone in the nursery that day when I'd heard a baby crying and someone screaming.

Evie stuck her head round the door. "Are you OK?" she asked and then noticed my bag still on the chair where Joe had deposited it. She went over to it and started taking out my clothes. "I'll lay these out to let the creases out. You can't be the Lady of the Manor Hostess greeting her guests looking like a sack of potatoes!"

"Thanks, but I don't care what I look like right now! I'd like to sleep for a week!"

"What about supper? Serena has something smelling tasty on the go. Shall I bring it up for you?"

I had to laugh at Evie's expressions. She knew how to handle my moods instinctively, and I'd miss her if I came to live here with the baby. But inadvertently, she'd helped me decide. I wasn't going to dress to impress. Nor would I go head-to-head with Rafaella and compete against her in beauty or power dressing to vie for Will's attention. He'd laugh if he saw me with cosmetics trowelled on. I had an acceptable dress for Saturday night and had brought smart casuals for the rest of the weekend. My task was to make everybody welcome and comfortable, and I was good at that. Rafaella was good at flashing her teeth and cleavage and tossing her super shiny hair. *Could I be just a teeny bit jealous?* If I couldn't match her assets, then I would not lower my pride by throwing myself between her and Will. If he wanted to fawn over her all weekend, that was his concern. If it became too much, I'd think of a way of making him aware of how incautious he was behaving.

"I'll be down in a minute," I conceded. "The last thing I want right now is for Serena and Joe to start worrying about me again."

∼

I was up and showered before I gave Serena any more work to do preparing breakfast for me. I'd wrapped a plastic bag round my hand and looked at the now grubby dressing which I'd hastily applied the day before yesterday. It didn't look very hygienic.

I knocked on Evie's door and when there was no answer, went in. Her bed clothes were flung back, curtains pulled back and window open.

The smell of toast rose as I went down the stairs to the kitchen and the fact that my stomach didn't rebel encouraged me. "Morning everybody," I said. Joe was tying his boots and Serena was making another list.

"Good morning, Clemency. Doctor Laidlaw rang a few moments ago; he's on his way to another patient and he said he'd call in on his way back."

"That's lucky then," I replied. "I was just about to take off this dressing, but Doctor Laidlaw can do it and hopefully all's well underneath now. Can I make myself a cup of Lady Grey tea, please? It'll be a change from ginger tea and it's not as strong as normal tea."

I sat with Evie and Serena, carefully nibbling toast spread thinly with homemade marmalade. No point in overdoing things.

"I'm going to clear away all the surfaces in here, so Brian has plenty of room when he arrives later," Serena announced.

"We can't sit round idly," said Evie.

"You can do the rounds with me. I'd like to see all the work Serena and Mollie have been doing in the last couple of days," I said to Evie.

"Oh, please, if you can check, we haven't forgotten towels."

Evie and I got up. "May as well start now," I said.

We met Mollie coming out of our bathroom with her basket of cleaning stuff. "Mollie, you are a star," I said. "Thank you so much for doing all this extra work we've loaded on to you. I hope it hasn't tired you out."

"Bless you m'dearie," she said, her little bright eyes twinkling. "Hard work never killed anyone, as my mother and grandmother used to say! I quite like all the excitement; it makes a change at my time of life!"

She stomped determinedly down the passage, and Evie and I just suppressed our smiles.

"When we've checked the rooms, I'd like to go into the library and just have another look for interesting facts in case our visitors are curious. And Honoria's Journal. It must be somewhere in this house. Hopefully, it's warmer than a morgue in there today!"

"The Family Tree scroll, map, and photo albums are in the long drawers. We'll have to make the small sitting room accessible to everybody as a quiet retreat."

On the top floor Joe had completed an amazing job in transforming the nursery into a comfortable bedroom and with the rocking chair adorned with cushions. I doubted whether I'd heard a child's distressed cries. Perhaps I had genuinely dreamed it. He'd done a decent job in the nanny's room as well.

Joe's voice echoed up the back stairs.

"Clemency, Doctor Laidlaw's here. I've put him in the sitting room."

"While you are with the good doctor, I'll disappear into the library for a while," said Evie. "Good luck!"

Doctor Laidlaw stood when I entered the sitting room and extended his hand. He wore the same homely Arran sweater and red cords from previous visits and smiled a welcome. After greeting him, I held up my hand swathed in the dressing. "I was hoping you'd have a look at this and if I can leave off the dressing now."

"Well, I think I'll check on junior's progress first and then we'll have a look at your hand."

How stupid of me. I'd forgotten his primary purpose and sat down obediently.

He went through the motions of blood pressure and routine questions and I lay back on the cushions while he listened with his old-fashioned trumpet instrument and the flames leapt quietly in the grate.

"He's got a good strong heartbeat and your blood pressure is fine. Are you experiencing much sickness?"

"Some days are good and some bad. I'm sure the bouts are getting less frequent."

"Good, it's important that you keep up mealtimes, even if they are small and often. If your blood sugar levels drop, we don't want you feeling faint again."

After reminding him of the date of my next scan, I showed him my hand. While he was donning surgical gloves, I explained the cause of the injury, obviously omitting that I believed the Twins had been behind the incident.

I winced a bit when he pulled off the last of the dressing. The wounds were healing. The stitches were meant to dissolve, but some had stretched the skin tightly, making the wounds red and angry looking. Doctor Laidlaw looked closely for signs of infection but was satisfied they were clean. He took a small pair of surgical scissors from their antiseptic wrapper and, before I could turn my head away in anticipation of some pain, he'd snipped the offending stitches and freed them from the skin.

"I'll put some new dressing on. It's too soon to leave the wounds open just yet," he said, dabbing my palm with antiseptic.

"That's a pity. We have quite a busy weekend coming up with lots of guests and I was hoping not to be bandaged up," I said.

"Oh, I can do discreet dressings," he assured me. "It's been a while since there was any kind of function taking place here."

While he rummaged in his bag for a clean dressing, I asked him about Will's birth.

"You mentioned before that Will was actually born here."

"That's right, he was a few weeks premature and his mother was due to give birth in London, but she had a car accident and I had to rush here when Geoffrey phoned urgently. I was a fully practising GP back them and I was able to bring a midwife with me as well, which was fortunate as William's start in life was a tad fraught, shall we say. Fortunately, he was a born fighter. Sadly, the same outcome wasn't to be with his older brother a few years earlier."

My hand jerked in surprise when I heard his words, and he apologised for hurting me.

"No, you didn't hurt me, Doctor Laidlaw; I didn't know Will had a brother."

"Sadly, he died at birth, my dear. Again, he was some weeks premature. And strangely, now I come to think back, Roberta was just returning from somewhere in her car and she crashed it into a tree coming up the drive. An ambulance was called on that occasion and Roberta was rushed to hospital, but nothing could be done to save the baby."

My blood ran cold.

"However, that was years ago now and you have much to look

forward too. I wish I could see young William again and offer him my congratulations."

"He'll be here on Friday and over the weekend. You are very welcome to call in any time to see him." I covered up my distress with pleasantries and offered him more coffee, but he stood up to gather his things together.

"Thank you, I might just do that, my dear. It would do me a power of good to see him strong and healthy and a very lucky man to find you." He shook my good hand, and I saw him out to the front door where his muddy Subaru stood.

"I'd like to check your hand again anyway," he added and then called a greeting as Joe appeared round the corner.

I had an appointment next week at the District Hospital for my hand to be checked, but I preferred Doctor Laidlaw, so I phoned the hospital to cancel it. As I closed the door, my hands shook. The discovery that Roberta had lost a child before Will's birth shocked me, and for a moment I stood in the hall oblivious to the gleaming floor and table bearing a huge bowl of bright daffodils and catkins. There'd been an entry in Geoffrey's diary that had puzzled me, and I wanted to see it again.

I grabbed the key to the study and ran up to the top floor. If Mollie confronted me again, it was none of her business. The study was as I had left it, and the woman in the cloche hat smiled serenely out of her portrait. *I must look through the photo albums to discover who she is.* I pulled out the 1973 diary from the desk drawer, murmuring an apology to Will's father for disturbing his study. There was the entry: *'Terrible day- Roberta in hospital- baby could not be saved.'* I sat down suddenly in the chair and gazed out of the small window at the bare tops of the trees that lined the drive. I was now convinced that Roberta had met with her two car accidents at the old ash tree and that the Twins were behind the crashes. Anger suffused me and I could have taken an axe to that tree there and then. It was irrational, I knew, but if the scene of that first accident in 1809 was removed, perhaps the spirits of those vengeful twins would not be able to feed on the negative energy surrounding it. My mind was in such turmoil that I only heard Evie calling my name when I was going downstairs to return the key.

"We were wondering where you'd got to," said Evie. "Serena wants to get lunch over in time for the caterer's arrival."

Lunch did nothing to suppress my thoughts.

"How did you get on with Doctor Laidlaw?" Serena asked.

"Oh fine, baby's fine, I'm fine. He changed the dressing on my hand and it's a nuisance that I've got to have it on when all the guests arrive, but he may call in again sometime over the weekend to see if it's healed enough to take off."

I could see Evie looking at me oddly, but I couldn't find it in me to put on a jolly face and crack jokes. I escaped while Evie was stacking the dishwasher and sat on my bed. *I'll have to leave here and return to London before an accident happens to me. One accident has happened already and there is no knowing whether I can prevent another one unless I remove myself.* It was vexing and frustrating because the house had possibilities for future use and I was growing to love it here despite the Twins.

Joe had explained that Harthill House didn't have planning permission to become a country hotel. It had been raised years ago in a Trustee meeting when Will said he wouldn't be living there. The house had never been connected to main sewers and the water supply came from a private reservoir nearby. All the properties nearby had hidden cess pits or sewage tanks which had to be emptied regularly by waste collection lorries. I'd screwed up my face in distaste and Joe had laughed!

In the distance, I heard the dogs barking excitedly and gathered myself together to greet Brian Chadwick. Joe led Brian and his men outside so they could unload the fridge freezer to take into the back entrance. A couple of portable hotplates were left in the space under the grand staircase, along with a stack of smart dining chairs. Evie and I carried table linen, and I watched as crates of crockery and glasses were carried from the van through the hall. And all the time as I went through the motions of checking and agreeing and nodding amiably, Doctor Laidlaw's words filled my mind: *"First baby could not be saved, Will was premature."*

When the very last crate had been stacked in the basement passageway and Brian explained that he and his some of his team would be arriving early on Friday, Serena supplied tea and biscuits and I was beginning to doubt whether I could manage a weekend of jollity with my colleagues and the overseas ones unless I shook off this feeling of doom.

"Are you sure you're ok?" asked Evie. "Did the doctor really say everything is ok? You seem a bit distracted. If you're worried about the weekend, Brian Chadwick looks like he could manage a royal banquet without breaking sweat and your guests will lap up every minute of their stay. If the weather's not good, maybe we can borrow your minibus driver to take people out."

"Oh, Mick, the minibus driver, I forgot all about him. He'll need somewhere to sleep. I hope he's not expected to stay in a hotel or bed and breakfast. I must ask Serena." I snapped out of my preoccupation with the past.

Brian and his crew were preparing to go and recovering my manners I thanked him profusely; they'd been too busy to notice me moping in the background. Joe led them out of the back door, and I explained to Serena about the minibus driver. She looked at her notebook of lists on the table and ran her finger down a page.

"There's the nanny's room on the top floor. It's a bit poky, but Joe located a mattress and Mollie and I gave it a spring clean only yesterday, so he can go in there and share the bathroom with Ben and Andy."

As I watched Serena consult her lists, I thought about the list I could make about my life at present:

Number 1: Undo Rafaella's spell over Will.
Number 2: Stop being sick and generally useless.
Number 3: Tell Mum and Dad about pregnancy.
Number 4: Tie Will down to arrange a wedding date.
Number 5: GET RID OF TWINS.

I switched attention to Serena again before I could add more to my mental list.

"Thanks, Serena, I'd better phone Will just to tell him there's room for the driver. I don't suppose he's thought about it either."

I texted Will. He was bound to be occupied showing them round somewhere. Surprisingly, he got back almost immediately.

> Brilliant, I forgot about him! Well done, Clem! We are all exhausted now, going back to the hotel for a rest! See you soon xxx

Chapter Twenty-Three

"It looks absolutely stunning!" Serena and I stood admiring the long table covered with a snowy cloth, the arranged place settings, folded napkins, glasses reflecting the glow from the soft lamplight and flames from the log fire. Candlesticks added height and in the middle was a tall silver cake stand that Joe had polished up on which black and green grapes were draped.

Brian and his crew had worked hard that morning putting up the table, arranging chairs and then laying up each place setting with care. He stood with his arms folded and a satisfied grin on his face.

"This is the biggest spread we've had for years," Mollie said. "I grew up with Master Geoffrey, but there were no grand parties until Miss Pauline got married and had her wedding reception here. That were a posh do. We all had to dress up in proper servants' uniforms. Master Geoffrey got married in London and brought his bride to live here and there weren't no parties after that." She looked momentarily sad, but said no more.

"I can't thank you all enough," I said, feeling unexpectedly emotional. "You've all had such a big upheaval recently."

"Seeing the house like this makes it all worthwhile," Joe briefly put his arm round my shoulder and squeezed.

"Wait till the weekend finishes and the clearing up starts and then see how you feel!"

"Well, let's all go down to the kitchen and have an early lunch, and then we can leave Brian and his helpers to get on with it." Serena had her sensible head on as always and we all obeyed except Brian, who excused himself to sort out his team who had taken over the basement corridor as a preparation place.

I looked at my watch again. Will had messaged earlier to say they were all on track and there was plenty of time to pick the others up from Salisbury train station. My phone rang again as we were going down the basement stairs. Looking at the caller display, expecting it to be Will or Kim, my heart sank to see Mother's name there. *Mum*, I mouthed to Evie, and she pulled a half-terrified expression.

I doubled back and went into the sitting room. Talking to Mum was never straightforward, and I felt a twinge of guilt for the long gap in communications.

"What can be so important in your life that prevents you from phoning your parents for weeks? We could be ill and you would never know. It surely can't be your little business keeping you so very busy every hour of the day and night." Mum didn't even give me the chance to say hello.

"Hello, Mum, how are you and dad? Yes, I am sorry not to have been in touch, but I'm sure Thomas would tell me if one of you fell sick. As it happens, I did have a bit of a tummy bug, which put me out of action for a time, but I'm fine now. No, I didn't want you to come up and look after me, Mum, in case it was contagious."

Mum rambled on for a while and I looked at my watch again. I needed to change into something decent to meet everybody soon. "Well, we have been busy at Tough Treks, Mum. We are negotiating a partnership with a similar outfit in the States which has taken up our time and Will has been going over there.... no, I didn't go, Mum, because of my tummy upset."

The conversation went on one-sidedly with Mum going on about visits to dentists and opticians and the unreliability of dry cleaners to do her sitting room long curtains. What I couldn't tell my mother over the phone was that I was pregnant, had dreadful bouts of sickness, was scared about a possible miscarriage, and was trying to restore myself in Will's enormous country pile. I wished I could. I wished my mother had possessed that wonderful intuitive maternal streak that would have had her rushing down to be by my side, supporting me and looking for effective natural remedies. If I told her over the phone, after a long time without speaking to her, it would only invite probable outrage and outpouring of her principled opinions. As Mum carried on, it made me determined not to be a remote mother, where nothing was ever suitable enough to give spontaneous affection. And whatever would she think if I said I was expecting a large party of colleagues for a celebration this very afternoon and had no time to talk anymore? Hurriedly I made an excuse that on overseas call was waiting for me and finished the call with a promise that I would ring again soon. "Love to Dad," I said before finishing.

Serena had kept a bowl of soup warm on the hotplate. Not that I felt like eating anything, but I forced myself. "My mother! I said lightheartedly, pulling a wry face. By her enquiring look, I recognised Serena was longing to ask if my mother knew about the pregnancy.

"We haven't told my parents I'm pregnant yet. Things have been uncertain, and I didn't want to tell them until I feel better, but we have plans to tell them soon."

A small table had been set up in the Drawing Room for afternoon tea. The room resembled a setting for a Jane Austen drama.

Joe entered through the front door with a large canvas bag full of logs for the hall fire. I moved off the fender while he filled up the log basket. There was a commotion from downstairs and Bess and Jasper burst into the Hall barking, followed by an anxious-looking Serena. The dogs had heard the minibus, even though it wasn't yet in sight. We all moved to the door, looking out expectantly, and my stomach flipped.

"I hope they all like dogs," said Serena, "and no one is allergic to dog or cat hairs. It would be impracticable to keep them shut up in our flat all weekend. I've already had to tip them out of the kitchen into the boiler room while all the food preparation is going on."

No one replied as at that moment, the minibus crunched onto the gravel and pulled up. Joe opened the door and two of the young men belonging to Brian's crew appeared. "We'll help carry bags," one of them stated.

First out was Will, and the dogs raced out to him. Then, one by one, the combined teams climbed out and stood looking up and around in total amazement. Two of Rafaella's team already had cameras out. I recognised Dunc Downing by his hair as he videoed the teams assembling and waited as Mick and Hugo pulled out luggage. We all moved towards each other and I felt extra courage in the company of Evie and Serena and Joe. Before I could decide how to greet Will, he enveloped me in a tight hug. I was so happy at that moment all my confidence flooded back as I kissed him! If I'd been a dog, I'd have capered around like Bess and Jasper! Then I turned to the others and set about shaking hands, laughing, asking all the routine greeting questions. I gave Kim and Ruby hugs as they stood round eyed.

"All I can say is Oh. My. God!" said Kim.

"Wait till you see inside!" I laughed. "We'll show you your rooms and then catch up!" I addressed them all and stood aside as they entered Harthill House. Rafaella lingered slightly and then turned to give air kisses on my both cheeks. "You are one lucky girl!" she said, sweeping her arms to show the house. "And you are looking so much better than when we met at the airport."

"It's lovely to see you, all of you," I responded warmly. "I have to confess to lots of nerves about arrangements, but everyone has pulled out all the stops."

Everyone stood in the hall, looking around with awe. Even Will looked pleased, pointing at the stuccoed ceiling and describing it to Jimmy. Joe said something to him and Will led the way to the stairs, with Brian's lads following with luggage.

"Some of you are this way, some that way," laughed Joe as we divided up. I went with Serena and Kim, Rafaella and Ruby up the main staircase, with Evie taking some of the lighter luggage. Will hesitated before joining Joe going up the back stairs. "Most of you are in the South Wing," called Joe, "but you all might as well come this way first."

"It's like the boys' dorm and the girls' dorm on different floors," joked Evie as our little group admiringly went up the main staircase. Kim and Ruby were shown into their room first and didn't object that they had to share a bed. I was glad to have Evie alongside as we showed Rafaella to her room. She stood on the threshold, and I could tell she was impressed.

"Have I got the master bedroom?" she observed. "It sure looks like it. It looks sumptuous! And a huge bathroom attached too. Are you sure I haven't turfed you out of here, Clemency? And Will?"

"No, we are just a couple of doors down the passageway," I said. I wasn't going to volunteer the information that Will had a separate room. After all, he appeared so genuinely pleased to see me, he might not use the Orchid Room after all.

There was a babble of voices as the others made their way down the back staircase en route to the South Wing.

"We'll leave you to settle in and then come down to the Drawing Room for an English tea," I said to Rafaella. "Thank you for doing so much to make us all feel welcome," she said. "We're all going to have an awesome time this weekend!"

Evie and I raised our eyebrows at each other as we went back along the corridor. "I'm just going to get something," I said, opening the door to my room. "I'll see you in the Drawing Room in a couple of minutes." I let out a relieved sigh. The first part was over successfully. I crossed to the mirror to tidy my hair and glanced out of the window automatically. Only grass and shrubs and trees and, I cursed, shadowy figures by the trees......

I knocked on Kim and Ruby's door on the way down. Ruby had all manner of stuff strewn over the bed ready to put away and they came down with me, exclaiming and chattering. I had been worried in case their personalities clashed, but they were relating well to one another.

Rafaella caught up with us, running lightly down the stairs, her hair bouncing around her face and shoulders as we went to join the others.

The drawing room glowed in the late afternoon sun, which was slowly sinking behind the western ridge. Will looked over as I entered with all the women and his eyes fleetingly sought Rafaella's before settling on me. I went up to him. "I haven't had time to tell you that you are in the Orchid Room, if you want it." I left the invitation open.

"Yes, Joe told me. I've slung my bags in there for now."

The others were looking around the room and remarks like 'awesome' and 'truly magnificent' flew around. Brian and Serena and a couple of helpers came in, and I introduced Brian to Will. "I am honoured to be here in such a grand house," Brian said as they shook hands. "You must be a very proud man."

When everybody had filled their plates and taken cups back to seats, Will said that although we knew who we all were, it would be good if everyone gave a little information about themselves after we'd filled our faces. "I'll go first!" he added, after seeing a couple of reluctant grimaces.

I found myself next to Rafaella on one of the yellow silk sofas with Evie on my other side as a prop or bodyguard; she'd recognise any situation where I might need baling out.

"OK, lucky for all of you, I'm not one for speech making. I'm more of an action man," said Will. Rafaella gave a low chuckle beside me and Hugo and Ben cheered. "It's great to see you all here, and I know we are all going to have a great weekend."

The New Yorkers were much more confidant and gave brief but comprehensive facts about their lives. Ben and Andy and Kim managed a couple of sentences each and Evie made everyone laugh when she said she didn't know half the present company and she didn't even possess a bike! "I'm not a lover of bikes, but Clemmie is my best friend and if you feel the need to be bored to death with historical snippets, I'm your woman!"

Rafaella spoke in a low voice that captured everyone's attention at once as she spoke of her family and how blessed she was with all her team and how she so looked forward to becoming part of a larger happy team. Her speech should have wrapped up the introductions, but all eyes then focussed on me.

"I just want to welcome everyone to this beautiful house, and we want you to enjoy the weekend. Especial thanks go to Serena and Joe, and Brian and his team and Mollie, who isn't here yet, but you won't escape from her." Someone laughed. "They're the ones who've done all the hard work to make this weekend happen."

There was applause and a few whistles and I had got away without saying a single thing about myself! Well, what could I say: "Hello, I'm Clemency. I'm engaged to Will, but you wouldn't know it. We may or may not get married and, in case you are interested, I'm pregnant!"

Joe did the bit about safety, as he knew what the fire alarms sounded like and where the nearest exits were. After that everybody drifted around, drinking tea and coffee, looking at pictures, gazing out of the window and generally chatting together.

～

Dinner was informal, and anyone could sit anywhere. A place had been left for me to sit next to Will. Rafaella held court at the other end of the table, with Hugo on one side and Matt on her other. It was good to see Joe and Serena sitting amongst us on that first evening. Joe had given Matt a hand with the evening milking so he wouldn't miss the meal. Rafaella and Hugo seemed to be vying with each other over tales of mishaps and client peculiarities and that end were laughing uproariously.

Our end was a lot quieter. Will was subdued and only came out of his preoccupation when Serena kept up a conversation. Since our spontaneous greeting when he arrived, I'd spoiled it when he'd come to my room before dinner and I'd mentioned my mother phoning me and making me feel guilty as usual. He'd glanced at my still bandaged hand as if I'd reminded him of his guilt. "Is it still painful?" he'd asked.

"No, Doctor Laidlaw redressed it yesterday and he may call in tomorrow."

"You didn't say anything about the baby to your mother?"

"Of course not! You know what she's like when she's in her accusatory moods. I couldn't really get a word in, even if I'd wanted to tell her. Can you imagine her reaction to the news that she had a pregnant unmarried daughter?"

"Clem, you know this isn't a good time to discuss things. I promised...."

"There's never going to be a good time or place, is there, Will?" I burst out, exasperated. "You'll want to spend more time with..." I nearly blurted out Rafaella's name, "with the New York team, making more plans and routes. I'll have to carry on as usual as if there was no baby or wedding or……" Tears threatened as I fought to get a grip on my emotions.

Will put his arms around me. "Come on, Clem, it's not as bad as that. I did promise and we will sort out something soon, really. Put your glad rags on and a brave face!"

"I'm still holding you to that promise!"

At the dinner table, I tried to do justice to Brian's catering skills. His Coq au Vin was delicious and judging by the nearly empty plates the others had enjoyed it too, as well as the veggie alternative. Evie sat next to Ruby in animated conversation. There was a happy buzz all down the table.

"I'm going to give a little speech to discuss what's planned for the rest of the weekend. It shouldn't take long." Will said.

I took his hand while the plates were being cleared away. "I'm sorry about my outburst earlier," I said into his ear. "Bit stressed, I suppose."

He squeezed my hand. "I'm sure I'll survive," he grinned.

While Brian and Joe were topping up glasses and the dessert was being served, Will asked if anyone was interested in a couple of walks the next day. Everybody was enthusiastic and so it was decided that Will would take half of us up the hill to the top of the downs where, on a clear day, the hills of the Isle of Wight could be seen. Joe volunteered to take the other half down past the chapel and to the river. Then in the afternoon, the groups would swap around. After tea on Saturday and before dinner, we'd all get together for a group chat about the partnership. Rafaella added that she and Will would do their best to answer questions and talk about any concerns. Will glanced at me at that point. Rafaella obviously thought I was just an appendage.

"I'll come up the hill in the morning," I declared. "I've only been downhill so far! Please feel free to do your own wandering on Sunday morning," I called down the table. Matt caught my eye and put his hand up.

"If anyone wants to see the lambs on Sunday morning, that's fine by me. We'll be getting them ready to go out, so maybe a few extra hands to guide them into the field will be useful."

By the nodding of heads and buzz of conversation, I reckoned Matt would have more helpers than he'd bargained for.

After dinner, most of the mixed group headed for the Drawing Room, where coffee had been laid on. Will and Hugo, Rafaella and Jimmy were grouped together. Although Rafaella sat casually, her arm rested along the back of the sofa so that if Will leaned back....

I chatted with Kim and Ruby and Evie for a bit, then excused myself to thank Brian in the kitchen. He was drinking tea with Joe and Serena.

"My crew has gone home; clearing up was done in no time. They'll be back for tomorrow breakfast and then dinner as Serena has insisted that everyone serves themselves tomorrow at lunch. I think I might offer her a job with my outfit! I'm for my bed now. Don't get up Joe, I remember the way to my room!"

I headed up to my room. Making an effort to hold or follow a conversation was beyond me at this time of night. I'd been tense all day, anticipating mishaps, but as I prepared for bed, I was more than happy that the weekend was going to be a success.

~

When I woke, the other side of the bed was empty. I threw on the bathrobe and ran along the passage to the Orchid Room, my heart beating a little faster than normal. If there was no answer, there were two possibilities: Will was up and about already and the other I didn't want to think about. The door opened and Will stood, half-dressed already.

"I peered in on you last night, but you were snoring," he said, giving me a light kiss. "It was late by the time we all got to bed, so I didn't want to disturb you. Are you ok so far? No throwing up? I don't know whether to go round knocking people up or just hope they all make an appearance."

"I expect they'll be up and ready for breakfast already," I said. "And I don't snore!"

Will raised an eyebrow, kissed me quickly, and pushed me out of the door. "If you say so," he said, grinning.

As I showered and dressed, I blamed to my wild imagination dreaming up something between him and Rafaella. Will had been affectionate and attentive to me and Rafaella had reclined amongst her phalanx of male admirers. *God, I'm being such a bitch.*

Last night's lateness and perhaps an excess of alcohol in some cases had not diminished the cheerfulness of both teams. They were all up and in the small dining room helping themselves to the range of choices, from full English to croissants, accompanied by fruit juices, cereals and lots of tea and coffee. My stomach reacted unfavourably at the sight of so much food at that time of morning. I dipped a ginger tea bag in a cup of hot water and sat as far away from the sight of sausage and bacon as possible.

Rafaella hadn't eaten either, but remarked that the coffee was very good. Evie waved to me from the other side of the table, where she sat next to Ruby. They certainly seemed to have a lot to talk about. When Will asked if everybody was geared up for walking, there were exclamations of agreement.

Mollie appeared as we all headed out of the dining room to get togged up for our walks. She seemed more diminutive than ever amongst the tall crowd, but she wasn't at all fazed and began clearing away with Serena and Brian. I had a feeling that while she was making beds and cleaning bathrooms, Mollie would probably discover more about our visitors than me.

A row of boots and trainers were lined up by the back stairs, awaiting owners. When everybody was togged up and sporting an eclectic mix of headgear, we divided into our two groups. It was like a school field trip and I couldn't help asking if everybody had their clip boards.

Our groups set off; those going down to the river with Joe turning right outside the front door and the rest of us setting off down the drive. I linked arms with Will and Rafaella strode on his other side. Mick, our minibus driver, had hurriedly decided to go with Joe's group and said he'd spend the afternoon cleaning the minibus.

As we approached the ash tree, my grip on Will's arm tightened. He must have realised why I needed to attach myself to him, because he squeezed my arm to his side. The grass was still churned up where Will's Range Rover had come to an abrupt halt. Some of the others were exclaiming about the size of the old ash and were taking snapshots of it. Logically, my brain was telling me it would be almost impossible for the Twins to attempt mischief surrounded by a large group unless the tree itself fell on top of us. The thought sent a shiver down my spine. Two jackdaws flew out with croaks of alarm. More photos were taken of Mollie's little lodge cottage and although the twisted chimneys were mock Elizabethan, it was hard to convince the Americans they were a Victorian addition. A black and white cat sat on the inside sill of the bay window, watching with wide green eyes as we trooped past.

The way up to the top of the downs was a long but gentle gradient and reaching halfway, we could look over the fields and woods towards the river westwards. Harthill House itself was hidden by the many trees that surrounded it and Jimmy spotted the spire of Salisbury Cathedral away to the northeast. It was good to feel fresh air again with a gentle breeze that felt like silk passing over my cheeks. Rafaella asked if I was ok so far on the walk as we stopped to look back over the valley and far ridge.

"Yes, I'm enjoying it," I said truthfully. "I'm hoping I'm over the worst of the sickness now. At least I hope I am. It can strike anytime."

The Shadow Watchers

"Have you made any plans for the future?" she said casually, looking over the undulating Narnia-like countryside spread below us. I looked sharply at her. Was she fishing for information? Had Will been unburdening himself to her?

"Nothing definite yet," I answered, just as casually. "We're waiting a little until all the routes are finalised and we've got definite bookings." I guessed she had a shrewd idea that our personal plans were nebulous.

Will shouted for us to hurry as we weren't at the top of the downs yet. We passed ploughed fields and hedges and went through a copse full of hawthorns and blackthorns. The blackthorn blossom was beginning to emerge in a hazy white mist. The view to the north was now hidden by the woods but open towards the south, the sky filled with huge white clouds. We could see hills far in the distance to the south, which Will assured us was the Isle of White and confirmed by looking at the top of the triangulation point made of concrete set incongruously in the middle of the track, marking the highest point of the down.

"We could go on further and find a folly built a couple of hundred years ago, which used to be part of the estate, but it's too far and across the main Southampton road," said Will.

The track continued through the middle of the ploughed field on either side of us and disappeared into another belt of trees. It was strangely silent up here. There was no wind in the trees and no birdsong. As we turned to go back, a battered Volvo estate car emerged from the trees, driven slowly. We all stood on either side of the track to let him pass, but the Volvo slowed to a halt and the driver's window wound down. The driver, an elderly man, sat so low in the driving seat he could barely see over the steering wheel. He poked his bobble-hatted head out of the window.

"Are you lost?" he asked in a surprisingly cultured voice. I'd taken him for a local resident and expected the slow drawl of Wiltshire.

"No, we're just out for a ramble," I answered because he had focussed on me. I wondered if he might be the local gamekeeper accusing us of trespassing on private land and turned to Will for help. The man scrutinized my face for long seconds.

"You have the sight, my dear," he remarked as casually as if he was remarking on the weather. "You might need my help one day." He turned away and rummaged on his dashboard. He handed me a hand printed card. I took it automatically, but I was rooted to the spot. "That's where I live," he jerked his thumb back the way he'd driven. "I don't have a phone, but I'm here when you need me."

He fixed me with an amiable gaze, nodded, wound up his window and proceeded down the track.

The others burst out laughing. Andy said: "You didn't tell us you had a warlock living up here, Will!"

"A real English eccentric!" exclaimed Dunc Downing, grinning in the direction the car, now trundling slowly downhill.

"He vanished in a puff of smoke!" laughed Ben.

I pocketed the card silently.

"What was all that about?" Will asked. "I didn't hear what he said clearly."

"I didn't really understand him very well myself," I lied. "He wanted to know if we were lost and he lives back there."

"There is an old farm bungalow in the clearing," said Will, looking towards the trees. "I think a stock man used to live there, and then it was empty for a time. I remember now from one of the Trust meetings that we rented it out.

"Is this your land as well?" asked Dunc and Will nodded reluctantly. Dunc and Andy whistled, and Ben tugged at his forelock. "Better call you squire from now on," he laughed, bowing.

Andy insisted on having a look at the 'warlock's' abode. We rounded a thick holly bush that hid a very ordinary and run down bungalow with whitewashed walls which had turned grey with weathering, and a tiled roof. It was more neglected than sinister, and we all turned to go down. Rafaella had been quiet throughout the exchange and eased herself alongside me as we spread out along the track.

"What did he mean about the sight?" she asked pointedly.

"I have no idea." I struggled to make light of it. "He said he had no phone, so perhaps he relies on seeing people. I wanted to quicken my pace and catch up with Will, and Rafaella obviously took the hint.

"He seemed a weirdo to me. Don't wander around up here by yourself, will you?"

"No," I agreed, "I most certainly won't!"

The encounter had put the others in a jocular mood and conversation ranged from witches, wizards, Lord of the Rings, online war games, and more practically, mapping this way as a trek route. I was grateful for the distraction and my hand kept fingering the card in my pocket. Thankfully, nobody had seen it or remarked on it.

Lunch was a noisy affair with the groups comparing their walks and our group joking about meeting the local wizard. Will couldn't put them straight because he did not know who the man was, either. Someone asked if he could have driven from the main Southampton Road, but Will said the track got considerably rougher through the wood and was not suitable for vehicles. When Joe came in late to help himself to soup and bread and cheese, Will asked him who was the tenant in Flint Cottage up on the downs.

"Oh, that's Osborne Stafford; he's lived there for years now. He's been a tenant since your father's time," Joe answered.

"And is he a witch or a warlock?" put in Andy jokingly.

Joe regarded him seriously as he considered his answer. "I don't think you can call him that," he protested mildly, "but he does investigate paranormal activities. William's father told me he'd written papers and books about the subject."

Joe addressed Will. "I've been to check the property a few

times over the years and he has no electrical equipment up there. He insisted the power supply was cut off, and he cooks on bottled gas and has a wood-burning stove. I don't think he has a phone line up there either."

"I told you – a warlock!" chortled Andy. I wished he'd shut up. Fortunately, the subject came to a natural end when the conversation buzzed with other topics and Will was keen to get the groups moving out again on the afternoon walks so that we could hold our group chat after tea. I excused myself from the walk down to the chapel and mill. Memories of that cold, dark day still made me shiver. Besides, I'd had good fortune not encountering the Twins either way this morning, but may not be so lucky this afternoon.

'You have the sight,' Osborne Stafford had told me. How had he come to that conclusion?

Rafaella seemed to cheer up considerably when I said I wasn't coming on the walk. She'd have Will all to herself. Chaperoned, of course, but I'm sure she'd manage to cosy up to him. She had been uncharacteristically quiet so far, but I was sure she'd been assessing Will and me – how we responded to each other and how much time we spent together so far.

Evie looked me over as she shrugged on her parka. "Are you ok? You look pale."

"I'm fine. I think that was the longest walk I've done since I've been here," I said. "I'm seriously unfit, which is not good. You'll enjoy going uphill instead of down, but there are no ruins to excite and delight you!"

"I'll have you know everybody listened intently when I gave them a brief history of the chapel and mill and what's left of the old manor house. Ruby can't get enough history. Her parents were born in Romania, which is full of mysterious places, and she says she misses it now she's based in New York."

"I'm glad you have a willing student who's eager to listen to you instead of me having a moan after a while!"

"I'll stay with you if you like," said Kim. "If you need help to set up for the group meeting...."

"Kim, thank you, that's kind! But this is a break for you, so grab it with both hands and get that London pollution out of your lungs!"

Jasper and Bess, who had been lying in front of the fire in the hall, suddenly realised they were going out again and weaved in and out of people and waited by the front door, eager to be off.

"Be sure to give our regards to the warlock, if you see him," called Andy as everybody set off in different directions. The sun had disappeared, but the afternoon was still bright with a slight chill in the air. I waved them off and shut the door. It was not completely silent; there were noises from the kitchen as I headed downstairs and some of Brian's team were about to set up tea in the drawing room. I met Serena in the boiler room.

"It's going ok, isn't it?" she said, and I agreed. "He's such an easy chap to work with." Serena nodded her head in the direction of the kitchen and I smiled. What Serena meant was that by and large Brian fell in with Serena's suggestions.

Everybody was busy, so I went upstairs, rummaging in my jacket pocket for the card handwritten in spidery writing.

Dr Osborne Stafford

Flint Farm Cottage, Bridgeford, Salisbury,

Wiltshire

Paraphysical Investigator

What in the world did that mean? I powered up my laptop, curious to find out who he was. There was a reference to a Stafford Osbourne, an eighteenth-century dilettante. Then I spotted a heading: Osborne Stafford Paraphysical Laboratory, Wiltshire, and clicked on it.

Osborne Stafford born 1922 in Lincoln, England. Studied physics at Oxford University and gained a doctorate after research into natural phenomena which cannot be rationally explained within parameters of current physical theories. His theories, although widely read, were not always well received by fellow physicists as he believed unexplained physical phenomena could be caused by electrical activity.

Nevertheless, he has many followers who have visited his laboratory in Wiltshire. In one of his published papers, he wrote: 'I am a trained physicist, gaining my doctorate at Oxford University. My ongoing studies of paraphysical phenomena, which I believe are caused by electrical energy, required an environment free of interference from other electrical sources. Flint Farm is a perfect location where I have investigated, observed, and measured phenomena outside of accepted physical parameters. With help from my students, my experiments include telekinesis, telepathy, teleportation of material objects, direct voice, auras, and paranormal activity.'

There were more paragraphs, but I didn't read them. I sat blinking at the screen. It was peculiar that he'd singled me out this morning. Perhaps it was a coincidence that put me in his path this morning. Could I consult him about the Twins' paranormal activity?

I jumped when there was a tap on the door. It was Serena. "Doctor Laidlaw is downstairs Clemency. He asked if he could check you over? I've put him in the sitting room."

I closed my laptop gratefully and went to greet the good doctor. "I'm getting too used to all your attention," I said as he stood up to greet me. "I'll miss you when I return to London!"

"Well, I pass this way several times a week and you are a very special patient, although patient is not the correct description. I hear you are in the middle of a busy weekend, so I won't detain you long."

"Most people are out on walks at the moment, so it is a very good time."

"I'm sorry to have missed William once again. He is very elusive."

I hid a smile at his apt description of Will. He unbound the wrapping and declared satisfaction with the wounds on my hand. "As long as you keep it clean and dry, the scars should heal quickly. A small dressing will suffice now. And now we'll just have a little listen to make sure Junior is faring well."

He took my blood pressure and listened to the baby's heartbeat, said he was happy with results and would leave me in peace.

"Don't hesitate to get in touch with me when you return here later. Or after the baby is born, whichever is the soonest!"

I wished all doctors were as kind as Dr Laidlaw and I said I'd let him know when I was back.

My underlying worry was whether Will wanted to marry, despite his protestations and promises. The doctor was right. There was something very elusive about Will's attitude. The last thing I wanted was to force him into a shotgun marriage.

Voices sounded from the main staircase hall. Will had brought the walkers in the back door and they'd shed coats and boots downstairs. They dispersed in several directions to go to their rooms before coming down to tea.

I bumped into Will by the stairs and dragged him into the sitting room for privacy. I showed him my hand.

"That's a relief," he breathed, stroking my arm.

"Baby's fine too, according to Dr Laidlaw, and it's not long before the next scan. I know the baby will be a boy, otherwise the Twins wouldn't be hanging around."

"The Twins?" Will frowned. He'd obviously forgotten about them. Changing the subject rapidly, he asked, "are you coming back to London with us tomorrow?"

"I haven't given it any thought," I said with a jolt. "This house is growing on me, but practically I will be better off in London and I can get back to work."

"You mustn't rush back." Despite his assurances, I sensed Will's preoccupation.

"Shall we see if tea's ready? With all this accessible food I'm permanently hungry!" he said, making for the door.

My patience unravelled. "Whatever's bothering you, Will, please tell me before you disappear again," I said to his back. An imperceptible jerk of his head made me believe he'd heard, but he continued to the Drawing Room and I followed him with a sigh.

More noise and loud barking heralded the arrival of the other group. They were all taking off shoes and boots. Evie spotted me.

"We saw no sign of your mystery warlock friend," she called out. "We even walked as far as his cottage, but no car was there and we didn't want to look like trespassers peering in his windows. He might have cast a spell around it!"

"I wish you wouldn't keep calling him my friend," I said, still smarting at losing my cool with Will. Now was not the time to alienate him. "I quickly looked him up and he calls his cottage a para something laboratory and apparently does psychic experiments."

"Ooh," said Kim, "I should steer clear of all that if I were you!"

Evie narrowed her eyes. "He could be useful with the *you-know-what's!*"

"Tea's ready," said Serena from the door to the Drawing Room and we all crowded in.

Chapter Twenty-Four

The discussions after tea focussed on updates to social media platforms, and mainly on our separate finances. Rafaella, to my mind, implied we were struggling financially when she suggested putting our overseas costs on the tab. Wondrously, I kept my cool, and we dispersed without arousing animosity. I slipped away, but not before noticing that Rafaella's eyes followed me. Kim intercepted me before I reached the door and slipped her arm in mine. "I could tell you were mad at Rafaella's remark about keeping costs on the tab. It was insensitive of her. We aren't the poor relations in this partnership!"

"My thoughts exactly," I said, grimacing.

"I have kept my eye on accounts all the time you've been here and they are very healthy. Did you know Andy had a degree in Statistics? He's helped me with forecasts. Now I'm just on my way upstairs to have a Skype conversation with my daughters. I'm going to tell them a bedtime story before we go down to dinner. It's about a princess who lives in a big palace with a magic staircase." Kim indicated the stairs as we stood at the bottom. "Every time the princess goes up the staircase, she sees a doorway glowing and when she goes through the doorway, she is in a different place. Last night, she found herself in a field of unicorns and they had a lovely time playing. Tonight, I think she'll find herself with lambs. I can take photos of the lambs tomorrow morning and show them to the girls when I get home tomorrow night!"

"I'll bear you in mind as a storyteller when I can't get mine to sleep in a few months' time!"

"He'd better start expanding soon, then. You are still far too thin for my liking!" Kim kissed me on the cheek and ran up the stairs.

Thank you, Kim, you've done the trick of cheering me up.

I headed back into the Hall, now busy as Brian and his crew prepared for dinner later. Evie and Ruby headed towards the library with their arms round each other's waists. It wasn't the simple affectionate reassurance that Kim had just shown me. It looked much more intimate. I'd noticed how well they were getting on and had remarked to Will that they were almost joined at the hip. Realisation hit me so hard that I staggered. How could I be so stupidly blinkered and naïve? All the years we'd been friends and shared and I had had no inkling. Evie had never had a boyfriend – she'd always joked she was married to the job she loved. She'd been there all the time, supporting me, comforting me, cheering me up, and I'd treated her like a big sister. Had she been waiting for me to reciprocate her feelings? I loved Evie, but not in the way she needed, but she'd never betrayed her feelings to me. Now seeing her with Ruby, I felt a fresh upsurge of affection for her. I wanted to rush up to them both and wish them well. While all these thoughts and feelings surged through me, they disappeared into the library. There'd be plenty of time to talk to Evie and I felt selfish that my own needs had eclipsed those of Evie's.

A few people still relaxed in the drawing room, while others disappeared before getting ready for dinner as we had told them to wear their glad rags tonight. In the bedroom, my laptop was still powered up and I refreshed the pages about Osborne Stafford. My mind shied away from his paranormal activities, and I shut down. As I went to the windows to close the curtains against the night, I instinctively looked down into the gathering darkness. The only thing that mattered was that I was safe in this house amongst friends, but where was Will?

I picked up my phone and saw several missed calls from Uncle Daniel. I swiftly called him and he answered almost immediately.

"Hi, it's Clemency. Are you alright? I saw you'd been trying to get hold of me?"

"I am very well, thank you Clemency, but I was getting a little anxious that you weren't picking up."

"It's been a little busy over the last couple of days and I haven't always been carrying my phone around. Are you sure everything is ok?"

Daniel laughed, "Yes, really, I am fine. I wanted to ask you a question, but I fear it may be a little late."

"Ask away, I'll help I can."

"You kindly asked me to lunch tomorrow, and I refused. Now I wonder if it's too late to accept your invitation?"

I laughed. "Is that all? Yes, of course you must come, Daniel. Brian has been catering so well for us all throughout the weekend. I'm sure another mouth won't be noticed!"

"Ah, excellent! The other question is also delicate. May I bring... a friend?"

There'd been a slight pause over the friend, but I didn't hesitate to answer. "Yes, of course. You'll both be very welcome. Lunch is prompt at one because the New York team are leaving later in the afternoon to catch their flight back to the States. If you can get here earlier, it will be lovely to see you and your friend," I added, amused. Perhaps he'd been hiding a companion somewhere.

There was a slight tap on my door and Will came in. He had cobwebs on his sweater.

"Where have you been, festooned in cobwebs?" I drew back, hoping spiders weren't attached.

"Showing the lads the old kitchens. We stuck our heads up that great chimney!"

I laughed with relief. He hadn't been holed up with Rafaella. I had to stop having these suspicions.

"I've come to apologise, Clem. I was out of order before. I must be more strung up about this new deal than I thought. Am I forgiven?"

He looked very sheepish, and I climbed off the bed and put my arms around him. I needed him, that was the truth, and we stood swaying for a few minutes before kissing and then I pushed him away. I wasn't letting him have his own way so easily. "We have to get ready for dinner; I haven't had a bath yet."

"That's what I came to tell you. Rafaella has bought champagne from Brian and asked if we could all get together before dinner for a toast."

I raised my eyebrows. "No champagne for me, but I can manage on water, and by the way, Uncle Daniel is coming to lunch tomorrow, so you'll be able to catch up with him."

"Well, it will be good to see the old boy again, I suppose. I'll leave you in peace now and see you later." He pulled me to him and gave me a deep kiss. I could feel myself responding before pushing him away again, and he winked as he went out.

I sighed when he'd gone. Is this what it would be like from now on, uncertainty, arguments, making up? Our previous life had seemed so uncomplicated. We were both conflicted.

If we weren't having a baby, would I still marry him? The thought crept so insidiously into my mind, it took my breath away.

After a quick shower, I sat playing with my hair; did it look better up or down? I was still pleased with my green dress and with a bit of help from trusty cosmetics, I was ready to play the hostess again. There was a light knock on the door and thinking it was Will, I called out. "Nearly ready!" The door opened, but it was Evie who came in looking unrecognisably neat in a grey trouser suit with a red top underneath. Her thick hair had been styled, and I suspected Ruby was the artist.

"I've come to say so sorry for neglecting you, these couple of days," she began, but I cut in quickly.

"Don't be sorry, Evie. I can see you are enjoying yourself. You and Ruby seem to have a lot in common, and I'm really pleased for you."

"I came to tell you before you hear rumours. I'm not ashamed or sorry."

While I knew what she was telling me, I looked surprised. "You've nothing to feel ashamed about, Evie. I saw you and Ruby together after tea and I must admit, it was a bit of a lightning bolt moment, but then everything slotted into place. I am so pleased for you, really, and I still love you as my best friend."

Evie had tears in her eyes, and that started me off as we hugged. "Now I'll have to put more mascara on," I said, letting go and laughing.

"I thought you'd be upset. I feel like I've been hit by a ton of bricks and so does Ruby, but we just seem to click."

"I'm so happy for you, truthfully. You deserve your chance at happiness at long last, but I still expect you to be my best friend, big sister, and matron! But Evie, what's going to happen when Ruby goes back tomorrow? It seems so unfair now you've only just met."

"That's the next thing to tell you! Ruby has swapped her flight until later in the week. She's asked Rafaella and of course she was OK about it. She's coming back to London to stay and we can do the town together. But I came to see what your plans were for tomorrow. Are you staying here or coming back with us?"

I hadn't yet decided, but if Evie and Ruby needed precious time together, I'd stay here. Evie grinned with pleasure and we hugged again when I told her.

"We're having champers before dinner, courtesy of Rafaella, so be sure to toast yourselves as well," I said.

"You are still my bestest buddy and I love you," said Evie, her eyes shining again. There was a brief knock and Will entered. "Hi Evie, I've just come to collect this lovely lady," Will said. "And you do look lovely, Clem. And you too, Evie," Will bowed chivalrously.

"You've scrubbed up well yourself," conceded Evie, and indeed Will looked very handsome in a dark blue suit and blue shirt which complemented his eyes.

"I'll leave this mutual admiration club and see if Ruby is ready," said Evie, drily. She kissed my cheek and left the room.

Will looked quizzically at me. "Is it true? There have been some whispers flying around."

"Yes, and if somebody dares to make snide remarks, I'll punch them in the face," I said with asperity.

"Whoa," laughed Will, putting his hands up in placation. "I haven't heard any such remarks. Good luck to them both. I sometimes wondered if she had a pash for you; she was always so fiercely protective of you. Now, are you ready?"

"She will always be protective of me, so watch your step, Mister!" I said lightly.

We processed down the grand staircase like actors in a period drama, joined by Rafaella and Hugo and Evie and Ruby. I secretly wished Hugo luck in drawing Rafaella's attention away from Will. There was a roar of voices coming from the Drawing Room as if our groups had multiplied. I half expected applause when we appeared, but conversations continued. The men all wore smart jackets or suits and Sam sported a bow tie, white shirt, and a grey silk waistcoat under his suit. Kim looked stunning in a dark sequined jacket with a high mandarin collar and her black hair gleamed in the candlelight. Serena looked elegant in a high-necked blue jersey dress, and Joe looked uncomfortable in a suit.

Candelabra had been positioned strategically at intervals along the dining table, on the old oak side table and in sconces which I hadn't noticed before. The effect made the high-ceilinged room look smaller and more intimate. Something shifted inside me as I saw how this hall would have appeared two centuries go.

Over by the side table, one of Brian's helpers poured champagne into glasses, smartly dressed in a white shirt and black waistcoat, and next to him stood a diminutive Mollie. She wore a black dress with a stiff white collar and cuffs and a white apron. I remembered her saying how she had to dress like a 'proper servant' for some occasion years ago; it must be the same outfit. A white frilly cap would have completed the look, but her hair sprang defiantly about her face in a wiry white halo. The sight of her made me giggle. Rafaella beckoned Will, and he meekly went over to her. She took one of the full glasses and raised it high. Immediately, there was a hush.

"Friends and colleagues: tonight, we are going to toast success, friendship, and a great host and hostess. Go get your glasses and raise them with me."

There was a little scrum as everybody collected a brimming glass. I took a glass, but there didn't seem to be any alternative to champagne. I held it anyway; nobody noticed it was empty because I was at the back of the crowd. Rafaella held her glass up. "To new friends and good trekking," she said, and everybody all dutifully roared back and took deep gulps.

"To new adventures," called Will and everybody repeated and swigged.

"To our wonderful host and hostess," called Rafaella and there was a lot of whistling, cheering, and slapping of thighs while more quaffing took place. From my position at the back, it looked very much like Will and Rafaella were holding court. She looked both sultry and regal in a low-cut and contoured silvery silk dress, which shimmered in the candlelight. Glasses were refilled and there was a general buzz of conversation again. Eventually, one of Brian's staff sloshed orange juice into my glass, and I found myself next to Mollie.

"You certainly look the part tonight, Mollie," I laughed. "Will you be cleaning the bathrooms dressed like this?"

She gave me a little push. "I haven't worn this for years, but it still fits," she said proudly. Then she took my arm. "A little word of warning, though, me duck. Keep your eye on that woman," she said, jerking her head towards Rafaella, who was resting her hand on Will's arm. Before I could respond, Mollie took up a wicker basket to collect dirty glasses.

I looked around for somebody I could talk to, anybody to take my mind off her words, and Brian Chadwick appeared by my side, immaculately dressed.

"Cover your ears now, my darlin', Joe was after finding this old gong for me. That'll get everybody's attention." He winked and produced a small brass gong from behind his back. He stood by the door to the Drawing Room and gave it a very professional beating. Everybody turned, startled.

"Ladies and Gentlemen, dinner is served," he announced in his soft Irish brogue. "Gentlemen, please wait until the ladies are seated before sitting yourselves. The places are named so if you would like to find them now...."

Someone touched my elbow. Matt had arrived. His shock of hair, normally hidden under a beanie hat, had been tamed into submission and he looked very handsome in a dark suit and shirt. "Haven't worn this for years," he admitted. "I was afraid it wouldn't fit!"

"Everybody's made a grand effort," I remarked as I saw his eyes linger on Rafaella's low necked dress moulded to her figure.

There was a scramble to find names. Naturally, I was not to sit next to Will, being the hostess. I was at the foot of the table with Hugo on one side and Jimmy on the other. Will stood at the head, trying not to look like the reluctant owner of a large historic house, with Rafaella on one side and Ruby on the other. Brian's helpers moved to help the women or 'ladies' be seated, which cracked Evie up.

The courses were exquisitely served and everybody was eating and drinking appreciatively. Hugo and Jimmy kept me laughing with tales of daring do and stupid accidents that had happened to them on their travels and what they had done before trekking filled their lives. I toyed with the food, managing to look as if I was eating a lot and it was truly delicious. Rafaella and Ruby were holding spontaneous conversations across Will at the top of the table. When I caught his attention, his eyes held a strange glitter, but it may have been the candlelight.

Ben was drawing something for Evie, and I hoped it wasn't on one of Brian's pristine linen napkins. I was happy to see Serena and Joe relaxed and chatting. Matt caught my eye and gave me a thumbs up sign.

Dinner was coming to an end; I could see Brian and a couple of his team bringing coffee and tea with little dishes of mint chocolates. They were so efficient, clearing away unobtrusively.

Suddenly Hugo stood up. "Before we all leave the table, and I know we've already toasted everything and everybody, but I'd like to say an extra thank you to Will, Clemency, Serena, Joe, Mollie, Brian and his merry band of helpers..." If he was going to add anything he was drowned out by clapping, whistling, and stamping of feet and Will held up his glass to Hugo with a grin, while Brian dipped his head in acknowledgement and the helpers looked embarrassed.

Dunc Downing then stood up. "From someone across the pond, it's been a revelation to see how you poor Brits live." His voice was drowned out by hoots of laughter from our team, and

Ben heckled him. "You need to see what's in my fridge before making assumptions."

Dunc held up his hand in acknowledgement. "What I need to see is the inside of a proper British pub. Mick here," Dunc indicated Mick, the driver next to him "Mick has offered to drive anybody who wants to join me to an Olde Worlde English pub in Salisbury which Matt has lovingly described. Mick has been on diet cola, so he is safe to drive! So, are there any takers?"

"Yes!" Hands shot up and chairs pushed back eagerly. In a remarkably short time, people disappeared and reappeared shrugging on coats. Will stood by my side, also wearing a jacket. "Are you coming?"

"I'm sorry," I said apologetically. "But I'll probably fall asleep with my head on a table. And I can't drink alcohol, anyway!"

"Better not wait up then." Will kissed my cheek and joined the little crowd by the door. Even Joe was going. Serena, Matt, and I looked on as they cheerfully went out, sending a blast of cold air into the lofty Hall. We three looked at each other with wistful smiles.

"Joe felt he had to go to make sure they didn't get lost! He said he wasn't sure how well William knew Salisbury! Wasn't it a lovely meal? It doesn't seem possible we only have lunch to go tomorrow. The weekend has gone so quickly."

"I feel like a spoilsport not going," I sighed. "I feel like an old lady ready for her bed!"

"You look nothing like an old lady in that gorgeous dress and I'm a party pooper as well!" said Matt ruefully. We looked at each other and burst out laughing. At that moment, standing so close together, something in Matt's expression made my heartbeat quicken up.

"I have to go, reluctantly, so I can be up for milking before the crack of dawn – your lot will probably be just going to bed when I'm getting up!"

As we walked down the stairs to the basement, we met Mollie outside the kitchen, from which noises of clinking crockery and voices could be heard. Mollie confronted him. "What you be doing up so late, Matthew? You'll never be up for the milking."

"I know Nan," said Matt, grinning. "But I don't have many opportunities to enjoy an evening in good company these days!"

Mollie's eyes flitted from Matt's face to mine, then she harrumphed and turned away. "Seeing as you're on your feet, you can walk me home then!"

Serena appeared out of the kitchen "Mollie, I can give you a lift. You don't need to walk; you've been on your feet all night!"

Mollie looked undecided, then said grudgingly, "well if it's not too much trouble...."

Serena laughed. "Of course it's not; I thought we'd already decided. I'll meet you by the front door."

Mollie and Serena went to fetch coats.

"Thanks again, Clemency, I really have enjoyed these last couple of evenings." Matt said.

"It's going to be very quiet next week," I said.

"Are you going back tomorrow?" he asked, not looking at me.

"No, I'm staying a few more days."

Matt grinned. "Good, we've got used to you being part of the family now!" As he opened the back door, he turned to face me and, thinking he was going to kiss my cheek, I turned my face. Our lips met. Hastily, we pulled apart and I could feel my face flaming.

"That was nice," Matt said wickedly. "I'll see you at lunch tomorrow. I'm glad you're not going yet. I've kind of got used to you being around. Oh, and the offer of seeing the lambs still stands if anybody is up before lunch!" He touched my arm and was gone.

I stood while my face flamed and my lips tingled. What on earth was I doing? The thing was, I didn't feel embarrassed – I felt happy.

Although I'd cried off going to Salisbury, I was still wired and wasn't ready for bed. Evie and Ruby had gone in the minibus and all Brian's crew was leaving after clearing up. I changed into leggings and a fleece jumper and went back downstairs to make hot chocolate. It was warm in the kitchen. The dogs had retired upstairs with Joe and Serena, but Tabby was asleep on the rug in front of the Aga. My mind shied away from treacherous thoughts. By the time the New Yorkers had returned to the States and we were all back at work, life would settle into normality again. Except for a baby and a possible wedding day...

I woke with a stiff neck where I'd fallen asleep with my elbows on the table and head in my hands. There were noises of voices and footsteps upstairs. It was past midnight. The pub goers had returned. I hastened up the back stairs, only to stop halfway up.

"Man, I think English beer went to Raf's head." That was Dunc's voice. They were obviously on their way to their bedrooms in the South Wing. "Did you see her draped all over Will? Man, he looked embarrassed. He didn't know where to put himself!"

"Yeah," said another voice that sounded like Jimmy's. "She's had the hots for him since he first came over. He's been the perfect English gent, though, behaving himself!"

"And why wouldn't he, Clemency is a darling!"

The sound of laughter faded as they moved away. I stood rooted on the stairs. My suspicions weren't completely unfounded then. Had Will behaved like a perfect gent all the time he'd been in the States? I carried on up the stairs to intercept Will. There he was coming through with Hugo, and Raf wasn't hanging round his neck. Instead, she was with Kim and Evie and Ruby, all laughing and chatting.

Will saw me and his face lit up. I could have sworn he was relieved to see me.

"Clem, I thought you were bushed!" he said.

"I came down for a hot chocolate." I answered, linking arms with him. Hugo said goodnight and walked off down the corridor, linking to the South Wing. Will and I headed the little procession going up the grand staircase with the other women behind. At the top, I firmly guided him down the passage to my room before he headed off to the Orchid room. Evie and Ruby parted with a hug and she accompanied Rafaella along the passageway. Outside my room, I turned and gave Evie a hug and touched Rafaella on the arm, wishing them a cheery goodnight.

Will didn't put up any resistance as I closed the door behind me.

"I'm not drunk," he said, sitting on the bed.

"From what I've just heard from the others, Rafaella might have had one too many."

Will looked guiltily sheepish. "What else did you hear?"

"That she was throwing herself at you, but you were 'the perfect English gent'!" The corners of my mouth turned up. Now we could face the truth.

Will covered his face with his hands and fell backwards. "God, I was so embarrassed! With all our mates around with their eyes on stalks!"

"Why, has she thrown herself at you in private?"

Will shot up. "What? No, well, she kind of has a way of making you think...." He stood up and strode over to where I still stood by the door. I was shaking slightly.

"I swear nothing has gone on between us. Honest to God, Clem!"

And then I took him in my arms. I'd looked into his eyes and I believed him. We undressed and got into bed. Will had his arm round me, but we didn't make love. He cleared his throat. "She told me it didn't matter anyway because she was getting married."

I shot up in bed, staring down at him, dim in the darkness. "What?"

"I don't know. I can't remember what I said to her. Everybody was boggle eyed at her draped all over me. Then she went all huffy and said she was marrying some Italian Count. She said he had been waiting for his divorce to be finalised. Evie rescued me." The bed shook. *Oh God, is he crying?* Will erupted into laughter.

"Evie came over as I was trying to tactfully extricate myself and said in my ear that if I did anything to hurt you, she'd cut my balls off!"

I spluttered, and we both cried with laughter. *Thank you, Evie! You are my knight in shining armour!*

"She would too!" I said, wiping my eyes on the duvet cover. We both went quiet.

He scrubbed his hair with his free hand. "It did kind of focus me, though. We'd better make plans for the wedding," he said to the ceiling.

I sat up again, amazed. He continued, still gazing upwards. "We'd better set a date before the baby comes along. Ma will keep nagging me, even if she's back in France. And it will be better to do it before all the treks get going, especially the ones planned for North America."

This time, he turned to look at me. "We could have the ceremony in the chapel if you like, and we have room for guests. You could ask Brian Chadwick if he would do the catering for the day. And you need to tell your parents."

I was speechless. I just stared at this man lying beside me in bed, telling me all the things I'd longed to hear. Tears sprang to my eyes.

"Was that a proposal?"

"I suppose it is," he said, glancing quickly at me. Seeing tears running down my face, he frowned and drew me to him. I could feel his heart thudding.

"If you are just suggesting we get married at your mother's insistence, I won't do it, Will."

"I wouldn't play with your feelings like that, Clem. I've been a roving adventurer for long enough and it's time to think about what you want. Christ, Clem, I have a horrible feeling I'm growing up!" He gave a lopsided grin.

I studied him solemnly. Alcohol had probably helped to loosen his tongue, but he was facing truths at last and I respected that.

"Thank you," I said simply, kissing his nose.

"Better get some sleep. Another big day tomorrow." He turned on his side, away from me, yawning. I lay in the dark, feeling happy and suspicious at the same time. Another treacherous thought slid into my mind. *If Rafaella had got Will into a quiet corner and draped herself all over him, would he have responded?* I'd never know the answer to that question.

In the morning, we both woke together as a door banged somewhere in the house. Will looked at his watch. "God, it's late!" he said, jumping out of bed.

"Come and have a shower in my bathroom," I said, wrapping my bathrobe around me. He donned his trousers, grabbed his wash bag, and followed me down the passageway. Luckily, my shared bathroom was empty. We showered together, but Will was in a hurry to dress.

"We should get a licence to hold marriage ceremonies here in the house," I said as Will quickly shaved. "I've had plenty of time to think about how we can bring the house to life again. We could offer people the chance to run day courses here: history, creative writing, art classes – I'm sure Evie would like to help and maybe your Uncle Daniel. We could organise musical events and picnics outdoors or hire the house out to TV and movie production companies; it's perfect for historical dramas..."

Will shoved some foaming shaving cream into my mouth. "For pity's sake, woman, let me get used to the enormous fact that I've just proposed to you!" he said, wiping my face with his towel and tweaking my nose.

"See you downstairs," he said and left me still wrapped in my towel.

Chapter Twenty-Five

Outside the ground was white with frost The azure sky arched overhead with not a cloud in sight. There was a quiet atmosphere at breakfast, as everybody realised the weekend idyll would soon end. Will, Jimmy, and Hugo had laptops and were preparing to map out routes in the drawing room after breakfast. Rafaella, in jogging gear and trainers, appeared fresh faced after a quick run 'up the hill' and appeared unfazed after her 'lapse' last night. She disappeared when she saw Will and the others with laptops and reappeared moments later with hers.

Joe put his head round the door and asked if anyone wanted to go down to the barns shortly as Matt and he would be putting ewes and older lambs in the field in front of the house shortly, and there were a few willing volunteers.

Ruby had requested a last visit at the chapel and river, and reluctantly I agreed to accompany them.

Once outside, and away from the others, I spontaneously gave Evie a smacker of a kiss on her cheek.

"What was that for?" she said, eyes wide in surprise.

"Last night," I replied enigmatically. "You gave Will such a fright, he proposed!"

Evie doubled up with laughter. "Brilliant! My threat had the desired effect! Seriously though, Rafaella was all over him most of the evening and she's not unattractive...."

"I have never known Rafaella to be so...so...what is the word I am looking for?"

"Forward?" suggested Evie drily.

"Uninhibited!" announced Ruby. "Rafaella is so cool and always in control."

"Except when she tried our ale," said Evie.

"She said she did not care for it."

"Well, she didn't show any embarrassment this morning, but thank you again, Evie!" We followed the faint track down to the Chapel, keeping the fence boundary on our right.

We climbed over a stile into the back of the grounds surrounding the chapel. In the bright sunlight, the chapel, the gravestones and even the angel hidden beneath the bower of emerging leaves had lost the melancholy and foreboding of our last visit on a cold grey day. Cowslips nestled between gravestones and there were cheerful yellow celandines everywhere. Daffodils bordered the churchyard. The rooks were as noisy as usual, and the calls of robins and blackbirds resounded as well as other birdsong I didn't recognise. On impulse, I picked a few daffodils and while Ruby was inspecting gravestones with Evie; I went over to the stone angel and lay the daffodils by her cushioned feet. I thought of the poor girl, Frances, and her sons lying there and instead of fleeing in terror, I wanted to bring comfort to her. Stupid, I know, when she had been dead two centuries, but I recognised a feeling of something – kinship, empathy? Definitely some kind of bond between us.

"I should have brought the key to the chapel," I said, still feeling a glow after Will's words about holding the ceremony here. It had last been used for his father's funeral service.

We wandered down to the Mill and stood looking at the rush of water in the sluice where the millwheel would once have operated. A long modern bridge spanned the river over the weir and the noise of water spilling over it drowned out any birdsong. The disquieting atmosphere down here made me uneasy. Evie pointed out a pair of little grebes which disappeared under water perilously close to the weir and emerged further upstream. "There's no trace of the boat house here, but there are some nettles growing, a sure sign of human activity...."

"Are you prepared to tolerate Evie's one-track mind?" I said jokingly to Ruby. "She will drag you through cemeteries and ruins mercilessly."

"Oh, I will love all that. We have lots of history in Romania. It is a very romantic country for myths and legends."

Ruby joined Evie armed with a stout stick, but on seeing the little pool, images of the nightmare I'd had of the twins forcing me into the water sprang into my mind and I backed away. I turned up the track, which would eventually come out into the field opposite the house. Signs of spring were everywhere, with green shoots emerging from the dead leaves and fallen twigs. I stopped and listened to the birdsong, with the sound of the river rushing over the weir in the background. Evie's voice grew fainter, but I sauntered slowly on. I hummed the words to an Abba song.

Trees and bushes now screened the Mill and the river, so I turned to go back before Evie missed me. I froze at a movement in the bushes to my left. Turning my head slightly, my eyes locked on to the eyes of a small deer similarly immobile. Its coat was winter dark. Joe had told me deer frequented these woods and from his descriptions, I guessed this was a muntjac. I couldn't reach my phone to take a photo without alarming it, but sensing my movement, the deer silently turned and ran off. Smiling, I set off to tell

Ruby and Evie. Dear Evie, she had struck gold with Ruby. She deserved happiness in a relationship, and I liked Ruby. She was kind and funny and sensible.

Two walkers appeared from the direction of the river. With a horrible jolt I recognised them: the Twins. My legs turned to jelly. I was rooted to the spot. *I've got to scream for help.* My throat constricted. I couldn't run towards Evie and Ruby; the Twins blocked my path. The way they moved was totally unnerving. As they walked, their legs made no contact with the ground. They were now close enough to touch, and I was still paralysed. They didn't flicker and fade like ghosts in a movie. They looked substantial and malevolence emanated from them. Tears streamed down my face. They knew me: the insolence in their eyes and the decayed teeth in rictus smirks nauseated me. Their smocks were torn and filthy, and I just stood and waited for the stink of death and rot to overcome me.

That apprehension released my fear. Anger suffused me. "Bugger Off!" I yelled. "Go back to where you crawled out of and leave me in peace! Fuck off! Leave me alone!"

And they vanished as if a hologram projection had been switched off.

Hurried footsteps sounded, and I clenched my fists. Evie and Ruby ran round the bend, and I went limp with relief.

"We heard you shout," panted Ruby. "Evie thought you'd fallen."

"No, I just told the Terrible Twins to bugger off," I said calmly, and then started laughing and crying hysterically. Evie grabbed my arm and through my tears I could see Ruby looking alarmed.

"We need to get her back," said Evie. "You support her other side."

"They just appeared right in front of me, Evie, and when I told them to bugger off, they did!"

Another fit of laughter convulsed me, but I was not hysterical anymore. Evie stared at my white face.

"Good for you, girl. Stand up and fight them!" She leaned over to Ruby, who was now looked totally flummoxed. "I'll tell you later," she said.

I felt a slight twinge in my belly and stopped laughing. Had my total fear harmed the baby? The Twins might still have the last laugh on me. *Please let my baby be safe.*

The walk back was blessedly uneventful, and sanity returned. "I'm so sorry," I apologised to Ruby. "You must think I'm unhinged."

"I will explain to her later. You had one hell of a scare," said Evie comfortingly. "And we won't talk about it in front of the others."

Upstairs, I splashed water onto my flushed face. When would those apparitions leave me alone? I was right to feel fear. Evil emanated from them.

Evie must have said something to Will, because he stuck his head round the door as I was changing. "Evie said you were a bit upset.... you're not still brooding about Rafaella and last night, are you?"

"No," I hesitated, then blurted out, "I ran into the Twins and they gave me a fright."

"Twins? Oh!" A shuttered expression crossed his face, but he rubbed my arms. "You'd better come back with us later, then. I've decided to see them all off at Heathrow."

"I'm not coming back just yet," I said. "Evie and Ruby are having a few days on their own before she flies back, and I thought I'd give them a bit of space."

"Come back to my place; I don't want you on your own in this house."

"I'm perfectly safe in the house," I said, nettled. *But for how long?*

I took his hand. "Honestly, I'll be fine. I don't want to leave Serena and Joe with all our mess to clear up while we swan off. You can come back and pick me up after Ruby's flown back to the States. You aren't planning on flying over to the States right away, are you?"

Did Will hesitate? "No, I must show my face at our office, I seem to have been flitting here and there for ages and I need to sort out our treks before I go on my first trek with Raf." He leaned in as if to stave off a protest from me. "And you need to phone your parents and arrange for them to come down here. I'll pick them up and drive them down – it'll be a mystery tour for them – then you can come back with me. We can arrange the wedding when we get back home."

Home. I was beginning to think of Harthill House as home, but I was relieved that Will hadn't suddenly had second thoughts since last night.

"Guess who Uncle Daniel's mystery guest is?" he said with a strange expression. "Ma!"

I looked a bit surprised because he nodded. "Yeah, I'm surprised as well. She phoned me earlier to apologise, as she didn't want to spring a surprise on me in front of all our guests. Very considerate of her. I hope she doesn't start nagging about dates again."

"We can tell her we are getting round to making plans. In fact, let's see if Kim is in her room. She'll have the year planner on her laptop and we can look at some weekends before your trek in the States, or right after. I can then ask Brian if he is free to cater for us if we give him some dates to consider.

Will shrugged. "I suppose now is as good a time as any."

I tapped on Kim's door and in next to no time; she had the year planner up on her screen and tore a page from a notebook to write down dates in late March, April, and May.

"Do you trust me to make tentative arrangements?" I asked

Will as we headed downstairs again. "I really don't want to waddle up the tiny aisle in the chapel. And if you can placate your mother, she'll be over the moon. Hopefully, so will my parents," I sighed.

"I'm not getting married to please parents!" Will protested. "But it makes sense if we present them with a fait accompli, then we'll get less hassle from them."

"But we'll only tell your mother today in private so she can return to France in a better state of mind. We won't say anything to the others at lunchtime, I promise!" I could sense Will's reluctance. "I'm really excited!" I whispered and leaned in to kiss him and he quirked an eyebrow at me. The threat of the Twins faded.

Joe appeared at the foot of the stairs.

"Mr Williamson's car has just arrived. Thought you might like to greet him yourself."

The hall had once again been set up for lunch with a white tablecloth and bowls of primroses placed down the length of the table and a tall vase of blue irises in the middle. Through the open door to the drawing room, most of the others were chatting.

Uncle Daniel was opening the passenger door as we went out and Roberta climbed out, adjusting a dusky pink pashmina as she straightened. She kissed me on both cheeks before hugging her son.

"I'm sorry to spring my arrival on you, but I am flying back tomorrow morning and as I had telephoned Daniel, I invited myself. You've told me so much about your venture I wanted to meet all your colleagues."

"No worries, Ma, it's good to see you again and you too, Uncle Daniel. Come and meet the gang. You'll only remember a few names, but it won't matter, as they are all leaving after lunch. Oh, and while we are outside and out of earshot, Clemmie and I have got some dates in the next few months for the wedding. We're having the ceremony in the Chapel and the reception, only a little one, here, if Brian, our caterer, agrees."

I tried to hide a grin unsuccessfully as Will got the announcement over as quickly as he was able. Roberta immediately hugged me and then Will, and Uncle Daniel shook our hands. "I'm so pleased it's sorted," Roberta said, looking relieved.

"Please don't say anything in front of our guests though, either of you," said Will as we headed through the door. "We need to get dates fixed first."

"Of course, but I am just so happy for you both!" said Roberta, linking arms with the pair of us.

Lunch was a jolly affair even though the weekend was ending and the next time the two teams saw each other would be on Skype. Matt joined us eventually after a late successful birthing, which happened after most of the ewes and older lambs had been moved. We could see them in the field in front of the house; the lambs and mothers were making a lot of noise adjusting to their new environment and the lambs were very frisky.

I caught Ruby glancing at me thoughtfully a couple of times and guessed Evie had told her about the Twins. Rafaella sat between Andy and Ben, who fastened on her conversation with awe.

Eventually, the hall was crowded with people, luggage, dogs, and catering staff clearing away lunch. The minibus was parked in front of the door and Mick was stowing luggage. There was a lot of hugging and promises to keep in touch: not just on Skype, but also on Facebook.

I was surprised when Will took me to one side while everybody was stashing luggage and themselves on the minibus.

"Come up to London with Evie when she leaves," he said, and I frowned at his serious expression. "You can stay with me while Ruby is still around. Phone your parents, drop the bombshell on them, and then we'll go and collect them at the end of the week to bring them down here." He looked down towards my hardly existent bump. "You could get away with not telling them about the pregnancy until they are here.... your mother will be so flabbergasted by the house, she might not react so much to the news."

He was right, of course. I was relieved that Rafaella was returning and it would be just Will and me again. I knew he'd be flying to the US soon to trek, but by that time, our wedding arrangements would be complete.

Rafaella waited till almost everybody had boarded the minibus. "I must congratulate you on the success of this weekend, Clemency. It has been truly fabulous and we'll remember it all when we're back at work."

"It's all down to Brian and the others. I really had little to do in all the work involved, but it has been a lovely weekend." As she air kissed me, I said, "And I believe congratulations are in order on your news! Whose wedding will be first, yours or ours?"

Rafaella flushed, and a little frown appeared between her eyes fleetingly. "Shh, it's still a secret from my team, but Nico and I are planning a wedding soon."

I tried to suppress a mischievous smile.

The occupants of the minibus were waved off by a little crowd of us. Ruby was tearful, saying goodbye to her colleagues. "They are my New York family," she said. We all stood and waved until the minibus disappeared round the long curve of the drive.

"Stay for a cup of tea," I urged Roberta.

"Thank you, but I have a seat reserved on a train, so Daniel is driving me straight to the station. Thank you for lunch, Clemency. I loved meeting all your colleagues; now I know why William loves the career path he chose. They are all so full of energy and enthusiasm. I felt quite old listening to them!"

'Old' would not be how I described Roberta. Her blond hair was cut in a neat bob with a slight flick at the ends just resting on her shoulders and kept from flopping over her face by a blue velvet covered hair band much loved by the English country set. Her blue eyes so like Will's swept over me and she suddenly embraced me.

"I am so pleased that Will has come to his senses, and the wedding is going ahead. Let me know the date you decide on and I will come over and help you in any way I can." She hesitated, as if unsure whether to continue. "And about the other troublesome matter, well, just be very careful and don't stay here any longer than necessary. Daniel is at the other end of the telephone if you need to talk."

After farewells to everybody, Daniel's car trundled sedately down the drive.

Brian's crew had efficiently cleared away all traces of lunch, folded down the tables and stacked up the chairs, ready to be packed into the van with the rest of the catering paraphernalia. As he walked round the drawing room looking for stray glasses or coffee cups, I asked him about catering for a very small wedding reception sometime in the next couple of months.

"My sweet wee girl, I'd be delighted," he beamed. "But you must give me some dates very soon, as April, May and June are very popular for weddings, fetes, and events. I wouldn't want to let you down. I'll be delighted and all to organise your own special celebration."

If I'd had any thoughts of resting, they were quickly dashed by Evie.

"Ruby was concerned about your episode with the Twins this morning. I had to tell her in case she blurted something out at lunchtime."

"In Romania, people are very superstitious about the supernatural," Ruby said, with no embarrassment. "Priests are always being summoned to homes and buildings and as you know, we have folk-lores which have been passed down through generations."

I suppressed a grin as the thought of vampires flitted through my mind.

"I think what Ruby is trying to say without being presumptuous is that you should confront the problem and not try to hide away from it," said Evie, touching me on the hand.

My first reaction was to say thanks. I'll handle it in my own way, but Ruby looked so concerned that I felt I had to reassure her.

"Well, I told them to bugger off," I said lamely, "but I don't know if that would banish them for good."

"That's why we collared you just now. Why don't we go to see this psychic thingummy bloke who lives up the hill? He, of all people, surely must have some answers."

My stubborn response was immediate. "What now? I...I don't feel ready to confront him. He's a stranger. And we can't just go up and see him without making an appointment."

"You said he hadn't a phone," countered Evie. "So we can't make an appointment. Come on, Clem, what have you got to lose? If he's not in, so be it, but if he is, he might know what to do."

I capitulated grudgingly. I could plead nausea or tiredness, but Evie would just keep nagging. She grabbed our arms and swept us out of the door. Joe was out at the front of the house, helping Brian with the last of the equipment.

"We're just going for a quick spin," I called over to him before Evie told him where we were going. "Please tell Serena that we are so full of lunch. She mustn't cook us anything tonight."

"The fridge is full of leftovers. Just help yourselves. I know Serena wants to watch a movie on TV this afternoon."

As Evie drove carefully uphill on the stony track, my stomach was churning. We'd passed the old ash without any incident, but I didn't have a clue how I was going to address Osborne Stafford.

His car was parked in front of the dilapidated bungalow and my heart sank further. *Clemency Wyatt, you are such a coward. Get a grip. I don't have to do anything I'm uncomfortable with.*

Evie and Ruby jumped out expectantly; I emerged more

cautiously. The scuffed front door opened, and Osborne Stafford emerged with a smile on his creased face.

"Three young damsels, my afternoon is blessed! May I offer any assistance?" His focus settled on me again, and I shuffled to the front before Evie took charge. "We're sorry to disturb you without warning," I said and took a deep breath as he looked expectantly at me. "My name is Clemency Wyatt and these are my friends Evie and Ruby. We're staying at Harthill House... and there's... I'm experiencing a little problem..."

"Little!" Evie muttered behind me. "That's an understatement!"

"You are the young lady I met yesterday. You must come in and explain yourselves," said Osborne matter-of-factly. "But before you enter, may I presume to ask that you switch off your mobile phones if you are carrying them? I would rather there be no extraneous energy present inside."

There was a bit of fumbling about as we dragged phones out of pockets. When he was satisfied, he ushered us inside. As we passed him, he hardly reached my shoulder. His fine white hair stood up in tufts and patches of shiny scalp showed through. Osborne was wearing a tweed jacket with a large herringbone pattern and it swamped him. The small hallway was narrow and dark and we had to press against a wall to allow him to shuffle past us in his stout slippers and lead us on. I pulled a face at Evie to show my unease. He led us into what presumably was the main living area of the bungalow and there was a collective intake of breath from the three of us. The walls which might once have been white were now a shade of greeny grey, and sketches and diagrams of various sizes were stuck around the walls, but what stopped us in our tracks were the slivers of silver foil hanging in strips at random intervals from the walls and ceiling reflecting and stirring in the draft from the open door.

Osborne moved piles of papers, books, and journals from a

faded blue sofa and beckoned us to sit down. "Tea first, I think, to break the ice and then you can illuminate me on the reason for your visit," he said pleasantly, as if he was receiving a visit from his grandchildren. He pushed back a heavy rug hanging in a doorway to reveal a small kitchen. From what I could glimpse from my position, it was very neat, in complete contrast to this living room. Plates and cups and dishes were stacked neatly on wooden racks attached to the walls, which were at least free from aluminium foil. Without speaking, we looked at each other and took in the rest of the living room. A bookcase sagged with books and magazines and a battery powered lamp sat on top with an array of torches. A plain table, again covered in books and piles of paper and pots of pens, stood under a window which was hung with a steel blind. Branches of a bush or small tree with new green leaves swayed in the wind outside and scratched the panes of glass disconcertingly. The room was also stiflingly hot as a wood burner set into the fireplace blazed fiercely.

Osborne returned with a tray carrying tea things and a plate of chocolate biscuits. As he paused to find a surface on which to set it, Evie came to her senses and jumped up to clear away sheaves of papers from a leather pouffe.

"You are lucky; sometimes I get so carried away with my research I forget to replenish supplies. I was on my way to the supermarket yesterday when I passed you. It was you, my dear, wasn't it?" he said, looking at me and I nodded. Evie was still on her feet and sorted out the crockery and handed us the steaming cups. At least it looked and smelled like tea. After offering us the biscuits, which I refused, but Evie and Ruby accepted, he bit into one hungrily.

"I can see you are all shocked by my surroundings," he remarked. "My research students from long ago all had the same reaction, but all quickly got used to the arrangements. I don't do as much research nowadays and I only get occasional visits from people who have read my published works and are curious to find out more about The Flint Farm Paraphysical Research Laboratory. They are all as amazed as you and cannot believe the amount of work on the paranormal carried out in this so-called primitive environment."

Ruby couldn't contain her curiosity. "I do not understand what you mean about paraphysics?"

Osborne beamed with delight, and I realised he was relishing the fact that he had a captive audience. "You have heard of physics?" he addressed Ruby. "Perhaps you studied it at school. I have a doctorate in the subject and lectured for some years until I realised paranormal phenomena could not be explained or contained by the theories abounding at the time of classical or modern physics."

Ruby frowned, while Evie and I sat with bland expressions. Perhaps Evie was mentally kicking herself for dragging us here and subjecting us all to a science lecture.

"'Normal' physics is not yet capable of explaining, proving, or disproving the existence of paranormal activity. Consciousness can act without physical forces intervening. Dowsing, mediumship, telekinesis, or the ability to move objects at a distance by mental power or other non-physical means and healing: they and many other forces are all part of the mystery of the multidimensional nature of reality. I became increasingly aware that my scientific colleagues were sceptical about my pursuit of paraphysics as a logical study of the nature of consciousness. So, I resigned my post and set up my lab here in the late 1960s and I've been here ever since."

"And have you proved anything?" queried Evie.

"Ah, my dear, you will have to read my publications about the many experiments I carried out with willing volunteers and students of the paranormal. Then you can draw your own conclusions."

"But where is your laboratory?" asked a bewildered Ruby. Folklore in Romania was a more romantic option than quantum physic lectures in a rundown bungalow in Wiltshire.

Again, Osborne laughed. He really was enjoying himself. "This is my lab." He swept his arm around the untidy room. "I don't need test tubes and Bunsen burners and chemicals. My experiments all stem from here." He tapped his forehead. "I shut out extraneous electrical influences to concentrate on the consciousness of unseen matter."

I felt Evie jerk as she glanced round the room and I quickly came to the same conclusion. No phone, no electricity and aluminium foil to seal out unwanted 'forces'.

Osborne Stafford seemed to realise that we had comprehended perhaps a smidgeon of what he'd said. "More tea, and then it is your turn," he nodded at me and took the teapot into the kitchen to boil more water. We'd seen bottled gas cylinders standing against the outside wall when we'd entered, so presumably that was his source for cooking and lighting. He stood in the doorway as he waited for the kettle to boil. "I won't detain you any longer than you wish. If you want to know all about string theory and my attempts to address the multidimensional nature of reality and the non-physical aspects of reality, I will give you some of my old journals. Things have progressed somewhat since my initial experiments and I am proud of my achievements in this little-known branch of physics."

He returned to the kitchen to fill the teapot.

Ruby had taken hold of Evie's arm and I was worried that she was getting frightened. "Don't worry, we won't be long now," I whispered, hoping to reassure her.

Osborne returned, and we went through the homely motion of

filling teacups again. He indicated the biscuits and took another for himself.

"Forgive me for saying, but I sensed your distress yesterday. I can see the auras surrounding people and yours was – how shall I put it – a little jagged."

I steeled myself. We wouldn't get out of here until I'd explained. I did not know what a jagged aura looked like, so hopefully Stafford would offer advice and we'd escape. Already, the light in the room was fading. Stafford added more logs to the wood burner, lit a fat candle, and sat patiently.

"I'm staying at Harthill House for the moment. It's the home of my fiancé, Will Payne-Ashton." Osborne nodded. He'd lived here for decades and paid rent to the estate, so he must obviously know about the house and its inhabitants.

"I want to know how to get rid of ghosts. They stalk me on the grounds of Harthill House. They are evil and malicious and caused an accident to happen in my fiancé's car. They've been around for centuries and accidents, sometimes fatal, have happened to former residents of the house. They mean to harm me and the baby I'm expecting." I wanted to be as succinct as possible. I didn't want to hear about more physics.

"Psychokinesis," breathed Osborne.

"We know who they are," Evie butted in. "We've been researching the family history. They are twins born in the year 1812 to the youngest son of Sir Horace Barnard who built Harthill House and I'm pretty sure they're harbouring resentment because they were excluded from inheriting the house and estate. We have photographic proof that they existed. The reason we came to you, sir, is to ask your advice on how we get rid of these entities." Evie finished. "They can't be allowed to harm Clemmie or make her leave."

Osborne finished his tea and sat looking thoughtfully at me for a few disconcerting minutes.

"I am flattered that you summoned up the courage to visit the warlock up the hill," he began and we all shifted uncomfortably. He gave a high, girlish laugh. "Oh yes; the locals called me that and I have even been investigated by the police in the early days of my research because the few neighbours I have were quite concerned by the number of young females who often asked them directions to here. They were all research students, of course, and there has never been any impropriety.

I believe that ghosts, as you call them, exist on another plane and you have connected with them on that plane, my dear. I have never carried out any experiments to exorcise them, that has never been in my remit. If these apparitions had caused disturbances indoors, I might have suggested the old-fashioned word, poltergeists. They rely on charged atmosphere for spontaneous occurrences."

We all sort of sagged in disappointment. My first instincts had been right. There had been no point coming here and being subjected to a lecture on the paranormal.

"But I have a circle of like-minded associates with whom I conducted experiments and still do on a limited basis now, for my long-distance experiments, one of whom practises mediumship and she lives not far from here. I can offer you her details and it is up to you to contact her if you so wish."

Evie was looking at me encouragingly and a part of me wanted to get the problem sorted one way or another, while the other part wanted to shrink back in horror and disbelief that I was considering consulting the occult.

"That's very kind of you," I murmured and Stafford went to the table to rummage around. He located a Rolodex- an old-fashioned cylindrical object carrying index cards as a filing or address system. He found what he was looking for, wrote down details on a scrap of paper, and handed it to me.

"You might also try mind control yourself. Despite your fragility, you are, in fact, a strong person."

We all stood up, and I held out my hand to thank Osborne Stafford. He had a surprisingly strong grip for one of such small stature. The others did the same, and he saw us out into a now dark and chilly evening.

"Watch out for potholes on the way down and visit anytime," he called as Evie pulled away in a flurry of gravel and small stones.

It was too dark sitting in the back of the car to make out the address Osborne Stafford had written for me. Ruby was quite animated talking to Evie. "I might have to speak in Romanian for a while just to express myself," she laughed. "You have just confirmed what most foreigners think of the British: eccentric, mad or both!"

"Eccentric, but interesting," said Evie, forcing herself to slow down as we descended the rutted track. Very few lights shone in the dark countryside. "I might just look up his theories and experiments in those journals he spoke about. I bet they are online, even though he doesn't approve of 'electrical' influence. I was very tempted to ask him about his experiments but thought we might be there all night, and that was something I didn't fancy at all!"

The entrance to the drive loomed up, and we passed Mollie's cottage, windows lit behind drawn curtains. I shivered as I thought of the contrast between normality and the paranormal. In the headlights, the old ash tree appeared larger and hung over the drive. I closed my eyes; childishly, I thought if I didn't see the Twins, they wouldn't see me. Nothing happened because Evie came to a halt outside the house. The caterer's van had gone, and the windows were shuttered. The portico light came on as I tried the door: it was locked. I took out my phone to contact Joe and remembered we'd all switched off. As soon as I'd switched on a list of missed calls and messages came up.

The last one was from Serena:

> We are having an early night as all cleared up now. There are plenty of leftovers in the fridge for your suppers. Joe says to use the back entrance as he's left it unlocked for you. See you in the morning!

We used our phone torches to light the way down the steps, under the wing, and through the courtyard. Stars pricked the night sky. It was strange with no dogs dancing around us, but the kitchen was warm and welcoming. Serena had laid three places and left a bottle of red wine and we all decided that scrambled eggs on toast was the quickest meal to prepare.

Evie opened the red wine immediately and apologised to me as she and Ruby took appreciative sips while I looked longingly at the bottle.

"Was the visit up the hill a waste of time, Clem? I thought he might have had a few tactics we could try or that he'd offer to come and visit.," Evie said, forking up scrambled egg.

I fished out the scrap of paper from my pocket. He'd written in his cramped, spidery handwriting: Dorothy Bidwell, Medium, Dottie's Magical Emporium, Burley, Hampshire.

There was a phone number too, and when I handed the scrap to Evie, she shouted with laughter. "Dottie's Magical Emporium! Oh, this just gets better and better! But seriously Clem, it's your call. If you don't want to do anything more, I'll understand... but maybe a brief trip to the New Forest won't hurt. Ruby would love to see the ponies, wouldn't you?"

"Ponies?" asked bewildered Ruby, who'd helped herself to another large glass of wine.

I laughed. "I bet you wish you'd got on the plane with the others after all this," I said. "Well, I suppose a trip to the New

Forest would be good, but if Dottie's Magical Emporium is too much, we are coming straight home. Poor Ruby has already had her fill of eccentrics!"

"Deal," said Evie, and held up her glass in a toast.

Chapter Twenty-Six

We helped strip beds and collect laundry the next morning, and I mentioned to Serena that my parents might be coming for the weekend. "If it's too soon after all this weekend, I can always arrange another."

"No of course it's not too soon; it won't take long to freshen up the master bedroom for them," said Serena. "It will be lovely for them staying here."

It was then that I told them about our wedding plans and there was a lot of hugging and congratulations.

"Brian has agreed to do the catering, providing we can get the right date for him and in all honesty, there won't be many guests."

We left a little later to investigate Dottie's Magical Emporium. I told myself it was always good to have an open mind in all things. Once we'd cleared Bridgeford, the open vistas of the New Forest spread before us. A thin veil of cloud covered the sun. Ruby was delighted to see the promised ponies and cattle immediately after crossing one of many cattle grids. Some congregated on the very edge of the road. Speed limits and warning signs alerted an apprehensive Evie in the driving seat.

The heathland gave way to forest, and we drove along under canopies of budding branches and fern covered banks. The village of Burley spread along a main street and as we drove through, avoiding a gathering of donkeys standing in the middle of the road, Ruby spotted a tearoom and a gift shop next door with the name painted above the windows: Dottie's Magical Emporium. Evie parked nearby.

"Now what do we do?" I asked as we stood by the car.

"Go in and browse? Or is that too obvious?" suggested Evie. "Dottie will think we're just day trippers looking for souvenirs."

A bell jangled loudly as we pushed open the door. A miscellany of gifts was displayed: books, gemstones, jewellery, figures of faerie creatures and mythical beasts. Water colours adorned the walls and racks of filmy and woollen scarves hung alongside the bookshelves. Dream catchers made of coloured glass, shells and feathers spun and tinkled in the draught from the door.

Ruby made a beeline for the figures of mythical beasts, seeming genuinely interested as Evie and I stood taking everything in. Despite the quantity of goods, it was not cluttered and each subject of interest was displayed to the best advantage. There was a jangling noise from the back of the shop and a tall woman emerged through a beaded glass curtain. In my mind I had conjured up a stereotypical image of a medium as depicted in movies and TV: short, stout, ample bosomed, wild-haired and wearing thick glasses, in fact very like Sybill Trelawney in the Harry Potter movies. The woman who came towards us was tall and model slender. Her face was unlined, so she might have been anywhere between 40 and 70 years old. Her greying blonde hair was done up in a neat French pleat and she wore a long grey cardigan and slim fitting jeans. She wore bright red lipstick, shockingly bright, against her pale complexion and silver hooped earrings dangled from her ears.

"Good afternoon. Are you happy to browse, or can I help you

find something in particular?" she said in a cultured Scottish accent.

"Both really," I gabbled as Evie and Ruby seemed engrossed in the books and jewellery. I waved the piece of paper towards her. "I was given this address and your name by Osborne Stafford......" I began hesitantly.

Dottie, if indeed this elegant lady was Dottie, broadened her smile. "Ah, dear Osborne, he said I was to look out for some young ladies who needed my advice."

Evie shot me a startled glance. How had Osborne contacted her at such short notice if he had no electronic means? Surely not by psychic means? "Wow, that was quick," I blurted out. "We only saw him yesterday afternoon!"

"He does possess a mobile phone, more often switched off than on, because he does shun electrical interferences. It was I who insisted he have one in case of emergencies - he is isolated up there and getting rather frail, although he gets very annoyed when the subject is brought up. Did you know he is 90?"

"I'm afraid we don't know him very well," I murmured.

She suddenly put out her hand. "I am Dorothy Bidwell, Dee, owner of this splendid emporium. I am afraid Osborne could not remember all your names, but he was concerned about one of you."

We all shook hands with Dorothy, who suited this name rather than the abbreviated version, and as she fixed her friendly gaze on me, I felt myself relaxing a fraction.

Dee looked at her watch, then went to the door, locked it, then turned the sign to Closed.

"I don't suppose I'll get much more custom on a Monday afternoon out of tourist season," she said. "Come through to my sitting room and you can tell me anything you wish to. And if you see something you would like to purchase, we can sort that out before you leave."

She drew back the bead curtain separating the shop from her private quarters and we all trooped down a passage. Dee opened a door at the far end and daylight flooded the passage. A large bay window identical to the one in the shop overlooked a garden, and the trees of the forest lay beyond a tall hedge. Bird feeders hung in front of the window from which blue tits and chaffinches vied for the nuts and seeds inside. A glowing fire warmed the room and a sofa and a winged armchair flanked the fireplace. Paintings of birds and flowers and forest scenes decorated the walls, and an easel stood opposite the window with a half-finished painting on it. Roberta's paintings in the gallery in London sprang to mind and I thought that these two talented women would have a lot in common with each other.

She pointed to the sofa, and we all sat in a row, while Dorothy removed some embroidery from the chair opposite and sat facing us. Evie stared at a framed photo of a glamorous young couple in white outfits. The girl wore a white mini dress popular in the nineteen sixties, revealing very long legs clad in knee high white boots.

Dee picked it up. "Yes, that is me in my youth."

"You were a model; I recognise the photo. I've seen some of your outfits in an exhibition at the V&A," Evie interrupted, grinning broadly. "And is that the rock star, Johnny Bidwell?"

"Yes, I was a model known as Dee Graham. My agent thought Dorothy was terribly 'uncool' for the swinging sixties! That's my husband, Johnny Bidwell. He was a singer in a rock band and, as was the norm in those days, we married in haste! I was eighteen and Johnny twenty. This is us on our wedding day. Johnny is dead now...." She replaced the photo and sat down. Apart from grey hair replacing the long blonde tresses under the floppy hat in the photo, she had lost none of her model slenderness and gracefulness.

One day, I'd ask her how she had made the transition from model to medium and emporium owner.

"How can I be of assistance to you?" she asked calmly.

"It's Clemency's problem," said Evie. "It might be best if Ruby and I browsed in your shop, if that's ok, so you and she can talk together without us hanging on every word."

"Yes, of course," said Dorothy, "that's very thoughtful of you."

There was an embarrassed silence on my part when Ruby and Evie left.

"Just start at the beginning. It's always best," said Dorothy encouragingly.

So I did, starting with my shock pregnancy and threatened miscarriage, being deposited at Harthill House by my fiancé who had never told me about his house in the country and hadn't expressed any feelings about my pregnancy. Dee listened carefully while I explained about feeling its history all around me at Harthill House, but it did not make me feel uncomfortable apart from the nursery where I heard screaming and a baby's cries. I recounted all the encounters with the Terrible Twins, as I'd christened them; all occurring outdoors and how I'd felt instinctively they wanted to harm me. I told her about my nightmare, so real and a warning and the accident in the car with Will. I told her of my shock when we found a photo of the Twins who had been real and living once and had names. I related how Evie's fascination with family history and background researching archives had led her to believe that the twins' appearances had something to do with them not inheriting the estate.

"Will's mother left Harthill House to live in London after several so-called accidents and she and Will's uncle are very reluctant about me continuing to live there. Because I'm pregnant, you see, and I think the same thing happened to them, but they aren't telling me the full story because they don't want to frighten me. I think the Twins were so bitter about not inheriting when they were alive that they've put a curse on male heirs down the line."

I sat back, having run out of words. Dee remained silent; her eyes closed. "You probably think it's all implausible and improbable, like Will."

"No, on the contrary, Clemency, I think it is all too plausible."

"Osborne said 'entities or ghosts are not his field of investigation, that's why he recommended you. I don't honestly know what you can do. Do you do exorcisms or séances? Without insulting you, I know nothing about mediums."

"Except what you have seen on TV and in films." She gave a short laugh. "There are protective practices I can give you, such as learning mantras and using herbs and special gemstones, but I really would like to visit the sites of disturbances before I can give any advice or help."

"Serena and Joe, who manage the house and estate, don't know about any of this, so it'll be difficult explaining what you are about. Would you need to see inside the house? I've only ever encountered them outdoors."

"I'm sure we can think of a valid reason for my visit without going into details if you wish," said Dee, and I felt my face flushing with embarrassment.

"Is your fiancé sympathetic about your sightings and feelings?"

"Well, he listened, but he doesn't really understand. He's preoccupied by our new partnership with a company in New York, and if I'm honest, I think our new business partner is a bit too familiar with him. I'm afraid it's made me suspicious."

"Has Will given you any sign that he reciprocates?"

"No, he said he was really embarrassed when she came on to him after a drink too many."

"If he told you that, it appears to me he's not hiding anything from you. Keep talking to each other. Trust and honesty are paramount if a relationship is to last."

I smiled. Dee Bidwell should also add agony aunt to her umbrella of roles.

"Also, these twins might well still seek some sort of retribution, even if the law included female first born heirs. If I could come to visit tomorrow morning, we can begin a plan of action."

She seemed so decisive and confident that my spirits rose.

"Thank you," I simply said.

As if on cue, there was a light tap on the door and Evie poked her head round. "Are we disturbing you?"

Dorothy looked at me, but I was happy for Evie and Ruby to rejoin us.

"In that case, I'll put the kettle on," said Dorothy, and disappeared into the kitchen.

"Ruby has got an assortment of gemstones for you to choose," said Evie as Ruby laid out the stones on the rug in front of the fire.

"Each has special properties for healing, combating negative energy, strength," said Ruby, lightly stroking the stones. I looked at the different coloured stones glowing softly in the firelight and wished that just by carrying some of them round in my pocket, my problems would be solved. They were all different colours and the only one I was sure about was the pink rose quartz, which I picked up and cradled in my hand. I separated out a few more that I was drawn to. Neither Ruby nor Evie told me the names. "We'll ask Dorothy to advise which is best in the circumstances," said Ruby.

Tea was accompanied by a fruit loaf. "Vegan," Dee announced. Ruby polished off two slices with relish.

"New York food is excellent if you are willing to pay a lot. I am experimenting with English food and so far, I am happy to report its excellence also!" she said, responding to our amused faces.

"Are these the gemstones you are choosing?" asked Dee, looking at the little pile. I nodded. Whatever she said about them, I wanted to keep them.

"Rose quartz is good for restoring trust and harmony in relationships and for promoting self-worth." She quirked an eyebrow at me and pointed to each stone without touching them as she described their properties. "You've picked out a 'rough' Amethyst, which is excellent, as it is said to hold more power than the smooth. It's incredibly powerful and protective against negative attacks, so a good all-rounder for protection and well-being. Obsidian is another powerful stone which will protect against physical and emotional attacks. And I see you've picked out the Carnelian. If you put this with your other stones in a little pouch, it acts as a cleanser to your other stones and it's also good for personal creativity and motivation. Jasper empowers the spirit, combats negativity and stress, and promotes courage and confidence. I don't think I could have chosen any better for you, Clemency! I'll give you a pouch to keep them in and always carry them around."

Evie insisted on paying for them and Ruby had also chosen a selection for herself.

"Now, when will it be convenient to visit," asked Dee. "I can do very early tomorrow morning and open the shop a little later. The evenings aren't light enough yet. I am closed on Wednesdays, if that fits better."

I looked at Evie. "We should be going back to London tomorrow."

"I can be there tomorrow morning at 8 o'clock. It really won't take long for me to latch on to anything unusual in the house and the grounds."

"I feel awful asking you not to tell Serena and Joe what you are doing," I said, almost squirming with embarrassment.

"I can say you are a colleague of mine who is an avid historian." Evie volunteered.

"I promise I will explain to everybody in due course," I apologised. "It's not in my nature to deceive, but Joe and Serena have been so good to me and I don't want to give them any more anxiety on top of keeping me well these last few weeks."

Dee nodded. "I understand. I can reassure you I won't be

hurling myself around brandishing crosses and chanting incantations," she said with a humorous twinkle in her eye.

∼

Sitting in the back of the car as we returned, I could see Evie glancing at me from time to time in the rear-view mirror, but she didn't comment. She and Ruby had plenty to say to each other. I fingered the bag of stones which I'd taken out of my pocket and rubbed them gently through the soft velvet pouch. I was sceptical that such simple things like gemstones could produce such powerful protection and aid confidence or courage, but maybe one just had to trust for them to do their work.

I was worried about Dee trotting round the house and grounds under the watchful eyes of Joe and Serena. Joe would be quite phlegmatic about the visit, but Serena would be suspicious. She had a natural wariness about her. And Mollie – above all else, I didn't want Mollie knowing anything about the visit. Hopefully, Dee would have completed her tour before Mollie appeared for work.

Then we were turning up the drive, passing the lighted windows of Mollie's cottage. There was a tremendous bump, and the car lurched alarmingly sideways so that even strapped in, I felt as if I was being thrown to the other side of the car. Evie stopped dead and there was a jerk as she stalled with the car still in gear.

"Bugger!" she hissed. "I hope I haven't hit a poor deer. I didn't see anything, did you?" She released her seat belt while addressing Ruby, who shook her head and opened her door. A spasm of terror passed through me and I was reluctant to either get out or stay in the car.

Evie was staring at something on the ground in disbelief. The headlights enabled us to see a large limb of a tree behind the car.

"How could this be?" Evie exclaimed, one hand on top of her head.

I shook my head. Ruby said quietly: "If that had fallen a second earlier, we would have been under it. Look at the size of it!"

I started to shiver violently and looked around wildly. I knew who or what had been responsible for this near miss. I was still clutching my bag of gemstones.

Ruby saw my distress and took my arm, pointing to the bag. "Looks like they've started protecting you already," she said incredulously.

"We must tell Joe before anybody else drives into it," said Evie. She walked round the car, inspecting the wheels and the body. "No damage, thank God, just a few twigs on the roof."

Just like there was no damage to Will's car the other time there'd been a near miss in the same spot.

Because we were standing under the old ash tree.

Joe and Serena were both in the kitchen when we burst in and were given the usual ecstatic welcome from Bess and Jasper, although Tabby fled at all the commotion. Evie told Joe about the fallen limb of the ash tree.

"Right, I'll get Matt out and his tractor, and we'll drag it away." He went out to pull on a jacket and boots. "Any damage to your car?"

"No, nothing, not even a scratch. It's a miracle," said Evie.

"That must have given you all a shock," said Serena, eyeing my ashen face. "Come and stand by the Aga and warm yourself, Clemency. You look as if you've seen a ghost."

"We never saw or heard it fall," said Evie. "Just felt a bump and I thought I'd hit a deer or badger."

"Joe and Matt will clear it away in next to no time," said Serena. "We'd better ask a tree surgeon to check it over. It is quite ancient."

"Would you mind if I had a whisky or glass of wine, Serena?" asked Evie. "I think I need fortifying."

Serena told Evie where to find supplies.

"You'll feel better after a bit of supper," Serena said as she lifted a large casserole dish out of the oven. "We were going to have ours and then leave some for when you got back, but we can all eat together now."

The last thing I needed was a heavy supper, but I had no desire to cause Serena any concern over me refusing to eat.

"It's good of Joe to move the branch now," I said at last, leaning on the hot Aga and rubbing my hands. "We met someone who knows Evie in Burley, and she is quite keen to see Harthill House. She's going to come very early tomorrow morning before she starts work and before we leave. I hope you don't mind."

"Why should I mind? You are soon to be mistress and free to do what you like here," said Serena and set plates on the hotplate of the Aga to warm. Something in her tone made me glance sharply at her.

"Serena, I don't know what the contract or arrangement is between you and Will and the estate Trust, but I'd never be able to look you in the eye if you are worried that I might dispense of you and Joe after we're married. You must stay here; this is your home!"

Serena caught some of the anguish in my tone and stopped fiddling with cutlery and turned towards me.

"I can't say it hasn't crossed our minds what your plans will be for this place, but I can say that as I've come to know you in these last few weeks, I know you wouldn't act unfairly."

Two little bright spots had appeared on her cheeks as she spoke and instinctively, I reached out to touch her arm. "Whatever happens, you are needed here until you decide for yourselves about your future."

"That's what Joe said. He said it wasn't in either of your

natures to get rid of us! If I may presume, do you think you could say the same thing to Mollie as well? She's unsettled also," said Serena, picking up the cutlery again.

"Yes, of course. It's odd getting used to the feeling that I'll have staff here as well as at the office in London. We had to reassure them about their jobs as well after the merger with Rafaella's outfit. I'll just nip upstairs now, before supper."

Dee had given me a slim book on the power of crystals and a printout, probably from a bigger volume, about how to cast a protective circle. I blinked at the title and sat down heavily on the bed, shaking my head in disbelief that in a couple of days I'd progressed from being an anxious hostess to a seeker of arcane laws. I threw them down, went to the bathroom and when I returned, I almost chucked the booklets into the recycling bin. I'd always been pragmatic, rational, and always confidant that any problem had a logical solution.

Yet here I was trying to assimilate ghosts, curses, crystals, and magic all at once, with no pragmatic or logical solution in sight. I unfastened my jeans, which were getting uncomfortably tight and opening the pouch, poured the gemstones onto the bed. They lay glistening, and I gathered them up in my palm. They were warm, but that was probably because they'd been snug in my pocket rather than emanating power and protection. There I went again, being sceptical; but as they lay comfortably in my palm, I closed my eyes and tried to empty my mind of everything, concentrating on the crystals. Was I imagining an increasing heaviness and warmth? My beeping phone brought me back to the present, and I tucked the crystals back into their pouch. Maybe they had given protection from that falling limb. I'd give them another chance.

Kim had messaged, saying everybody was back at work, facing reality with a bump, and thanking me for such a special weekend. There was also a voicemail message from Will, brief and to the point as usual asking when I was arriving and had I phoned my parents yet. "Love you," he'd ended. I sighed. Did I have the strength tonight to phone my parents?

There was a brief knock, and Evie stuck her head round the door.

"Matt and Joe are back – the drive's all clear now and supper is ready."

We clumped down the broad staircase. "I mentioned Dee was a colleague of yours interested in history," I said. I suppose we should all be telling the same little lies."

"That's almost exactly what I said to Serena, and she didn't turn a hair about it."

Serena had set the hot dishes on the hotplate and we all helped ourselves; Joe and Matt politely waiting for us to fill our plates before diving in. The chicken casserole was delicious, herby, and lightly garlicky. The others also had jacket potatoes, but I gave them a miss.

"That was a seriously large chunk of ash that came down," said Joe. "It's a good thing we had chains to drag it away with the tractor. We'll go down tomorrow after Matt's finished milking with chain saws. I suppose the upside is that we'll have a good supply of logs."

"I couldn't see any signs of rottenness, although we'll be able to see better in daylight," Matt added, piling butter into his jacket potato.

"We had no warning," said Ruby, "just a bump. Evie thought she'd run into a deer."

"I'll call a tree surgeon tomorrow to check the whole tree over. We can't have any more of it suddenly coming down. I hope we don't lose it. It's older than this house."

I remained silent and, glancing at my closed face, Serena asked if we'd enjoyed the trip through the New Forest.

"Oh yes, the ponies are cute and I wasn't expecting to see so many cattle around too," enthused Ruby. "And Burley is a little gem tucked away in the forest."

"You get a fair few nutters attracted to Burley in the summer," remarked Matt.

"Excuse me, nutters? What is this word, please?" asked Ruby and we all couldn't help laughing at her pronunciation.

"Crazy people," Matt stated, "people with obsessions about weird things. Hippy types go there because of its connection with witches and witchcraft."

We three didn't dare look at each other.

"It has a very nice tea shop and gift shop," I offered weakly.

"Yes, and we bumped into an old colleague of mine, so it was all quite providential really," said Evie angelically.

Chapter Twenty-Seven

"We had a narrow escape last night coming back from seeing you," said Ruby to Dee Bidwell as she unfolded herself from her Fiat 500. "Did you see a huge branch in the drive as you drove past? It smacked down just after we passed. I think Clemency's crystals were doing their job protecting us!"

"Yes, it was rather large. Joe was there and introduced himself. I sensed something had happened near the tree. There are lingering memories of fear and grief and anger."

Glancing at me, Evie said: "An accident happened there a couple of centuries ago. A carriage ran into the tree and some family members were killed."

"Ah," said Dee thoughtfully. "Maybe when the activity has finished there, you can take me down again, Clemency?"

I ushered everyone inside. "Serena has left tea and coffee in the sitting room if you have time."

"That would be lovely, thank you," said Dee, admiring the hall as we passed through it. "My friend Jonathon, who runs the bike hire, is opening the shop for me this morning so I don't have to rush round here like a lunatic – unless you need to get away yourselves?"

"No, we are fine for time," said Evie firmly.

Ruby cleared away our drinks and Evie, Dee, and I began our tour of the house. Evie gave a potted history as we stood in rooms, but I could tell Dee was concentrating on residual memories and remained silent. I hoped Mollie wouldn't appear; she'd be even more huffy if she was introduced as another historian. She'd been busy yesterday morning, and Serena insisted Mollie had today off.

On the top floor, I fitted the key into Geoffrey's study door and stood back. Evie had not been in here and peered round with interest.

"Oh dear," said Dee, closing her eyes. "The poor man; there is a lot of sadness in this room. I think he brought all his sadness and worry in here."

I recalled the entry in Geoffrey's diary – 'terrible day' – but said nothing. I would not be disloyal about Will's mother and father and their relationship. We were quiet while Dee closed her eyes and her lips moved. Then she nodded and smiled and went out. As I locked the door, I hoped she had provided some relief for Geoffrey's evidently restless spirit. Evie's phone rang, and she went downstairs to answer it.

The nursery looked more cheerful, newly decorated and furnished with curtains, pictures on the wall and a two single beds, now stripped, between the windows. The rocking chair stood in a corner.

Dee breathed in sharply and looked at me. "Have you felt something in here?" she asked.

"Yes," I said simply.

"Tell me what you felt or saw."

"I didn't see anything. I wasn't feeling too grand and sat in the rocking chair. I must have nodded off, and I heard screaming, crying, wailing, and a baby's cry. It was horrible at the time, but I thought I must have dreamt it. Mollie says this is the nursery where all the babies and toddlers were looked after years ago."

"There has been illness here and tragedy, death, such loss - unbearable pain of loss and grief……" Dee closed her eyes and took my hand. "I've put a protective bubble around us," she said. "You must follow the instructions I gave you and do the same."

She scrabbled in her bag and brought out a metal box and extracted a strange bundle and her lighter. "Smudge," she explained, "dried sage leaves. When lit, they cleanse and remove bad energy. There is a person here who is feeling unbearable grief and cannot find peace. She has suffered and continues to suffer. I can only try to ease her grief."

She lit the bundle, and I sat in the rocking chair as she walked round the room wafting the soothing aromatic smoke and reciting quiet words I couldn't hear. I closed my eyes and felt a sense of peace surround me. After a few moments Dee said, "I would advise you not to use this room for your nursery, Clemency. May I return and try to communicate with this poor soul, although I don't think she is the only one who has suffered tragedy here?"

I remembered the inscription at the foot of the angel in the little churchyard: 'May Our Lord Jesus Christ and Mary, his Virgin Mother, ease her Great Grief'. Did Frances' grief still linger in this room and goodness knows how many others who'd lost babies? Poor Frances.

"I have never seen apparitions of the Twins inside the house," I said as we descended the back stairs to the basement. Dee peered into the little pantries off the long corridor.

"My, this is a busy passage; this is the heart of the house and has such good energy," she said.

"Oh, I'm so glad you said that; I feel the same; as if the servants are still bustling about getting on with their daily tasks!" I said. "Shall we go outside now? I can indicate some places where I've had encounters with the twins."

"Of course, they're the real reason I'm here. If you see them, just hold my hand and I'll project a circle."

I told Dee that I was convinced they were responsible for the branch falling from the tree as we walked through the garden to the gates where they'd loitered. She said she could pick up faint presence.

"I felt very different energies when I passed the ash tree," she said. "Shall we walk down there?

The sound of a tractor reached us at it trundled up the farm drive with a trailer full of logs on the back. We would be undisturbed by the ash tree. Despite feeling agitated at approaching the tree, still huge despite losing one of its outspread limbs, I had the crystals in my pocket and Dee's reassuring presence. She walked around the girth and I saw she still had smouldering leaves in her hand. Two jackdaws flew from their perch on a lower branch and she greeted them as if they were friends.

"There's a residual feeling of bitterness, resentment and rage mixed with pain and suffering. I think these entities are hiding from me. They recognise I can feel their presence and resist me trying to tune in. When you see them, you immediately go into panic mode and you're fearful. They are feeding on that, I'm afraid, Clemency. I'm not sure if I can get to the bottom of their resentment or send them on to a quieter plane."

"They are bitter because they think their father should have inherited Harthill House and, by rights, passed on down to them. Evie worked it out from the family tree. There was a family tragedy when a carriage collided with the ash tree and threw the line of inheritance sideways through a female."

"Hmm, isn't that the case in so many successions throughout history?"

"It's silly really because there's no title and a lot of the estate was sold off."

"I wouldn't think the Twins are aware of that in their bubble of warped time. Let me think of how I can help more or of somebody else with experience of such hauntings."

"I feel it's more of a curse on all the poor women who've carried the so-called heirs. I love Harthill House, but perhaps like Will's mother, I'll be safer away from here. And my son when he is born," I said quietly.

Dee stood with her eyes closed, but I could see from her pale face that whatever she was projecting or praying was unsuccessful. The twins' auras of bitterness and anger were too strong to break.

We walked back up the drive. "How do you cope?" I asked. "How can you live normally when you can feel all these emotions?"

"It's the same as having visitors in your house; once I ask them to leave, they're out of my head. Sometimes I must deliberately tune out, otherwise it would be like having a head full of clamouring souls. I have to be firm."

Evie and Ruby were striding towards us.

"How are you getting on? Sorry I had to leave, a call about work." She grimaced, then asked Dee if she would like another coffee.

She looked at her watch, then at me. "Thank you, but not for me. I was just telling Clemency that I will think and pray about her problem, but I ought to get back."

Drops of rain were just starting to bounce off the grass and trees, and we hurried back to the house.

"Stay positive; remember your crystals and your mantras. Here is my box of smudge. Use it where you have encountered the entities. I know you doubt their efficacy, but if you keep your mind calm, it will make a difference. I promise to keep in touch." She gave me a quick hug as if to reassure me and climbed into her car.

"She said she couldn't contact them; she said the twins were hiding from her," I said flatly to the others as we watched her car disappearing down the drive. Despite her advice, I wasn't feeling too positive about the visit.

"Well, you'll be away from here shortly," said Evie. "Get your stuff together and then we can get going."

I stared around my bedroom. I wished now that I hadn't been to see Osborne Stafford or Dorothy Bidwell, although I liked her a lot. Dee had just highlighted all the same places that I had felt or seen something, inside and out of the house, but it would be good to get back to the city. I felt strong enough to return to work without fear of the Twins stalking me. I decided to leave some of my clothes here as I'd be back at the weekend with Mum and Dad.

My phone call to my parents the night before had gone reasonably well, considering all the questions mother fired at me. As soon as dad had uttered the word wedding on the phone, Mum had snatched the receiver from him and started her grilling. Naturally, she had wanted to know why now and I'd countered with the reply, why not now? She was suspicious about the weekend visit, but I could hear dad in the background calming her down.

There was a tap on the door and Serena entered with some garments I'd washed and dried yesterday.

"Sorry I only met your friend briefly," she said. "I hope she enjoyed her visit?"

"Oh yes, very much. And as she only lives in the New Forest, we can see her again hopefully."

"I hope you'll stay for lunch before you all head off. It'll seem very quiet after the weekend. Could you stop off at Mollie's just to say goodbye? I told her not to come in today as she did so much over the weekend and although you'll be back next weekend, I think she would appreciate the gesture." Serena looked embarrassed at her suggestion, but I reassured her it would be no trouble.

I hoped Evie wasn't in a tearing hurry to get away and I sent her a text rather than go looking for her. As I checked the cupboard, I spotted Geoffrey's satchel on the shelf. I dragged it down, glad I'd found it, otherwise I would have gone back to London with the key to the study still in my pocket. The leather was badly scuffed, but Will might find it useful and a legacy from his father. I undid the large buckles and peered inside. No wonder it was heavy, it was filled with ledgers or books. Maybe they were some of Geoffrey's account books.

I opened one stiff backed ledger at random. The date 12th March 1814 was inscribed on the page and underneath, elegant decorative script filled the page. Random words: sheep, cattle, storm, and Gerard leapt off the page. I flicked back to the front of the book. There on the first page was the title: "Harthill House 1810-1815" in the same flowing script and underneath, her name: Honoria Barnard Payne. I'd found Honoria's journals, and they had been under my nose all this time! I rooted out another journal and opened it at the front. This one was dated 1807-1810. In the year 1809, the accident had happened when several family members were killed. I had to fight the instinct to delve into the journals right there and then, but time was against me. I carefully put them back in the satchel and put the satchel in the small case in amongst my clothes. There would be plenty of time to scan through it and then share with Evie back in London.

Mollie was cleaning her windows when we stopped outside her lodge cottage to say goodbye and thanks for all she had done. She nodded and even as I said I'd be back at the weekend she'd said enigmatically, "Oh, aye, we'll be seeing a lot more of you than you realise yet."

Chapter Twenty-Eight

Will was cheerful when he'd picked me up from Evie's, where I'd gone to collect a few more bits of clothing and toiletries. A stab of jealousy had briefly shot through me that someone else – Ruby- was sharing our flat and claiming Evie's attention, but I pushed that emotion from my mind immediately. It was Evie's turn to experience happiness now.

I needed to regain confidence before returning to work, so I turned down Will's offer to drive me and battled with public transport. Will usually cycled in anyway. Travelling in was an ordeal of queues, crowds, traffic. I'd only been 'in the country' for a few weeks but already displaying a country person's shock at busy city life!

When I sat in front of my computer, I feared that Kim would have finished all the tasks so I'd be redundant, but I needn't have worried: the seasons' bookings were building up and Ben wanted me to edit bloopers and discrepancies on the webpages he was redesigning.

Kim insisted I called it a day when I started to flag in the afternoon and I gladly made my way back to Will's flat, again experiencing a twinge of regret about not returning to my own place. The journey on public transport exhausted me. I made a cup of chamomile tea and lay on the sofa for a while. Brian Chadwick had messaged me with his only available dates: alarmingly few to choose from. After phoning Will, still at the office, we agreed on the 24$^{\text{th of}}$ March, both of us registering panic at how close we were to that date, but I was able to confirm it with Brian.

I contacted Serena straight after. "I'm worried about finding someone to marry us at such short notice," I said anxiously.

"There are several denominational ministers in Bridgeford," said Serena. "I know them all through going to various events, so would you like me to find out if any are free on that date?"

"That would be a load off my mind," I said. "I don't really care who marries us as long as it's legal!"

Serena laughed. "I'll see if I can pull some strings and get back to you."

I texted Will to bring home a takeaway that evening because the fridge was depressingly empty. It had been lovely being waited on by Serena and Joe, but now I needed to stop acting like the lady of the manor and apply myself to domesticity.

The ledgers in the satchel had that familiar musty smell of second-hand bookshops. The book coverings might have been made of calfskin; Evie would know. The pages inside were foxed and slightly brittle. I'd learned from Evie to turn the pages of old books with clean hands. Why had Will's father put them in the satchel? Was it possible that he was going to take them to an archivist or return them to the library? Maybe he'd had doubts about the original inheritance stipulation. And the thought struck me that maybe he had put them in his satchel prior to destroying them.

Settling on the sofa again, I read the first entry written in such an elegant script:

Twentieth Day of April 1807

Gyles has expressed his most serious concerns regarding Edwin. Instead of attending Dr Eldridge's lectures in Salisbury on the management of rivers and water meadows, Edwin declared he wasn't a farmer and cared not to become one. He was absent for the whole of the day. He returned home for supper and gave no answers to his father's questions on Dr Eldridge's lecture and excused himself shortly after eating. Dear Papa, who was dining with us, said it was abundantly apparent that the lad was not suited for the business of running an estate. Gyles was already furious at his son's behaviour and was about to argue with Papa, but I gently laid my hand on his arm, which had the fortunate result of restraining him. Dear Papa has not been in good health recently. He picks at his food and even refused the excellent port which Gyles keeps. I worry that the death of Mama has taken a greater toll on him than we have feared. Edwin's absence from Dr Eldridge's lectures became apparent when a messenger arrived this evening with a missive from the good doctor expressing his concern that Edwin was not suffering a malady causing his absence. Gyles begged our leave and hurried from the dining room. Bartholomew and Edmund were attempting to hide sly grins, and I felt obliged to reprimand them. Dear Papa then engaged them in a conversation about seed drills and Edmund instantly seemed to grow in stature as he expounded on the benefits of sowing using the new machinery rather than casting seeds by hand which were not evenly sown and mostly eaten by birds and vermin. My dear Cousin Edmund is almost like a brother to Bartholomew and despite his youth is so enthusiastic about new methods in agriculture that I could see dear Papa's face brightening at their conversation. Tolly and I exchanged indulgent smiles, But I was exceedingly pleased that my dear sisters, Anne and Grace were supping in their room tonight as they are such timid creatures that any uncomfortable behaviour at the table and Gyles' irritation with Edwin would have caused them megrims.

It was a diary. Honoria had kept a diary of the happenings at Harthill House and the first entry in this particular journal was certainly informative. Just in that first entry I established that son Edwin bunked lectures, Honoria's father James was not well, her husband was mad at Edwin, her other son and her cousin smirked at the prospect of Edwin getting a rollicking from his father, and Honoria's sisters were of a delicate constitution. Instead of being bored, I wanted to know more. I laid my head back on the cushion before embarking on another entry.

Bang! The noise startled me and I jerked awake, totally disorientated. "Clem?" Will was calling from the hall and as he entered the sitting room, he switched on the wall lights so that I sat squinting in the brightness.

"Why are you sitting in the dark?" he demanded as he dumped several cardboard bags on the coffee table.

"I must have dozed off; what time is it?"

"Time to eat. I brought a takeaway – yours is a non-spicy veggie option with rice so it doesn't upset you. What's this?"

Will picked up the journal which had slid to the floor when I'd sat up in alarm.

"It's a ledger from Harthill House," I said. "I was going to let Evie study it for a picture of social history two hundred years ago. I found it in your father's study. I hope you don't mind me bringing it here."

Will shrugged. "History isn't my thing! Nice bag though. I seem to remember Dad had a bag like it. I might find a use for it." He leaned over and kissed me. "I'll get some plates; let's eat before this all goes cold."

∼

The Shadow Watchers

By the end of that first week back in London, plans were progressing. A special license to marry in the chapel had been applied for and issued. I'd spoken to the non-denominational minster from Bridgeford, the only minister available for that Saturday in March, and booked her going on Serena's character reference. Laura Cartwright was approved to conduct the marriage service, so we didn't need an official registrar as well. Brian Chadwick needed to know how many people to cater for and sent a range of menus via email. The guest list would not be extensive; as well as our work colleagues, my parents, brother and his family. Will only had his mother and Uncle Daniel and all at Harthill. Ruby had negotiated with Rafaella in extending her stay in the UK by working at the office with us, so that she could attend the wedding.

"And she is going to pay my wages while I'm here and work remotely for her!" said a jubilant Ruby.

I added Dr Laidlaw and Dorothy Bidwell to the guest list. Will had no objections. He was happy for me to continue with the arrangements. A thought struck me. "Do you think we should invite Rafaella?" I said, preparing to be generous.

"No," said Will abruptly.

"Have you had a disagreement with her?" I persisted. Even at the office, Skype calls seemed to have shortened considerably.

"No," Will said again, "she's busy preparing for treks before I go out to join them." He took another swig from his nearly empty bottle of lager. "She's getting married soon."

My mouth dropped open. "What? Before our wedding?"

"I don't see why it matters," he muttered, eyeing his empty bottle. "She mentioned it in the minibus to Heathrow. I thought she was tipsy when she told me that night in the pub just to make me jealous, but apparently it's to some Italian Count."

Relief that she wouldn't be coming to our wedding was overshadowed by the fact that it was obvious Will still harboured feelings for her.

I put down my pen and stood up. Holding out my hand, I said, "I'm off to bed. Are you coming?" Will put aside his magazine and took my hand.

"Good idea," he said.

Saturday dawned fresh and spring-like, certainly in our part of the city, and I hoped the sun would still be shining when we drove up to Harthill House with Mum and Dad. They lived in Bromley, so it meant a bit of a detour out of the city to avoid congestion charges. We set out early to avoid traffic.

We were offered coffee when we arrived at their house in a quiet residential road and refused because Will explained he didn't know how busy the motorways would be on a Saturday, especially the M25 if we were to get to Harthill House by lunchtime. Serena had kindly offered to prepare lunch, just soup and bread and cheese and leave it for us to serve up in the dining room and she would also do a casserole for supper which would cook slowly in the Aga. She obviously sensed that she and Joe should stay in the background initially until Mum and Dad settled in.

Dad was happily chatting to Will in the front of the Range Rover. Mum and I sat in the back quietly at first, then the questions started. It didn't help that I'd left nothing for Mum to arrange – the guest list was decided and the catering completely taken care of. Mum sniffed, saying that caterers in her opinion would always let one down over arrangements, but I said Brian Chadwick was local and good. Mum persisted in wanting to know why we'd suddenly sprung it on them. I'm sure she was fishing, but I just didn't want to tell her about my pregnancy in the back of the car, and certainly nothing about requirements of entailments set out in ancient Wills, so I exaggerated Will's upcoming trips to the States and Europe and that we honestly weren't left with many dates to choose.

"At least let me help you choose your dress," insisted Mum, and my heart sank. I hadn't really given a wedding outfit much thought, but I relented and agreed.

"Good," Mum said, looking a little more agreeable. "I'll come up to town one day next week and I'll make appointments at wedding outfitters. You are my only daughter, so I need to see you dressed properly. Cost is not a problem".

Will had been listening to our conversation because I caught sight of the big smirk on his face in his rear-view mirror.

Dad probed Will about the location of his house and Will would only commit to saying it was a few miles south of Salisbury and that his parents and grandparents before that had lived in it. "It's been kind of empty since my father died," Will explained. "And my mother went to live in France so she could do her painting."

"Oh dear, will it be full of cobwebs and mice?" said Mum, mentally arming herself with mop and bucket and dusters and preparing to shame our slovenly habits.

"No, it's all taken care of, I promise," said Will, smiling. "You just have to enjoy the weekend."

At last, as we wound along the road following the river towards Harthill, both my parents took more interest in the countryside. Several times Will had to pull in to let vehicles and farm traffic pass and then suddenly we were swinging right up the drive and my heart began beating faster. I think Will cottoned on to my trepidation as he caught my eye in the mirror.

"What a lovely little cottage!" Mum exclaimed as we passed Snowdrop Lodge. There was no sign of Mollie either in the garden or in her window, but smoke was drifting up into the clear blue sky. The old ash tree overshadowed the drive, looking sadly lopsided after losing one of its boughs, but was still large enough to make me shiver. My hand slid into my pocket where I'd placed the crystals and I inwardly murmured one of the mantras Dee Bidwell had given me. We sped past, and I let out a sigh of relief.

"Is it much further?" Mum asked, thinking I was in discomfort. "We both might need a loo soon!"

"Almost there," said Will cheerfully. Between the lime trees lining the drive, first the chimneys and then the roof became visible before disappearing behind the large stand of tall beeches and oaks at the final bend of the drive.

"That looks like a big house. I wonder which lord lives there?" said Dad.

Will drew up with a noisy skid on gravel. He got out and ran round to open Mum's passenger door. Dad descended, looking up at the red bricks glowing in the sunshine.

"Is this a hotel? Are we having lunch here? Looks very grand," Mum said, staring at the many windows. Will got between them and put his arms round their shoulders.

"Maureen, Arthur, welcome to Harthill House, the ancestral home of the Payne-Ashtons!"

Mum stared incredulously at him, then turned to me. "You've never said a word about this!" she said accusingly. She looked about to burst into tears and I put my arm round her. "Mum, it's ok, really".

As if on cue, the front door opened and Bess and Jasper burst out barking, whole bodies wriggling. Dad bent down to pat them and received an ecstatic lick on the nose from Jasper. Joe and Serena emerged, and Mum blinked.

"This is Serena and Joe, who manage the house and estate while I'm away. And Bess and Jasper, of course! This is Clem's mum and dad, Maureen and Arthur Wyatt."

Mum's face went through a range of expressions as she struggled to comprehend.

"Let's get inside. I'm sure we could all do with a cup of tea or coffee." Serena said after shaking hands. I caught Serena's eye and nodded towards Mum.

"There's a nice warm fire inside. William and Joe will bring your luggage. Don't worry," she said in a soothing tone.

We managed to get Mum inside, although she resisted. Dad was inside in a flash and stopped dead in the hall as he took in the size, the huge fireplace, ablaze with crackling logs, the alcoves, busts, and plaster swags. Behind him, Joe and Will came in with our small collection of bags.

"You're a dark horse, Will," said my father. "And have you got a title hidden under your belt as well?" His eyes twinkled as he clapped Will on the back.

"Definitely no title," said Will firmly.

Serena and I guided Mum, followed by my boggle-eyed dad, to the small sitting room. The sun made the pink walls glow and Mum plopped down on the sofa. There was a tray set out and Serena withdrew to fetch pots of tea and coffee. Dad, unable to contain himself, wandered out of the room. While Will and Joe were upstairs with the bags, Mum looked as if someone had hit her in the stomach.

"If it's any consolation, Mum, I only learnt about this place about a month ago." I said. "So, I haven't been keeping it a secret from you."

"It's just that, all this time you and Will have been courting I've felt he wasn't good enough for you..."

"Will has never felt the need to flaunt his history, and it doesn't make him wealthy either. He still needs to earn a living because the estate is run as a trust and needs to provide income as well."

Serena returned with pots of tea and coffee and quietly slipped out again. I poured tea into two cups, one for Mum and one for me.

"When you told us the other night about your plans, the first thing that came into my head was that you were pregnant." Mum's eyes had been roving about the room but fixed her eyes on me when she uttered the word 'pregnant'.

There was a pause while I handed Mum her tea. "Yes, I am, Mum. The baby's due at the beginning of September."

I don't know what Mum was about to say, but her expression was disconcertedly frosty. If I expected hugs and happy tears, none were forthcoming. Fortunately, Will came in with Dad, who stood by the fire with a happy grin while Will poured coffee for them both.

"Mum has just guessed correctly that I'm pregnant," I said. There was no use waiting for a suitable time to make the big announcement now; might as well get it all out in the open.

Dad's jaw dropped, then he put down his cup to hug me. He shook Will's hand and tears started slipping down my cheeks. At last, I didn't need to hide my secret from them any longer.

"We were going to make the big announcement over dinner when we'd shown you around so you could get used to the shock of the house and then the wedding plans. Don't you think it'll make a wonderful venue?" said Will.

"It's perfect, isn't it, Mo?" Arthur hadn't registered that Maureen wasn't joining in the enthusiasm.

"I'm just wondering why you didn't think fit to tell my daughter that you owned a stately home. Let's face it; you've had plenty of years together to do it. Or hadn't you planned on staying with her until she told you she was pregnant?"

There was a shocked silence. Dad and I both said, "Mo" and "Mum!" simultaneously. Will looked stunned. Mum sat straight-backed, defiantly looking at her future son-in-law, who I wouldn't have blamed if he'd sent her packing. Yet although my stomach was twisting into knots, was there a kernel of truth in her outburst?

Will reached for my hand. "Clem and I have been a couple for years, as you rightly say, Maureen. I've never said anything about my family home to her because it has never occurred to me to do so. My childhood was spent mainly in London with my mother and I only came here to stay with my father during school vacations. When I went to University visits here were few and far between. I didn't ask to inherit Harthill House, but it is my millstone and now Clemency has said yes to becoming my wife. It will be a shared millstone. I can tell you she already loves this house more than me, Maureen. If it hadn't been for her convalescing here because of her awful morning sickness and miscarriage scare, who knows? We just might have carried on as we were in London."

It was a long statement, and he squeezed my hand tightly, maybe for support. Mum's expression softened a little, but as soon as he mentioned morning sickness, she went on the attack again. Arthur sat wearily on the other end of the sofa, drinking his coffee.

"Morning sickness? Miscarriage? Good Heavens! Why didn't you let me know?"

"It was a spur-of-the-moment decision. Clem wasn't well. I had to jet off to the States on a business deal and I knew she'd get rest and be looked after by Serena and Joe."

"She should have come home. I'm her mother. I should have looked after her, not some... strangers."

"Mum!" I couldn't let her carry on like this. "I'm sorry I've upset you. When Will whisked me off here, I'd only just come back from the hospital. I was upset and ill and couldn't put two thoughts together. He wanted what was best for me. Joe and Serena are two of the kindest people you could ever meet. Mum, please let's not quarrel. This is supposed to be a weekend just for all of us to share in our good news."

"Hear, hear," said Arthur. He came over to me again and hugged me, and I let the tears soak the shoulder of his best tweed jacket. "Sometimes you go just too far, Maureen," he added. Mum sniffed.

"Can you show me where the ladies' room is, Clemency," she said, standing up, and I wiped my nose on my sleeve and stretched out my hand to her and without a murmur she took it.

I led her up the grand staircase, and her head was swivelling round. I led her along the passage to the main bedroom and opened the door. Mum gave a little gasp. "The bathroom's through there. I'll just go to the bathroom next door and come back for you, Mum."

Mum was inspecting the rosewood bureau when I returned. Serena had placed a bowl of blue hyacinths on it and their scent was heavenly. Mum always, always had a propensity for turning any situation on its head and making it all about her. It would probably have been an easier option for Will and me to have quietly married, had the baby, presented it to the grandparents, left, and got on with our lives.

Mum turned, looking pale and a little red eyed. I hoped I wasn't in for another of her diatribes.

"This is a lovely room, love. It's nicer than some hotels – not that we've ever stayed in many," she added hastily. "Are they all as palatial as this one?

She fiddled with the edge of the curtain. "All this and finding out about your baby and your hospital visit and the wedding has all come too suddenly for me to cope with. You know how I like to be on top of everything. Well, you've managed to discombobulate me. But it is your life and we are still your parents, so we'll stand by you. I had a miscarriage before we had Thomas, so I know all about distress."

"I didn't know that Mum. I'm sorry. But you're soon to be grandparents again. It's going to be alright; I promise." Holding out my arms, we hugged, an event that I could count on one hand. "I was never going to keep things secret for any longer, only I was nervous in case something happened to the baby. Anyway, come and get some lunch. I bet dad and Will are starving!"

We went down the back stairs. "This house is like a maze; I'm sure I'd get lost in it!" said Mum.

"This is the servants' staircase; it goes from the top floor all the way down to the basement so they didn't disturb the household and guests. We'll give you both the grand tour after lunch. I can see Dad is champing at the bit already!"

Will had taken Dad into the dining room, which had been laid up for us and on the sideboard stood a tureen of soup, warm bread, cheese and cold meat and salad. There was beer and juice and fruit as well.

"I thought we'd have to make our own lunch," murmured Mum.

Will had been eying her warily, but when I nodded and raised my eyebrows at him, he relaxed and pulled a chair out for her. "Serena is also an excellent cook." He was about to add something, then stopped. If he'd commented on how she'd coaxed me into eating nourishing meals, it might have set Mum off again.

As we tucked into herby tomato soup, Dad let fly with all his pent-up questions. How old was the house, who built it, who lived here at first, how did Will's family come to live in it?

Will launched into the history, embarrassed at first, but judging by Dad's rapt expression, he gave a good potted history.

"Clemmie unearthed the family tree. She probably knows more than me about the history and she also found some old diaries, didn't you, Clem?"

"Yes, I'll show the family tree later on if you're still interested," I said.

"Now, do either of you want to rest, or would you like a guided tour of the house?" asked Will, gathering plates and bowls together. Mum, I was pleased to see, had regained her composure and had more colour in her face.

"You bet!" said Dad enthusiastically, and I was a little more optimistic about the rest of the weekend.

"I'd like to thank this –is it Serena? for lunch first," said Mum. We loaded lunch stuff onto the trays and Will put them in the dumbwaiter and as it clanked its way down, Dad went down the stairs to the basement to see its arrival.

"He's like a schoolboy," sniffed Mum.

"It's good to see him enjoying himself. We really are sorry for the shocks, but now you're here, just relax!" I said.

Joe emerged from the kitchen to take the tray. Mum offered to do the washing up, but Joe said there was a dishwasher for that.

Will asked Joe if he'd accompany them around the house. "You know the place better than I do," Will said wryly.

Serena looked a little warily at Mum as she had sensed the atmosphere earlier, but Mum was enthusing about the size of the Aga and the old-fashioned Welsh dresser full of antique plates and jugs.

"We spend a lot of time in here during the day," Serena explained. "We live in a flat on the top floor and it's just not practical to keep going up and down. When you've finished your tour, come back down in here for a pot of tea."

Mum bent down and scratched Tabby's head. We all heard the loudest purring.

∼

Will and I fell into bed much later. I was exhausted emotionally and, to his credit, Will had kept up the attentive son-in-law and host duties. The tour of the house raised many questions, especially from Mum, mainly concerning the cleaning and maintaining. She was very persistent in wanting to know whether Serena would continue to cook and clean after the baby was born. "I hope so," was all I could say. I didn't want to get into a discussion about whether we would ever live here.

"You'll be the proper lady of the house, won't you?" she said, looking pleased.

"And you'll both be welcome to stay any time. There's plenty of room!"

"I won't be able to keep your father away," Mum commented drily.

We had dinner in the dining room. The lamps captured the rich red of the walls and, with the glasses and china, we might have been in a five-star hotel. Mum even had a large glass of red wine, which made her face glow and when we proposed a toast to the plans for the wedding, and an expected grandchild, she didn't make any deflating remarks.

As we lay side by side in bed, we both sighed with relief. "It nearly turned into a disaster this morning," I said. "You were really great, thank you!" I turned and kissed him. "I hope I don't turn into my mother," I mumbled sleepily into his chest.

"Never!" he declared, bundling me to him.

Chapter Twenty-Nine

At breakfast I could only manage a weak cup of ginger tea, and Mum granted I was doing the right thing to keep nausea quelled. After yesterday's emotional outbursts and eating more than I usually did to keep Mum's suspicions at bay, resulted in the usual tedious trips to the bathroom earlier. Dad and Will sat down to a good breakfast in the dining room and, as Mum sipped her tea after a bowl of porridge, she remarked how quickly one could get used to this sort of lifestyle. I'd let Serena know that we were taking the parents to lunch in Salisbury before she began preparing a roast, but before then, we were going to look at the chapel. I still had a job assimilating the fact we were to be married, and in the chapel, and very soon.

A bright and sunny morning heralded another early spring day. Dad admired the workmanship of all the old keys on the board outside the kitchen as Will selected the chapel keys. He took a photo just so he "could look at it and admire the workmanship of such utilitarian objects". Mum had obviously forgiven Serena for usurping her place looking after me and was chatting animatedly in the kitchen.

As we drove past the ash tree, there was a movement and I sucked in a breath and clutched my bag of gemstones. It was Mollie dressed in an old mackintosh and headscarf.

Will slowed and opened the car windows.

"Morning, my lovelies," Mollie said, her bright eyes raking over us. "I be just collecting kindling that was left behind when they sawed up the bit o' old tree that fell down."

"Mollie must be nearly eighty, yet she still comes up to the house to help Serena with cleaning," I said when we drove on after introductions. "She and her husband, who's dead, used to do all the farming, but now her grandson does it all."

"I'm surprised we haven't seen anything of Matt," said Will. "He's usually up at the house on some pretext, usually when there's food around!"

"Well, it's only when he and Joe are busy together and Serena always makes enough soup to feed an army!" I'd seen a lot of Matt during my stay and felt a need to defend him although I'd never detected any animosity between either of them.

The track down towards the chapel and river was still as rutted and muddy as when Evie had driven down and dad joked that the wedding guests would be better off travelling to the service by tractor and trailer otherwise there'd be a lot of punctures and broken suspensions.

"That's not a bad idea actually, Arthur," said Will. "There's not a lot of room to park and everybody can travel together!"

"It won't be so good if it's raining and I don't fancy sitting on smelly hay bales in my finery," grumbled Mum. Will and I exchanged glances. It was a good idea, and we had time to work on the suggestion.

We halted outside the little chapel and dad jumped out with his phone camera ready. "It's very attractive," he said, admiring the flint and stone chequered walls. With no tower or steeple, the chapel looked compact, tucked into the corner of the churchyard, protected by crumbling walls with the trees in the wood crowded up against them. The mullioned windows pleased dad, even though there were boards over the glass. He clicked away and exclaimed when he saw the date set in the brickwork over the window at the west end. "Roman numerals- MDCLXV. Don't tell me, let me work it out!"

As Evie had already told me the date, I waited as dad worked it out. "1665," he announced triumphantly. Will twirled the big key in his hand. "I wonder if the key is that old as well."

We processed up the path to the porch protected by the rusting iron grill, which showed signs of being kicked and battered by would-be intruders. Will struggled with the padlock and the hinges squealed shrilly. The church door looked solid and aged. After a bit of fiddling with the lock, he pushed the door, which opened with theatrical creaks and groans. The darkness reached out to us with a smell of mustiness and age. Most churches smelled of wood and incense and polish, but this chapel had been kept shut for decades apart from occasional use. I shivered despite the warmth of my padded jacket, and I felt Mum do the same. Will moved towards the wall by the door and felt around for light switches. Suddenly, the interior was illuminated weakly by two chandeliers suspended from a central beam, their crystals dark with age and accumulated dirt.

There was just room for a few rows of plain wooden chairs facing the chancel, divided into two sections to leave an aisle in the middle. The stone font looked ancient, with eroded leaves and doves at the base. At the chancel end was a bare stone altar topped by a broad slab of marble which overhung the base. There was no altar cloth, candlesticks or crucifix, which added to the general atmosphere of neglect.

"Are you sure you want to get married here?" whispered Mum, voicing my first reaction at the chilly interior.

"It will look much better when the windows are uncovered,"

said Will. "When my......the last time a service was held here, the windows let in a lot of light. That window over the altar is stained glass and original. If I remember correctly what my father told me years ago, it depicts the Virgin Mary. The church is named The Chapel of St Mary the Virgin."

"Lovely name for a lovely little chapel," remarked dad looking around.

I'd noticed sconces on the walls and a pair opposite each other in the tiny chancel. "We'll have candles and lots of flowers. There must be some form of heating, surely."

Dad was wandering round the walls and shone his phone torch on plaques set in the wall. "These all commemorate your forefathers, Will," he said. "And there are a couple of monster radiators, one on each side, so there must be a boiler somewhere." He spotted a door in the wall beside the chancel step which opened into a brick lean-to housing an ancient-looking boiler. A wooden cupboard stood against a wall with a chair forlornly next to it. Mum tried the cupboard. It was empty apart from wooden coat hangers hanging from a rail and kneelers with threadbare cushions on top.

"These look quite old," she remarked, peering at the tapestry work. "They would look quite nice if they were restored. Look, this one has lilies round the edge, and that one looks like a dove..."

"There's a nice project for you, then, Mo," said Arthur, "you like needlework."

"Well, there's a lot of preparation to be done in here," said Will, heading for the porch. "I'll have to see if Joe is up to it and that boiler will have to be serviced to get it working." He switched off the lights and we went out blinking and surprised to see that it was still sunny outdoors. Will looked in a hurry to leave the place. Maybe he remembered his father's funeral and his reluctance to acknowledge that Harthill House and the estate now lay in his responsibility.

We soon warmed up back in the kitchen, clasping hot drinks to us.

"The chapel will look brighter when the windows are uncovered, with lots of flowers and candles and the altar covered with something," I said brightly to convince myself as well as the others. There must be special altar cloths and a crucifix and candles somewhere. I wasn't religious, but the chapel needed its identity. I'd glanced at the far side of the churchyard as we went back to the car. The statue of the angel was hidden behind a tangle of fresh green leaves. Frances' babies had probably been baptized in the chapel and how many babies before and after? And all the funeral services, especially for those poor babies......I dragged my mind away from morbid thoughts.

We collected our bags and packed them in the car so that we could return to London immediately after lunch. I wished I had invited Uncle Daniel to lunch with us.

When I came down from the bathroom, Mum appeared from the kitchen with an enigmatic smile on her face.

Will and Joe made a list of essential jobs to be done and were optimistic that all could be accomplished.

As we drove past the ash tree, I attempted a protective bubble around the car. There'd been no sightings of the twins, thankfully, but instead of feeling reassured, I just felt more suspicious about their absence.

Mum and Dad loved Salisbury Cathedral with its soaring spire and surrounded by the elegant houses and gardens of The Close. The morning service had finished, but the organist was still playing and the sound filled the interior. Mum suggested this would make a better wedding venue than a poky old chapel. We wended our way through the shop and into the cloisters on our way to the Refectory. Despite the sun and blue sky, the Cloisters were in shadow but Dad happily took photos and read all the information signs. He was interested because a copy of the Magna

Carta was kept at the Cathedral, but Mum said he had to save looking at it for another time. I glimpsed Uncle Daniel just about to exit the Cloisters. I ran to intercept him before he disappeared and his face lit up when I caught up with him.

"Clemency! How lovely to see you, my dear. Are you here on your own?" he said, embracing me gently.

"Have you time to meet my parents? They're just here for the weekend. We've set the date for the wedding – no not in the Cathedral," I laughed as looked impressed. He politely greeted my parents.

"I hear congratulations are in order," he said, shaking Will's hand. "And you are looking very much better, my dear," he said, addressing me.

"She should have come home to us where she would have been looked after," Mum bristled.

Uncle Daniel looked apologetic as he explained he had to leave as he was expected to lunch at friends and said his goodbyes.

"Expect an invitation soon," I called after him and he lifted his hand in acknowledgement. We took our table in the Refectory for lunch.

~

Mum was as good as her word. She phoned next morning and said she had arranged visits to three bridal salons, all central. I had to bite the bullet and hope the experience wasn't too excruciating.

The next day I met her at Oxford Street Tube Station. She was dressed in a very smart coat with faux fur round the neck and wrists and a feathery fascinator. Mum was clearly out to impress. I on the other hand, was dressed in black trousers and padded jacket and boots; Mum looked askance at me but refrained from criticism. My only contribution was my tamed hair, gathered into a French braid. After all, I might be in my underwear for half the day. My stomach roiled at the thought of trying on creations mum liked and I didn't.

By the afternoon, even after a light lunch, my energy levels had depleted looking at so many styles of dresses. I was tempted just to choose one so that the experience would be done and dusted. However, one creamy, lacy one with an entwining leafy motive enhanced with gold thread caught my eye. It wasn't tightly fitted, so when I expanded there was room for a bit of a bump.

"I worry that the chapel will still look old and musty on your wedding day," she said.

"Joe and Will have it all under control," I said.

"Serena and I have come up with ideas for flower arrangements, so I'll be up before the wedding to help her arrange them. Serena and I are quite like-minded."

I suppressed a smile. The usurper was now forgiven.

"Do you mind if we liaise with Will's mother about flower arrangements? She's very keen to help as well...." I added.

∽

Once back at Will's flat, I bundled some bedding into the washing machine and brooded on how these tasks were dealt with by Serena and Mollie back at Harthill House. I'd have to get used to calling this flat home. My flat sharing days with Evie were over. Ruby would eventually return to the States, but Evie was free to decide what to do with her life and her relationship with Ruby. She might even decamp to the States, even though she loved her work here.

There were so many possibilities of making Harthill House earn its keep and I could easily work from there. Joe had shown me the office above the old stables and it was well equipped with hardware. There would be no worries about childcare, especially if

Serena and Joe agreed to stay on. I sighed. If only Will was more positive about the place.

The very real problem of the Twins receded while in London and if I followed Roberta's and Daniel's advice, I would be safer here, too. But the pull of Harthill House was irresistible....

Evie's phone call rescued me from my thoughts churning round like the washing machine. "Ruby's going back to the States next week," she said without any preamble.

"When was this decided?" I asked, as there had been no mention of it in the office.

"She's going back for Rafaella's wedding. I thought you and Will must know about it."

"I'm not in the office today. We knew she was getting married, but not the date."

"It's next week! Ruby said she'd be back for your wedding but you know how things are - once she's back in New York there'll be a hundred things to keep her there."

"There's still time for her to get back, so don't fret!"

"Yeah, sorry to dump on you. We'll have to get together soon."

"Before you go, Evie, Mum asked me to ask you if you would like to be my bridesmaid."

"Bollocks to that!" Evie said, without a pause.

"I promised I would ask! I knew your answer!" I laughed.

"I expect your mum has chosen your dress with a ten-metre train as well. Well, it won't be me carrying it!"

At least Evie had cheered up when we ended our call.

The front door banged shut as Will entered with his bike. The entrance hall was too narrow to leave it there and susceptible to theft.

"I suppose you've heard about Raf's wedding? Part of me thinks she's doing it practically at the same time as ours to trump us." He kissed me on the cheek on the way to the fridge for a lager, as I chopped vegetables and onion for a stir fry.

"It's no big deal. Has she invited us?"

"No, and I wouldn't go, anyway. It's too close to our wedding and the first trek."

"It doesn't affect our plans," I shrugged. At least Will wasn't looking moody.

"Joe phoned to say he and Serena were cleaning the chapel this weekend. Let's go down and give them a hand," Will said. "I don't feel as if I've been pulling my weight."

We left London in a shower of hail on the Saturday morning and by the time we were on the other side of Salisbury the sun had reappeared. Catkins danced wildly in the strong breeze. Seasons were so much more apparent in the countryside. As Will accelerated up the hill approaching the drive, all my muscles tightened and I had to fight to keep my breathing steady. In London it was easy to dismiss and forget about the threat and menace of the Twins, yet here we were going up the drive passing the old ash tree and we were easy targets, Will, me and the baby all in the same car.

"Well, the ash is still standing," said Will as we drove past and I opened my eyes but still clutched my crystals. One of the resident jackdaws flew past the windscreen and Will braked hard to prevent the bird slamming into the windscreen. *Please, not a bad omen,* I begged.

My phone rang as we pulled up on the gravel. It was providential that we were here as Brian Chadwick wanted to finalise catering and asked to call in that afternoon.

"We'd better get down to the chapel now, if that's ok with you, Joe?" said Will.

"Shall we walk there?" I suggested. The thought of passing the ash tree several times in one day unnerved me.

"Are you sure you're up to it, Clem?" said Will.

"Yes, I'm not an invalid," I said defensively.

On the way down the side of the field, I kept a surreptitious lookout for the Twins. Sheep were grazing in this field and the young lambs bounded around. Dog violets, celandine and primroses nestled against the fences.

There was the ritual of unlocking the doors and Joe, and Will fetched out an extending ladder. Matt had run to join us and helped Will unscrew the boards on the windows with a battery powered drill.

"It's too risky to leave the boards off," said Joe. "Vandals are a menace even in the countryside."

With bated breath, I stepped inside. Joe flicked the light switches, and I looked around with an ever-widening grin on my face, and I gripped Will's hand. The light from the cleaned windows transformed the little chapel. It was so much lighter and airier than our last dismal visit. The noonday sun transformed the coloured glass in the east window and the reflections glowed on the tiny chancel and altar, which looked cleaner but was still unadorned. The west window looked more imposing now it, too, was clean.

"It took us a while to clean them," said Joe proudly.

"I hope we didn't need permission to clean the chandeliers," said Matt, and looking upwards, I could see that the glass pendants glittered. "Serena insisted we take them down so she could wash all the pendants. All Joe and I could think of as we unscrewed them was that episode from Only Fools and Horses!"

"You've done wonders," said Will. "You should have shouted for me to give you a hand sooner."

"We've got a boiler engineer coming on Tuesday to service the boiler. Serena found invoices and receipts in the Trust files and it was last serviced about 5 years ago, so hopefully it won't be any trouble."

"It all looks under control, thanks to you two, and with the walls left to wash, and a lot of dusting and polishing, the chapel will be more than ready by the 24th," said Will and as there was nothing more to do, he switched off the lights. It would take quite a while to replace the boards across all the windows, as only one person at a time could go up the ladder.

"Why don't you go on ahead, Clemency," suggested Joe. "You can tell Serena we'll be right behind you for lunch."

I hesitated. My mouth went dry at the thought of walking back through the fields unprotected. I had my crystals in my pocket and I stood looking at the gravestones while I tried to remember how to cast a protective circle around me. The little churchyard looked tidier than the last visit; someone, probably Joe, had trimmed the grass around the plots and stones and spring flowers bordered the path. There were even shiny spikes of bluebell leaves thrusting up. The angel stood secluded in its bower, protecting its charges.

Taking my phone out, I called Evie. When she learned we were at Harthill House; she said she'd drive down and help with cleaning. "I'm at a loose end, anyway. Now Ruby's flown back, and I know where I can get lime wash for the walls, so I'll bring some with me."

I'd walked behind the chapel and froze as the faded names on a moss-covered gravestone leapt up at me.

George and Wilfred Barnard
19th April 1812 – 6th June 1912

There was no inscription, just the dates, but I felt winded. Curiously, I noted they had both died on the same date. My eyes scanned the trees and shrubs over the walls, half expecting to see the mocking faces of the Twins....

Will locked up the chapel, and we started back.

"Evie's coming to give a hand," I said. The sun reappeared from behind a bank of clouds and the woods were full of birdsong.

"Good, the more volunteers the better," said Joe. "It'll all be done by tomorrow afternoon."

After lunch, the three men went down to the barns to muck out while Serena and I waited for Brian Chadwick.

"Are any of your American friends coming over?" asked Serena.

"Only Ruby," I said. "Rafaella's getting married on Tuesday, so Ruby's flown back for that."

Serena looked at me as if deciding to say something. "Well, I'm glad she's settling down," she said at last. "I didn't approve of the way she monopolised William and ignored you."

Mollie had observed Rafaella's attention towards Will as well. How many of the others had noticed?

"Perhaps she's pregnant," said Serena just as the doorbell rang and the dogs raced up the stairs in a cacophony of barking. I gripped the back of a kitchen chair as a weight seemed to plummet through my body. I breathed in through my nose and out through my mouth as Serena reappeared with Brian. He kissed me on both cheeks. "It's lovely to see you again so soon, my wee girl!"

Serena put a teapot and mugs on the table, and Brian opened his laptop. It wasn't long before all the menu options had been chosen.

"I'll give my favourite girl a special discount and throw in breakfast and a Sunday lunch for your guests who are still here," he said with a twinkle in his eye. "And might you be after having a bit of a ceilidh after the reception?" he asked. "I can organise supper snacks. And I can recommend a good group that'll have you all on your feet in no time!"

He fished out a card from the pocket in his laptop case. "Have a look at this group performing on YouTube," he said. "And they don't charge the earth either. I'll finalise the menus for you and be in touch very soon. Take care of yourselves, now."

When he'd gone, Serena told me to go and have a rest as I looked pasty faced.

In the small sitting room, I fed the fire with more logs. I

fetched my laptop to look at the YouTube offering of the group Brian had mentioned so that I wouldn't dwell on Serena's words about Rafaella, but I couldn't help it. What if Will and Rafaella had fallen into bed on his trips to the States? She had been proprietarily possessive on the weekend visit. What if she had fallen pregnant and it was Will's and that was why she was marrying in haste? Normally no one cared about these things nowadays, but Rafaella was marrying an Italian Count for goodness' sake with a good family name and pots of money. And he had been in Italy for months, according to Ruby, so any child would be unlikely to be his....... I stared at the fire as thoughts whirled round my mind. *Was I ever going to be free of doubts? Should I be even going through with this marriage to Will?* I stood up, sat down, and was saved from my thoughts when my phone buzzed and it was Evie on her way.

It was Evie who put my mind at rest. At supper she regaled us with details about Rafaella's forthcoming marriage: her future husband had wanted the ceremony at the family palazzo near Lake Como, but as he was now divorced, it had been easier to obtain a licence in the States.

"Why the haste?" I had to know.

"According to Ruby, Rafaella wanted the wedding out of the way so she could go on the first trek of the season to show Will and then afterwards she and Count Niccolò are going to Italy for a few months and then a late honeymoon in Thailand. Apparently Niccolò collects and sells antiques and suchlike, so it is a business trip for him as well."

"Lucky for some," observed Matt. "Will she be a Contessa when she's married? Where are you going on honeymoon, Will?"

Will looked helplessly at me. "I think it'll have to be on hold because of me going over to the States and then trek season will be in full swing. And Clem's still got to be careful with the baby..."

"So, it'll be Casa Harthill House for you then, Clemency?" Matt said mischievously.

Getting ready for bed that night, Will tugged off his socks and threw them onto the chair. "Do you mind about not having a honeymoon? We've got a lot on in the next few months and once the baby's born, you'll have your hands full. I'm thinking that Raf, Rafaella will need cover for treks while she gads about with her husband. She does all of them usually."

"I hope you're not suggesting you go over to the States to cover for Rafaella on every trek?" I said sharply.

"No! There's Hugo, Ben and Andy to cover." He leaned over, switched his lamp off, then put his arm round me.

"Better get some kip, lots to do tomorrow, love."

Our day of cleaning and lime washing the walls went without a hitch. Serena had located a large box in the junk room which contained an altar cloth, thankfully not moth-eaten, silver candlesticks and a small silver cross and I was content with the simplicity.

～

We all watched the live video recording of Rafaella's wedding ceremony in the office. It took place at the home of her parents and it was a very lavish affair. Huge urns of big showy plants were dotted around two large marquees on the lawn and the entrance to the marquee in which the actual ceremony took place was adorned like a bower with greenery and flowers, even though there were still traces of snow all around. The many guests were dressed fashionably and Rafaella looked stunning in an off the shoulder ivory cream silk column dress with a fan like train.

Five small flower girls attended and her soon to be husband, Count Niccolo, was dressed in a white frilled shirt and a coat with tails. He was predictably darkly handsome and looked Rafaella appraisingly up and down as she walked down the middle of the marquee with her father, accompanied by the music of a string orchestra.

"I hope you aren't expecting such grandeur when you come to our wedding," I said to Kim, who was watching, enthralled. My own feelings were mixed: I wasn't resentful that obviously no expense was spared on her big day, but our small affair in the chapel paled into insignificance in contrast.

"This is a celebrity wedding!" she answered. "I bet it'll be in New York celeb magazines!"

Will raised his eyebrows in agreement as Andy commented it was all a bit over the top and we all reluctantly returned to our screens.

The next day was the day of my ultrasound scan. Will sat ill at ease in the waiting room amongst the other women and some partners. When it was my turn, the sonographer asked if we would like to know the sex of the baby if it was lying in the right position. I agreed readily. Instinctively, I knew my baby was male because of the Twin's attention. Will nodded, his attention focussed on the screen and equipment. The sonographer chatted while I lay on the bed with my midriff exposed and she apologised for the cool gel. Suddenly the screen filled with grainy shadows and then the shape of the baby emerged as she passed the probe over my belly, now much bigger than my last scan.

"There's the head. Oh, looks like you have a thumb sucker here! Shoulders, fat belly. Ah, I think we can safely say you have a little chap tucked away."

Although I knew we had a son, my eyes were still filled with tears. It seemed incredible that this tiny being was active inside my womb. Will had been holding my hand and his grip tightened as the little limbs moved on the screen. As she continued, she pressed quite hard with the probe on parts of my abdomen to get a better image, and I winced. She calculated the measurements and declared him a bonny size.

We celebrated afterwards in the hospital café, Will peering intently at the scan print outs inside my file.

"Little Billy looks cosy, doesn't he?" he declared, grinning.

As soon as Will named his son, the baby became real instead of being a foetus that had had a precarious start, and I began crying again.

"We won't go back to the office," Will said. "Let's have a walk on Hampstead Heath and a meal out to celebrate!"

Chapter Thirty

Our wedding day! Will was banished from my sight as soon as he went downstairs on Mum's command. As a traditionalist, she did not believe in the groom seeing his future wife before the ceremony and he dutifully moved his gear for the day into Hugo's room in the South Wing.

Serena and Kim insisted on helping me dress and in the end, Mum, Roberta, Evie, and Ruby were all ensconced in my bedroom quaffing champagne. Nerves had driven me into the bathroom earlier, but I gratefully accepted a couple of fortifying sips of bubbly. Then Dad and I were the only ones left in the Hall apart from Brian's crew busy in the kitchen and the old dining room in the South Wing, which I hadn't been allowed to see how it had been set up.

Joe and Matt had arranged a tractor and trailer and the small crowd scrambled aboard the trailer cheerfully as they sat on hay bales covered with rugs, with greenery festooned over the sides. Joe hired a neighbouring farmer's son to drive the tractor, and he had entered into the spirit by wearing a bowler hat and gaiters. My two nephews forgot to sulk about having to dress smartly and chattered loudly. They had arrived with my brother Thomas and Anna two days before and had been super excited when shown to the farmhouse where they were staying, following Matt when he went to check the ewes and lambs and when he called in the cows for milking, racing to open and close gates.

The older guests, besides Mum and Roberta, included Uncle Daniel, Dr Laidlaw and Dee, and they squashed into the silver Range Rover which had once belonged to Will's father. Will drove and Hugo was in the front passenger seat as his best man.

Alone in the Hall with Dad, he turned to me. "I never thought a day like this would arrive," he said. "I imagined you and Will cycling round the globe until your limbs got too creaky!"

"And now not only have you got to give your only daughter away, but look forward to another grandchild!" I said and was surprised by the sudden lump in my throat.

"Well, I'm proud of you, lass," said Dad, patting my hand. "Always have been and always will be."

Joe waited out front by his sparkling Defender, talking to Brian.

"Aren't you looking as fresh and pretty as a May morning?" Brian said as the three men fussed around me as I climbed into the vehicle.

"Get on with your Irish Blarney, Brian, but I don't know how we would have managed without you!"

The chapel had responded to the TLC it needed. The scent of freesias and spring blooms filled the warm interior. Candles, twinkling chandeliers and sunlight filtering through the windows transformed and uplifted its atmosphere. I was amazed how crowded the chapel appeared. There weren't that many guests. With a shock, I saw some people were not solid. I couldn't stop my eyes roaming round as shadowy figures filled the little building. Instead of being terrified, I recognised them as spirit well-wishers. Together with the lilting music of the Galway Spinners and the wide smiles on the faces of our friends and relatives, I had tears in my eyes as I walked down the tiny aisle. Hugo had a grin plastered across his face. Will's smile was nervous, but his eyes locked on to mine as I walked towards him and all the doubts and suspicions I'd harboured melted away.

∼

"How are you feeling, Mrs Payne Ashton?" Will stood in our bedroom looking bleary-eyed in his shirt and socks very late that evening.

"Happy! It's been such a happy day!" I answered. Everything had been perfect. The sunshine, the lovely food prepared and served by Brian and his team, being surrounded by my friends and family uplifted me and the future looked bright. Hugo had presented us with a tiny outfit comprising cycling shirt and shorts during his speech.

"Couldn't have gone better," he said, swinging me round by my waist. "But, Christ, I'm exhausted -and I think I may have had one too many." He sank onto the bed.

"Counting the number of times you stood on my feet in those reels, I'd agree with you!" I said, hanging my dress on the cupboard door. The Galway Spinners had played such lively music, everyone had been on their feet most of the evening.

I turned, and Will was lying on his back on the bed, snoring loudly.

"There may be two of us feeling queasy in the morning," I murmured, climbing in beside him.

Chapter Thirty-One

Will departed for his first trek in North America shortly after our wedding, fired up in anticipation, while I mooched around the flat, unable to settle, despite going into the office most days.

Serena phoned saying a local festival director had been in touch asking if it was possible we would allow a classical music event on the grounds of Harthill House because the original venue owner had suddenly cancelled. Serena and Joe wouldn't agree without our permission and the director had asked if he could visit. The festival Director's name was Simon Treloar and when I phoned to invite him to Harthill, he sounded delighted. We arranged a meeting the following Sunday. On an impulse, I invited Evie and Ruby if they were free that weekend and they readily agreed. "But are you willing to drive us there, Evie?" I asked hopefully.

"Of course I will. I don't fancy trains and taxis," she asserted.

All the while I was in London, the malicious stalking by the Twins could be set aside. Will was oblivious to them, even though he'd acknowledged at last that I could see them, but as my pregnancy progressed, I was filled with foreboding that they'd make more attempts to harm both Will and me. Despite the growing dread, my heart lifted when Evie drove up towards the house. The green of spring was such a welcome contrast to the bricks and mortar of grimy London streets. As usual, the dogs were ecstatic in their welcome.

Serena held me at arm's length. "I do believe this child is asserting itself at last!" she said, appraising my loose jumper and leggings.

It was true. I was acquiring a definite roundness, and I was looking less gaunt. Lunch was without Joe and Matt, who had gone to a farm in Somerset, demonstrating new milking methods. The three of us headed out, but instead of going down towards the chapel and river, we took a path that led behind the stables following the river northwoods. The woods were older here with silver birch the dominant tree and the leaves were translucent in the afternoon sunshine. Primroses flourished and bluebells stretched away into the distance. Birdsong was everywhere, and we breathed in deeply. When we came to the bottom of an incline the trees thinned out to reveal the silver thread of the river. Ruby lay flat and took photos of bluebells and the bright yellow marsh marigolds in the boggier spots. Our path descended gently again to the ruins of a building choked with nettles and ivy and brambles.

It was a pleasant walk, and I felt an easiness which I didn't feel around the perimeters of Harthill. Instinctively, I knew this was not Twins' territory.

We arrived at an old brick-built bridge over the river. It had five bar gates at each end, as if to deter people using it, but there was a well-worn track over the bridge. We all climbed over the gate, looking at the slow current of water underneath. It was a tributary, or cut of the main river, which was further over and much broader. On the other side of the bridge, a herd of black and white cows grazed on the lush spring grass of the water meadows. Some gazed curiously in our direction as they ruminated.

Upriver we could see the roofs and chimneys of the next farm at Withycoombe and trees crowded the banks, some trailing branches in the water. On a spring day such as today with a warm sun, blue skies and all shades of burgeoning green, life was good. A splash sounded near the bank and a shiny sleek head cut through the water. "An otter," I breathed incredulously. "How wonderful. I wonder if there are babies."

"Where will you live after the baby's born?" asked Evie. "Why don't you spend your maternity leave down here and come otter watching! Then you won't be tempted to take the poor tot into work with you!"

"I might just do that," I answered Evie. After a fear free walk, I was easily lulled into a feeling of security. "And there's the bonus of an extra pair of hands – Serena's. She has experience of bringing up babies and I'm a bit nervous of what to expect plus there's room for mum and dad to stay – Mum would be very upset if she never got to see her new grandchild often!"

"And Billy's new aunties will be visiting too!" announced Evie.

As if he could hear what we were saying, I felt a sudden movement, and clutched myself.

Evie held my arm immediately. "What is it?"

"I think little Billy just kicked me!" I laughed.

It was an easy walk back and my body was stronger than the previous anxious months. We emerged from the friendly birch wood to go through the last gate. On the other side of it stood the Twins with their sullen, angry faces. I lurched to a halt and couldn't breathe. I opened my mouth to try to gulp air down, but my throat closed. Panic rose in me like a dark tide as my chest constricted. Evie bent me over. "Breathe in. Count to five. Breathe out slowly," she instructed. As my eyes focussed on the grass under my feet, I gulped down air, coughed and my heart's frantic rhythm slowed.

"Where are your crystals?" asked Ruby. She had sensed what I had seen. I'd grown complacent to danger and had left them in the flat.

"Remember your mantra. Remember how to cast the protective circle that Dee taught you."

Ruby was calm, her warm hand on my shoulder as I wildly searched my memory for Dee's instructions. I closed my eyes and tried hard to focus. Gradually, my breathing became less ragged, and I stood upright with my eyes closed as Evie and Ruby held on to me. Bird song filled the woods, and I opened my eyes. The Apparitions had gone.

"I wish we could see those bloody Twins," said Evie. "We'd be able to warn you. Are you ok to carry on?"

I nodded. I had to try to focus on my bubble of protection until I got inside the house. My future turned bleak again.

Suppertime was cheery with the return of Joe and Matt. We took our drinks up to the sitting room. The evenings were lighter, but the warmth of the day had gone.

"I have a surprise for you," I said to Evie, who raised her eyebrows questioningly. I ran upstairs to fetch the Journals which I'd brought with me. As I glanced out of the window at the darkening field and woods beyond, no Twins stood in the hazy shadows, but I could have wept as my visions of living in a country idyll were dissolving because of spectres of the past.

Evie practically snatched the Journals from me and carefully leafed through them. "My God, Clemmie, where have you been hiding these?" she crowed. She began leafing carefully through them, but Ruby urged her to read aloud some extracts.

Ruby and I settled back on the cushions as the fire blazed and threw shadows on the walls. Evie revealed glimpses of life in this house two hundred years ago.

Chapter Thirty-Two

Honoria's Journal

Grand-mère, Mémère, constantly remonstrated with me that I was too headstrong for une jeune fille. I was but twelve years of age at the time. Mémère was always beautifully turned out with never a hair out of place, whereas my long dark tresses were always coming unbound and I would tear the ribbons out impatiently. Hannah, the little maid who served my two sisters and I was only a year older than me, yet she clucked and fussed when I returned home with dirty hands and mud on my boots, tears in my skirts and twigs in my hair.

Yet every evening at dinner, the whole family would assemble in the dining room, presided over by Grand-père and Grand-mère. Grace was said in French in deference to Grand-mère. She was very proud of her heritage and gave lessons in that language to all her children, those who survived, and her grandchildren. Grand-père was English, Sir Horace Barnard, and even in their old age you could see how much he still adored her and often deferred to her wishes and decisions, except in the matter of farming. Grand-père was primarily a merchant, importing and exporting grain, wool, and silks. He owned a wharf in East London on the broad Thames River with ships that sailed to the East, returning with exotic silks and spices. His other vessels plied backwards and forwards to the ports of the Low Countries. He was rich and well respected for his fairness in trade. He met Mémère in London where her mother and father of the French aristocracy were being entertained at court, and soon she was betrothed to Grand-père. Mémère told us of the grand house in which they resided by the banks of the Thames, but as more children were born Grand-père looked for land in the countryside where it was free of London's deadly miasmas.

That was how Harthill House came into existence. There had been an old house and estate in Wiltshire by the river Avon. Petherick Manor had fallen into ruins and the land neglected because the owner had been a Royalist in the time of the first King Charles, and he had died in one of the battles between those loyal to the King and the Parliamentarians. His daughters had lost their inheritance. Henry Petherick's brother Edward had managed to buy the land because he supported Oliver Cromwell's Parliament and he worked to restore the estate fortunes and added a mill and a chapel. When ill health forced him to retire, his daughter and her husband struggled to continue. When her husband died, Petherick's daughter was forced to put up the estate for sale. Fortuitously, it was at the time my grandfather's agents were searching for land and he saw the prospects for good agriculture and sheep rearing. He wasted no time in building the grand house in which we now live called Harthill House, as there are plentiful deer in the woods around us.

I have sketched and painted Harthill House from many different angles and it is always pleasing to look at. Grand-père set the house on a bluff facing south and west rather than rebuild the old manor by the river as he foresaw flooding and the trees that abounded all around would have a dampening effect on any dwelling built there. The mill and the chapel are still in good condition, and Mémère loved the chapel right from the beginning. It is dedicated to St Mary the Virgin and of the catholic faith which pleased Mémère as she was also of that faith and every Sunday all the family rode or walked there.

My family is so extensive that I sometimes wonder how we are all housed. Mémère bore ten children, and seven survived. My grandfather added two wings to the main house, which were joined by long galleries lined with portraits and statues. On wet or inclement days, we children held races from one end to the other to the annoyance of the servants.

My grandparents and parents were convinced that having outdoor exercise invigorated mind and body which is why even now as I grow old, I keep to my routine: going on my daily walks checking the chicken coops, advising the gardeners in the kitchen garden and orchard, inspecting the readiness of crops, and casting my eyes over the flocks and herds. My father, James managed the estate for grandfather so I accompanied him from an early age. I had four siblings: my sisters Anne and Grace are older than I but have an impediment in their minds that prevents them learning. They spend most days doing simple tasks like hemming napkins and darning hose. Mother had soft dolls made for them and they endlessly dress them and make believe they are real babies. If my mother is distressed by their condition, she never admits to it and is practical and patient with them. My younger sister Violetta and brother William died of painful throat croup in infancy. William was my father's heir, so he was much distressed by his passing. I am sure my father liked to take me around the estate because of my wilful and headstrong tendencies and forthright opinions.

My Uncle Guy, whose name Mémère always pronounced in the French way, Gee, was the eldest son and heir; he and my father argued much about the best practices on our farms. Guy wanted to preserve the old ways, but my father was always interested in learning about new crop rotations and the new machinery which would facilitate work in the fields. When I should not have been listening, I heard Father confess to Mother that he always worried about his position after Grand- père passed. I heard him tell Mother that Guy was not so passionate about running the estate as he was; although Uncle Guy had reassured him that Harthill House was ever my father's home. Nevertheless, I knew my father felt insecure and that was his reason for driving progress.

It was on a visit to Grand-Père's wharves with my father that I met Gyles Payne, who was overseer of all the unloading and loading of cargoes and the warehouses. At first sight, I thought him a common citizen because his attire was hardly that of a respectable gentleman. My father thought the world of him, as did my grandfather. When I commented that he looked rather rough to be responsible for all the business carried out in the family name, my father answered that there was not a more trustworthy person this side of the river; that he was a man of good name and I should never judge a person on appearance only.

I became Gyles Payne's wife in the year of our Lord 1789 and one year later our son and heir Edwin was born. We lived in the grand mansion that my grandmother and grandfather had first lived and I tried hard to take to the life of London's gentry. In truth, I grew bored of taking tea in the salons of affected ladies whose only interests in life were the acquiring of new gowns and fripperies and how terribly hard it was to find reliable servants. Gyles worried about trade because revolutionary powers in France were persecuting royalty and nobles and he was not alone in his fears for that country.

My beloved Grand-Père died some years ago, and Guy and James were successfully running the estate and businesses together. In the year Edwin was born, Uncle Guy's health suffered and my father worked tirelessly at Harthill. My cousin Horace, who was the eldest son of Guy, enlisted as an officer in the British Navy in dangerous times.

I was overjoyed when Gyles responded to Papa's plea to join him at Harthill House after the death of Uncle Guy. Gyles appointed his deputy as overseer at the wharves and warehouses and together with our sons Edwin and Bartholomew, we journeyed home.

It is heartbreaking that Mémère, Grand-Père and my mother no longer fill the house with their presences. My Aunt Marie-Thérèse is chatelaine now. She is a gentle soul who much prefers to sketch and paint, but manages to keep all the servants at their tasks.

We had a suite of rooms in the South Wing and Eleanor, Guy's widow, lived in the North Wing with her son Horace - when he was home from the sea- Horace's wife, Priscilla and their son Edmund. Eleanor was also the daughter of a landowner and liked to help at milking times and lambing. She was a merry soul. Then there was James' brother Laurence, who was Professor of Botany at Oxford University. He and his wife Joan often travelled to the East in search of rare specimens, so they rarely stayed at Harthill House although rooms were kept for them. My Aunt Helene resides in the Main House also. Her husband, Henry Wallington, was tragically robbed and murdered by thieves who held up his carriage in Hampshire. She lost the child she was carrying and came to live at Harthill. She and my Aunt Marie-Thérèse are companions. Helene is also a gifted artist and they sketch together often.

There is a last brother, my uncle Gerard, who is much younger than his brothers and sisters. Because he was the youngest offspring, he was allowed many liberties which his siblings were not. He was sent to study at Oxford, but soon wasted his allowance on gambling and I am ashamed to admit to his penchant for keeping company with women of ill repute. He would return to Harthill House to show remorse and beg more allowance, then disappear again and repeat his bad habits. My father never knows where Gerard resides in London because he leaves lodgings suddenly to find another lodging, most probably owing rental, which he cannot pay.

I still look back with sadness at the deaths we have borne here at Harthill House. My beloved Aunt Marie-Thérèse died some years ago, quietly, as if not to cause us any fuss. We have had to appoint an upper housemaid, Spears, to oversee the duties of the maidservants and the running of the household in her place. The butler, Mr Hobbs, is responsible for the footmen. I envisaged managing the household, but as I insist on overseeing the accounts for the estate, it was deemed too onerous a task for me. Spears, the upper housemaid, heeds my authority.

My uncle Guy passed many years ago; he was never of a healthy disposition and after the death of their son Horace in the naval battles off Trafalgar, Eleanor, and Horace's widow Priscilla returned to Eleanor's home in the county of Kent. Gyles and I are now the legal guardians of Horace's son, Edmund, who is of an age with my younger son Bartholomew.

The death of my uncle Laurence was followed shortly after by the death of his wife Joan in Oxford. In their travels abroad, they were purportedly infected by disease and died of consumption at their home in Oxford. They had no offspring and although many of their collections are housed at the University of Oxford, some of their illustrated accounts are now in the library here awaiting the attentions of my father.

My second cousin Edmund is now the heir to Harthill House. As I write, I try to stifle my feelings of bitterness: not towards Edmund himself because he is as dear to me as my own sons and his enthusiasm for the future of the estate fills me with hope. My bitterness is directed at the indisputable fact that my father, who has toiled all his life to keep the estate and the businesses in London active and prosperous, must let Edmund take precedence. I feel grieved also that my prodigious efforts to ensure we are bringing in healthy profits go unrewarded.

My mood is sombre today, remembering those who have gone to the arms of the Good Lord.

Our elder son, Edwin, is causing us much heartache. Gyles does not yet know the trouble he has expedited, and I am mindful not to burden him. Edwin is headstrong and wilful. Mémère castigated me for these same qualities of character many years ago and taught me how me to channel them into good works. Unfortunately, Edwin has not channelled his wilfulness in the same way. He ignores duties around the estate and is quite honest, saying he is not interested in farming or the business in London, of which Gyles was expecting Edwin to take over.

Edwin rides out often. I know he meets other dissolute men for drinking and gambling, and I have upped his allowance on many occasions to pay his paltry debts. I fear he is taking after James' profligate brother Gerard, who we surmise resides still in London.

To my chagrin, my upper housemaid, Spears, came to me yesterday. Without preamble, she accused my son of causing her daughter, Mary, one of my chambermaids, to be with child. I immediately flew to my son's defence and accused Spears of lying, or in my own words, that she must be mistaken. Spears did not capitulate and stood calmly with her hands crossed before her. I felt a desire to send her packing immediately but recognised that I must not appear discomposed before this woman.

I asked how she could be so certain and she answered that Mary and Edwin had been secretly trysting for some months, unbeknownst to her own mother. I write the words she spoke while they are fresh in my mind. "My daughter is honest, my lady, as you know. Master Edwin professed to love her and promised he would gain consent from his parents for her hand in marriage."

I was appalled that he would even think that, but strove to keep my features composed. Spears continued:

'When Mary discovered she was with child, Edwin told her no one would believe her if she told her elders of her plight. He said she was just a maid with loose morals, like all the rest.'

I cast my mind back to when I had last seen Mary. I had had occasion to reprimand her only yesterday because she had not laid the fire in the dining room.

'I will speak with Mary and I will speak with my son,' I informed Spears. 'You may leave now.'

Spears cast me an uncertain look, but curtsied and left without saying another word. When she had gone, I found myself twisting my handkerchief in consternation.

In my heart, I feared the accusation might be true. I knew certain advantages were taken of the maids, but no harm ever came of it.

I rang the bell pull, and a footman entered. ''Fetch Mary Spears,' I said tersely.

I sat at my bureau and pulled a sheet of paper and a quill towards me. There was a knock on the door and the footman reappeared, ushering in Mary. He bowed and left, but I thought I detected a smirk on his face. They all know, I fumed inwardly. Mary timidly approached my desk, her hands twisting together. She did look woebegone, and she did look plumper, something I had failed to notice.

'What is all this nonsense, Mary?' I asked, not unkindly.

'Oh, madame, I am ashamed to bring trouble to the family,' she began, tears forming in her large blue eyes.

I waited. I needed to hear a confession from her own lips without being prompted by me and I write her words:

'Master Edwin promised he would marry me, Madame, honest. He brought me gifts, ribbons and lace and this pretty necklace.' She pulled out a chain from beneath her high collar and I blinked. At the end of the delicate silver chain was a flower called the forget –me-not, or myosotis, fashioned in silver and sapphires. I t had once belonged to Aunt Marie-Thérèse.

'Give that to me," I snapped furiously. 'It does not belong to you. It once belonged to my aunt and you are fortunate that I do not dismiss you on the spot for thieving.'

Mary swayed and went so white I thought she would fall into a faint. Manners prevailed on me to grasp her arm and lead her to the nearest chair. She was shaking and tears now fell fast.

'Master Edwin said he had chosen it especially for me, as the blue matched my eyes. I swear on my life I never stole it, Madame!' She suddenly clutched her belly. 'The baby kicks all the time, Madame. Sometimes I think he wishes to be out in the world.'

'How many months gone are you, Mary?' I asked reluctantly, as the dreadful truth dawned on me.

'Master Edwin first courted me on Midsummer's Day last after hay making, Madame.' Her eyes shone with tears, but a small smile played on her lips as if she was remembering the event. My swift calculations caused me to gasp involuntarily. Mary's babe could arrive any time.

'Mary, you must go to your home now,' I said. She looked bewildered. 'You must obey me now. I will speak to your mother and I will arrange for a midwife to visit you. On no account must you resume your duties here.' Mary lived in the small hamlet northwards along the river bordering onto the estate that belonged to our neighbour, Lord Brownhill. We had not the space for all the servants to live in and the track along the river was well used.

More tears fell, but instead of summonsing the footman again, I went in search of Spears myself. She had not gone far and was hovering in the Great Hall ostensibly checking for dust on the surfaces of the polished tables. Silently, I beckoned her, and she followed me into my sitting room.

She could not look at her daughter, and I saw her displeasure as well. I gave her instructions and arranged for a stable boy to saddle a mare to carry Mary along the river. As they prepared to leave, I informed her I would pay the midwife and for any necessities in bringing a child into the world. Spears nodded and curtsied. In chests in the attic, I knew there were several layettes from our own family births which I would speedily pass to Mary.

When all was quiet, I asked Hobbs to seek Edwin. I realised I knew not his whereabouts these days.

Suffice to say, my conversation with Edwin did not go well. Edwin merely shrugged and said that Mary was to blame, that she enticed him and he could not help himself. He denied promising to marry her and spread his hands when I questioned him about the necklace. In the end, he departed. I have not yet informed his father.

Mary bore a son not two weeks after I sent her home. She is residing in the home of her sister in Withycoombe until she resumes her duties here. I could not in all honesty leave her to live on charitable donations and, according to Spears, the sister has agreed to rear the child. They have named him Johannes. I have supplied garments and a sum of money for the child's well-being.

He is my grandchild.

April 1809

I sit here with the empty pages of my journal before me. I have attempted many times to set down the horror that has befallen me and failed. I must gather my faith and strength and set down events as they happened. I feel if I write an account of that terrible day, perhaps it may assuage my grief a little.

On a sunny spring morning at the start of this month, Gyles gathered Bartholomew, Edwin, and Edmund to set out the short distance to Lord Brownhill's castle by the river travelling down the muddy road leading to Salisbury. They were to meet and discuss improvements in farming methods such as the new seed drills, a machine that harrows when pulled by horses, improvement of seed stock, looking into improving sheep breeds, inclosing, and the state of markets. Maintaining the water meadows was of paramount importance as the river ran through both our estates, and Gyles hoped Edwin would take responsibility for the river keeping. However, Edwin, although agreeing to accompany them, refused the responsibility of water meadows, saying with contempt that such a venture was beneath him. Gyles was appalled at his son's attitude and told him to go to his room. Edwin's face was suffused with colour as he was reprimanded in front of his grinning brother and cousin. He stalked away without apologising to his father. So Gyles and the other boys set off in the phaeton. Gyles and a groom controlled the two horses, and the boys sat in the back. It would have been a squeeze if Edwin had accompanied them. Later, I saw Edwin ride off on his chestnut. At nineteen years of age, he is becoming very arrogantly disobedient, and I had still not informed Gyles of Edwin's natural son.

I was resting, and the afternoon sun was lowering in the west. Suddenly, I heard a great commotion and voices shouting. Rousing myself and ready to administer reprimands, I went through to the Great Hall. Oh, I can barely bring myself to write another word......

The groom was staggering onto the forecourt with a body in his arms, lying limply. One of the footmen ran to assist, and then other servants were running from different parts of the house. I recognised my Bartholomew by the gay red waistcoat he was wearing that day. I ran towards them, shouting for help. Nearly all the house servants were outside. The groom staggered inside and I ushered him towards the salon where he could lay Tolly on a chaise longue. Spears appeared by my side.

'Send a horse and messenger to the Physician Birch,' I shouted and Spears motioned to a male servant. Tolly was laid on a chaise longue and the groom dropped beside him. I t was only then that I saw the long gash in the groom's arm and blood streaming down. I heard Spears tell a maid to bring water and cloths quickly as I turned my attention to Tolly. He was deathly pale, but there was no blood on him I could see. Leaning over, I could hear very faint breaths and I took his limp hand. 'You will be well soon, my dear,' I crooned. Even with a horse galloping, it would take some time for Physician Birch to arrive. All I could do was apply a cool cloth to his forehead. He was damp with perspiration but cold to the touch and my heart quailed. What if he had been injured inside? Who could tell such a thing? It was only then that I realised Gyles was not here, nor Edmund. What had happened to them? The groom sat while Spears bound his arm and I turned on him furiously.

'What has happened? Did you drive the horses too fast? Where is my husband? Where is Master Edmund?' The groom could not meet my eyes. Hobbs shook the man's shoulder roughly, despite his injury.

'Address my lady, Booth.'

The groom, Booth, looked up and in a voice so quiet that I had to lean towards him, addressed me, his eyes still downcast.

'My lady, we were coming up the drive at a sedate pace. In truth, I had slowed down because the young masters wanted to get down and race the carriage up the drive. Mr Gyles said to let them down as the young rascals had had to sit still and attend to the business of the meeting all afternoon. Then, then...' he faltered and looked up at me and I saw the fear in his eyes.

'As we came up to the old ash tree, someone jumped out from behind the tree. I thought it might be Master Edwin, but I could not swear to it. The horses spooked. After that, it took all my strength to control them with Mr Gyles trying to help. The horses raced straight towards the tree and at the last minute shied away, but... but the carriage slammed straight into the trunk. I was thrown and lay winded. When I rose, I saw poor Mr Gyles lying by the tree, blood all over his head. I couldn't see where Master Edmund was. The horses had dragged the carriage on its side a little way and I saw young Master Bartholomew lying over the side. He was crying out, so I ran to him first and picked him up to get help. I ... I don't know what happened to Mr Gyles and Master Edmund.'

By now the poor man was shaking with the shock he had undergone, but I was out of the door and running down the drive. Sharp stones dug into my slippered feet but I heeded not the pain.

As I drew near to the ash tree, there was a crowd of servants, some kneeling, and some standing. A stable lad was holding the horses, and another was detaching the carriage, which lay smashed on its side, with a broken wheel a distance away. Somebody tried to hold me back, but I pushed them away violently. Two people lay on the blood-soaked grass: my beloved husband Gyles and my dear cousin Edmund. I knew instantly that there was no breath left in their bodies. I heard screaming. Hands held me as I knelt beside my husband. It was me screaming. I was half carried away from the scene, although I heard one of the land labourers saying he was going to fetch the farm wagon. I could not bear the thought of my beloved husband lying in a dirty farm wagon. As I was being half carried, I heard shouts and regaining some sensibility. I turned and saw Physician Birch in a gig accompanied by a young woman. As they approached the ash, they came to a halt, and the physician jumped down. He examined the bodies, but he shook his head and I knew he would confirm they were both gone from this life. They made room for me in the gig and we progressed to the house while I tried and failed to inform the good physician of events. All I could repeat over again was to save Bartholomew. I had hardly the strength in my legs to go to the salon where my son lay. He had not moved, and he was even paler than when I had rushed out. I saw a maid weeping and Spears still gently bathing his head. Physician

Birch bent over my boy, laying a hand on his chest, taking his hand in his own. His companion, who I presumed was his daughter, produced a small mirror which was held in front of Bartholomew's mouth and nose. After a few minutes, he turned to me. 'Madame, I regret to inform you that there is nothing I can do for your son. Sadly, he must have expired shortly after being brought here.'

I gripped the arm of a chair and tried to control the scream of despair that rose in me. The young woman took me gently but firmly by the arm and led me to a seat.

'I am also extremely distressed to have to inform you that there was nought I could do to save your husband and the other young gentleman. I would deduce from their injuries that they received fatal wounds resulting in almost certain instantaneous death. I am so very sorry, Madame.'

The young lady still held my hand, and I snatched it away. I wanted to run and run and howl.

It was silent in the sitting room. Evie had stopped reading aloud. When Evie had spoken of the ash tree, I gasped. I could feel goosebumps all over. The fire had died down and the sound of a log collapsing into ashes made us all jump. Even Evie looked a little shaken.

"That poor family and the poor mother," whispered Ruby. These were Will's ancestors and this woman Honoria was painting such a graphic picture of the ordeal of that family.

"I'm going to make some hot chocolate and then we'd better turn in," declared Ruby.

∼

Honoria's words had unsettled me, but I had to meet Simon Treloar. Evie showed Ruby the old derelict kitchens while I poked around the old family sitting room above it. It was situated in the southern corner of the main block and two walls had windows looking south and west. There was a big open fireplace, empty apart from scatterings of soot and twigs. Sofas and large-winged armchairs, dusty with unuse, filled the room. There was an old-fashioned radio with cut off wires and shelves in the alcoves on either side of the fireplace held a few dog-eared books, board games and jigsaw puzzles. The dusty floorboards were covered by a large, worn carpet. It would make a bright homely family room, especially with an evening sunset streaming in. Mentally, I envisaged Will and I and our child or children re-establishing this room as a family retreat.

I met the Festival Director with Serena and Joe. It was just warm enough to have coffee on the terrace outside the Drawing Room, and Simon's eyes measured the garden and the vistas beyond. After pacing around the stretches of lawn, Simon returned to us grinning happily. "I had a feeling in my bones that this location would be perfect. The festival goers couldn't have a nicer spot to picnic and listen to music," he declared. "I did panic when the original venue owners cancelled."

His reassurance that all aspects of Health and Safety were taken seriously and after a brief consultation with Joe and Serena, I agreed. Terms and conditions were soon sorted and the date in June settled. We shook hands. I'd just managed my first booking for Harthill House.

No sooner had his car pulled away, my phone rang. It was Dee.

"I will be passing Harthill after lunch after picking up stocks for my shop," she said. "I was hoping you were there so that I may call in?"

"Yes, I am. How fortunate! It will be lovely to see you again".

"A fortuitous coincidence," she laughed. "I have not forgotten your dilemma and would like to stop at the old ash tree to commune with your adversaries."

"Oh, please try," I said, not knowing what else to say. Last time she'd tried to communicate with them, they had 'hidden' from her probing. Dee did not want me near the tree while she communicated and I agreed. They would focus on me and I would hinder Dee's attempts. When I told Evie and Ruby, they were pleased that Dee was initiating action, but I wasn't convinced. However, if anyone could reach out to the Twins, Dee had the power.

Obviously, we delayed setting off back to London after lunch and waited fretfully in the Hall. Eventually her Fiat pulled up outside and Dee emerged, as elegant as ever, but her eyes were troubled and her face pale. We dragged her down to the kitchen for restorative tea.

"I could do with a wee dram," she grimaced, sitting down heavily. My heart sank.

"They are cunning and wily," she admitted. "They were very aware of my presence and intentions and sat outside my sphere, but their malevolence was tangible."

She took my hands. "I am so sorry I could not make a difference. You must carry your crystals, use your mantras and protective bubble whenever possible. Be vigilant."

Dee departed shortly afterwards, disappointed at her failure. I was dismayed, but not surprised. Dee was right about being vigilant. The Twins would not be so easily distracted from their intent.

The journey back to London was subdued. Ruby and Evie tried to involve me in their chatter, but Dee's visit had depressed me. My misguided vision of living at Harthill was fading rapidly.

Once back in the city, I needed little persuasion to stay over with Evie and Ruby. Will's flat still did not feel like home to me, and I didn't want to be alone.

After we'd eaten scrambled eggs with avocado on toast, Evie produced the Journal again.

. . .

May 1809

I perceive that while my mind cannot settle on any one task or duty, my pen continues to scribe. Even now, after the funeral of my dear departed, I find myself repeating the words of the rector, Mr Draycott, at the graveside. They bring me comfort in these dark days:

'Forasmuch as it hath pleased Almighty God of his great Mercy to take unto himself the souls of our dear departed brothers: Gyles Payne, Bartholomew Payne, Edmund Barnard, here departed , we therefore commit their bodies to the ground: earth to earth, ashes to ashes, dust to dust: in sure and certain hope of the resurrection to eternal life through our Lord Jesus Christ, who will transform frail bodies that they may be conformed to his glorious body, who died, was buried, and rose again for us. To him be the glory forever.......'

I am resolved to build a fitting monument in remembrance.

Those words, solemn as they seem, give me strength to continue and strive. I also need strength at this grievous time for beloved Papa, who has been ailing for some time, has now taken to his bed. The shock of the accident weakened him so that I fear for his life now. I am beset with anxieties: once Papa departs from this earth, the inheritance of the estate will rest on the shoulders of my son Edwin. My uncle Gerard suddenly arrived to attend the funeral of my loved ones and he and my father spoke angry words afterwards. Papa would only relate to me that his brother was eager to read the Wills.

I have designed a fitting monument to our dear departed with help from my aunt Helene, who sketched a most majestic obelisk to be placed in the Ladies' Bower.

When the good Doctor Birch had departed this morning after attending to Papa, my son Edwin begged an audience with me. He has avoided me ever since the accident and seemed at first to be most subdued. I believe it is the shock of losing his father, brother and cousin and he rides out often. I fear estate duties will be an excessive burden to his careless spirit.

'Mother', he addressed me boldly. 'I wish to formally step out with Miss Birch with the intention of marrying her.'

I am astonished. Miss Birch, Frances, the physician's daughter! Miss Birch has accompanied her father on numerous occasions since the accident. I have formed a good opinion of her. She is gentle and compassionate. I was harsh with her on the day of the accident, but she has been nothing but solicitous to me, nonetheless.

'I would like to ride out with her and her father, of course.' Edwin continued. We have talked much when she visits with her father and she is the sweetest person I have ever met.'

It has not been often of late that I have concurred with my son, but in this instance, he impresses me with his wisdom. Frances Birch will tame his wayward manner. Even in my mourning, I have had to think of a suitable marriage for Edwin. He is now heir to the estate after the death of my beloved papa. I had hoped for a union where the bride would bring a rich dowry so that the estate monies are not drained, but the Birch family are gentlefolk. The good physician himself is the second son of Sir Brenton Birch, who is the largest landowner in the county of Somerset.

I agree to Edwin's suggestion and propose that we arrange to call on her family soon. If I succeed in securing the betrothal, then I can pray for heirs to safeguard our inheritance. Edwin is puffed up with pride and swaggers out.

I hope that Edwin will now begin to take his responsibilities seriously.

January 1810

Snow lay on the ground on the day of Edwin's marriage to Miss Frances Birch. Our little chapel of St Mary the Virgin was still dressed in Christmas greenery: holly, Christmas roses, evergreen branches, and with the many candles, the cold and dark were dispersed. The rector, Mr Draycott, performed a happier service than the last instance of my beloved husband and son's funeral service. I am still in mourning for them.

Miss Birch was a most modest and becoming bride. She had a circlet of sweet-smelling winter jasmine on her head and a fur cape around her narrow shoulders. I had to strain to hear her vows, and I noticed her mother dabbing her eyes.

Edwin has grown into manhood in this last sad year and is tall and broad, his hair tamed into a queue and his voice loud and confident.

After the wedding, Edwin and Frances danced reels to the fiddlers' tunes in the large salon in the South Wing and they made a handsome couple as we clapped to the music.

I had wondered whether it was my duty to speak with Edwin about marital duties now that his father is gone, but I quelled my initial embarrassment. Edwin is not an innocent; has he not fathered a child already, who now lives in the house of my maid Mary's sister at Withycoombe, along the river? By all accounts, the child is thriving. I laid emphasis on his duty to produce heirs quickly. It has come to my attention that my uncle Gerard had been consulting lawyers in London.

March 1810

Praise be to the Good Lord in Heaven! Frances is with child. She has been most unwell, looking very pale. I have advised her to rest often so as not to harm the unborn infant and she answered that she has not the spirit to be very active. Sometimes I hear a warning voice in my head that Edwin is not gentle with Frances. She seems to have diminished in spirit since her marriage, but she is still but sixteen years of age and has led a most sheltered life with her parents and brothers.

January 1811

An infant boy was delivered of Frances in late November. The midwife was fearful for both mother and child. I have engaged a wet nurse to live in, as Frances has been very fragile these last anxious months. Edwin has not been patient or indeed outwardly loving towards her. I have heard whispers from the servants that he struck Frances on occasion when he could not have his way with her after giving birth and he has since visited Mary Spears. When I confronted him, he did not deny the rumours and grew flushed and angry, declaring that a wife has no right to refuse a husband. Despite entreating him to show kindness, I recognised sorrowfully that my son has a volatile manner. Putting aside my own repellent feelings that I should have to speak of such matters, I coldly advised him to be discreet in his needs.

Frances and the baby are very weak. Her father, Doctor Birch, advised that his daughter would be better cared for under his roof, but I would have none of that. How Edwin would react to such a scheme cannot be borne.

My father is also ailing, and the good physician informed me that his illness has progressed to the stage of imminent mortality. I succumbed to moments of pity for myself, encumbered with a wayward son, a sickly daughter-in-law and grandson, and to add to my distress, I was informed that Gerard intended to marry soon. I see through his devious plan- he will marry and produce an heir just in case Frances' baby dies. It is all too frustrating.

February 1811

We are bereft. Edwin's baby son, Frederick Edwin, or Freddie, as we began to name him has died. His breathing grew worse and despite the physician's administrations, he could not save him. Death hangs over this house. Doctor Birch insisted that bloodletting was not conducive to the recovery of Papa and I allowed him to administer opium to ease my father's pain.

Two coffins lie in the Great Hall. One holds my dearly beloved Papa, James. I helped Spears and Hobbs wash and dress him. His poor face, which was lined with pain for too long, is now smooth and peaceful. I must be thankful that the Good Lord has released him of his earthly travails. The other coffin, so small, holds the tiny body of Frederick Edwin, aged nine weeks. I was present in the nursery when he breathed his last, struggling breath. The wet nurse wept copiously. 'He would not feed, my lady, he just would not take my milk' she cried, fearful that I would lay the blame for this child's death on her. Frances sat as frozen and white as another corpse. Even her lips were bloodless. She did not weep or utter any words.

The two coffins were put in the farm wagon, clean and draped in black cloth, and the household walked behind it to the chapel, to be received by the Rector. In the church, Edwin held the coffin of his son in his arms. Even he appeared to be in a state of shock. Frances did not attend.

The letter lies before me on my breakfast table. Uncle Gerard is coming to visit to pay his respects to his departed brother, buried in the grounds surrounding the chapel. Freddie is buried with him in the family plot, as it seemed too heartless to dig a lonely grave for the infant. A memorial stone is being prepared.

Edwin burst in. He sat and helped himself to coffee and cream. 'Is Frances coming down?' I asked. She has not left her room since the death of Freddie.

'Maman, I am at my wits end with her. She does not speak and I must shout to make her listen.'

I indicated the letter. 'My son, we are under a grave threat from your grand uncle. He is bringing his bride here. If she produces a son and his lawyers in London find the succession in his favour, we are undone. We, **I**, have striven for the success of our lands and our holdings in London. I will not let this man ruin our lives. He is a wastrel and will sell everything to fulfil his wicked gambling habits and other things I cannot bring myself to speak about.' I watched Edwin flinch. I was uncomfortably aware that there were comparisons in their natures.

'Edwin, you and Frances must produce another heir. It is imperative that we do not lose, **you** do not lose your inheritance.'

Edwin nodded. I could see that the thought of being disinherited and losing everything was appalling to him as well. He took my hand and raised it to his lips and told me he would not disappoint me.

I am troubled advising Edwin to force poor Frances into another pregnancy so soon after little Freddie's death. I am not a heartless woman, but I am determined that Uncle Gerard or any of his progeny do not lay hands on our inheritance. Grand-père and Grand-mère and my father and I have striven to continue the success of Harthill House Estate and the businesses on London Wharves. Edwin is now forced to act in the interests of his inheritance.

March 1811

My agent in London informs me that Gerard's bride is a well-known strumpet called Lily Stokes. She plied her trade in the dismal streets of Shoreditch, so I expect Gerard was a regular client. It is reprehensible that he could stoop so low.

Frances looks pitifully thin and sad. My heart reaches out to her. I addressed her as a loving mother and emphasized that now she was a dear member of the family her duty was to produce an heir. I explained about the devious plans of Edwin's grand uncle but she simply said that she knew her duty, and painful as it may be as she looks so fragile. I patted her hand and nodded.

April 1811

At last, Frances is with child. She does indeed seem happier, although dreadfully sick some days. I heard gossip in the kitchens that now his wife was with child she was happier because her husband leaves her alone and uses obliging Mary Spears. I am appalled and repelled but I will not admonish Edwin, as he has fulfilled his promise to me.

Of course, we had to lay on a feast for Uncle Gerard's visit. He arrived with his bride on a bright April day with new green leaves on the trees and lambs and calves in the meadows. His bride is very pretty in a common way and dressed most garishly, with overly rouged cheeks and lips, and bows and paste gems in her hair. I am also shocked by my uncle's appearance. Although he is my father's youngest brother, he has the appearance of an old man who has led a most dissolute life and his face is as red and coarse as a pauper. His clothes are old and dirty. My heart quails when I think of how he would gamble away our inheritance.

Lily Stokes has begun to act like a haughty lady. She looks down her nose at the servants and does not deign to thank them at any time. She is, of course, much younger than her new husband and clings to his arm when they are walking. When she was introduced to Edwin, she curtsied prettily, then fluttered her eyelashes at him. I am most displeased by his flattered reaction.

When Gerard was introduced to Frances, he said most cruelly that she looked near starvation. I informed him civilly that Frances was with child and occasionally felt unwell. Gerard's face turned a darker red than its habitual shade and he almost glared at his simpering wife. I was most gratified that his expression implied that his wife was not yet enceinte.

When they left in the carriage to visit the little churchyard, nobody else accompanied them except Booth, the groom.

For supper that evening, I had invited the Rector, Mr Draycott, and Lord Brownhill as well as my two sisters and Aunt Helene. I could not envisage a meal with Gerard and his wife alone with Edwin and Frances. I do not know how we would manage a civilised conversation.

Both Gerard and his wife drank a lot of wine during the meal. Thanks to Lord Brownhill and Mr Draycott leading dull but distracting discussions ranging from the wars on the Iberian Peninsula and the magnificent hero Admiral Nelson, conversation with Gerard and his wife was brief. Unfortunately, as Edwin was at the head of the table, his guest on one side was Lily Stokes (it pains me to call her by her married Barnard name), and the pair of them conversed with heads almost touching and Lily fanning herself, giggling unbecomingly and fluttering her eyelashes. Really! She could not help employing her strumpet ways, leaning over to expose her low-necked gown. Frances picked at her food, but Helene engaged in discussions with the Rector about painting and sketching, of which they are both accomplished and Lord Brownhill tried valiantly to amuse Frances with tales of his new spaniel pup who is very mischievous.

Port was served at the table on my instructions as I did not want them to retire to the Gentlemen's Parlour with Gerard accosting the other men and setting out his rights to the succession. Both the Rector and Lord Brownhill excused themselves soon after to ride home when Lily suggested some card games.

I asked Gerard what time they were leaving in the morning so that they could break their fast before the carriage departed.

'Honoria, my dear, we plan to stay a while longer if that is acceptable to you. The lease on my accommodation is ending and I intend to look for a larger residence now that my wife is with me and there must be room for future offspring. That may be temporary, of course.' He looked directly at me and I recognised his implication instantly.

So, they are installed in the North Wing and I have appointed a maid and a manservant to see to their needs. In my room later, after my maid had brushed my hair and hung up my gown, I dismissed her, then picked up the hairbrush and hurled it at the wall with a howl of anger.

"Wow," laughed Evie, "Honoria is seriously peeved! Not surprisingly, she's been the mainstay of the family fortunes and suddenly she realises she is possibly going to lose it. In those days, if you lost your income and your house, you really were on the cobbles. There was no state funding to prevent you from starving. It would have meant the Workhouse for many people. Can you imagine Honoria letting matters get to such a state? We know obviously that she doesn't lose the estate, but she can't see that yet. Shall I go on or shall we all turn in?"

"It's like ending on a cliff-hanger, but my eyes keep closing," I admitted.

"Come back here after work, Clem, and we'll try to get as far as we can with the journal," said Evie, yawning.

I readily agreed; listening to Honoria's voice was compulsive. I kept seeing the photograph of her straight-backed and stern faced in her old age, still proud.

My phone rang, startling us all. It was Will.

I sat in my old bedroom, now stripped of all my belongings and possessions, and looking like any other spare room.

"Clem," shouted Will, although the reception was clear. "I'm so sorry I've been out of touch. Some areas had no signal at all so I thought I'd wait until we were back in civilisation! How have you been? I hope the nipper is behaving himself!"

Will sounded happy and fizzing with energy. Before I answered, he broke in. "The thing is Clem. Rafaella's broken her ankle when she collided with a boulder. It doesn't sound much of an injury, but she had to be airlifted off by helicopter, because we couldn't bring her down with the bikes. We have a couple of days to go on this trek and she was supposed to be leading another one almost immediately afterwards. Naturally, she's out of action for that trip and the others are committed to other treks so I volunteered to take her place. Jimmy Jordan will be Trek Leader, so I won't be leading everybody over precipices. I know I should have asked you first if it was ok, but a decision had to be made before the trek got cancelled or postponed. It'll only be for another eight days or so and then I'll be coming home. Are you mad at me, love?"

I sighed but said no, I wasn't mad at him.

"I'll try to stay in touch as much as I can on this trek," Will promised before finishing the call.

Lying in bed, recalling Dee's defeated face, saddened me more than Will's prolonged absence. I would never be safe at Harthill.

Ruby and I travelled in to work together the next morning. Our own trek leaders had to be rearranged to compensate for Will's absence. Apparently, Rafaella was likely to be in plaster for at least three months.

At the end of the day, we picked up a takeaway meal on our way back to the flat. It was just like old times going back to my old home.

Frances is rallying. She has colour in her cheeks at last and looks rounder. Edwin is all but ignoring her, and that causes me some disquiet. He is much in the company of his grand uncle now and the two ride off together at times. I pray Edwin is not gambling; Gerard's influence over my son is more than I can bear, and I am constantly praying that they do not strike some sort of deal about the estate.

My life is no less easy with the presence of Gerard's wife, Lily Stokes. She sits with Frances, Aunt Helene and I some afternoons as we embroider or mend linen, but she has no talent for such things and sighs and requests Madeira wine and cake. She has asked for gin, but I have informed her we do not keep it in the house. The reputation of gin parlours in London made some areas of the city extremely unsavoury and unsafe. She continues to behave like a strumpet whenever Edwin is present, although she is very clever, concealing her behaviour in front of her husband.

The memorial obelisk to my beloved husband and son and dear cousin Edmund has at last been erected in the Ladies' Bower. The Rector led a thanksgiving service for their lives and blessed the obelisk and I shed tears of grief again. Gerard was full of condolences, but I perceive his false sincerity.

My life since that awful accident has altered considerably, and I feel a tremendous burden upon me. Booth the groom had been spreading the rumour still that Edwin was responsible for the accident; that he had jumped out from behind the ash tree and made the horses spook in fright. I cannot hold with such behaviour and dismissed him with three months payment.

Late September 1811

I had taken tea with Frances, her mother, Helene, and Lily. Frances is looking healthy again and walks regularly with her little terrier, Jackie. She often expresses her desire to ride her little mare, Blanche, but both her mother and I are horrified that she should consider it in her condition.

'I have never had the opportunity to ride,' Lily butted in. 'And now I suppose I never will now that I am with child at last.'

I am afraid that the fear which I have felt daily since their marriage exploded in my bosom so that for several moments I could not catch my breath.

'Honoria, are you well?' Mrs Birch asked anxiously.

'A crumb, my dear, I will be quite recovered in a moment.' I drank some tea but my throat was quite closed.

Meanwhile, Lily sat back with a smirk on her face, knowing that the news had caused me consternation.

Frances expressed her delight, forgetting the threat any babies born to Gerard and Lily would have on her immediate fortune. 'Two babies in the house! Do you know when yours will be born?' she asked innocently.

'I think April,' answered Lily, coyly. 'Gerard is quite beside himself with pride.'

'Mine will precede yours then,' said Frances, feeling the roundness of her belly. 'He is expected to be born in December, according to Papa. At least I hope it is a son. I don't want to disappoint Edwin.' A shadow passed over her features and I knew she was thinking of the last sad baby.

'You must join us in making layettes,' I said heartily, and Lily's expression turned from feigned interest to boredom in the blink of an eye.

November 1811

Lily's belly is already distended more than Frances' even though she is yet a few months into her pregnancy. She struts around demanding refreshments and Spears has voiced her disquiet to me that Lily sits in the kitchens picking at the prepared foods and quite upsets cook.

My days are filled with anxiety about the future. Edwin does not pay so much attention to Lily now she is with child, but it does not stop her from playing the coquette. He pays hardly any attention to his own wife besides polite enquiries after her health. I know I should not have such wicked thoughts, but I have night panics that Lily's babe may be Edwin's. It is beneath my dignity to ask him and he would deny it.

December 1811

We have confined Frances to bed until she is brought to term. Her father is quite anxious for his daughter. I cannot tell her to be of good heart because I know she suffers still from grief over Freddie and fears for this child.

I visited Lily in their rooms in the North Wing. The boys are endlessly carrying in logs for the fires as Lily complains of the cold because she cannot move around a great deal. Indeed, she is of such great size already and I wonder if the prediction of the birth was wrong. The midwife who attends Frances says she is sure Lily is carrying twins. The door to her sitting room was open, and a maid was clearing a tray of tea and the inevitable refreshments. I paused as I could see my uncle's legs stretched out before the fire. Lily was in intimate conversation with Jane, her maidservant, as if they were equals (which they most certainly are!). Jane was telling Lily with a giggle that Mary Spears was with child again and guess who the father was.

Lily answered immediately – 'It is Edwin's child, naturally.'

The maid Jane said scornfully, 'you are right, madam. Master Edwin cannot keep his hands off her. We have all witnessed him. She is too foolish to slap him away. He has tried to have his way with many of us, but she is the only one who is willing. She has told us she loves him and his wife does not.'

Gerard gave a loud guffaw. 'That will please his hoity toity mama!' and they all laughed, even Jane.

'When is the bastard expected?' asked Lily.

'Judging by her size, I reckon she must be in her sixth month. She tries to hide her belly behind her aprons, but we are not blind!' laughed Jane.

I turned on my heel and fled down the passage before they knew I was there, my face flaming and my temper boiling.

I needed something to still my shaking hands, but I would not succumb to drinking Madeira or sherry before dining, so I summonsed Spears.

She knew the reason for her summons because she curtsied slowly but could not meet my eyes.

'I have just heard a most malicious rumour from a maidservant,' I said. 'Tell me; is it true that your daughter is with child again?'

Spears lifted her head. 'Yes, my lady.'

'Is she betrothed to someone I do not know about?'

'No, my lady.'

'Has she informed you who the father may be?'

Spears hesitated and looked away. 'I cannot say, my lady.'

'Has she informed you when she thinks the child may be born?'

'I would say February or March, my lady.'

I rose and went to my bureau. In a small pouch I had put five pounds. It seemed a trifling amount, but to a maidservant it was more than a year's income. I gave the pouch to Spears.

'Give this to Mary. I want her gone from this house by evening. Then you will find a servant to do her duties until another is appointed. I must say that I am disappointed in you as well, Spears. You do not seem to have instilled moral conduct in your daughter.'

Spears flushed red as she took the pouch. 'May I respectfully suggest you instruct your son in moral conduct also, my lady,' she said proudly. Before I could respond, she unhooked her bunch of keys and put them on my bureau. 'I will go this evening also, my lady. I will care for my daughter.'

She turned to go. My anger died as swiftly as it had arisen. Before she reached the door, I called her name involuntarily, and she turned warily. I went to the bureau again and scooped up more crowns and a guinea. Spears did not move when I thrust them into her hands.

'I am sorry,' I said, for I was. 'This is no fault of your own.'

Tears sprang into her eyes, and I was horrified to find them in mine as well. She took the money and curtsied and left. I went to the hearth where a fire burned, but I shivered despite the heat. I closed my eyes briefly, then pinched my cheeks, straightened my back, and went down to the basement. The servants would be in uproar. I sought Hobbs the butler and informed him of the two dismissals. His eyes widened, but he said nothing. I asked him who would be best to replace Spears.

'Emily Partridge might do, my lady. She is a good girl who gets on with her work and causes no fuss.'

'Then appoint her immediately and tell her to find someone to replace Mary Spears until we appoint new servants.'

I turned from him immediately before I could read the expression on his face. I needed to find my son.

December 1811

I insisted that the house was filled with greenery for the Christmas season and the rooms were filled with the clean sharp scent of pine from cut boughs. I am required to put on a show of Yuletide good will despite the delicate situation I find myself in.

Frances' travails began a few days before Christmas. She has been confined to her room, but her father was summonsed and a midwife from Bridgeford, that village being nearer in distance than Salisbury.

Edwin removed himself to the stables to await news. Since my tirade against him, he has been quieter and has ceased to spend time in the company of his grand uncle.

I entered Frances' room lit by candles and exceedingly warm. Frances was being walked round the room, but she was evidently in distress and both the midwife and her father were supporting her. The birthing chair which has been much used in this house stood ready with clean cloths surrounding it. Her father informed me that birth was imminent.

Frances was led to the chair, moaning and her father gave her instructions in his gentle voice, which made Frances shake her head from side to side. The midwife, who had been present at all manner of births, looked on with irritation. Suddenly, Frances let out a shrill scream. The midwife peered under Frances' gown. 'The head's visible,' she announced with satisfaction. With much cajoling, Frances lowered herself onto the birthing chair and the midwife knelt at her feet with clean cloths in her hands. I remembered my own birth pangs and gritted my teeth against her screams.

Then, with a slither, the midwife caught the baby and wrapped it. Dr Birch took it from her and scooped birth liquid from its mouth and massaged its tiny chest. I did not know whether it was male or female. A long shaky wail came from the baby and Frances' father rubbed it briskly with the cloths, while the midwife looked askance at such roughness.

He tenderly wrapped the child and gave it back to the midwife. Then he helped Frances onto the bed and massaged her belly until the afterbirth came away. He inspected it, much to my distaste and seemingly satisfied. He wrapped it and threw it on the fire where it sizzled and spat.

Frances lay back, exhausted. 'You have a son,' Doctor Birch said, cradling her head and beckoning the midwife. 'A fine healthy son.'

Frances lay back with a sigh to rest. I looked at her newborn son. He was tiny, with delicate features apparent even on his little red face. I prayed that he was healthy. It was imperative for our future that he was healthy. Nevertheless, I asked the doctor if we should have him baptised straightaway. He hesitated, then concurred.

'It would be prudent to err on the side of caution.'

Frances' maid servant Dora was waiting outside the door to administer to her mistress's needs after her labour. Then I sent a footman to fetch Edwin from the stables.

Two days after the birth of her son, the minister baptised him

Robert Horatio Payne. I had engaged the services of a wet nurse even though Frances insisted on suckling the babe. It was distressing to watch as the infant did not seem to receive nourishment at her breast and he would turn his head from side to side restlessly, snuffling.

We celebrated Christmas quietly. The Great Hall was festooned with winter fir and holly, the red berries shining brightly. The holly trees are laden with berries this year, portending a hard winter. A group of fiddlers and singers arrived from Bridgeford and cheered us with Christmas music. Cook roasted a huge goose and Lily stuffed herself: the sight of her chin and fingers shining with goose fat turned my stomach. Frances remained in her room and ate very little.

Little Bertie gives us great concern. He lies quietly but snuffles all the time and his cry is too weak for a healthy baby. He brings up his milk and so needs constant feeding by the wet nurse.

Thus, we enter the year of our Lord 1812. It began to snow on New Year's Eve and the shepherds and stockmen of our and neighbouring estates are out each day searching for sheep and cattle in difficulties and because the drifts are so deep; they have been herded into the barns where they can eat hay. Fortuitously, the summer grass provided a good yield of hay for fodder but I pray this weather does not linger.

January 12th, 1812

The day began with a promising wind from the south, melting icicles and turning the compacted snow into slushy puddles. Doctor Birch managed to ride through the slush and went immediately to the nursery. I gave instructions to lay another place for the doctor for dinner and heard a commotion from the upper floor. I hurried up the servants' staircase, and the commotion turned to screaming. As I entered the nursery, I was met with a scene I will never forget.

Frances sat in the rocking chair, the tiny bundle wrapped in swaddling clothes clutched to her breast and it was she who keened, a relentless sound that made my ears hurt. The wet nurse sat in a heap on the floor sobbing into her apron, which covered her head. Doctor Birch knelt by Frances, trying to ease the babe out of her arms, but she clutched him more tightly and screamed hysterically. In such circumstances, I would administer a sharp slap to the person screaming and it would shock them into silence. However, it was immediately apparent that something was dreadfully amiss with the child. Most of the housemaids had gathered by the nursery door in various states of distress. I sent them away sharply with a message for a footman to find Edwin at once.

Then I went over to Frances and laid my hand on her shoulder. I addressed her in as firm a voice as I could muster. 'Frances, let me have Bertie, please. Daughter, let your father and I look at your son.'

My firmness worked, and she handed over the hapless bundle. I immediately handed him to Doctor Birch, but I could feel no warmth or movement. Frances was rocking backwards and forwards as if still nursing her child, still emitting the horrible keening noise. Her father laid the baby in the crib and unwrapped his swaddling clothes. His indrawn breath came out as a sob and it told me all I needed to know. I bent over the crib. The face and lips of the little mite were colourless and his little limbs stiff. Bertie must surely have passed from this world some hours ago and there was nothing the doctor could do now. Silent tears coursed down his face, but the look he gave me was accusatory. I knew he was thinking that if Frances and the babe had moved back to the family home, perhaps there would have been a chance for his survival. I dismissed this thought. The baby's constitution had been weak from birth, and I had feared he would not live.

When Edwin rushed in and saw his lifeless son, his anguish tore at my heart. He stood over his inconsolable wife and I quailed at his words to her.

'Why did you allow this to happen, madam? How could you let another baby die?' Frances was too distraught to respond, and I laid my hand on Edwin's, which he shook it off angrily.

Doctor Birch stood in front of Edwin, tall and straight. 'Good God, Edwin, show respect for your wife at this time.'

The doctor knelt at his daughter's side, taking her hands into his own and I knew this is what Edwin should be doing, but Edwin had stormed out, dashing away angry tears.

It was heartbreakingly sad listening to Evie read Honoria's account and both Ruby and I had glistening eyes. I remembered waking from my doze in the rocking chair in the old nursery hearing the shocking sound of screaming, and a baby's distressed crying. I shuddered, gently rubbing my stomach, reassuring my son that all was well......

January 15th, 1812

I tried to persuade Frances to remain at the house for the funeral, but she refused.

The funeral cortege was silent and sombre. The minister, Mr Draycott, greeted us solemnly at the door of the little chapel. Edwin led, clutching the tiny coffin to his chest and, with the minister's help, laid it on the altar. After his outburst, Edwin has been assuaging his grief in drinking with his grand uncle. Frances entered, supported by her mother and father, and I followed on Gerard's arm, weighed down with grief and guilt and fear. Lily did not attend, as it would be too distressing in her condition. As many of the servants and footmen that could be spared shuffled into the chapel, eager to pay their respects.

The weather was inclement. After the snow, rain had set in and the skies were heavy and grey. Even the candles in their sconces failed to brighten the gloom in the chapel as the minister intoned the sombre words of the service and afterwards we processed to the newly reopened grave of my father, my husband, son and first grandson for the committal. The minister intoned the words which offered us no consolation or comfort as the rain dripped down from the leaden skies and lifeless trees. Frances was dry- eyed, stiff, and silent. She had uttered not one word since the passing of her child.

I had questioned the wet nurse after the death and she had haltingly told me that when she had gone to the crib to lift the babe out for his early morning feed it had been empty. Frances was holding the babe to her breast, but he was not breathing. The wet nurse had spoken with shock that the babe was dead and that was when Frances had started screaming.

We returned to the house in the carriages. Doctor and Mrs Birch accepted sherries but there was no conversation between us. They took their leave and Frances' mother tearfully embraced her daughter, who remained as immobile as a statue. Edwin drank more than was polite on such an occasion.

Eventually, I was able to retire to my room. Frances was escorted to her room by her little maid Dora, and I hoped she would have some respite from grief in sleep. Every bone in my body ached as if I was old and feeble. I lay on my bed, but my mind continued to work, giving me no rest.

Only this morning, before the funeral, Gerard had approached me holding letters. His bearing was humble, but his eyes sparkled with triumph.

'I have letters from my lawyers,' he began.

'Surely not today of all days, Uncle,' I said, holding up my hand to forestall him.

'Of course, it is so very regrettable. However, my situation has become much clearer and my lawyers have new advice.'

'Please come to the library after breakfast tomorrow, Uncle.' I begged. 'Today is for sorrow and grief.' He bowed and tucked the letters into his waistcoat, but his face as he left bore ill-disguised triumph.

I knew immediately what advice the letters would hold. Edwin had no heir. When Lily bore her child or twins, as was forecast, and they were male, then the estate would be entailed on the eldest male. If only Edwin had wed someone more robust than dear Frances.......

There came an urgent tapping on my door. I was tempted to ignore it but I rose reluctantly and issued a command to enter. Dora, Frances' maid servant, bobbed in a curtsey. Her face was flushed most unbecomingly and her cap awry.

'Begging pardon, my lady, for disturbing you. I was wondering if Mistress Frances was in your company.'

'Frances?' I asked sharply. 'She is resting in her room after her ordeal, just as I am.'

'Begging pardon again, madam, but she ain't - isn't. I took her up, my poor mistress, and helped her into the chair by the hearth. I went to fetch a tisane and when I returned, she weren't there. I have looked in all the downstairs rooms and even in the kitchens and pantries but nobody has seen her.'

'Have you asked Master Edwin? Perhaps he has taken her somewhere quiet.'

Begging pardon, my lady, I saw Master Edwin ride away as I was on my way to make the tisane.'

'Where is Jackie?' I asked. Jackie is Frances' little terrier who follows her everywhere.

'He is not in her room or the nursery, madam.'

'Well, there you are then, Dora. Your mistress has taken Jackie outdoors. He has been shut in all morning. Have some footmen go round the gardens to ensure they are safely found.'

'Yes, my lady.' Dora dipped a hasty curtsey and disappeared, looking relieved.

I could not shake off my unease. My windows looked south across the farmland and towards the distant rising ground of the New Forest. The weather was not conducive to taking the air. I hastened to Edwin and Frances' rooms in the main house hoping to find that Frances had returned and was resting. The rooms were empty; the fire burned low; the clock ticked loudly and rain spattered the windows. The Ladies' Bower and the Obelisk were opposite their windows. It was a constant reminder of my husband and dear son and it stood pale against the rain darkened tree trunks and dull evergreen hedges. I had a presentiment that she might have gone back down to the chapel and the grave of her sons in her grief.

I turned to issue instructions for someone to go to the chapel when I saw two envelopes lying on the salver on the small table near the door awaiting collection. One was addressed to me and one to Frances' parents. My fingers shook as I picked it up with such foreboding that it took all my resolve to slit the letter open with the knife on the salver. Frances' handwriting was very neat, with round childlike strokes.

My Dearest Maman,
You have shown such patience and kindness to me, and I have come to regard Harthill House as my home. In these last two years, I have become a wife and mother. Two years since I was an innocent girl who was happiest on my little pony, Blanche, accompanying dear Papa on his big bay, Roland. Papa used to tease me about Blanche having to trot faster to keep up with him and we had such fun racing each other across the downs.
It was in the unhappiest of circumstances that forged our

acquaintance, and it is through our shared grief of losing dearly beloved ones that enables me to speak what is in my heart to you.

Dearest Maman, I loved your son Edwin to the best of my ability, but I have failed in my duty as a loving wife and thus, I can never forgive myself. I have watched him grow angry because I know how much Harthill House, the estate and YOU, Maman, mean to him. I realise the cost of keeping the estate and your businesses flourishing has been a great burden to you. Edwin admitted he has no head for business, but with your support he was safe in the knowledge that all would be well. He informed me about the threat to the entailment of the estate with the arrival of his grand uncle Gerard and Lily, his wife. Edwin made it clear that while I provided heirs, the estate would remain in safe hands.

Now that promise of inheritance has come to nought, and the fault lies with me. I wish with all my heart that I had been a stronger wife, able to bear him healthy sons to fulfil his heart's desire. I have been unable to provide healthy heirs and have failed in my duty as a wife and nurturing mother. The deaths of my beloved sons, Freddie and Bertie, have broken my spirit and the torment and suffering of bearing and losing more children is more than my body and spirit can endure.

You must not take any blame on yourself, my dearest Maman. The fault lies with me and me alone.

From your Truly loving Daughter,

Frances.

The tears that spilled down my cheeks wet the paper, and the words blurred. I shook so badly I had to clutch the back of a chair, but I could not compose myself. I ran from the room screaming for servants, for Edwin, for anyone.

We scoured every part of the estate: every man and woman calling, poking under bushes, searching stables, barns, attics, and cellars.

We were all soaked to the skin. Edwin had not even donned his coat and his hair, shirt and breeches clung to him and his face was leeched of colour.

'It is all my fault,' he said every time our paths crossed. 'I was too harsh with her. I blamed her; I told her she must put aside grief to do her duty.'

There was nothing I could say or do to comfort him. It was my burden of guilt as well. It became too dark to see, and the flaming brands and lanterns were diminished by the rain and foul night.

We spent a sleepless night, and at first light of dawn the search began again. The weather relented and a pale, washed-out sky arched overhead.

Doctor Birch had been summonsed. I could not in all conscience conceal the terrible situation, and he brought some of his own farm hands. I handed him the letter Frances had addressed to her parents. He turned away from me as he read it and his shoulders shook just once. He did not relate to me the contents of the letter and I did not enquire. He gathered his men to join the search.

Edwin insisted I stay indoors for my health, for after the rain yesterday I felt a cold chill wrapped around all parts of me, but I would not consent and had donned sturdy boots to continue.

Before noon, as a weak sun illumined the sodden fields and woods, there was a shout from beyond the Ladies' Bower. Some of my farm hands escorted the miller, Mr Dunworthy, a fat man whose breath laboured as he was rushed up the track. He was twisting his hat in his hands and mopping his brow with his neckerchief.

'My lady, Sirs, you must come,' was all he could utter, and his distress was so great I ran past him with Edwin and Doctor Birch overtaking me on the muddy, slippery track leading to the mill and the river.

Mr Dunworthy's workers had discovered Frances in the river, caught in the reeds and overhanging branches. They had been alerted by hearing whimpering and small barks and on searching had found a bedraggled, shivering Jackie lying on the bank close to where poor Frances floated.

Someone tried to bar my way, thinking I would be too distressed, but I pushed him out of the way. Frances lay floating face down, wearing the same coat and dress she had worn for the funeral. Her bonnet and shoes were lost, and her long hair was tangled in the weeds at the edge of the river. Her father jumped in, regardless of the cold and depth, and lifted her up out of the water. Willing hands helped lay her body with great gentleness on the bank and all around the men were silent, some openly weeping, caps in hands, shocked at the tragedy. Jackie wriggled free from a stockman's arms and crept up to his mistress, whining and pawing at her clothes. Edwin was distraught and knelt by his wife, cradling her cold stiff hands, and I thought he was about to strike the poor creature, but he could not stop weeping.

A bier was found by the miller and Frances' poor body was reverently laid upon it and we processed through the dripping woods to Harthill House.

Mr Dunworthy caught the arm of Doctor Birch as he set off behind the bier and whispered into his ear. The doctor started and in sotto voce he seemed to instruct the miller. Mr Dunworthy tugged his forelock and returned to the mill.

'What is it?' I asked the doctor, as he seemed unable to move. He looked at me with such contempt I reeled back a pace. 'The good miller informed me that there were stones in the pockets of Frances' coat. I have instructed him to keep his counsel, and I will reward him handsomely. Frances will be awarded a Christian burial. After that, madame, you should look to find yourself another physician.'

He stalked off. We both knew from our letters what Frances intended, but if it was known she had taken her own life, no minister would allow her to be laid in consecrated ground.

1st February

I scarce take note of dates now. Days have passed and a great sadness lies over the house. Even Gerard and Lily have remained quiet in their rooms, but I have no doubt that my uncle is plotting and planning. The letter Frances wrote lies in my bureau and I take it out, as if by re-reading her words, I will see something different and she will return with Jackie, wet from the rain but brave and resolute about her future. Jackie lives with the groom now, as Edwin could not bear to see him nearby. It took all my courage to show Edwin her letter. He had received no note from her and when he read her words; we wept together. 'I was wrong to marry her,' he railed. 'I could not deal with her quietness and forbearance. I should have wed a strong woman who could bear children without fuss.'

'I presume you mean poor Mary Spears,' I snapped back at him. Edwin had the good grace to look shamefaced.

'At least she did not shrink away from me, as Frances did, as if I was a monster.'

The Rector came. If he had his doubts as to the cause of Frances' death, he heard the same story from our lips as from her father: Frances had taken Jackie for a walk to palliate her distress and had somehow tumbled into the river.

I cannot write about the service for that poor child. She is buried at the edge of the churchyard. Both our families have arranged to have a memorial raised and permission has been given for her two babes to be re-interred with their mother.

Some days after the burial, Gerard emerged looking obsequious, holding papers in his hands. He was so sorry to have to bring up matters after such sad events, but………

Of course, he has been corresponding with lawyers and Wills examined. I was so irate after his damnable speech my grief was dispelled and I strode back and forth racking my brain for means to defeat his plans. Gerard even gave us the choice of staying on once he inherited or finding a quiet place to live out the rest of my life. When Lily bore his sons, there could be no more disputes.

I opened a drawer for paper to draw up some sort of plan. Frances' letter fluttered to the floor and as I picked it up, her words stood out clearly. 'I wish with all my heart that I had been a stronger wife, able to bear him healthy sons to fulfil his heart's desire.'

Edwin's angry words echoed in my head: 'I should have wed a strong woman.' My response had been bitter: 'You mean someone like poor Mary Spears,' and Edwin had replied that at least she did not shrink away from him.

Mary Spears had already borne a son, and her next birthing was imminent. I had not taken the trouble to enquire about her health these last few months, but I realised I had stopped pacing, my heart pounding alarmingly in my breast.

My first impulse was to dismiss the preposterous notion that had entered my head, but the more I tried to dispel it, the possibility became more insistent. I realised I would do anything to ensure the safety of Harthill House and its estates. Uncle Gerard would fritter away his inheritance. Edwin and I would be forced to live elsewhere on a meagre existence. And what would become of my dear sisters who needed gentle, loving care, and my aging Aunt Helene? No, I would not allow any calamity to befall these women who were dependent on me alone.

The grief which consumed my whole being fell away, and I stood straighter, and my mind cleared. First, I needed to speak to Edwin, then proceed to London to see our lawyers.

∽

The bad news from our lawyers in London was that the claims of Uncle Gerard were legal and could be upheld in any appeal. Edwin's claim as male heir was also legal and the Will of my grandfather, Sir Horace, clearly stated that the estates were to be entailed on the male heirs of his son James and thereafter. A great burden was lifted from my person when these words were uttered. Edwin was still dispirited and downcast because I had not yet told him what was on my mind.

We retired to the house of our overseer at the wharves where the Barnard ships, and warehouses lay. We were warmly welcomed despite lack of communication since all the tragedies that had recently befallen. After taking a glass of Madeira and seed cake which our host's wife put before us, she retired and we conversed with Mr Waterhouse about the business and profits, which although were handsome, had not risen greatly because of the conflict with Napoleon and the Peninsular Wars.

Mr Waterhouse was most anxious to appraise me of plans to build new wharves for our ships as the old docks had been in use for centuries and loading and unloading was becoming overcrowded, costly, and fraught with danger from river pirates.

After a pleasant hour looking at figures and the plans for the new wharves and expressing my trust in his decisions, I begged for a quiet room where I could converse privately with my son. We were shown into a small parlour where a coal fire warmed the room and a small case with glass frontage shone in the firelight. Inside were perfectly made models of ships of all ages and countries. My host modestly explained that after finishing the construction, his wife and daughters had helped him to paint them. He lit the lamps on the small table and said he would have the maid serve us coffee and we would have total privacy. Edwin and I examined the models and the shelf by the fire, which contained books on all subjects. The maid brought in a tray of coffee with cream and sugar and began to pour, but I said I could manage and thanked her. I was silent as I poured the coffee and added cream and sugar to fortify myself for the forthcoming conversation. Edwin was growing impatient, questioning my need for privacy. I went to the door, opened it and, seeing that the passage was empty, sat down and told Edwin what was on my mind.

At first he sat blinking like an owl, as if unable to comprehend my words. When I emphasised the outcome if nothing was done, he gulped at his coffee, then twisted his hands in consternation.

'It is a big undertaking you ask of me, Mama,' he stammered, rubbing his brow. I looked at my first born, heir to Harthill House. All his life, he had rebelled against responsibility. He had assumed he need not do anything because all would be taken care of without his necessity to contribute. Instead of feeling angry at his shortcomings, I realised he had an inherent weakness. I vowed there and then to live to a good age so that I could guide my son and his future.

'Do you seek the alternative, Edwin?' I asked gently. 'Do you desire a life of poverty and watch your mother and aunts suffer poverty at the profligate hands of your wretched grand uncle? Once you had feelings for Mary...'

'Mama, I would not wish to see you, or my aunts suffer.' He hesitated, drew in a long shaky breath, then said firmly: 'So be it, Mama. I will do your bidding with good grace and God grant me strength.'

I rose and embraced him, tears in my eyes and was startled to see tears in his eyes also.

'I am sorry, Mama, I have caused a great deal of trouble and will do all I can to repair the ills caused.'

'All is not solved yet, but the sooner we return to Harthill House, we can put our plan into action.' I pulled the bell rope and when the maid appeared, I asked her to fetch our host as we wished to take our leave.

Mr Waterhouse expressed concern about the lateness of the hour for our return to Wiltshire and when I glanced out of the windows, I was surprised to see darkness without. Such had been the urgency of the business of the day I had not thought of the hours passing. He insisted that we stayed with him and his family that night and return early on the morrow. Our groom would be lodged comfortably in the coach house attached to the premises of the warehouse. I had no heart to refuse, even if my need to return lay urgently in my mind. We passed a pleasant evening dining with my host and his wife and daughters. The eldest daughter was betrothed but the two younger sisters were pretty and held intelligent conversation, even disagreeing with their father who looked amiably on. I saw Edwin watching them covertly and felt a pang of pity for him; either would make eligible consorts for him, but that door was now firmly closed.

By good fortune, the day's weather was clement for our return to Wiltshire and we made good speed. My impatience grew as we neared Harthill House, but I needed to be calm before I approached Mary Spears and her mother. Gerard was at his simpering best greeting us on our arrival, which I ignored.

On our arrival home, despite the lateness, I sent a missive to Mary Spears that Edwin and I would visit the next day to ascertain her health and offer any assistance. I was not surprised to receive a short note from her mother saying that her daughter was in good health, that her time was near, and thanked me for my concern. I read from the tone of the note that she would prefer no interference from us. Nevertheless, the next morning Edwin and I set off in the small carriage, alone.

Edwin was very nervous and with good reason. He had not set eyes on Mary Spears since her dismissal, so when we were received by a reluctant Mrs Spears and ushered into the small but neat parlour of the old farm building by the river, we were both unprepared by Mary's appearance. She stood with difficulty as we entered, and Edwin's eyes were drawn irresistibly to the great swelling of her belly. It was impossible to conceal, and she wore a plain brown dress which flared out under her generous bosom to accommodate the swell. A clean white apron stretched across her belly. Her hair was neatly tucked into a white cap and a stray curl peeped out. Her cheeks had spots of red on them, caused by either her condition or on seeing her former lover again. Her whole appearance was healthy and a testament to fecundity. She curtsied as low as she was able on our admittance and kept her eyes downcast. Mrs Spears bustled in with a tray of tea and homemade wafers.

'We thank you for your concern about Mary, madame, but we are managing most ably, thank you.'

I accepted my cup graciously.

I observed Mary casting glances at Edwin from beneath lowered eyelashes and saw her colour rising. If I was not mistaken, she still carried feelings for my son.

'I will speak plainly, Spears,' I said and realised that I had forgotten her first name, so used was I to using her last name during her service. Then I proceeded to inform Mary and her mother about the situation at Harthill House. If Gerard and his wife became master and mistress, then there would be no doubt that this cottage which I had given rent free as part of guilt payment to Mary and her mother would be taken from them. Mary gave a frightened moan and stifled it with her hand, and I observed Edwin's hand creep out to allay her fear. Then I set out the details of my plan, which if carried out, would solve all our futures.

Mrs Spears dropped her cup loudly onto the saucer and held her hand to her cheek. Mary half rose. There was a silence broken only by the crackling flames in the hearth. Mrs Spears drew in a deep breath, but I was amazed when Edwin spoke. He rose from his seat and knelt by Mary. He took her hand, and when she tried to snatch it away, he lay his other hand gently on top.

'Mary, my behaviour has been reprehensible over my lack of respect for your welfare, for which I now humbly beg your forgiveness. I speak with all honesty now, Mary, to tell you that when I was in your company you did make me very happy, and it was only because of our positions that you had to suffer.'

He glanced at me, but I was holding my breath.

'Fate has stepped in and now I would very much wish to repay your loyalty and loving kindness towards my firstborn son with you and to redress the hurt I have caused you. Mary, I cannot dissemble any longer. Will you do me the honour of becoming my wife?'

There were three gasps in the room; one from me, one from Mrs Spears, and one that sounded like a low-pitched shriek from Mary. Edwin still firmly clasped her hands. She looked beseechingly at her mother. Mrs Spears, to her eternal credit, was nodding. 'Mary, this is your decision to make and I will abide by it, whatever it be.'

Mary looked wildly around her. 'How can you think of marrying me with this?' She put her free hand on her swollen belly.

'That is precisely why it is imperative that you marry as soon as possible, Mary,' I said clearly before Edwin could speak again. 'A son born to you after marriage to Edwin will inherit Harthill House and its estates.'

'And then as soon as it's born, whether it be a boy or a girl, you will cast me off again!' Mary's tears ran down her face and she dashed them away angrily.

'No, Mary. I promise you that when we are wed, I will look after you and our children for the rest of my life.'

I had never heard Edwin speak so sincerely, and I looked pleadingly at Mary.

She took Edwin's hand and placed it on her belly. Edwin looked shocked at feeling movements, but he did not pull his hand away in revulsion.

'I know there is a boy in here because he gives me no rest day or night! Promise on the life of my son that you will honour your intentions.' Mary looked both fierce and fearful at the same time, but Edwin laughed.

'You need not fear, Mary. I will uphold my intentions honourably.'

Just then, there was a commotion beyond the room, and the door was flung open. A sturdy, yellow-haired boy of about three years of age rushed into the room. 'Mamma' he cried. 'There was frogspawn in the pond. Aunt Meg helped me put them in a pot and I can watch them grow!' He seemed unaware that his mother had company and climbed awkwardly onto her lap. Only as he lay there and Mary brushed his hair back with her hand did his thumb creep towards his mouth as he solemnly regarded his mamma's visitors.

'Johannes, this is your father and grandmother who have come to visit. Shake hands with them like a good boy you are.'

Johannes did indeed climb down and approached Edwin. Edwin held out his hand with a rare smile on his face. 'Are you really my father?' he asked boldly.

'I am indeed. And I hope that we can see each other more often from now on if you are agreeable.'

'Would you like that, Mamma?' he asked shyly, and Mary nodded, blinking back tears.

Mrs Spears clapped her hands. "Now Johannes, go and see your Aunt Meg and get those dirty hands washed.'

Johannes bowed to Edwin, and me and ran out of the room.

'He is beautiful, Mary, and I recommend you for his good manners,' I remarked.

'I cannot leave him here if I am to be wed,' Mary burst out.

'Indeed not, Mary. He shall live with us as our son at Harthill House,' said Edwin. I had never seen him so agreeable and sent a silent prayer to thank the Lord for his gracious mercy.

'We will obtain a Common Licence for the marriage. I will apply to the bishop and choose a church, for it is expedient that people should not know until after the marriage.' Seeing Mary's mother looking troubled, I added: 'We must all keep this secret until after the ceremony and Mary takes up residence at Harthill House. Master Gerrard or his wife must not know of our plans, for they will seek ways to prevent the marriage. We will take our leave now, and I or Edwin will apprise you of the date and place of marriage very shortly. Remember, it must be our secret.'

I had no option but to insist on secrecy for Mary and her mother had no idea of the lengths Uncle Gerrard might go to prevent Edwin and Mary from marrying.

February 1812

It is done. Edwin and Mary were married in a quiet church on the outskirts of Salisbury where none knew our faces. Apart from the Rector, the only other witnesses were Mrs Spears, Mary's sister Meg, her husband, myself, and the old church deacon. We drove back to Harthill House; snowdrops brightening the hedgerows and catkins dancing merrily from trees. We drove carefully, as Mary was most uncomfortable as we tried to avoid the deepest ruts in the muddy lanes.

I had asked Hobbs to prepare a small table with sherry and

pastries for a celebration. Uncle Gerard and his wife had been unaware of our departure as Edwin and I had walked to the stables for the coach and then had picked up Mary and her family. Young Johannes had been lodged at his uncle's farm cottage further down the river.

Mary gratefully accepted Edwin's and the coachman's helping hands to descend from the carriage and, once in the salon, sank into a chair by the fire. Despite her great size, she had carried herself graciously in a voluminous dark green taffeta dress covered by a fur-trimmed cloak.

After we had partaken of a little sherry and a few morsels, we felt somewhat restored and I pulled the bell rope for Hobbs. When he appeared, I instructed him to fetch the maidservants and footmen.

'Mary, dear, you must now play the part of the lady in this house and together you and Edwin must greet the servants as their new master and mistress.'

Poor Mary. She paled alarmingly but stood as Edwin offered his arm and they faced the door together as all the servants trooped in. They managed to hide their astonishment very well, but I expected downstairs would be a babble of gossip for days. If I heard any ill words about Mary's new position, they would answer to me.

After they had bowed and curtsied Edwin dismissed them. I detained Hobbs and asked to if he would be so good as to escort my uncle and his wife to these rooms. He bowed and left.

'There is one more ordeal you must suffer today, Mary,' I smiled, trying to instil confidence in my voice.

'We must appraise my uncle and his wife of your news. Edwin knows it will be a grievous blow to them and they may be discourteous to you in their surprise.'

'If they insult Mary, I shall have them escorted from the premises forthwith,' huffed Edwin.

'We must be delicate until the birth of your child,' I warned him. If Mary bore a daughter and Lily bore a son or sons, it would all have been in vain for us. I felt quite lightheaded at the thought of such a catastrophe.

'Be seated, Mary,' I said. 'You need not stand to greet my uncle and his wife. You are equal now.'

Mary gratefully eased into the chair. 'Once we have given our joyful news to them, you must rest; you have had a long day.'

Edwin helped himself to another sherry. It was as much an ordeal to him to confront his grand uncle.

After a long moment there was a tap on the door and Hobbs entered. 'Mister Gerard and Mistress Lily,' he announced.

'Thank you, Hobbs,' I said brightly, 'offer my uncle and his wife a glass of sherry and refreshments, if you would be so kind.'

The sight of two burgeoning bellies was almost overwhelming. Lily had grown fat as well and looked quite monstrous. Edwin put a hand on Mary's shoulder, either to give her courage or to stop her from rising and curtseying. Lily's eyes bore into Mary's unpleasantly. I straightened my spine.

'Uncle and Lily, please help me toast Edwin and Mary on their marriage and join with me in wishing their good health and fortune.'

Gerard's face, which is florid at best, now turned choleric. Instead of drinking his sherry, he slammed it down, spilling it. 'What joke is this, Honoria? That wretched girl, Frances, is barely cold in her grave. Who is this floosy sitting here?'

Edwin flinched, and his face flushed angrily.

'Uncle, you are here by my kind invitation. Please do not resort to insults under my roof,' I said icily, but my heart pounded so rapidly in my breast I could scarcely speak.

'Mary and I wed this day, Uncle, and we hope for a safe birthing for our child soon.' Edwin spoke calmly, although his high colour belied his emotions.

Lily, meanwhile, had finished her sherry and helped herself to the assortment of delicacies served by Hobbs. He stood by implacably calm, but his eyes were on me and if I gave the word, he would most certainly endeavour to remove Gerard.

'If the situation is untenable, dear Uncle, you are quite free to find other accommodation,' I smiled sweetly at him. I was determined he would not better us. Mary sat frozen in the chair. Her hands rested on the arms of her chair, but her knuckles were white.

'My felicitations to you both,' Gerard snarled, bowing to Edwin and Mary. Then he turned to me.

'I see through your scheming, niece, and I can assure you that you cannot win this game. Meanwhile, I must fall on your hospitality a while longer, at least until my dear wife has safely been brought to bed. Then we shall take stock of our situations. Come, my dear, let us leave the happy couple to their nuptials.' The scorn in his voice apparent, Lily rose with great difficulty, helped by Hobbs while Gerard stalked stiffly to the door. Hobbs opened it for them and, with a nod from me, left to escort them back to the North Wing.

A grim silence followed until Mary, in a tremulous voice, said, 'I don't feel well at all. I think I need to lie down.'

'Are your travails begun?' I asked anxiously, my hand on the bell rope to summon a footman. The midwife lived in Bridgeford and I wished that we still had the services of Doctor Birch.

'There are no pains, but I do feel faint,' said Mary. Edwin proffered her a glass of sherry. 'Drink this, it may restore you a little,' he advised. 'We'll summon a maidservant to help you to bed.' He looked at me enquiringly. In all the rushed preparations a maid had not been appointed for Mary.

'I'll summon Dora,' I said, pulling the rope. Since her mistress Frances' demise, she had been given duties in the laundry, which I knew displeased her. She would be glad to be appointed lady's maid again. When Mary had been helped to the bedroom by Dora, who was her usual sweet self, Edwin sat down by the fire, throwing another log onto it with force. 'By God, you are right about Gerard; he is a knave and a varlet. How dare he call Mary a floosy when his own wife is a common prostitute!'

'My son, he was caught in a disadvantaged situation. We have called his bluff, and he has now shown his true colours.'

'We should have them thrown out immediately,' 'Edwin raged.

'As a Christian, I cannot be uncharitable and see Lily suffer because of her husband's foolish ways. I'm afraid we must allow them to stay under our roof until she is delivered. By then your son will have been born and Gerard will have no claim.'

'Unless Mary bears a girl child,' said Edwin gloomily, downing another sherry.

'You must not think of that. You must be strong now. Uncle Gerard will not let your life be easy, so you must be on your guard and be clearheaded.' I removed the sherry decanter from his reach.

'Go and sit with your wife now, Edwin. She needs your strength and love and patience. Her life has just been turned upside down.'

Edwin raised my hand to his lips. 'Dear Maman, do not fear. I am fond of Mary and will treat her well.'

An attack of cramp and a kicking child pulled me out of Honoria's discourse. It was very late. When I heard of poor Frances' drowned body guarded by her little dog Jackie, I immediately remembered the afternoon when I'd seen a distressed dog running up and down the riverbank. Now I knew I'd had a ghostly premonition.

"Let's carry on tomorrow night," I said.

Despite the late hour, sleep didn't come easily. The shadows of Honoria, Frances, Edwin, Mary, and Gerard seem to hover at the foot of my bed in the darkness and their history was as fantastic as any romantic fiction. Yet it was all real and I was now part of this story. Strangely, these people were Will's blood relatives, yet his part in the drama was remote. When our baby was born, another chapter would be opened. An image of the leery faces of the Twins swam into my mind and I shivered. Two hundred years of history was condensed into this moment, and my part in this family history was yet to be played out. I had a bad feeling as I tossed and turned.

Honoria's Journal

March 1812

Mary's travails began yesterday, and the midwife in attendance hovered about the bed. Little Johannes had been taken to the stables to feed the horses and help the groom muck out and to play with Jackie so that he would not hear the moans and shrieks coming from his mother. Meg, Mary's sister, wiped a damp cloth over Mary's brow and her mother, whose name I now knew was Alice, held her daughter's hands. The room was stifling as a fire had been kept going day and night since Mary had been brought to bed a week ago. We could not open a window as March winds roared round the house and tossed the rooks' nests from the high branches. The midwife lifted the sheet and inspected Mary yet again. 'Mary, I do believe it won't be long now,' she announced. I had employed a midwife from Salisbury in the end, and she had lived in this past fortnight. "Tis time for you to walk about a while. The little mite will be encouraged to make an appearance.' She lay cool hands on the mound of Mary's abdomen, feeling the contractions which made Mary moan louder.

Supported by her mother and sister, she shuffled across the floor. Her waters had come early this morning, and the midwife had said to me that the birth would be a little harder, the longer it endured.

'The babe's head is in the right place; all will be well.'

Mary rested on the edge of the bed, and the midwife inspected her again. 'I see the head,' she announced triumphantly. Mary was laid back with the help of her sister and mother, while I could only look on and try to suppress my anxiety.

After many exhortations and encouragement to push, Mary gave a shriek, and the baby slithered out into the hands of the midwife, who rubbed it down with cloths and a ragged cry was heard.

'It's a fine boy, Mary, praise the Lord!' The midwife handed the mewling baby to Meg who rocked it gently, crooning. Mary moaned again: 'The pain, the pain!'

The midwife placed her hands on Mary's abdomen and pressed quite hard. 'I do believe there is another child in there,' she said in surprise.

Mary continued to writhe and shriek and I wished that good Doctor Birch was present. At her next inspection, the midwife saw the next baby's head and gently held it while telling Mary to push.

In a flurry of birth liquids and blood, a second son was born. He cried heartily from the first breath and we all sighed with relief. Once the midwife had checked him, she turned her attention to Mary, who lay exhausted. 'Fetch hot water and clean linen,' the midwife instructed, and I was only too glad to leave the room to give the order. Edwin was pacing the great hall and rushed to the foot of the staircase as I instructed a maid servant.

'You have twin sons, Edwin!' I smiled triumphantly at him. 'The midwife says they are both lusty. Mary is resting. You shall see them presently.'

'Twins!' he uttered in shock. He closed his eyes in relief. He had fulfilled his obligations.

The midwife set to cleaning Mary with the warm water and

clean linen. 'Bathing will help the healing and prevent infection. It is not a common practice yet, but it seems sensible to me.' She had inspected the placentas as I remember Doctor Birch doing with Frances and wrapped them to be taken away. Mary was helped to a chair while the bed was stripped and new linen placed on it by two maidservants and Mary helped into a clean nightgown and fresh cloths beneath her. Her colour was returning to normal as we helped her back into bed.

'Rest now, 'said the midwife, 'but tomorrow I will assist you to your feet as I believe that lying abed for too long after birthing does not aid the healing. I will watch her for bleeding,' she addressed me.

I was rather alarmed by her statement, but as she had acquitted herself admirably, I decided not to gainsay her.

March – April 1812

Mary and Edwin's twins continue to grow lustily, and my fears about their health are receding daily. They have been named Julius and Samuel, and Samuel is by far the noisiest. Mary is a most patient mother and allows Johannes to stay with her whilst feeding the twins, which takes up most of the day and night. Edwin is taller in stature as he strides around and is at last taking more interest in estate matters. My uncle and Lily keep to their rooms and we have not dined together since the birth of Edwin's twins.

One fine day at the end of March, Jane, Lily's maid servant, sought me out and handed me a note. 'I am to await a reply, madame,' she said, curtseying.

The missive from Lily was written laboriously in a hand unused to writing and quite brief.

'Dearest Honoria,' I read. 'I am in sore need of your advice. I would be grateful if you would spare me a moment of your time in my rooms as soon as you are able. Gerard is away in Southampton on business and will be away these two days.'

Gerard on a business journey! I nearly snorted in front of Jane, but as I was intrigued, I informed her I would visit forthwith.

The aspect from the windows in my uncle's and Lily's chambers in the North wing overlooked the back of the stables, the kitchen garden surrounded by beech hedges, and the woods running down to the river. In spring and summer there was the advantage of the westering sun, but the height of the trees cast a gloom in all the rooms, which made them seem darker than those in the house and South Wing. The fire in Lily's sitting room blazed and Lily was ensconced on a settee covered in rugs. In the few weeks since I had last seen her, I could not believe that she could grow any larger and a part of me felt pity.

Jane hovered nervously, and Lily asked if I would take tea with her, to which I agreed. When Jane left, Lily almost wept. 'Dear Honoria, I am at my wit's end. I am most uncomfortable and now I am so afeard that the babes are too big to come out normally. I am feeling pains most days, but they have come to nought, but I think my time is very near.'

I nodded in acquiescence and waited for her to continue.

'I have heard the servants speak highly of the midwife who attended Mary. Gerard has arranged no help for me yet, but I would so very much like a midwife to be present as soon as able. I thought perhaps his journeying might have been to seek a physician, but he said it was private business.'

Gambling, more likely, I thought. Jane returned with tea and pastries for Lily. She hovered about her mistress, but I looked hard at her and she hastily left the room.

'Lily, I would not have you suffer more than you are now, despite the froideur between my uncle and myself. I will enquire if the midwife who delivered Mary is available and I will also seek the attendance of a physician.'

'Oh, thank you Honoria,' she said, tears rolling down her cheeks. 'I feel so lonely here and I am in fear day and night. I can hardly walk these days.'

'I will enquire about the midwife forthwith, rest assured. I am sure when your time comes, all will be well.'

She wiped her eyes with the corner of her skirt. 'How are Mary and her babes? If I could walk, I would visit her to see the bairns. I have no reproach against you, Honoria. You have been kind and given us a roof over our heads. Before we wed, I lived in sorrowful conditions. Your uncle visited me when it suited him. I was overcome and grateful that he chose me for his wife.'

She stopped suddenly, afraid to divulge any more information and my coldness towards her thawed a little.

'I will send for Mary and the babes to visit you and you will be much cheered by their company.'

I drank my tea and departed. Lily had not asked to be in the middle of a feud between Edwin, myself, and Gerard, and despite her manufactured airs and graces, now Edwin had heirs. My confidence had been much restored. I knew that Lily and Mary would be grateful for each other's company.

April 1812

'Twas fortuitous that the midwife was able to attend the very next day, and I obtained the services of a physician who had worked together with the midwife on several occasions.

Three days after our conversation, Lily was brought to bed. Her travails were arduous, and I did not attend. I had learned from the midwife that Lily had birthed before, but I did not enquire what became of the offspring nor if the father was Gerard.

The physician needed to use instruments to enable the first baby to pass. Gerard had taken himself to the stables with a bottle of brandy and all avoided him.

At last, I was summonsed, along with Gerard. Lily had been delivered of twins, both sons and very large. They had suffered no damage, but Lily was weak and bleeding and the physician and midwife remained to watch over her.

Gerard was more than tipsy and extremely jubilant. 'Two sons to match Edwin's!' he chortled. 'We are back to stalemate, Honoria!'

Edwin wanted to evict them now that the birth was over, but I had to overrule him. Lily would take time to heal and I could not see her suffer through no fault of her own.

In the next few months, the servants were busy attending to needs of babies and mothers and I focussed on the affairs of the estate, guiding Edwin gently so that he would not suddenly grow tired and bored. He was interested in the shipping and wharves in London and visited as often as he could. I felt a small suspicion in my mind about the one remaining presentable unmarried daughter in the Waterhouse household. Naturally, I ensured that Mr Waterhouse reported directly to me and I was proud and gratified to hear that Edwin was most serious in his interest and showed much keenness.

Lily and Gerard continued to live in the North Wing, but I insisted they paid rent from Gerard's allowance. Lily and Mary became friends as they had much in common and the sound of four noisy babes drove me to my quiet rooms often.

My sisters Anne and Grace love the babes. Mary and Lily allow them to sit near the cribs in the nursery and they are content singing simple lullabies, whilst the two nursemaids hover nearby. The sight often moves me to tears.

To assist Edwin and with his agreement, I appointed a steward for the stock and agricultural duties necessary. Master Alfred Crane lives in the farmhouse and works hard with the livestock and fields of crops, and is most trustworthy. Edwin is, I think, relieved to defer to his knowledge and experience.

"Gerard must have lived there permanently because his twins worked on the estate when they grew up," I said. "And they were in that photo in the album."

"And Gerard must have influenced his sons against the succession for them to be still troublesome now," said Ruby.

"Despite the fact he had a permanent roof over his head, he was obviously still embittered and passed it on to his sons."

"There seems to be no obvious solution; even Dee admitted she couldn't see a way through," I sighed. *There is a solution for me. Keep away from Harthill House.*

"Did it not come to the attention of either of you that the name Crane suddenly popped up?" asked Evie.

"Matt and Mollie have both said the family has lived on the land here longer than Will's forefathers," I said. Just as Will and Matt were friends, it seemed fitting that they were both linked through a shared history.

Chapter Thirty-Three

It took some time to adjust to the present after nights of listening to Evie read from Honoria's Journals. Her words had conjured up images of life at Harthill House two centuries ago and I could not shake of awareness of playing an integral part in the continuing drama.

I returned to our flat and had a thorough cleanup, neglected since Will's departure. I threw out old stuff from the fridge and replenished it and filled jugs with tulips to make an imprint, even though my heart wasn't in it. Late spring was well and truly established at Harthill House and I wanted to be part of it, despite the Twins. I stood in the spare bedroom trying to imagine it as a nursery with primary colours and a frieze round the walls. Mum kept nagging me - when were we going to buy essential things for the baby?

Will arrived with souvenirs from New York, including a blue plush elephant with enormous ears. He was always restless after a trek. Winding down to mundane admin at the office was difficult for him and at this time of year he always focussed on the next trek.

One night after we'd eaten, he announced that he'd start decorating the spare bedroom before the next trek in a week's time.

It was my cue to broach the subject of finding somewhere more suitable.

"What's wrong with here?" Will asked, looking bewildered. "We've got two big bedrooms and this sitting room is spacious as well. And Ma might want to stay here when she's next over. It is her flat, after all."

"There is nothing wrong with it, Will," I said. "And your mother likes staying at that hotel where we had dinner." I didn't want him to go stubborn on me now. "I've had plenty of time to think things through while you've been away." I listed the drawbacks of living in this flat with a baby in tow.

Will stared at me morosely and I sighed inwardly. He really had never made many difficult life choices.

"We'd never be able to afford a house anywhere in London even if we got a good price for this place, and further out would be astronomical as well," he said. "Plus the fact that Ma owns it so I can't sell it without her say-so."

"You already have a house in the country," I said.

Another uncomprehending stare. "You'd really want to live at Harthill House with the baby? What about these ghosts you keep seeing, or have they gone away?"

"No, they are still there and a problem, but instinctively I feel it's the right thing to do. I just know it will be a struggle if we live here. Serena and Joe are on hand there, and I can work remotely while the baby is small. And you won't need to give up this place."

I knew that Will would not commit to living at Harthill House full time and would have to accept more absences. The Twins bothered me more than I cared to admit. When the baby was born, he would be another threat to them. Why was I drawn to Harthill when we would be safer here in the city? I was letting my heart rule my head and chose to ignore the warning voices inside me.

"I'm sorry, Clem. I've got to admit the logistics of living with a baby here hasn't been my main priority. You could stay at Harthill for your maternity leave, I can see now that it would be good for you to have Serena and Joe on hand, you'll be safe with them, and there'd be room for your Mum and Dad to stay too whenever they want. I'd come down to Wiltshire at weekends and, after a few months, we can see how it's working out."

I relaxed visibly. "I'd like to do that. Harthill has grown on me and the all the countryside around it. Our baby will get lots of healthy fresh air instead of exhaust fumes!"

I didn't confide in him about my continuing anxiety about the Twins. I went into the kitchen to clear up and Will's phone rang. He answered it quickly. I heard 'Hi, honeybee, how's it going?' before he got up from the sofa and headed into the bedroom. My insides turned to water, and I gripped the edge of the sink. Rafaella. 'Honeybee'. Still keeping in touch despite distance and her injury. And in keeping with my churning insides, I was given a fierce kick.

"That was Rafaella," Will said, coming into the kitchen and picking up a tea towel. "She sends you her love and apologises for keeping me away an extra-long time and hopes the bump is coming along well."

"Oh, right," I said. Perhaps it wasn't a private conversation expressing love and longing after all. "I hope her ankle is healing."

"She's got to have another op soon and will be off her bike for longer than she expected. I said she must let us know if they're short of Trek Leaders. Don't worry, I won't volunteer myself all the time!" he said, looking at my expression. "Come and sit down. You look done in."

I sat beside him on the sofa and he wrapped his arm round my shoulder and I leaned into him. "I'm going to be away a lot during the summer while you and titch here," patting my bump, "are going to have to struggle on without me so I'm going to try to be as helpful as I can." He kissed the top of my head and I snuggled in. That was the biggest declaration of commitment I'd heard from him so far.

~

Will came with me to my next antenatal check. All the baby's vital signs were good; he was a little larger than the average at this stage and he appeared to be very active. Will beamed proudly that there was another action man on the way! A couple of days later, Will and Andy departed for their trek in Southern Spain.

The days flew by. The trek season was well under way and two or three of our team were constantly abroad, either in Europe or the US. Will was back in time for the Music Festival at Harthill and was impressed by the professional organisation. A small dome had been erected for the musicians with raised staging and clever lighting. We wrapped up against the chilly evening breeze, which did not faze the festival goers enjoying their upmarket picnics, and the music, singing, and lanterns on poles all contributed to a magical evening. We were embarrassed when people came and thanked us as both of us were new to this type of experience, but even Will acknowledged that more events on a similar scale could be beneficial.

Ruby returned to the States at Rafaella's request, which gutted Evie, but we all hoped it would be temporary.

Will was asked to do one more trip in the States. Rafaella's ankle was slowly healing, but she was nowhere near fit for cycling. She worked in the office a few days a week, which was good news for Evie because Ruby returned to us. Rafaella had reluctantly acknowledged that being in London with Evie was Ruby's greatest desire and let her go. Shortly after that, Rafaella announced that she and Nicco were leaving for their European tour and a replacement for Ruby had been found. Her name was Lenny, short for Leonora. She had a very strong Brooklyn accent, but like Ruby, was a whiz with figures and had a wicked sense of humour.

By mid-July the City teemed with tourists. After a particularly hard day when I'd spent ages getting back to the flat due to crowds and traffic hold-ups, I decided it was time to decamp to Wiltshire for the duration. Will was home and he agreed I'd be better off at Harthill. We drove down the next weekend and I was amazed how the seasons had progressed. I was admiring the leaves on the lime trees lining the drive when we spotted Mollie by the old ash and all my senses prickled. However, she was just returning from her cleaning stint at the house and after greetings; I turned to wave. I blinked hard several times as she appeared to be accompanied by two tall companions in rustic clothing. I glanced at Will but he obviously had noticed nothing and my foreboding increased, although I tried to focus on the trees in heavy summer leaf and beginning to produce their fruits.

Will stayed for a couple of days, helping Matt at the farm before going back to prepare for back-to-back treks with Ben. After that, he'd be around for a short while before embarking on a long trek to Northern Greece and Macedonia with Hugo. He wouldn't return from this trek until late August and I told him I was worried that he wouldn't be back before the baby was born.

"Yes, I will," he said confidently. "You aren't due till the beginning of September and I'll have been back ages before then! Stay here and help Serena and I'll be much happier that you're not on your own. And Dr Laidlaw is on hand as a bonus."

Although I felt guilty abandoning them at the office, I was able to keep in touch daily and between them, Ruby and Kim could capably run a battleship.

Afraid of becoming complacent, my wanderings were kept within the confines of the gardens, watering peppers and tomatoes in the greenhouse, and weeding and hoeing round courgettes and other vegetables, always looking constantly over my shoulder.

Mum and Dad came to stay and Mum was at last satisfied that I'd ordered nursery stuff. Dad and Joe moved my bedroom around to accommodate a crib and a small chest of drawers with a changing mat on top. A baby bath was put in the bathroom next door and a sturdy buggy was housed downstairs outside the small sitting room. Mum insisted that I should have a bag already packed for hospital even though I still had weeks to go.

Serena took me on a shopping trip to Southampton to buy lots of baby garments and essentials. It was an exhausting day, but productive. We were chatting as we turned up the drive to home, so I hardly had time to register the misty shapes of the Twins that materialised in front of Serena's car. She drove through them, completely unaware. In shock, I turned to look out of the rear window, half expecting to see bodies on the ground, but of course there was no sign of any presence, human or otherwise.

After lunch one day, I sat outside on the sunny terrace, basking in my first taste of summer here. The leafy trees now obstructed the view of the obelisk and instead of snowdrops by the fences, seeding cow parsley grew in profusion. But it was the sound of birdsong which amazed me. A couple of months ago the sound of jackdaws and rooks dominated, making Harthill feel sinister, but today there was a cacophony of bird calls coming from the woods and beyond.

Matt appeared round the side of the house, minus filthy overalls and looking respectable in jeans and a checked wool shirt unfastened to reveal a black t-shirt emblazoned with a Led Zeppelin logo. He dropped into the chair beside me.

"I can't take in all the birdsong," I said, indicating the woods. "I'm a real townie and feel ashamed that I can only identify blackbirds, robins and pigeons!"

"Nesting is more or less over," Matt said. "Martins nest under the eaves round the house and the stables, and swallows around the barns."

"Dear me, I'll have to buy myself a bird spotting book." I laughed.

"I can lend you my books. I've got loads which I've had since as I was a lad. Better still, I can take you through the woods and point out the songs personally! I've got a bit of spare time before milking. How about an introduction now?"

We let ourselves out into the field and once on the track through the Ladies' Bower, the bird song grew louder.

"Should have brought the binocs," Matt said, stopping to point upwards.

"Woodpecker," I whispered. "I've never seen one up close."

He identified more birdsong from invisible birds. "We'd better get back to the track before we get engulfed in nettles." He took my arm to steer me through the tangled undergrowth, which had sprung up rapidly since my last visit. I was busy unsnagging myself from brambles full of small hard blackberries, so when I looked up, I saw by the gate the distinct outline of two forbidding shapes.

"Oh," I yelped, grabbing Matt's arm.

He held me firmly. "Watch your step, Clem. Don't want you tripping up," he said, all the while steering me towards the gate. I began to panic. How was I to go through the gate with the Twins blocking it? And Matt was oblivious. Taking a deep breath, I thrust my hand into the pocket containing the gemstones and chanted silently. I closed my eyes and when I opened them again, the apparitions were gone. I sighed in relief, almost forgetting Matt by my side, who was looking at me curiously.

"Sorry, funny turn, but I'm ok now," I lied. His eyes flicked towards the gate and he looked as if he was about to say something, but changed his mind. He took my hand and led me across the field.

Matt came to lunch next day carrying a bundle of books.

"I've got a couple of bird and wildflower books for you and wondered if you were up to listening in the woods again." He wore the same checked shirt but today he wore a Metallica t-shirt and I laughed.

"What's funny?" he said, smiling.

"I just don't see you as a head banger!" I said, indicating his t-shirt.

"You don't know me very well, then," he huffed. "Even the cows have got used to the beat now!"

"I'd love to hear some more birdsong," I said. I was safe in Matt's company, and it was good to go beyond the confines of the garden.

We forgot about time as Matt pointed out the calls of chiff chaff, greenfinches and made me try to identify the calls of the common birds like blue tits and chaffinches and sparrows.

"We must go down to the river, where there is kingfisher," he said as he guided me along the banks of a dried-up stream bordered with fading yellow flag iris.

He took my arm to steer me through overgrown shrubs and hillocky mounds. The more I was in Matt's company, the more relaxed I felt. He was so easy to talk to and his love of all things in nature was palpable and infectious, as was his sense of humour.

"Are you ok going through the gate?" he asked, and I turned sharply.

"What do you mean?"

"Just that yesterday you looked like you saw something or someone that terrified you."

I swallowed. Now would be a good time to unburden myself, and I felt Matt would be more understanding than Will.

"There might be something you can help with, Matt," I said, "but we'll need more time than I have right now. But thanks for asking."

"I'll always be on hand to help you," he said seriously and threaded my arm through his to guide me through the ordinary five-bar gate devoid of menacing presences.

Chapter Thirty-Four

The spikey needles on the Cedar of Lebanon don't make a sound when there's a breeze. I lay on a sun lounger in its shade on the south lawn looking up as the sun filtered through the branches, which swayed mesmerisingly in the warm breeze. It was peaceful, but as I lay there on that warm and humid August afternoon, our son decided it was time for one of his many footballing sessions. His little feet kicked and pushed against my ribcage, making me feel breathless and uncomfortable. I could see his movements as I lay on the sunbed. At my last checkup, the midwife had announced that he was 'a big lad' and I worried that a natural birth would be difficult, remembering how people had remarked how thin I was during those first horrible nauseous months of pregnancy. I was now booked in to Salisbury District Hospital where there was a well-established Maternity Unit.

Will had returned from a trek in Spain and immediately prepared for the next big one: a long trek through mountainous Greece and Macedonia with Hugo. It was challenging terrain, and all the trekkers who had booked were experienced.

"I'll be back in plenty of time for the nipper's birth," he reassured me.

Billy was quieter when I waddled around. I hoed weeds that continued to sprout around vegetables and flower beds and inspected the fruits in the orchard. The chickens were familiar with me now as I collected eggs. They had the run of the orchard, which was well fenced in as well as being hedged, but they were still shut in every night.

Encounters with the Twins since July had been at a distance where they'd lurked by the gates and in the tree shadows and I had hastily changed direction to head for the safety of the house. It was wearying being vigilant and even if I told Joe and Serena of my fears, there was little they could do to protect me. My crystals lay in their little bag beside the lounger, and I remembered to chant my protective mantras whenever I was outside.

I was listening to Dido's ethereal voice when an extraneous sound filtered through. I lifted out my earpieces and listened. Barking. Bess and Jasper must be with Joe somewhere. I settled myself again, and then remembered that Joe and Matt were baling straw after combining crops. Neither of the dogs would be allowed anywhere near the farm machinery.

The barking was insistent and urgent, and I was sure it was Bess. No one was around. Mollie had gone home after her morning cleaning and Serena had driven into Bridgeford. Inelegantly, I shifted my bulk off the lounger and waddled over to the gate. Matt had made me a stout walking stick and having been sceptical about needing it, it had proved very useful and gave me confidence for any encounters with the Twins. The barking was louder here and more insistent, and I knew something was wrong. Warily I entered the woods, calling, but the dogs were too far away to hear me. There was no breeze under the trees, and the leaves hung motionless. The drone of insects was loud as birds drowsed in the afternoon heat. I walked over the uneven track as fast as I could, my long summery skirt swishing against the masses of rosebay willow herbs and tall grasses that lined the path. The woods beyond the track were impenetrable with a wealth of nettles and brambles and thick undergrowth. I hoped the dogs weren't somewhere in there. Urgency drove me on, for I would never forgive myself if anything happened to either dog while the others were busy. They hadn't been lying under the tree with me, so I had assumed they were in the house. Despite my slow and panting progress, I soon headed downhill towards the river. Stupidly, I'd left my phone and crystals by the sun lounger. I mumbled the mantra repeatedly as I tried hard not to stumble in my leather thonged sandals, keeping one hand under my heavy bump and calling out to the dogs every few seconds. The glint of sunlight on water appeared through the tree trunks, and soon I could hear the rush of water over the weir. The track opened out and the old mill was ahead of me, but then I saw movement to my right. Bess was standing on the bank of the small inlet where the old boat house had once stood. She turned to me and started barking even more frantically. There was no sign of Jasper, and my heart thumped uncomfortably. I shuffled forward nearer the edge as Bess had her front paws in the shallow water. Then I saw Jasper. He was paddling a few metres out in the river, splashing water frantically but not getting anywhere. A branch of a tree trailed in the river and he seemed to be snagged on it. "Oh God," I groaned. If he freed himself, he might be caught up in the strong current and swept down the millstream or the weir. Using my walking stick as support, I stepped gingerly into the shallows.

"It's not too deep," I reassured myself. "If I use my stick for support, I can reach forward and grab his collar. Good boy, Jasper, stay there. Good boy."

I edged forward cautiously and gasped as cold water rose above my ankles and soaked into the hem of my flimsy skirt. "I can see the bottom." Talking out loud gave me confidence. "I'll be fine."

I bit my lips together as I was forced to edge out further. What had seemed no distance to where Jasper was trapped now seemed metres away and the current was stronger already, swirling around my calves. Bess had stopped her nerve-jangling barking. Thank goodness and the only sounds were my loud breathing and the rippling river. Jasper's frantic splashing seemed to have slowed down and I could see he was tiring. God knows how long he'd been in the river and why on earth were they down here by themselves? Irritability masked my fear as I moved forward again. The cold water rose to my middle as the bed shelved suddenly and I gasped and stumbled. I tried not to shiver as I planted my stick firmly on the bottom. Leaning forward, I grabbed Jasper's collar and tugged hard. The dog surged free and swam towards the shallows, then jumped out of the water shaking vigorously while Bess capered around barking joyously.

I don't have a clear recollection of what happened next. One minute I was bracing myself to turn round in the strong current and head back to the bank. Then I heard a crack and the branch of the tree above me snapped and thumped across my shoulders. Caught completely off guard, I toppled over into the water. The river surged over my head and I swallowed water. I flailed around in panic and managed to get my head above the surface, coughing and choking. The river surged past me at eye level, ominously silent, and I couldn't afford to move forward as the strength of the current tried to lift me off my feet. *If I lose control, I'll drown.* I'd lost the walking stick, but just behind me, the branch that had snapped was trailing in the water. If I could just get a grip on it, I would be able to drag myself towards the bank. I flailed one arm behind, trying to reach the trailing limb while trying to keep my feet steady. The water surged around me and hit me in the face like waves in the sea as I struggled to stay upright. I gritted my teeth and lunged for the branch. It held. Thank God! I edged towards shallow water. On the bank Jasper was whimpering and Bess growled. Oh God – the Twins were leering at me behind the dogs. My hand lost its grip, and I was face down in the river again with the current dragging my clothes into deeper water. *No, not my baby!* The description in Honoria's Journal of poor Frances's body in the river filled my memory, and I was paralysed by cold and terror.

All went quiet, even the sound of water a few inches from my face, and, as if Dee Bidwell was beside me, I distinctly heard her voice. *"Centre yourself, Clemency. Surround yourself with light. You are strong."*

Somehow, I gripped the trailing branch again and dragging myself into shallower water. I was so intent on saving myself I didn't look up to see if the Twins were still lurking. The bank was within reach and Bess, beautiful Bessie, reached forward to lick my face. I half laughed and half sobbed in relief. "Good girl," I said as I crawled onto the muddy bank, soaked, and shivering, but beyond relief that I was out of danger now. My strength had deserted me and I just sagged in the mud.

A searing pain shot around my back, and belly and I screamed. I knew at once what it was. The effort and struggle in the river had started contractions.

"No, not here," I gasped. "I can't give birth here, not with the Twins...."

Another pain gripped me and I must have passed out for a few seconds before another contraction roused me and I was aware that Jasper was lying next to me, wet, his warm panting on my cheek. I had to drag myself further onto the bank because my legs were still in the river. The effort was almost too much, but I had to do it. There was no other option. Had my waters broken? How could I tell? I was soaked to the skin and shivering, not just with cold, but with real terror.

I lifted my head, scanning the bushes, grasses, tree trunks and blue sky above me, praying for strength. *Just find the strength to get back to the house. I'm going to beat those Twins; my baby will not be born here.*

"I need to get to my feet," I said to Jasper, who was whining with flattened ears and I knew he sensed the Twins. "I need to lean on you to get up."

But I just couldn't. My legs were like jelly and my strength gone. Tears of frustration ran down my face. I was reenacting the nightmare I'd had months ago when I had been trapped in the river by the Twins, with my long skirt dragging me down.

The next contractions were not as fierce as the first ones. I put my hand between my legs to feel if the baby's head was crowning and gasped with relief when all I could feel was wetness. Where was Bess? I put my hands in the mud to push myself to my feet and shrieked as another contraction ripped through me. I lay there, shivering convulsively, my vision fading.

The thought of the Twins triumphant at last in their attempt to kill my baby sent adrenalin coursing through my body, and with grunts of pain and determination I dragged myself a few yards, at least clear of the river and rolled onto my side.

"You shall not win, you shall not win," I muttered through clenched teeth at another contraction. They were coming too close together. "Where are you Will, when I bloody need you!"

Now was the time to project a circle of protection around me. Jasper sat bolt upright and before I could grasp his fur, he shot off through the bushes. That was the moment I lost hope. I was alone and had to deliver my baby alone. Crying in pain, frustration, and fear, I lay in the mud. Did I hear voices?

"Help!" I croaked and then dear Bess appeared, tail waving furiously at the sight of me, followed by Jasper. They hadn't deserted me after all. Bess looked very pleased with herself, but I needed human help, not doggy help.

I closed my eyes at another gripping pain, and despair swept through me.

"Clemency, Clemmie, open your eyes, stay with us!" It was Matt, looking ashen with shock at my pitiful state, staring at my sodden clothes, wet and bedraggled hair, and mud all over me in complete disbelief. Joe's kind, concerned face appeared besides Matt's.

"It's ok, Clemency, you're safe now," he said gently. "Can you tell us what happened?"

"Baby," I gasped, tears of relief running down my face and into my ears. "Baby coming!"

I swore.

Matt seemed paralysed, then suddenly he was kneeling beside me. Joe similarly knelt and took my pulse. "It's galloping," he said to Matt, not so quietly that I couldn't hear.

"It's not safe to move her far now," said Matt. "Can you lift her shoulders up, and I'll lift her body? We've got to get her out of this mud onto some grass.'

He stripped off his shirt and lay it under my back on the grass, and Joe lay me down gently. I briefly felt Matt's warmth before my sodden cheesecloth shirt soaked through his shirt.

"Clemmie, I'm going to examine you," Matt said, leaning close to my face and taking hold of my hand. He had regained his colour, but his eyes were cloudy with anxiety. "Don't be alarmed. I won't hurt you." He got up and disappeared from my view. I looked into Joe's worried eyes as he knelt beside me. I saw the white smile creases round his eyes on his weathered face and streaks of white in his hair, which I'd never noticed before, along with bits of straw.

"He's gone to rinse his hands in the river, Clemency. Not the best of hygiene, but needs must in the circumstances. Can you tell us how you managed to get so wet?"

It was too hard to speak. The effort of rescuing Jasper

combined with the shock of seeing the Twins and contractions had drained all my strength. I shook my head helplessly.

"Jasper, river," I croaked and then Matt reappeared.

"Right, I'm going to take a peek. Is that ok with you, Clem?" I tried to nod. Everything was such an effort. Matt smiled at me so lovingly, I wept again.

"I promise I won't hurt you, but it's not safe to move you yet. Do you understand?"

I croaked, and Joe squeezed my arms as he supported me.

Gently, he lifted my skirt caked in mud. Joe produced a knife. "Cut it away," he said. "it's soaking and will only get in the way."

With infinite gentleness, Matt inspected me. "Baby's head is crowning," he said in a startled tone. "Now look, Clemency. You are in safe hands. You've seen me deliver lambs and I'm an expert with calving as well, so I promise you I will do all in my power to deliver your baby safely." The certainty in his voice calmed me.

He shifted into a better position. "Grip hold of Joe's hands. He won't mind if you hurt him."

"Clemmie, love, next time you have the urge to push down, push – I can see the top of baby's head."

"Don't let Twins... " I managed to mumble between gritted teeth.

"Twins? Are you having twins, Clem?" said Joe. His warmth was a comfort. But I shook my head. What I wanted to say was don't let the Twins harm my baby but they wouldn't have understood.

When the next contraction gripped me, Matt felt it with one hand on my belly. As it subsided, the urge to push came strongly.

"Push, Clemency," instructed Matt. I was so weak, but the urge was strongest and I closed my eyes. Pushing and swearing and squeezing Joe's hands like vices.

"Stop, stop, Clem," shouted Matt. "Take very short breaths, like panting, but don't push yet even if you feel you must."

"OK, Matt?" Joe's voice above me was calm.

"Cord," whispered Matt. He was sweating freely now, and he bent to release the cord from round the baby's neck.

"Pant, pant, Clemency," said Joe, and I tried to copy his breathing, while panic spread through me. Another contraction built to its powerful crescendo, and I writhed in agony.

"Wait, wait a few more seconds, Clem." Matt looked desperate, one hand cupping the baby's head, then his face cleared.

"I've done it, thank Christ," he said. "Ok Clem, next time, push as hard as you can. I had to turn little mite's shoulders as well," he said to Joe. Joe held me even more tightly.

"Squeeze my hands hard, love," he said. "See if you can hurt me even more!"

I was sure I hadn't the strength, but when the urge came, I gave a deep groaning moan and pushed.

"That's it, good girl, Clemmie, nearly there! Wow!" The baby slithered wetly into Matt's hands. "Clemmie, you've got a son, and he's a whopper!"

Matt was scooping mucus from the baby's mouth, cradling it against his chest as he did so.

"Well done, Clemency, love, I'm just taking my arms away a second." Joe pulled his shirt over his head and handed it to Matt, who wiped the baby down, then wrapped him in it. The baby gave a brief cry, then a proper wail, and both men grinned with relief.

"Good lad!" Joe said.

"Is he ok?" I croaked. Whilst I felt utterly drained, I needed to see my baby. "I'll lay him on your tummy, but first we have to get your wet shirt off so it doesn't soak the baby." Matt looked apologetic but set to work with Joe's knife, and the flimsy fabric ripped easily. He lay my son on my breast as he wailed. His little face was pink and red and purple, his eyes puffy and screwed up, his little nose squashed, his brows in a cross frown and his hair slick with mucus, but he was the most precious thing in the world to me.

"Joe, if you can just lift Clem's shoulders higher- we need to get the placenta delivered."

As Joe raised me, sitting behind me so that I could lean on his chest, I felt another contraction and gasped. Matt pushed on my belly and the placenta came free in mucus and blood. The dogs circled, sniffing.

"We need to get her to hospital," Matt said to Joe. "I can't cut the umbilical cord with this knife, too unhygienic and she's bleeding." He gathered up the flimsy remnants of my skirt and placed it to staunch the bleeding.

We all heard a wailing siren. "Hope that's our ambulance," said Joe. "I called for one as soon as we knew we couldn't get her back to the house. I'd better run back and guide them here, as they'll be waiting at the house."

Matt changed places with Joe so that he could support me, and I leaned on his chest. He put his arms around me and, despite his bodily warmth, I shivered uncontrollably again.

Billy wailed. Instinctively, I guided his little mouth to my nipple and after a bit of snuffling and fumbling, he suddenly latched on and an exquisite pain shot through me.

Matt's arms tightened around me and I looked up and, despite my shivering, smiled shyly. I was surprised to see tears in his eyes. "Thank you, Matt," I whispered. "You've just saved our lives."

He kissed the top of my head. "So, what's the little blighter's name?" he asked, wiping his nose with the back of his hand.

"Billy," I said as the newly named son sucked noisily. "He's going to be called Billy Matthew Joseph Payne- Ashton. I wish Will was here."

Another bout of shivering and faintness overwhelmed me. Matt immediately noticed and tightened his arms around me again. "Hang on in there, Clem. The paramedics are on their way."

My eyes closed with exhaustion and as Matt exhorted me to stay awake, I noticed Billy had fallen asleep.

Suddenly, the dogs barked, and Joe and two paramedics carrying backpacks and a folded stretcher appeared. Joe had obviously filled them in because one of them immediately set to work clamping the umbilical cord while the other lay the stretcher down on a dry surface and started unfolding blankets. They didn't comment on this half naked and soaking wet woman lying on a riverbank.

"Hello, Clemency, we'll take good care of you and your baby now. We'll take vital signs in the ambulance and attach a drip. You need a vitamin K shot as well, Clemency.

I heard the paramedic talking to Joe. "She's very pale and tachycardic and there's a concern with the blood loss, only it's hard to tell in this position, it's so wet and muddy."

"We drove down to the mill. it's a lot nearer than carrying her through the woods back to the house," said Joe to Matt, who was kneeling and rubbing my arms.

I was floating in a shivery, pain-free void, but I heard their voices clearly.

"Serena is on her way. She stopped off to visit an old dear who hasn't been well and now she's cursing herself for not being here."

"I doubt whether she could have done anything more," said Matt. "She wouldn't have known where to look. If it hadn't been for the dogs coming to find us..." Matt's voice trailed off. "She could have died out here, and the baby."

Joe put his hands on Matt's shoulders. "You saved her, lad, and her baby. That's all that matters now. What you need is a stiff drink. Christ, I could murder one as well!"

They both laughed and as the paramedics stretchered me and my son to the waiting ambulance, Serena ran up, having parked her car next to the ambulance on Joe's instructions.

"Oh my God, why is she in such a state?" she cried.

"Clemency love, you'll soon be ok. I should have been here. I'm so sorry."

"Is the father coming in the ambulance?" asked one paramedic as the other one began setting up a drip. There was a silence.

"Neither of us is the father," Joe volunteered, and I watched Matt turn bright red. "Clemency's husband is abroad and Clemency lives at Harthill House with us."

The paramedic turned to Serena.

"Would you like to accompany your relative?" he asked, and Serena nodded vigorously without admitting she was not a relative of mine.

She stepped up into the ambulance, then turned back to hug Matt. "Thank you, thank you."

"I'll just say goodbye to Clemency," he said.

I felt his warm breath as he kissed my cheek, and I gripped his hand in eternal gratitude.

Nobody else noticed the Twins skulking in the trees lining the river, their faces twisted in fury.

Chapter Thirty-Five

Little Billy was in an incubator in the Neonatal Intensive Care Unit. I was in the ward with a feverishly high temperature and I hadn't seen him since our arrival, but a cheerful nurse called Ume kept me updated on his progress.

My mother and father had anxiously rushed to the hospital, but I only had a vague memory of them as I drifted in and out of sleep. Will had been out of signal range in Greece, but on my third day in hospital and with my temperature close to normal again, Joe and Serena came to visit as they had every day, although in my semi-delirious state I hadn't been aware of their presence. Joe had managed to get in touch with Will. Because of their isolated position and a couple of punctures on the support vehicle bringing him to Athens, it would take another couple of days before he reached the airport, but he'd be coming as fast as he was able.

"Can I ask you what you were doing in the river?" Joe asked. It must have been bothering him, because Serena laid a hand on his arm. "I can't understand why the dogs were down there. Serena was sure they were in the house when she left."

"I never checked, love," said Serena guiltily. "I took them out early and I'm sure they had followed me into the house. I've been blaming myself all this time. You could have drowned. I'm so sorry, Clemency."

I put my hand out to hers. "Please don't blame yourself. The main thing is I had two superheroes who rescued me!"

I turned to Joe, who still frowned. "I heard dogs barking when I was on the sun lounger. I thought I recognised Bess' bark, and it sounded as if she was in some sort of difficulty. I knew there was nobody around I could call, so I just headed down the track. I did not know they were by the river until I saw Jasper tangled up in some branches hanging over the river and I just knew I had to get him out before... before he was swept over the weir." I stumbled over my words as vivid pictures of my struggle in the river and the realisation that the Twins were responsible made my throat and chest constrict.

"I can't believe Jasper would go in the river by himself," Joe railed. "Did you see anyone else down there? No, of course you didn't, otherwise you wouldn't have ended up in such a state. I'm sorry, love, I can't believe the dogs nearly caused a nasty accident."

I shook my head, trying to hide my distress. I wished I could tell them about my theory that the Twins had somehow lured the dogs into danger so that they could harm me and my unborn child. It sounded scarcely credible to me.

"They must have followed a rambler," Joe shrugged.

I was saved from further obfuscating by the arrival of Ume with a wheelchair.

"As your temperature's down and blood pressure's fine," she announced. "It's time to get to know your son!" In the Neonatal Unit, she lifted Billy from the incubator. He was free from drips and dressed in a Babygro and a little hat and mittens. As the nurse placed his warm little body in my arms, his violet eyes opened and he frowned up at me, focussing on my face with deep intensity. He was asking me where I had been for the last few days. Tears ran down my cheeks as I kissed his downy cheeks and little nose. Immediately he started rootling for food. For the first time since I'd held him to my breast soaking wet and semi-conscious on the riverbank, he remembered and latched on so ferociously that I winced.

"Told you he was feisty, didn't I?" Ume laughed. I forgot about Joe and Serena watching outside the unit, but I felt my face flush as I remembered lying in Matt's arms while Billy suckled. Had he been to visit? The last few days were so hazy, I couldn't recall.

Next day I was discharged. I'd bathed Billy and marvelled at his little body. His crib had been moved next to my hospital bed, and he'd had several feeds. He certainly was a hungry baby! Joe and Serena collected us and Joe carried Billy and installed him in the baby car seat, a gift from Mum and Dad, while I leaned on Serena. I was surprisingly weak.

As we approached the old ash, I broke out into a cold sweat. I had no crystals and I couldn't get a grip on myself to project a protective bubble. There were no shapes lurking, and I exhaled, holding onto little Billy's mittened hand and thanking our guardian angels.

Joe carried him upstairs, and I followed slowly, my leg and stomach muscles protesting.

"You'll soon be back in shape," Serena reassured me. "I'll bring you up a cup of tea."

It was a relief to lie on the bed with Billy asleep in his crib. There were emails, messages and cards congratulating the 'proud parents' and I was able to answer a few of them before he woke. He lay for a while, his eyes trying to focus on his surroundings and a colourful mobile hanging above his crib, and when I leaned over, I swear he recognised me by the way he wriggled even though he was swaddled in a soft blanket that Evie and Ruby had sent.

One message was from Evie.

> Let us know us when we can come up! His
> Aunties are dying to see little Billy!

And there was a similar one from Kim. I replied to both, saying they were welcome anytime.

Joe insisted on carrying Billy down the stairs the next morning, and I based myself in the sitting room. I was longing to get the Family room renovated for daily use.

The next day, after Billy had had his morning feed, I tucked him into his buggy and decided to give him some fresh air round the gardens. Serena had put all the stuff I'd left by the sun lounger when I'd gone looking for the dogs in my room. I put the crystals in the buggy and prepared my protective bubble. Terror of the twins now gripped my heart as the recurring memory of my ordeal in the river kept resurfacing. Each night I had woken in a sheen of perspiration and a thumping heart as I relived it, convinced I had been crying out during the nightmare. *I should have counselling; I'll invite Dee over.*

Perhaps Matt thought I'd been embarrassed by him delivering Billy, and was keeping away, but I needed to thank him. He'd waved from a distance several times and then hurried back to his tasks.

The sun was warm, and I sat under the cedar tree, Billy fast asleep, and we were joined by Serena who'd brought out a jug of elderflower cordial and homemade biscuits. He was such a good baby, sleeping between feeds, waking up hungry but not screaming. I loved lying him against my shoulder with his little head in the crook of my neck so that I could breathe in his sweet baby smell and feel his warm breath while I sang any song that came into my head. He still had that reproachful look in his eye sometimes and I had whispered to him, "I hope you look at your daddy like this when you see him. He needs to squirm a little and apologise for being absent." I'd sent Will a video. And luckily, his phone had a signal as he neared civilisation again. "He looks like Winston Churchill!" he'd replied.

I agreed. "But he'll start looking like himself soon!"

Molly's reaction had been unsettling. "Another babby for the nursery," she said, peering into his buggy. "I hope for the best for you all," she said enigmatically.

"He won't be going anywhere near that old nursery," I retorted. "You know it's haunted as well as I do!"

I wasn't expecting Mollie's reaction. She peered suspiciously at me.

"You've seen something up there?"

"I've heard screaming and a baby crying. I read a journal that tells that one of Will's ancestors lost her babies in that nursery. They died. And I've seen other things as well."

"Aye, a lot of babies have been unfortunate, but if the estate had gone to the rightful persons, none of this would have happened." Mollie had regained her gritty attitude. "That's why I wished you well. A wrong was done centuries ago and which should have been righted."

I stared openmouthed at her, but just then Serena appeared and broke up the tense atmosphere. Mollie smiled and went off with Serena, and I stood looking after her with a mixture of incredulity and rage building up in me. What on earth did she mean?

It didn't take me long to work it out. While Billy suckled, I remembered the words in Honoria's Journal. Honoria had been clever outwitting Gerard's ambitions but had given no thought to the consequences of how his deep-seated grudge would be passed on to his own twin sons, Wilfred and George. And those twin sons were continuing the family vendetta, even to this day. I'd skimmed through Honoria's Journal before Billy's birth and read how the Twins had remained, working on the land, and how they'd had continual fights with Edwin's twin sons, Samuel and Julius.

Honoria had written that she was convinced they had caused the death of one of the twins, Julius, but nothing could be proved.

I was overwhelmed with dread and as my embrace of Billy tightened; he stopped sucking and fixed me with one of his penetrating gazes. I rocked him while trying to stem my rising fear. Now I understood why Roberta had fled from the house, taking a young Will with her. Accidents had happened to her during pregnancies. Uncle Daniel's wife had met with an accident at the house. How many more tragedies had happened that were unrecorded? I couldn't stay here now.

Mollie's veiled threat confirmed what I already sensed since my first interactions with the Twins: they didn't want any other male rivals. Even in death, their malevolence controlled the present. Crystals, protective bubbles: none of them would prevent their evil intentions and chanting mantras for evermore was a futile gesture. I wish I could have laughed at myself for being so unbelievably naïve. And the worst thing was I was alone in all this. Mollie must know, but she could or would do nothing. I doubted that Dee Bidwell could get rid of the Twins' presences. Even if the house was exorcised by a priest and evil spirits driven out, I would live in continual dread that they would return. Although nothing ever happened in the house, I couldn't imprison myself and my child. And I would be scared to have more children in case ...in case what? In case Billy met with an accident and I was set on the same path as Frances, destined to bear unfortunate male heirs? This was the twenty-first century, for God's sake, and there were no such things as ridiculous curses.

I had to take several deep breaths to quell my panic. Billy must have sensed my emotions because his little face puckered up. I didn't need to take immediate action. Will's mother was arriving any day now, and so was Will. I would go back to London with him to give me some breathing space. I would be more than sorry to abandon Harthill; I loved the house and the tranquil countryside around it. I had even made notes on how to use the house to its full potential.

My phone rang. "I'm at Heathrow just waiting for my bags," Will shouted. "I'm going to get a taxi all the way. It'll be quicker than faffing around getting the Range Rover."

"Oh, Will, I'm so happy!" I said, leaking tears. "And I have the Range Rover here at Harthill. I drove here with loads of baby stuff."

"Right, tell little Billy, Daddy's on his way! Love you both!"

I changed Billy after I'd fed and burped him and he'd fallen asleep. I left him on the sofa, wedged in by cushions while I went downstairs to tell Serena and Joe. Joe looked at the kitchen clock.

"It'll take him about an hour and a half by road, so no rush, love."

Serena sat with the sleeping baby while I tidied myself. I was still pale waking every night for feeds and after nightmares. I put some blusher on my cheeks and changed my shirt. Billy had managed to miss the muslin on my shoulder while being winded and had dribbled down my front and back.

My fears miraculously receded at the prospect of Will's homecoming, and I swear there was a little smile on Billy's face as I tucked him into the buggy. "It's wind," laughed Serena.

The day was overcast and still. Joe was cleaning out his Defender and peered into the buggy.

"Off to meet Daddy at last," he grinned. As I pushed the buggy over the gravel forecourt, I had a foreboding. Last time I'd set out to meet Will, something had happened.

Stupid!

There was a strange whooshing sound and a noise of tinkling glass. I looked back at the windows but saw nothing unusual. Joe had heard the same noise and came a little way down the drive with me. He was soon striding away. The surface of the drive was uneven under the buggy wheels and I thought the motion would waken Billy. In the distance, I saw Joe quicken his pace and then break into a run. Someone was coming up the drive. "Will," I called happily. Perhaps he'd got the taxi driver to drop him off at the entrance. Only it didn't look like Will; this person was staggering and streaked with red.

"No!" I cried and ran, pushing the buggy as fast as I could. The dread feeling welling up made me stumble. Joe was holding the stranger and lowered him on to the grass verge as he put his mobile to his ear. Then he set off faster than I'd ever seen him run and I panted after him, my leg and stomach muscles screaming at the unaccustomed use. *No, no, no, please, no....* Blood covered the stranger's head, but he was conscious, and I was compelled to run on. "Don't go, love," he shouted. "It's a horrible mess."

Urgency and adrenalin drove me on. Where the old ash had stood, there was a gap and the huge tree lay right across the drive. Joe was somewhere among the mess of branches, scrabbling through them. And in front of the enormous roots of the fallen tree stood the Twins, facing me, smirking.

I stopped, paralysed. I wanted to reach the ruined tree, but I was afraid for my baby. I saw Joe crawling out backwards, his head bowed to the ground, and I knew. I knew Will was under that mighty tree.

"Bastards, you bastards!" I shrieked. "Cowardly, fucking murderers!" Joe heard me and ran towards me. The Twins were behind him insolent in their stance: no shouting or screaming would affect them in any way. Joe grabbed me bodily, trying to turn me away.

"It's Will, isn't it? He's dead, isn't he?" Joe stood mutely, his face and arms covered in scratches from crawling under the branches, and he just held on tightly to me. Somehow, we were trying to draw strength from each other.

"Ambulance is on its way," he croaked. But he wouldn't meet

my eyes and I knew it would be too late to save Will, and I sobbed uncontrollably.

"Sit down, love, there's nothing you can do. Sit with your baby." He led me to the grass, and I fell, my legs unable to hold me up. I remembered Billy in his buggy, but Joe had placed it beside me and even through my screaming and shrieking he'd remained asleep.

"Bastards," I yelled again. Joe was on his phone again. Later I found out he had been calling the fire brigade and police, and the ambulance he called earlier for the taxi driver. My body felt as if it was being torn in two; one half wanting to get to Will and the other half to escape with my baby from the paralysing malevolence of the Twins.

Suddenly there was a feather-light pressure on my shoulder. I stared round and there was Mollie, but instead of looking at her wrinkles, her face was smooth and her blue eyes were full of sorrow. I shook her hand off. If she had been honest with me from the beginning, none of this would have happened.

"I am so sorry, my lover," she said, and although she was beside me, her voice was faint. "This is all my fault. Those two hulking brutes are my kin and I should have controlled them a long time ago. I let me own feelings get in the way and now it's too late to make amends. You'll probably never forgive me and I don't blame you. God bless you and your babby. Let me deal with these two buggers now. I will take them with me and mark my words, my lover. I promise they'll not trouble you ever again."

Joe was gazing at the tree, stunned, and didn't appear to notice Mollie. Through my tears of grief and rage, I watched her march up to the Twins, diminutive against their hulks, her wild hair writhing like the snakes on Medusa's head and reaching up, she clouted them both around their heads. I watched, astonished, as she firmly placed herself between them, gripped their arms and dragged them round. Mollie turned her head, smiled an apology at me, and the three of them slowly receded. My head grew hot and my eyes dimmed.

∼

My mind deliberately blocked out chunks of what happened over the following days. The only reality was endlessly feeding Billy or clutching his warm, soft body to me. He was my anchor and the one tiny soul who saved me from a black pit of despair. I was aware of people gathering, Roberta, full of grief and remorse, Uncle Daniel, ever on hand to hold little Billy; my mother and father doing endless practical things like pushing Billy in his buggy because they felt helpless to penetrate my grief. Evie and Ruby were uncharacteristically subdued, looking into my shuttered face.

The funeral in the chapel was simple, and someone had filled it with late summer blooms. I remember telling Joe that Will wouldn't want anyone to wear black and accordingly, people came dressed in normal clothing, which of course did nothing to ease the deep shock that rendered everyone helplessly tongue-tied. All our team had come, trying to express sympathy to me yet struggling to overcome their own shock and grief. Some of our regular clients had turned up at the funeral, expressing their condolences by taking my hand or giving me the lightest of embraces. The biggest surprise which shook me a little out of my catatonic state was the arrival of Rafaella, her lower leg still encased in a supportive boot, accompanied by Jimmy, Dunc and Sam. As she embraced me, I felt her sobs, but I stood as stiff as a block of ice.

"I can't believe he's gone," she sobbed. "Will was so full of life and I ...we'll all miss him so much. This is so dreadful for you, Clemency."

There was nothing I could say or indeed wanted to say to her. She must have left sometime later after the refreshments had been served. I remember being embraced by Dunc and Sam and Jimmy as they shed unashamed tears.

Hugo had given a eulogy in the chapel, which had included light-hearted moments in Will's life which produced ripples of laughter. It hadn't been that long since he'd given the Best Man speech at our wedding. What I hadn't known was that Will had requested cremation, but although I knew I was being cowardly, I could not attend. Joe, Serena, Matt, Roberta and Uncle Daniel, and Douglas Pargeter from the Trust accompanied Will's body to the Crematorium the day after the funeral.

After the service, as Dad guided me to Joe's Defender, something caught my eye. In the shadows where the angel mounted eternal guard, I saw the form of a young girl, bonnet in hand, a sad smile on her lips……

Serena had laid on tea and refreshments, helped by Mum and Roberta. The doors to the drawing room were open as the day was warm and sunny. Conversations murmured around me. Mum pushed a plate of refreshments in front of me.

"Come on, love," she said. "try to eat a little. You are starving the poor mite as well as yourself." I took the plate from her, too tired to argue, and satisfied, she patted my arm. Then Matt appeared with a red-faced bawling bundle and he thrust Billy into my arms, sitting down beside me on the yellow silk sofa. An inconsequential thought flitted through my mind: *in a few months, this lovely old sofa will be covered with sticky fingerprints.*

"He's mighty hungry," said Matt. "He's been protesting for quite a while."

I draped the muslin that accompanied Billy's feeds across my shoulder and lifted my top automatically. If people were embarrassed, then tough, but apart from a few smiles in my direction, nobody looked offended. "Is it ok if I sit with you?" asked Matt. He stroked Billy's fuzzy head gently.

I nodded, wincing as Billy's powerful suck sent prickly pains through me. I turned to Matt. I really hadn't seen or spoken to him since the day of Billy's birth and I looked at his normally tanned face, so like Will's, yet so different. Today he looked pale, serious, and sad.

"Where's Mollie, your gran?" I asked, as Billy's suck grew less fierce now that he was filling up. His little fist rested possessively on my breast. "I need to thank her. She tried to comfort me that morning......" I couldn't finish the sentence.

Matt stared, frowning, as he reached out to stroke Billy's head again. He seemed unaware how near my breast his hand was, and it was such a natural action, I felt comforted by it.

"Gran? You don't know? Ah, God, no, of course you wouldn't..."

"What? What is it?" I asked.

"Gran died that morning, Clem. She died that same morning as Will... as ... Will." Matt struggled for words as I stared at him. "She had a massive stroke at home and never recovered."

It was my turn to look incredulous. "No, that can't be true," I said firmly. "She came up to me. I was screaming my head off. She said she was sorry she hadn't done something about them when I first came to Harthill. She said they were kin and then she marched them away."

"I've no idea what you are talking about, Clem, but Gran died at home that morning. I went round to cut her hedge after all the chores and found her on the floor. I couldn't help her. Perhaps if I'd been sooner, I might have resuscitated her. I just don't know. Anyway, I phoned for an ambulance and when I saw one going up the drive I sprinted after it, thinking they'd missed the Lodge. Then I saw what had happened to Will."

"I'm so sorry, Matt," I whispered. "I don't understand either, but she was definitely with me." I clutched his arm, and we sat silently with our own thoughts. *I must tell him about the Twins now.*

Billy lay back with a sated expression and I sat him up, his head lolling, milk dribbling from his mouth. I patted his back, and he gave a loud burp and bottom burp at the same time.

Matt and I glanced at each other and burst out laughing. It felt good to laugh again. Emotion suddenly thawed the icicles around my heart and enormous sobs burst from me uncontrollably. My mother took Billy as all my pent-up grief and guilt rendered me a sobbing wreck, nose and eyes running, and I couldn't stop. Poor Matt, alarmed at first, tentatively put his arm around me and then held me close with both arms. I fell asleep a little while later, still sobbing like a baby, and Matt never let me go the whole time.

Epilogue

Six years later

It was Billy's sixth birthday, and the table had been laid under the cedar tree, ready for an invasion of his classmates. Most had accepted the invitation to his outdoor party. Some were away on holiday as it was August and still on school holidays, but we were expecting a good number. This year I'd invited parents and younger siblings to bring their own picnics to save them from driving back and forth. The lawns were spacious enough to hold such a gathering; after all, the annual Summer Music Festival brought in a far larger audience.

The party was set for early afternoon, so Matt could do the evening milking. He and Joe had organised outdoor games. One game was an obstacle course using straw bales, and I hoped there weren't too many children who would hate having spiky straw all over them. There was a gentle fishing game and a ring toss game and a pyramid knockdown and build up game for two teams.

Serena and I had painted old plastic plant pots for the teams to knock down with balls and a race to build them up into a pyramid shape again. To end there was going to be a tug of war in which parents and children could take part together, and a Spiderman cake with candles. Hopefully, everybody would go home exhausted.

Billy charged around before everybody arrived, giving me time to reminisce.

I still suffered flashbacks and nightmares about Billy's birth and Will's death. Serena and Joe had looked after me and the baby like another set of grandparents and I clung on to Billy. Evie and Ruby visited often. Hugo took over from Will and although I was officially on maternity leave, I had doubted whether I would ever go back to the office knowing Will would never be there again, yet I did eventually return. I had no desire to return to Will's flat. Roberta had packed up all my stuff and brought it over to Harthill House.

Mollie had been true to her word: the Twins had never appeared to me again. That was the only thing that assuaged my grief: that Billy and I were safe at Harthill. There was no lingering malignancy where the ash tree had stood.

Dee Bidwell was a pillar of strength for months. She'd arrive and listen to my incoherent ramblings and then she'd take my hands, close her eyes, and we'd sit quietly while her healing strength flowed through me, calming me. When I railed about the uselessness of crystals and mantras and stupid bubbles, she insisted they had protected me. She told me that when I had been struggling in the river; she had suddenly sensed I was in danger. I remembered hearing her calm voice that had probably helped save my life.

"There you are, that's definitely proof," Dee smiled. She taught me yoga, which I initially resisted, but soon found therapeutic.

Billy's first Christmas was in the company of my parents, Roberta, Evie and Ruby. Joe and Matt had erected a Christmas tree in the hall and despite not feeling at all Christmassy, Serena insisted I help her decorate it with Billy grabbing at the branches, shrieking excitedly.

Serena wanted us to drink a toast to Mollie; her death had been overlooked because of the awfulness of Will's accident and Serena and Matt remembered her with tales of her life and mannerisms.

"She had second sight, you know," Matt had said, "and she was always saying we were connected to the family."

"She was. And you are," I remembered her words as I'd sat howling in the drive that terrible afternoon. "She told me when I came home from hospital with Billy that a wrong had been done centuries ago and someone had to right it."

"What?" Roberta started, her face paling at Mollie's words. Serena and Joe looked at each other in disbelief and confusion. They had known Mollie for years and Roberta had known her before them. Matt sat as still as a statue; his eyes fixed on the flames in the fireplace.

"Mollie appeared to me in the drive that morning," I faltered but had to finish. It was important that a lot of happenings were explained and a line drawn under events. "I thought she'd come from her cottage to help. She told me how sorry she was. She said it was all her fault, that she should have controlled the Twins. They were her kin, and they felt they had been robbed of their inheritance, and she had been sympathetic. But it wasn't Mollie, it was her spirit, because Matt told me a lot later that she'd had a stroke and died that same morning. She took the Twins away, and she kept her word. I haven't seen the Twins or felt their horrible presence since and there have been no more accidents. She righted the wrong herself" "

"What Twins?" asked Joe. He and Serena looked thoroughly

bewildered and I wouldn't have blamed them for thinking that my ordeal by the river and the shock of Will's death had unhinged me.

"The Twins were the ghosts of Wilfred and George Barnard." I said calmly. All my fear and horror at encountering those evil apparitions had dissipated and I could think logically again. "They were the grandsons of Sir Horace, and as males, they felt they were done out of inheriting Harthill House and estate. The estate was entailed on an elder son, James Barnard, and because he had no surviving sons, the estate passed to the male heirs of his daughter, Honoria, and their male heirs in perpetuity. It was a race for Honoria's son to provide heirs and there were terrible tragedies along the way, but Honoria managed to keep the estate in the hands of her father's successors. I think I must have been the only one who could see the Twins' ghosts," I said. "Apart from Mollie. I'm sure she guessed I was psychic because we had some weird conversations about the past."

Roberta had rocked backwards and forwards. "I knew there was something evil here," she said. "Things happened to me while I was pregnant that couldn't be explained and I lost a child." She momentarily covered her face with her hands, then spoke again more confidently. "When it started happening again after Will was born, I knew I had to get away. Poor Geoffrey never knew anything and such was my need to protect William that our relationship ended, even though I still loved him. My poor, poor babies..." she crooned, grieving for both her sons. I got up and placed the slumbering Billy in her lap. He would bring her comfort as he did to me.

Roberta's eyes were shiny with unshed tears. "Geoffrey's sister Pauline had an accident when she was pregnant. She crashed into that old ash. She died, and the baby was stillborn."

Poor Daniel. No wonder he advised me to leave.

Evie had fetched the Family History chart and the photo album. She turned the pages until she found the photo of the family sitting at the laden tea table under the cedar tree. The Twins were there facing Honoria, and I hadn't recognised them at first.

"This is Honoria, the Matriarch in the old sense of the word," said Evie, pointing as everybody leaned forward. "She was quite ancient when this photo was taken, but I think she was unable to relinquish her hold on Harthill House. I'm surprised she hasn't been haunting the place too. Sorry," she said as she saw the horrified expressions on Serena's and Roberta's faces.

"At least she wasn't evil," I said. "She was just scheming and manipulative."

Evie turned the page of the photo album and looked enquiringly at me. I hated them; they had done their worst, but they would never defeat me again.

The sullen faces and mean eyes of George and Wilfred stared out, caught in perpetuity.

"Poor Clemmie. I believed her when she said they were stalking her. We tried to help in a haphazard way, didn't we, going to see Osborne Stafford and Dee? We should have talked to Mollie instead," said Evie.

But would she have helped?

"I'm going to make more tea," said Serena, standing up. "All these revelations are rather upsetting and, in some way, make me feel guilty as well."

"And I'm just going to fetch something from home," said Matt, who hadn't said a word throughout the conversation. Perhaps he was regretting mentioning that Mollie was psychic.

Joe rubbed his hand through his hair. "I don't know what to say. I believe every word you've told us, Clemency, but all these years Serena and I have looked after the old place and never an idea of all these..." he searched for a suitable word, "undercurrents going on all around us."

"This house IS a lovely old house and there's nothing bad in it," I said, smiling, but resolved to invite Dee to burn her smudge sticks of sage in the old nursery with its sad atmosphere to pray for Frances and her babies.

"I don't know what could have been done for myself and poor Pauline when we suffered unexplainable accidents. I just knew I had to get away." Roberta stroked Billy's head. "He is so like Will as a baby and you don't know what a comfort that is to me."

I smiled. "I promise he'll be brought up surrounded by photos and stories of his daddy." Will had never held his son and aching grief rose in me again.

Serena and Ruby returned with tea and warm mince pies, and Joe wandered off to fetch beer.

Matt reappeared with a shopping bag. He carefully lifted out its contents and placed it in a space on the coffee table. It was a large bible, ancient in appearance. Evie leaned forward, immediately eager.

"I've had to make a start in clearing out Gran's stuff, and I'm not doing very well. I honestly don't know what to keep and what to throw away." He turned to Serena. "Can you spare the time to come down and advise me? I'm her only living relative, so I suppose I ought to hold on to some family keepsakes."

"Of course I will," replied Serena. "Just give me a shout when you're ready."

"Thanks, two pairs of hands will be better than one. While I was listening to Clemency's story, I remembered Gran's Bible, which was always on the sideboard. I don't think she was religious, but it is a family heirloom. And I remembered what I'd seen when I'd looked at it ages ago and it rang a bell."

He opened the Bible to the first blank pages and, written in several different handwriting was a list of names and dates.

"Oh, this is wonderful," breathed Evie, "family names in bibles are such a valuable source. I'll read out the names:

The first name written is Gerard Barnard, born 1750, died 1832. Married Lily Stokes 1811.

George and Wilfred Barnard, born April 1812 sons of Gerrard and Lily Barnard. Died 6th June 1912.

Wilfred Barnard married Joan Perkins in 1833. She died 10th July 1850.

Elias Barnard, born 2nd July 1834 only son of Wilfred and Joan Barnard."

"Perkins," said Matt. "That's the name which rang a bell. It was Gran's name before she married."

"George doesn't appear to have married. The family names go on until we get to a Philomena Barnard who marries Thomas Crane on the 20th of May, 1910." Evie said.

There was a collective indrawn breath from all of us at the sound of the name Crane. I looked at Matt. His lips were pressed together and his face was pale.

"Edward Crane, son of Thomas and Philomena Crane, born 10th March 1912

Thomas Crane died 16th September 1916 of injuries suffered in Somme Offensive, France

Edward Crane married Alicia Payne 17th March 1934."

"Payne," I interjected. "Edwin's surname."

"John Crane born 12th June 1935, son of Edward and Alicia Crane

John Crane married Mollie Perkins 15th March 1958

Jack Crane, born 21st September 1959, only son of John and Mollie Crane

John Crane died 11th November 1975

Jack Crane married Sandra Webb 2nd June 1979

Matthew John Crane born 5th October 1980, only son of Jack and Sandra Crane

Death of Jack and Sandra Crane in car accident 2nd January 2000."

"I suppose I ought to add the death of Gran in there," said Matt woodenly. "Gran was related to the Joan Perkins who married Wilfred Barnard, one of the Twins. She hinted on rightful place but we never took much notice of what she said. That's why she told you they were kin, Clem."

"Over the page there are all the names of family stemming from the Payne/ Barnard family," said Evie, glancing at Matt's expressionless face.

"Edwin Payne born July 1790, elder son of Honoria Barnard and Gyles Payne, grandson of James Barnard. Then there's a list on the Payne side of the family all the way until one Alicia Payne marries Edward Crane in 1934, and then the line carries on until the births of William and Matthew." Evie finished. "So you are distantly related to the Barnards and Paynes, Matt."

Matt looked around with a thoroughly miserable face. "What does it all matter now," he said and before any of us could answer he was on his feet. "Got to see to the milking. Thanks for Christmas and all that, and I'll let you know when I'm at Gran's cottage, Serena." He left abruptly, and I prickled uneasily. Billy was making angry cries as Roberta held him to her shoulder and I took him again to finish his feed.

"I'll build all this information into a proper tree; it'll be easier to assimilate." Evie said.

"But what does it all mean?" said Roberta in a bewildered tone. "Does it mean that Harthill House really belongs to Matthew?"

It was the sixty-four-thousand-dollar question that we all wanted to know, but dreaded the answer.

"It all goes back to the fight for inheritance between Gerard and Edwin," said Evie. "Edwin's grandfather, James had already put in provisos in his Will about male heirs of his daughter, Honoria and that seems to be the legal basis for the rest of his successors. If Gerard contested that Will, it mustn't have been proved, otherwise there would be no doubt that his line would have succeeded. Gerard was obviously so bitter losing an asset like Harthill Estate that he passed on his bitterness to his sons all the way down the line until it reached Mollie. To her credit, she never tried to indoctrinate Matt, as he's clearly unsettled by it."

"I've got to go and talk to Matt." I couldn't explain my uneasiness.

"He said it didn't matter, so why stir up trouble? The estate should be safe in Billy's hands now. All these terrible accidents and incidents should never have happened and so many lives have been lost or damaged." Roberta looked quite upset. All she wanted was a straightforward life for herself and her grandson, with no more complications.

When Billy had been fed and changed, I put him on his play mat on the floor again. He had already learned to turn over onto his stomach and lay kicking his legs and waving his arms, trying to reach his soft toys, so with two aunties and grandparents to watch over him, I slipped out to find Matt. It was dark outside; clouds covered the moon and wind sighed through the trees. I made my way to the milking barn. Although the threat of the Twins' presences had gone, I still gripped the torch tightly. Floodlights illumined the area around the yard and Matt was hosing the concrete after milking. His beanie hat was pulled low and his face set in a grim expression. Before I could say anything, he jumped in first. "It's best if I move on from here. There's too much baggage attached to me. I should never have brought the Bible over. I should have read it first. I'll stay while an advert is placed in all the farming mags and for the interviews. There'll be no shortage of suitable applicants...."

"Matt, slow down," I put my hand on his blue overalled arm, hoping he wouldn't shake it off. "What on earth are you talking about? You don't need to go anywhere. We need you here... I need you here. You, of all people, have no baggage attached."

"Your mother-in-law is scared stiff I'm going to take over the house and estate. I can't stay because it was my ancestors who caused your suffering......."

"Matt, stop. It was a shock to all of us. We were all surprised. But it changes nothing. You belong here, you are linked to the house and estate, and there's no way I'm going to attach any blame to you for what those horrible Twins did. Please don't think of going, Matt. I don't think I could bear it on top of everything else that has happened." I tried to swallow the lump in my throat and the prickle of tears. I longed to tell him how much I'd relied on his presence during Will's many absences, and if truth be told, since Will's death.

"Besides," I said desperately, "you've got to be here for Billy's christening. I would like you and Joe to be his godparents."

"Are you blackmailing me?" said Matt, but his face was clearing and he gave a lobsided smile. "But it'll be a privilege. Billy's going to be a little terror round here soon! I admit I'd miss him and you all...."

"He can be an extra pair of hands to you as he grows," I flashed back, a warm feeling spreading through me. "In fact, in the spring, you can teach me to help with milking and lambing. I can't sit and mope all the time. It places such a strain on all of you here.... I don't mind getting my hands dirty."

"You'll have a lot more than dirty hands if you really mean it," said Matt. "And little Billy will be covered in muck and mud and worse most days!"

It was as if a heavy load had been lifted from our shoulders. Matt took off his beanie and rumpled his already tousled hair.

"I can learn to drive the tractor," I began, then started laughing at his horrified face.

"But if you are serious, you can start by helping me walk the ladies back to the bottom meadow."

A half-moon appeared through scudding clouds. The air was

getting colder. There would be a frost later. I held five bar gates open while Matt herded the cows through. His dog followed closely.

He led me back through a different gate behind the stables and back onto the drive. Where once the mighty ash had stood, we could now see stars studding the sky. Matt and Joe had sawn up the entire tree and even the roots had disappeared.

"What do you think of creating a wildflower bed where the old ash was?" I asked.

"Sounds good to me. It will be like a natural, everlasting memorial to Will."

"Without dwelling on the past again, so many tragic accidents happened around that old tree. I think that's what drew the Twins there."

"Well, we'll ease the memories by planting living things. Good idea, Clem," and Matt reached out and squeezed my shoulder. I felt a lightness in my heart that I hadn't felt for months.

∽

On a blustery day at the end of February, I strapped Billy into his car seat and set off for Salisbury, parking near the Cathedral Close. Billy looked round eyed at everything as I pointed out cars and buses and people. We turned into Uncle Daniel's gate and his tiny front garden was full of delicate narcissi and late snowdrops. Daniel was expecting us and opened the door before I could knock.

"Welcome, welcome my dears," he said, smiling down at Billy. It was the first time he'd seen him since Will's funeral and I felt a guilty at leaving it so long. "Come in out of the chilly wind," he said, and I drew the pushchair into his tiny vestibule with a difficulty.

"If you hold Billy, I'll fold it down to make it easier," I said, handing over Billy. To my relief, Billy didn't struggle or cry. He inspected Daniel solemnly, then me, then touched Daniel's nose.

There were lots of objects within easy reach of little hands in the tiny sitting room, so I sat Billy on my knee with a toy animal which he pulled at. Daniel went into his kitchen and brought out a tray with tea things on it. He placed it on a shelf near the fireplace, well away from Billy. "I bought the plainest biscuits I could find with minimal sugar content," he said, producing a plate. "Can I give one to young Billy here?"

"I'm sure he'd love one," I said, and Billy squirmed in delight and set to sucking and biting and making a contented humming noise. He possessed two bottom teeth already and there were bumps on his upper gum where more would soon erupt.

"I must say he is very like his father, and he's very sturdy for his age. You deserve much credit for bringing him up on your own, my dear."

"I'm not really on my own. Serena and Joe are like another set of grandparents to Billy. I'm sorry we haven't been to see you sooner, Daniel, but I thought after your accident we'd better wait until you were properly better."

Daniel waved an impatient hand. "A stupid accident on my part. I tripped on the doorstep and banged my head on the wall. No lasting damage, just addled my old brain a little more!"

Yet Daniel looked more fragile than when I'd last seen him; his eyes were less twinkly, and I saw a stick propped up by his chair.

"How are you now, my dear?" he asked as we sipped our tea. Billy had finished his biscuit without too much mess and I handed him another to keep him occupied and retrieved wet wipes from my bag.

"I suppose as well as anyone who has been bereaved," I said. I didn't want to burden Daniel with tales of my nightmares, waking wet with perspiration and a thudding heart, pinned to the bed with fear. "Billy has been my lifesaver and we just get on with life.

And to keep occupied, I help in the house and sometimes give Matt a hand with milking and tidying up the cowsheds. There'll be lambing soon and I want to help with that as well. I need to keep as busy as possible."

"I heard about the shock when Matt found out he was related to the Barnards and Paynes," said Daniel.

"I think Roberta was more alarmed than I was. She assumed Billy's inheritance would be taken away from him, but Matt would be the last person to cause trouble over legalities. Successive Wills have been proved without challenge and I had a long conversation with the solicitor who handled William's Will. It was a shock to me he had made one and recently, too. He made it not long after we married, but he didn't tell me."

"Roberta forced him to make one so that the estate was entailed on his son."

For a moment, my mind drifted back to the reading of the Will, which had shocked me. As well as the house and estate going to his son, unborn at the time it was drawn up, I was to act as his executor until he came into the inheritance, unless in the event of my death before that, then The Trust would be his Executors. I was dumbfounded when Will left me his personal trust fund to manage and use as I saw fit, and I inherited his shares in several companies. One company owned land and docks at Wapping. Will had never assumed a mantle of wealth, and I needed several sessions with the solicitor to understand the extent of his inherited wealth.

"When I listened to Evie reading Honoria's Journal, it crossed my mind to ask you what happened to the ships and docks and trade on the river, and now I know."

"Ah, yes, Honoria's Journals - I looked for them after Geoffrey's death and they were hiding in plain sight all the time." Daniel gave a wry grin.

Billy had grabbed a leaflet from the arm of the sofa and was intent on screwing it up, fascinated by the texture and sound it made. He drooled unashamedly.

"Don't worry, it's only a flyer for an event," laughed Daniel. "He's enjoying himself! You won't possibly understand the remorse and horror we felt when Will died, Clemency. I wish we'd been more open with you about events that happened to us. You know all about them now, but it doesn't lessen the guilt we both feel. We just wanted to protect you."

I reached over and took his veined hand in mine. His skin was thin and wrinkled, and I didn't want to hurt him. I hoped the tragedy of Will's death wasn't the cause of his sudden frailty.

"I don't think there was anything any of us could have done. I twist myself up in knots with guilt, insisting we stayed at Harthill House, creating all the risks. If Mollie had been aware of the Twins' appearances to me, she might have controlled them sooner. It doesn't do any good to keep dwelling on it."

By now, the leaflet was in wet shreds and bits lay all over the carpet.

"Don't worry about clearing it up. It will give my nice lady, who comes in twice weekly, something to do; she's always telling me I'm too tidy."

Billy and I had a little tussle while I attempted to put him back into his all-in-one padded suit while Daniel unfolded the buggy. He kissed me on both cheeks and bent down to stroke Billy's head, and was rewarded with a toothy grin.

"I won't leave it too long before our next visit," I promised.

∽

William Matthew Joseph Payne-Ashton was baptised in the little chapel in the April. Birds sang, bluebells stood tall in blue scented hazes, primroses nestled in hedgerows and woods. During the happy service, Billy joined in with a lot of echoing shrieks and cries. I reflected on the number of services held here down the centuries, some joyful, like Billy's baptism, but other times full of tragic loss.

Mollie's lodge cottage, Snowdrop Lodge, had remained empty since her death. Matt and Serena had cleared and sent stuff to charity shops and Matt had auctioned some items on social media. I helped Serena in the house as much as possible, but she insisted I needed to focus on my plans for the house and suggested we advertise for help. Tenancy of The Lodge came with the job. Naturally, I was inundated with offers, some from people who mostly needed a roof over their heads. Eventually Serena, Joe and I narrowed it down to half a dozen applicants, and we interviewed them on different days, taking them round the house and the lodge after verifying their references.

At last, we arrived at employing Addy, who had worked for a family in Jamaica and had moved with them, first to London and then Wiltshire, to look after house and children. Now the couple's children had grown and left home and the couple had returned to Jamaica Addy and her husband, Neville, had lived in so she was looking for accommodation and a job. She was in her early fifties and looked strong and capable. Her husband had a separate job, but he would help at weekends if necessary. They moved into Snowdrop Lodge in the March and soon got to know the routine.

Dee Bidwell came several times to sit quietly in the old nursery and pray and meditate. "The atmosphere of unhappiness and sadness is growing less," she assured me.

Serena took on board the reason for Dee's visits with equanimity. I think she was learning to live with 'oddities' by now. Addy was more forthcoming. She too sensed 'presences', but in her opinion, they were friendly and she said she prayed for the 'poor lost soul' on the top floor. The sound of her hearty laughter booming round the house lifted our spirits. Little Billy loved to climb on her lap and she'd sing her native folk songs until he fell asleep.

The Shadow Watchers

~

The picnic party came to a rumbustious ending, with adults and children taking part in the tug of war and ending up sprawled, laughing, on the grass. We all sang Happy Birthday and Billy blew out the six candles on his cake and he handed out little goody bags to his classmates as Addy and Serena began clearing away. Rosie and Jamie had become fractious, so I led them off to have a nap, if possible, leaving Billy with Matt and Joe and Neville to clear away obstacles and party debris. He was happy riding his birthday bike around the lawns.

I settled the twins in front of the TV to watch CBBs and put the kettle on to make tea. I didn't hear the door quietly opening and shutting and squeaked when a pair of arms sneaked round my waist. I turned and Matt crushed me to him. In his hand, he held a bottle of champagne.

"While it's quiet, it's time to toast ourselves," he said, popping the cork as quietly as he could so as not to disturb the twins.

I grabbed two glasses, and we gratefully settled on the chairs on the sunny patio. Matt poured the fizzy liquid and lifted his glass. "To you," he said quietly.

"And to you too," I replied, clinking his glass. "You'll be weaving your way down the field to collect their ladyships,"

"No, I won't; Joe and Neville and Billy are doing the milking tonight. Joe gave me the night off.

"I hope Billy will be ok," I said anxiously. "He's been roaring around all afternoon."

"Neville said he'd look after him and bring him home when he flags. Knowing Billy, he won't give in easily!"

I looked at my husband's tanned face, framed by his blond hair, lightened by the sun, which now stood up after all the afternoon's activities. I studied the way his mouth seemed permanently turned up in a smile and how his smiling blue eyes met mine.

"I love you, Matt Crane," I said.

"And I love you, Clemency Crane," he replied.

Matt and I eventually married. From the time of Will's death, he'd unobtrusively supported me in practical ways. He'd also kept his distance. Later, he'd told me he fallen for me not long after I'd arrived at Harthill House full of insecurity and nausea. But as Will's fiancé and then wife, he'd kept his feelings for me well under control. I told him that whenever I was with him; I felt a spark of something. At the time, I'd fastened on him as a friend in Will's absence.

Matt said when he and Joe found me half drowned on the riverbank, he'd almost gone into shock himself and he'd realised how deep his feelings ran. That's why he'd been so distant after Will's death, as he knew he could never express his feelings. The night his family connections were revealed had been the catalyst to his decision to leave. "All those revelations nearly finished me off," he'd said. "You stopped me that night, and I didn't have the willpower to carry out my decision."

"I was terrified you'd leave me. You'd been my rock and I couldn't bear to lose you. It never occurred to me I loved you."

"Joe cottoned on to my feelings for you. He saw us both together and he and Serena had observed that you 'came alive' in my company. They tried to get us together in situations so we wouldn't be conscious they'd contrived them! I tumbled it though, but you didn't notice anything!"

"I did," I'd laughed. "But I couldn't betray Will, even though he was dead. I went through all the stages of bereavement: grief, loneliness, anger; but guilt was the main thing. He'd kept going away, not really understanding any of my fear and apprehension. His mother had to practically lay down the law for him to marry me so that his son could inherit Harthill lawfully. Will would happily have breezed through life doing the things he loved. I realised he had been self-indulgent, but I felt all this rage against him even though he'd died such a horrible death and I couldn't move on. I was full of guilt because if we'd have stayed in London nothing would have happened, but I was selfish because I loved this place. You helped to heal me, Matt. Without all of you, I couldn't contemplate life."

"Remember the rainstorm?" asked Matt mischievously, refilling our glasses.

Yes, I remembered the rainstorm. One afternoon I'd gone to fetch the herd while Matt readied the milking machines. I wore wellies but only a thin jacket as the weather had been mild. Out of nowhere, there was a tremendous squall of winds and rain. The cows ahead of me soon turned the turf to a muddy mess and in the murky gloom I slipped and fell several times. By the time I'd reached the barns, I was covered in mud and cow muck. When Matt saw me, he nearly fell over laughing. Then he'd controlled himself and told me to go and have a shower. Obstinately, I refused and carried on with the job in hand. "Suit yourself," he'd shrugged, but I could see him shaking with laughter.

After we'd cleared up, Matt herded the cows into the large pen before releasing them into the far meadow. By this time, I was shivering with cold and wet and anxious to get back to Billy. Matt was on his phone.

"Right, let's get you cleaned up," he said. "Serena said Billy is fine and in the kitchen with them. I'll take you back to mine so you don't traipse shit all over the house." He grinned again. He led me to the farmhouse. "You can drop all your clothes on the floor here," he indicated the conservatory.

I was appalled. "You're not going to hose me down here?"

"If you like," Matt said, straight-faced. "Or you can use the shower room just through there."

"Go away while I take these things off," I'd said crossly. I didn't know where to start; my clothes were stiff and slimy to touch. Even bending down to take off my wellies was nearly impossible.

"Come here, I'll give you a hand." Matt was serious now. He pulled off my boots, and helped me off with my jacket, covering himself in mire at the same time. Self-consciously, I turned to try to ease off my wet, stiff jeans.

"Sit on the bench," Matt instructed and tugged at the legs of my jeans until they finally slithered off. By now I was in a dither and wanted Matt to disappear, but I was shaking from head to foot.

"Show me the shower room and I'll manage," I mumbled. Matt was very quiet now, and I tried to pass him. He was looking at me with a strange expression and my heart thudded.

"What? What?" I said defensively. I felt alarmingly exposed standing in front of him in my underwear.

His hand reached out and touched my cheek. If I'd flinched, I think he would have pulled back and left me to struggle and that would have been that. But I didn't flinch. I was rooted to the spot, holding my breath, my eyes searching Matt's. His mouth brushed mine lightly. It was as light as a butterfly's wings and I closed my eyes, breathing in the earthy smell of animals and Matt's essence. This time he kissed harder and before we knew it our arms had wrapped round each other, pressing each other closer. Desire flooded through me so strongly I was glad of Matt's arms holding me up. Matt broke away first. "Are you really sure about this?" he asked, his eyes troubled.

I nodded, then said quietly, tears springing to my eyes. "I feel as if I've come home after a long time in the wilderness."

He lifted me and carried me into the shower room. He turned on the shower until steam dulled the glass cubicle. He gently removed the rest of my clothes and I stood shivering, not in fear, but in longing. He stripped off his own clothes swiftly and lifted me into the shower. The hot water sluicing over our bodies made us both gasp. Gently he kissed me all over. Then we came together, so naturally I felt no embarrassment or guilt. A warm bubble of happiness spread from my midriff to all my extremities and I kissed him joyously, water streaming over our bodies.

"I'm going to have to marry you now," he said gruffly, and I could only embrace him laughing and crying at the same time.

And so we married in the chapel the next July, and the weather could not have been more glorious. When we'd announced our intentions, Joe and Serena explained, "Thank God, you've both come to your senses at last!"

I nervously contacted Roberta, who had returned to France. When she had learned of Matt's connection to the family, she had believed he was a threat to Billy's inheritance. She'd soon come to accept that nothing had changed, but even so, by marrying Matt, perhaps she would feel that threat again. I was relieved when she gave her blessings.

"I must tell you, darling Clemency, that even early on I could see Matt's eyes light up every time he looked at you. I think it's meant to be, and I gladly give you both my blessing!"

Evie and Ruby also tied the knot, and Ruby was determined to become a UK citizen. Just after our twins were born, Ruby passed on the news that Rafaella was pregnant and her office had taken on another trek leader to cover for her. I had no doubt she would strap her baby on her back and cycle off as soon as she was fit.

I was horrified when twins appeared on my first scan, so deep was the trauma of the Twin's actions, but was relieved that I didn't suffer extreme nausea during the pregnancy. Rosie and Jamie were delivered safely in the Maternity Unit of Salisbury Hospital; once again, Matt was present during the birth, but the circumstances could not have been more different.

We lived in the farmhouse. It was more practical for Matt to be on site and I enjoyed being a farmer's wife and being involved. Billy followed Matt around, helping him do little chores. Billy called Matt by his name. He knew he was not his father; I'd explained when he was nearly three. Photos of Will were kept on display both at Harthill House and in the farmhouse, and he could watch videos of his dad on treks doing what he loved best. Photographs of our children showed two fair headed boys and a copper haired girl.

Billy shared Matt's ability to handle sheep and cattle and was already training the new border collie under Matt's guidance.

I took the advice of Uncle Daniel and wrote an account of all that happened to me since the fateful day six years ago when I first thought I had food poisoning. It was a cathartic exercise. Every year on the anniversaries of Will's and Mollie's deaths, we all go to the chapel and lay posies of wildflowers on their headstones and then I make a lone pilgrimage to where Frances and her babies rest and with the stone angel protecting them eternally, I lay a posy on her tomb and whisper to her from my heart.

I still have flashbacks and nightmares, but when I wake in terror, Matt's right there beside me and I know I am safe.

About the Author

Ellie Crofts began writing stories at an early age. Growing up near Liverpool she wrote her first book aged twelve about kidnapped children imprisoned in a cave in arid Spain, even though she had never been there. She moved to Devon as an adult and then Wiltshire. When her children were in bed, she wrote humorous family articles for a woman's magazine and had a children's story broadcast on local radio. Besides teaching, she has worked in libraries and as a housekeeper in a 'big' house and the glorious setting inspired her imagination. Ellie lives in Warminster with her husband and their border terrier, Dennis. The Shadow Watchers is her first novel.

More from Serenade Publishing

Songbird Series

Songbird

Heartbeat Song

Our Song

Brigadier Station Series

By Sarah Williams:

The Brothers of Brigadier Station

The Sky over Brigadier Station

The Legacies of Brigadier Station

Christmas at Brigadier Station

Heart of the Hinterland Series

By Sarah Williams:

The Dairy Farmer's Daughter

Their Perfect Blend

Beyond the Barre

The Outback Governess

By Sarah Williams

Primrose Series

By Tanya Renee

Prairie Sky

Prairie Nights

Prairie Fire

Prairie Hearts

Prairie Sound

Prairie Rain

With The Band

By Tanya Renee

Finding Direction

A New Page

by Aimee MacRae

The Spring of Love Series

By Virginia Taylor

Forever Delighted

Forever Amused

Forever Heartfelt

The Tooth Fairy Chronicles
By Victoria Rocus
Tooth Decay With A Side Of Fae
Toothaches And Wedding Cakes
Baby Tooth And Tangled Roots
Wisdom Tooth And The Awful Truth

It Happened in Paris
By Michelle Beesley

The Bondi Bubble
By Megan Krolik

White Butterfly
By Kim Foale

The Ancient Fire
By Ellen Read

The Love Healer
By A. K. Leigh

For more information and to buy autographed copies visit:
www.serenadepublishing.com

Acknowledgments

I would like to express my thanks and gratitude to Sarah Williams of Serenade Publishing for her advice, help, suggestions and assurance while writing this novel. Heartfelt thanks to my amazing family for encouraging me to finish the job, especially to my daughter Sarah for her book cover artwork suggestions and to my beta readers for pointing out the many bloopers and giving me thumbs up!